FLOWER GIRLS

FLOWER GIRLS

JANET DAILEY
BEVERLY BEAVER
MARGARET BROWNLEY
RUTH JEAN DALE

St. Martin's Paperbacks

FLOWER GIRLS

"Striking a Match" copyright © 1996 by Janet Dailey and Sonja Massie.
"To Love and to Cherish" copyright © 1996 by Beverly Beaver.
"Something Old, Something New" copyright © 1996 by Margaret Brownley.
"Something Borrowed, Something Blue" copyright © 1996 by Betty Lee Duran.

ISBN: 0-312-95940-0

Printed in the United States of America

St. Martin's Paperbacks edition / October 1996

10 9 8 7 6 5 4 3 2 1

Contents

STRIKING A MATCH

~

Janet Dailey
and Sonja Massie

Chapter One

"*G*od doesn't make mistakes," Reverend Dylan Gray said as he stood at the edge of the bluff, overlooking the sleepy, moonlit valley below.

His hands were shoved deep in the pockets of his jeans, the lambswool collar of his black leather jacket was pulled snugly around his neck, and a scowl creased his forehead. Although he was only in his mid-twenties, Dylan's hair had turned prematurely silver in the past six months. Some of the dear, elderly ladies at church had told him how becoming it was, how it made his pale blue eyes all the more striking. But the young minister hadn't been impressed, attributing his fading hair color to his recent trials and tribulations. This place would make him old fast.

"God doesn't blow it, because He's God," Dylan reasoned aloud. "I mean, it's impossible. Right? Right."

No one argued with him, because he was alone . . . blissfully, peacefully, deliciously alone. For a change.

At least, he should have felt at peace with heaven and earth in such a beautiful place. Stars twinkling overhead, the river flowing below like liquid moonbeams, the rich scent of pine in the air.

That was why he had hopped on his classic Harley-Davidson motorcycle and raced to the top of this hill that overlooked the picturesque village of Covington Falls, North Carolina: to commune with nature, with his Maker, and to get away from it all—more specifically *them* all—even more specifically *her*.

He shuddered and tried to shove the image of the grouchy, demanding old lady to the back of his mind. The thought of Abigail Covington did nothing to further his quest for spiritual tranquility.

So what if she was his church's primary contributor? Abigail Covington was a royal pain in the—

He quickly intercepted that thought, too. Dylan Gray was a minister of the Lord now, not a New York City street punk. It hadn't been an easy transition. After years of seminary and countless hours of prayer and soul-searching, sometimes Dylan wondered if the transformation would ever be complete.

"Forgiveness," he whispered, nearly choking on the word. "Love, patience, understanding . . ." He took a deep breath and looked up to the heavens. ". . . and if You could help me not to strangle her the next time I see her, that would be very helpful, too."

For a moment, Dylan listened quietly, waiting for a reply. Oh, he didn't expect the sky to unfurl and angels to trumpet. In his immediate vicinity, no bushes burst into flame. But he thought he heard a small, celestial chuckle; at least, he hoped he had. The good Lord had to possess a sense of humor. Why else would He have sent Dylan Gray—hell-raiser, rabble-rouser, adrenaline junkie, turned reverend—to a dull little place like Covington Falls?

Sin City, it wasn't. The worst scandal of the past five years had been the Friday night poker game behind Harry Beckett's barber shop, where the fellows had actually played for *money*. Miss Covington had found out about it and turned them in to the local chief of police, insisting they be arrested for breaking the city's no gambling ordinance. Dylan had been hauled out of bed at two in the morning to post bail for three of his deacons.

And then, there had been that uproar over whether the church's new carpet should be red or blue. Miss Abigail "Let's-Raise-A-Stink-Whenever-Possible" Covington had pronounced that scarlet was too stimulating, too risqué for a house of worship. As always, her cronies had sided with her, and although they were the minority in the congregation, they were the wealthiest and the loudest. Dylan had thought he was going to have a split in his parish after only three months on the job.

In a moment of diplomatic brilliance, he had suggested forest green as a compromise, pointing out that it was in keeping with the church's name: Chapel in the Pines. With only a minimal amount of grumbling, everyone had agreed.

Even now, he couldn't believe how petty people—one person in particular—could be.

"This isn't why I went into the ministry," he said as he strolled back to his Harley and threw one long leg over it. Settling on the seat and looking up at the stars, he didn't hear or sense a reply to his complaint. This time, not even a chuckle. "I was hoping to work with the gangs, the dopers, a few hard-core criminals and their victims. Something a little grittier than next Thursday's Ladies' Auxiliary luncheon menu."

No heavenly response.

"I'm dyin' here, Lord . . . of boredom . . . and that's the worst way to go. Couldn't I have something a bit more challenging than catering to a rich old busybody like Abigail Covington?"

Still no answer.

And Rev. Dylan Gray had spoken to the Lord often enough to know that, when there was no reply, it wasn't because the heavenly Father wasn't listening. Usually, it was because *Dylan* wasn't listening.

"All right, all right," he said. "I get the hint. Shut up with the griping, already, and get back to work. Right?"

This time he felt the divine nod.

Dylan started up the Harley's engine and savored the throbbing power of the machine beneath him. For a while, he allowed the old feelings to return: the exuberance of his adolescence, the reckless abandon, the naive sense of indestructibility reserved for the young at heart.

With a roar that split the silence of the night, he took off down the twisted road that wound back and forth down the side of the rocky bluff. The night wind stung his face, and his blood pumped to the rhythm of the bike as he wrung out the curves.

Abigail Covington, or no Abigail Covington, even a preacher man had to get his kicks now and then!

About two blocks from the chapel, Dylan Gray felt a jolt of adrenaline that had nothing to do with his Harley ride down the hill.

Something was terribly wrong.

Lights—flashing eerily, red and blue, against the church's stone walls. Sirens. Voices shouting. Smoke— black and acrid, filling the night air. Firemen—wearing helmets, masks, and bright yellow suits bearing the letters C.F.F.D.

And—

"Dear Lord . . . no, please," he whispered as he saw a stretcher being carried to an ambulance waiting at the curb directly in front of the chapel.

Immediately, Dylan thought of Mrs. Whittle, the church's secretary, a middle-aged sweetheart who had happily adopted Dylan on sight. But why would she have been working so late? When he had left about an hour ago, the chapel had been empty. He had been careful to lock up, as usual. What could have happened? How could a fire have started?

Jumping off the Harley, he left it at the edge of the chapel's parking lot and ran to the ambulance. Gratefully, he recognized one of the paramedics as a member of his congregation. The man was wearing the white uniform with a red cross on the shoulder, instead of his usual Sunday morning charcoal suit, but the wire-rimmed glasses and the cheerful smile beneath the black, bushy mustache were the same.

"Jim!" Dylan called. "Jim Pickard, what's going on? Is it Mrs. Whittle?"

Jim paid him no attention at first, as he was occupied with hanging an intravenous drip for the patient. Without waiting for an answer, Dylan hurried to the stretcher and peered down at the white-sheeted figure, expecting to see his secretary.

But Mrs. Whittle had a round, plump face with robust color, surrounded by curly dark hair. This face was gaunt, cadaverously pale, with white hair pulled back severely.

"Miss Covington," he whispered. "Abigail?"

A wave of guilt washed over him, as though his own negative thoughts only moments before might have caused this catastrophe. He had wished her ill, and, apparently, ill had befallen her. Somehow he felt responsible.

Feebly, Miss Covington opened her eyes. As she focused on him, her vague look gradually faded and an angry glare took its place.

"And where were *you*?" she said accusingly.

"Where was *I*? What do you mean? I . . ."

"If it hadn't been for that little girl, my roof could have burned down, right over my head, for all the help you were."

Little girl? What little girl? He turned away for a moment to survey the scene, trying to make sense of the chaos. Like yellow wasps, firefighters buzzed around the side of the Covington mansion nearest the church. Whatever flames there might have been seemed to have been extinguished by the fire company. But billows of black smoke and white steam continued to roll from the broken glass windows of the sun porch. "*Your* roof? Oh, it was your house," he said. "I thought it was the chapel."

"Goody for you. And I'll just bet you're mighty relieved." She slapped the paramedic's hand as he attempted to readjust the IV needle in her arm.

"I'm sorry for your loss, Miss Covington," he said with a degree of sincerity that actually surprised him. Although the mansion's mistress was difficult, the mansion itself was a graceful, elegant home, and he hated to see it suffer damage of any kind.

With the IV finally in place, Jim wheeled the gurney to the back of the ambulance. Dylan followed.

"Is she going to be all right?" he asked under his breath.

"Oh, yeah. She's too ornery to die," Jim replied, not bothering to drop his voice. "Just got a bit of smoke. Probably no more than she gets every day from those cigarettes she's always smoking."

"Don't go talking about me like I wasn't even here," she snapped, lifting her head to grimace at them both. "I may be old, but I'm not deaf."

"And, unfortunately, not mute either," Jim added as he shoved her into the ambulance. She was swallowed by the gleaming stainless steel and enamel white interior.

"If there's anything I can do, Miss Covington," Dylan began, "I'd be glad to—"

"You're darned right, you can," she shouted back. "Get that burned porch fixed for me, pronto. I want to be able to sit out there as soon as they let me out of the hospital. I'll pay for it, but make sure they don't rob me blind, or I'll—"

Dylan fought down his temper as Jim slammed the doors, cutting off the rest of her orders.

The two men stood, side by side, and watched as the ambulance pulled away.

"You know why she likes to sit out there on that porch," Jim said, his dark eyes twinkling behind his wire rims. "It's so she can keep an eye on everybody's comings and goings at the church. She doesn't have enough business of her own, so she's gotta mind everybody else's."

There was more truth to Jim's words than Dylan cared to admit. But he really shouldn't join in gossip, tempting though it was.

"With all her money," Jim continued, "she thinks she owns the whole darned town. And the chapel is her prized possession."

"She doesn't own the church," Dylan replied quietly. "No one does. It's a house of worship."

"Yeah. But we all know who pays the electric bill, the phone bill, and your salary, don't we, Rev. Gray?"

Dylan choked back the first words that came to his lips and waited for kinder ones to surface. "The Lord provides," he said. "We shouldn't question how He chooses to do it."

"Are you telling me that you don't mind that old biddy bossing you around like that?"

Did he mind? Dylan recognized an honest question when he heard one. It deserved an equally truthful reply.

"Yeah, sometimes I mind," he said thoughtfully. "But the truth is, Miss Covington needs help from time to time, like everyone else. But she doesn't have family and friends to ask."

"That's her own fault, from what I've heard," Jim interjected. "Over the years, she's chased them all away with her grumpiness."

Dylan shrugged. "That may or may not be true. But the lady is elderly and alone. She just isn't very tactful in the way she asks for assistance. I try not to let that bother me."

"But it does?"

Long ago, Dylan had determined to be honest with his fellow man, rather than try to play the "perfect" minister all the time. If they knew you at all, they would see that you, too, had frailties. Plenty of them. You might as well own up to it in the beginning.

"Sure, it bugs me sometimes. But my irritation doesn't keep me from lending her a hand when I think she needs it. Just like I would for you, Jim. Just like you would for me."

Dylan hoped his answer had provided a graceful exit as he turned and left Jim Pickard standing there with a contemplative and slightly confused expression on his mustachioed face.

He might as well check out the damage now and see

what he was getting himself into.

Seeing the devastation, he groaned. It was worse than he had thought, while standing in the street. Although the basic structure seemed sound, smoke had blackened the walls, floor, ceiling, and wicker furniture. The heat had been fierce enough to cause the paint to peel in places and most of the windows were broken.

Fearing the worst, Dylan hurried around the porch to the back to check the room's most valuable asset—the antique stained glass windows. The first time he had seen the beautiful panes, Dylan had admired the intricate workmanship, the traditional, yet stylish, representation of morning glories, wisteria, and lilies.

"Oh, no," he whispered as he stared at the sagging, melted lead, the blackened and broken glass. They bore no resemblance to the works of art he had enjoyed before.

Finding contractors to repair the rest of the damage would be simple enough, but he couldn't imagine how these windows could ever be restored or replaced.

Although most people who knew Abigail Covington considered her heartless, he knew better, and he knew she would be heartbroken to see this, if she hadn't already.

At least the lady herself had survived the ordeal. Thanks to . . . what had she said? A little girl?

Dylan glanced around, but saw only firefighters packing away their gear, and a few curious onlookers, standing at the perimeter of the yard. Miss Covington often shouted at anyone who set foot on her property, and it seemed she had made believers of her neighbors. Even though she had been carted away to the hospital, they appeared to be reluctant to broach her security.

After a walk around the house, Dylan decided that the building would be safe, left alone until morning. Only the porch had been damaged, and the door lock still worked. Just for good measure, he secured the porch door, too. Although there was nothing left that any burglar would want, he was fairly certain that Abigail Covington would have wanted it locked, so he felt obliged.

As he headed across the lawn toward the chapel, Dylan passed a copse of pines that bordered the two properties. Pausing, he thought he heard a sound coming from beneath the trees. At first, he thought it was a puppy whining, sniffling. Then, he saw the faint outline of a crouched figure at the base of one of the pines. A person.

"Excuse me," he said softly, walking in that direction. "Hey, what's going on?"

The shape was small. A child. A little girl, he realized as he drew nearer.

The little girl? he wondered. The one Miss Covington had mentioned?

By the dim light of the firefighters' vehicles and the distant street lamp, Dylan thought he recognized the long pigtails, the jeans, and sneakers. Although he couldn't discern details in the darkness, he knew he had seen the child playing in the neighborhood before. He knew those braids were bright auburn, the jeans were shabby, and the sneakers scuffed. When he had seen her up close before, he had noticed that her face was sprinkled with freckles and often smeared with strawberry jam.

Once, he had asked her name, but it had been months ago, and now he wished he could remember.

"Hello there," he said, trying to sound as nonthreatening as possible. She was obviously upset and didn't need to be alarmed by having a stranger approach her in the darkness. "Is something wrong?" he asked, stopping about six feet from her. "I'm Reverend Dylan Gray, from the chapel next door. We met once before, remember? Is there something I can do to help you?"

With a big sniff and a hoarse cough, she shook her head. "No . . . thank you . . . sir."

Well, at least she was well-mannered, if not particularly well cared for.

She continued to cry, her knees drawn up with arms folded across them. Her face was buried in the sleeves of her sweater, which was at least two sizes too large.

"Are you sure," he said, dropping to one knee beside

her. "People don't usually cry for no reason. If you're scared or upset, I'd be glad to talk to you about it. That's what I do for a living, you know."

She lifted her face to look at him. "Really?" she asked between hiccuping sobs. "Listening to people's problems is a job . . . I mean . . . it's like *work*?"

He sighed and nodded. "You have no idea how much sometimes."

"My name's Nikki," she volunteered, quickly warming to him. "Actually, it's Nicola Sarita Dickens, but my mom only calls me that when I'm in trouble." She paused to cough again. Her throat sounded dry and tight. "My mom works, too. She's a waitress at the truck stop. She calls it 'slingin' hash.' Her legs hurt a lot. Her feet, too. Sometimes I rub them for her when she gets home."

Dylan smiled. "I'm sure she appreciates that very much." He glanced down at the luminous dial of his wrist-watch. Nearly ten o'clock. "It's pretty late. Much too late for you to be out here all alone. Where do you live?"

"Two blocks away, on the corner of Ashwood and Chestnut."

"Maybe I should walk you home. Your mom must be worried, wondering where you are."

"Naw, she's working tonight, won't be home until after ten."

Dylan swallowed his indignation that the child would be left alone so late. He'd have a talk with Mom later. "Either way, you should be home, not wandering around out here in the dark. Come on, let's go."

He offered her his hand, and to his surprise she took it eagerly. Too eagerly. He would have to talk to her mother about that, too. Even in a quaint village like Covington Falls, children should be taught to be leery of strangers. To do less was to set them up as potential victims.

As they began to walk toward the street, Dylan smelled a strong odor of smoke coming from the girl's hair and clothing. She coughed several times, crossing the lawn. As they approached the light, he saw that her face was darkened with soot.

Again, he recalled Miss Covington's words. "Did you have anything to do with the fire tonight?" he asked.

She shot him a terrified look. "No! Of course not! I didn't—"

"I meant, did you help Miss Covington get out of her house? I'm only asking because she mentioned that a little gir—, I mean, a young lady, helped her, or she might have died in her bedroom."

The child hesitated before answering. "Well, I might have been the one who ran upstairs and told her about the porch being on fire. I might have helped her find her way down. The smoke was pretty thick and chokey . . . you know."

"You *might* have?" He wondered briefly why she was so reluctant to admit an act of heroism. Most kids would be busting their buttons to tell the tale.

"Yeah, maybe."

He wasn't going to let her off that easily. "So, did you?"

She simply nodded.

"Then, I think we'd better have the paramedics check you out. Sounds like you swallowed a bit of that smoke yourself. There aren't that many brave heroines like you in the world. We have to take good care of you."

She pulled her hand out of his. "No! I'm not all that brave. It wasn't any big deal, and I don't want any doctors to check me."

"I understand, but one of the paramedics is named Jim. He's a friend of mine, and he has kids of his own. A bunch, in fact. He's very nice and—"

"No, no, no! I can't."

"Why not?"

"My mom said I had to be very careful and not get hurt, because doctors cost a lot of money, and we don't have any money. She'll get really mad if she finds out I got hurt."

Dylan studied the child for a long time before speaking. "You know, when I was a kid, I lived in New York City, in an area they call the Village. One night, when I was about your age, I snuck out of our apartment. I was supposed to be in bed asleep, but my friend and I wanted to ride on this older guy's new scooter."

"What's a scooter?"

"Kind of a cross between a motorcycle and a skateboard," he admitted, suddenly feeling ancient.

"Oh, okay. Go on." She seemed eager to talk about anything . . . as long as it had nothing to do with doctors, or her having to see one.

"Anyway," he continued, "I took a flying leap off my friend's scooter, busted my head, and had to get five stitches in the local emergency room."

"Wow! Did your mom yell at you?"

"No. Neither did my father. But I had to work all summer collecting soda bottles and sweeping the drugstore and grocery market on our block to pay my parents back for that hospital bill."

"All summer?"

He nodded solemnly. "The longest summer of my life. But that's how long it took to make it right."

"Boy, that's a bummer. It's too bad you fell off and broke your head."

"No, it's too bad that I didn't obey my folks in the first place."

She cleared her throat, coughed a couple of times, and looked down at her battered sneakers. "So, what are you saying I should do?"

"I think you should go let the paramedics look at you, get whatever medical attention your body needs, and worry about making it right with your mom later."

Finally, she nodded. "Yeah, okay. But I'm telling you, she's got red hair, just like me, and she can really, really, really get mad!"

He chuckled. "What if I take you over to meet Jim, then while you're going to the hospital, I'll go wait for your mom to come home. I'll tell her what happened and maybe calm her down a little before she comes to pick you up? How does that sound?''

Reluctantly, Nikki agreed, and Jim took only a few seconds to decide that a trip to the hospital was in order. Dylan waved goodbye as the ambulance pulled away.

He paused for a moment, mentally clicking off his newly acquired responsibilities: talk Nikki's bad-tempered, red-haired mother out of killing her, find contractors to repair the damage done to the mansion, and, of course, try to find someone with the skill and expertise to repair those beautiful windows.

A challenge greater than the Ladies' Auxiliary Luncheon. That was what he had prayed for, only a short time ago.

In the future, when you ask for something . . . be a bit more specific.

Chapter Two

*F*or the past three hours, Zoe Harmond had sat in her van in front of the Victorian mansion, waiting for one Reverend Dylan Gray to appear. The old, oversized Dodge was comfortable enough to wait in, even to live in—which Zoe did—but she was growing impatient. As the sun sank into the forest of pines behind the house, her ire rose.

"A little late," was understandable, but this was ridiculous. Did he want his darned windows repaired or not?

For the fifth time, she pulled his letter from her glove compartment and glanced over it.

Dear Joe Harmond:

If this had been the first time she had ever had her name confused, she might have been offended. But it had happened all her life, and she had decided long ago there were plenty of other things in life to get perturbed about—like grossly late people who wasted her time.

She continued to read.

Thank you for your prompt response to my inquiry.

Of course she had responded quickly. Considering the vast amount of money to be made on this rare job, she couldn't risk losing it. The opportunity had arrived at the perfect time. The profits would provide the remaining funds she needed for her hiking trip across Europe next month. A lifelong dream—within her immediate grasp—if only she could finish the project in time.

We would like you to begin the repairs as quickly as possible, the letter continued. *I will meet you at the following location, next Friday evening, April 17th, at four o'clock.*

"Okay, Rev. Gray," she said, looking around the deserted yard. The only movement was that of the oak trees swishing their leafy petticoats in the evening breeze. "I'm here, raring to go, but where are you?"

Two hours ago, she had knocked on the doors of the house: front, back, and side. On her circuit around the house, she had checked out the burned porch and its damaged windows. They would prove a challenge, but a welcome one. Once they had been beautiful, she could tell. And it would be a pleasure to restore them to their original splendor—if Rev. Gray arrived before she became too old and feeble to do the work.

She had even tried to rouse someone at the chapel next door, since that had been the address on the letterhead of his correspondence. No one had answered at the small apartment behind the church, which she assumed was the rectory. She supposed the reverend lived in the mansion next door. After all, he had been the one to contact her. Why, she didn't know, since he didn't seem to care if he met her.

Of course, after three hours, she was entitled to just drive away. It would serve the old codger right. Although she didn't know for certain if he was a codger, old or not, she wasn't feeling generous enough to give him the benefit of the doubt.

But if she were to drive off in a cloud of righteous indignation, where would she go? The nearest campground, where she could park the van and maybe get a shower. It was a primitive lifestyle, to be sure, but one she had grown accustomed to over the past two years.

Living in a van, even a well-equipped one like hers, was a trial at times. But Zoe was a gypsy, by ancestry and spirit. A rover with no ties, few responsibilities, and more freedom than anyone she knew.

Besides, roughing it here in the old Dodge allowed her to save money for her hiking trip. The ultimate escape. Supreme freedom.

After shoving the letter back into the glove compartment, she reached behind the seat into her goodies stash and pulled out a bag of trail mix. Munching on the nuts, dried fruit, and toasted coconut, she watched as the clock on her dash clicked slowly downward to seven-thirty.

Reverend Dylan Gray was rapidly becoming her least-favorite customer—and she hadn't even laid eyes on him yet.

With a sigh of exasperation, she tossed the bag onto the passenger seat and opened the van's door. As always, it screeched on its rusty hinges and grated against her nerves. The truck needed a lot of work, but if it could just hold on another month, she would find some nice pastoral junkyard for its retirement.

The rays from the setting sun were staining the house's pearl gray siding a delicate pink. She didn't have much more daylight left, thanks to the wayward reverend. Maybe she could take a closer look at those windows, at least determine how she was going to remove them. She would have to lay them flat on a table to do the repairs. Sometimes, just removing old windows that had been cemented into their casings decades ago, could be the most difficult part of the operation. Zoe was eager to see what sort of challenge she would face.

But when she tried the porch door, she found it locked. Who bothered to lock their house in a sleepy little town like this? Was the minister afraid someone would rob him? From the looks of the mansion, he wasn't one of those holy men who had taken a vow of poverty. Maybe he was a stingy, wizened miser who spent more time counting his coins than reading his Bible.

Her estimation of him was diminishing by the moment.

Frustrated, she jiggled the doorknob, resisting the urge to give it a swift kick. Then, she pounded on it again with her fist, knowing no one would answer, but enjoying the release of some of her stress.

"Excuse me, lady," said a small, feminine voice behind her. "There's nobody at home right now."

"Yes, I can see that, thank you," Zoe replied, far more brusquely than she had intended. Turning around, she saw a young girl, about eight or nine, standing in the middle of the cobblestone walk. The child cringed at the sound of her voice, and instantly Zoe felt ashamed; she hadn't intended to be so harsh.

"I'm sorry," she told the girl. "It's just that I've been waiting here for someone since before four o'clock, and I'm a bit irritated."

"I know. I saw your van parked here when I got home from school. My name is Nikki," she said.

Zoe recalled herself at that age. Like this child, she had been long and lanky, all knobby knees and elbows, a bit tattered around the edges. Her own braids had been dark brown, not red, but they, too, had been tied with bits of mismatched yarn at the ends.

Her heart went out to the girl, knowing how it felt to be so poor you couldn't afford ribbons or fancy barrettes. There hadn't been much money for extras in the foster homes that Zoe had been shuffled between for most of her childhood.

"Are you waiting for Rev. Gray?" Nikki asked.

Zoe noticed a twinkle in the girl's eyes and briefly wondered about it.

"Yes. How did you know?"

Nikki shrugged thin shoulders and looked pleased with herself. "I just figured it out by myself, because he's been meeting lots of people here—people who build things and fix things—ever since the . . ." She glanced down at the ground and shuffled her sneakers. ". . . since . . . you know, the fire."

"Yes, I can see it did a lot of damage."

"Only to the porch!" Nikki interjected. "It didn't hurt the rest of the house or the lady who lives here."

"I'm glad to hear that. Where is she?"

Again, the girl wouldn't meet her eyes. "Miss Covington is still in the hospital, but she'll be back home soon. She didn't get burned or anything awful like that."

"So, why is she in the hospital?"

"She breathed some of the smoke, but not too much. Rev. Gray said they're mostly just keeping her there so they can watch her. She's old, and she had a heart attack a long time ago."

"Speaking of Rev. Gray," Zoe tried the window to the right of the door, just to see if she might be able to slide it open, "do you have any idea where he might be?"

Nikki nodded, swelling with importance. "Oh, yeah, he's gone to the hospital."

"To see Miss Covington?"

"No. He went because there was a bad car wreck downtown this afternoon, and some of the people who were hurt go to his church. He seemed really worried and sad when he left. That's probably why he forgot about meeting you here."

"Mm-m-m . . ." In a spirit of fairness, Zoe had to readjust her opinion of the minister a few notches to the right. Maybe he wasn't an irresponsible nitwit, after all.

"What are you supposed to fix?" Nikki asked, watching curiously as Zoe tried the window to the left.

"The stained glass panels, down there at the end," she told her, grunting with the exertion of tugging on the window. As she had feared, the heat had warped the metal and wood, and it refused to budge.

"Do you need to get inside really bad?" Nikki asked.

"Well, sort of. I came all this way to look at the windows, maybe even begin working on them, but now I can't even get to them."

Nikki stepped closer to her, glanced around, and lowered her voice conspiratorially. "I might be able to help you . . . get inside, that is."

"Really? That would be great."

With an uncertain look toward the church, Nikki said,

"Do you think it would be all right with Rev. Gray? I don't want him to get mad at me."

Zoe didn't want to get the girl into trouble, but she really wanted a closer look at those panels and a head start on the work. "Do you think he would mind?" she asked.

"Naw. You're a nice lady, and you aren't going to steal anything or do anything bad to the house. I think it would be okay. Come here . . . I'll show you a secret, but you have to promise not to tell anybody."

"Cross my heart and hope to die."

Nikki grinned and motioned her to walk around to the back side of the porch. She knelt on the grass beside the house and pushed some branches of an azalea bush aside.

Kneeling next to her, Zoe saw a decorative panel of white metal filigree, the entrance to a crawlspace beneath the porch.

"See, it has screws right here," Nikki said, pointing to the four corners. "But they're really loose. If you even pull on it, even a little bit, it comes right off."

"So it does." Zoe watched as the girl deftly removed the screen and set it aside. "And how do you know about this?"

Nikki grinned, wrinkling the freckles on her nose. "I saw the plumber crawl in there one time, to fix something. He had to use a screwdriver to take it off. But he didn't put it on good when he left. He was in a hurry to go, because Miss Covington yelled at him. She told him he wasn't doing a good enough job and she was going to shoot him with her granddaddy's shotgun."

Zoe nodded thoughtfully. "That would cause *me* to leave. No doubt about it."

"Follow me," Nikki said, sounding as authoritative as a jungle safari guide.

A moment later, she had crawled inside the space, and all Zoe could see were the well-worn soles of her sneakers.

On her hands and knees, Zoe slipped through the opening and under the house. The grass had been damp and cool with evening dew, but beneath the house, the hard-packed earth was dry and dusty. A musty smell filled her nose, and Zoe tried to take shallow breaths.

She couldn't see much in the relative darkness, but she heard Nikki rattling some sort of metal latch. Hinges squeaked, a trap door opened, and a square of dim light appeared above them.

"See," Nikki said proudly, "a secret passageway, just like in Nancy Drew books."

The girl hauled herself through the opening, and Zoe did the same. They were inside the porch, staring at the charred damage around them.

"Wow, it looks even worse from in here," Nikki said woefully.

Zoe noted the dark, skeletal remains of the fine wicker furniture, the fancy flower pots that now sprouted only mangled, black vines which must have once been lush greenery.

"Such a shame," she said. "Do they have any idea how the fire started?"

Nikki shot her a quick look. "I don't think so," she replied in a hushed voice. "It was probably just an accident or something."

"Like a short in the electrical system?"

Nikki nodded vigorously. "Yeah! Something just like that." Suddenly, the girl began to fidget, shifting from one foot to another, sticking her hands in and out of her pockets, as though not knowing where to put them. "If you don't need me anymore, I think I'd better go home now," she said.

"Oh, sure, no problem. I'm not going to stay much longer myself. I just wanted to check out these windows."

"Now, don't tell anyone about the secret passageway," Nikki said, as she lowered herself through the trapdoor near the rear of the porch.

Zoe's promise seemed very important to the child, so she quickly gave it. "I swear. Thanks a lot."

"You're welcome. See ya."

A second later, the freckled face, the braids, and the shy,

lopsided grin disappeared. Zoe found herself alone. And, although that was her usual state of affairs, she was surprised to discover that she missed the girl's company already.

Oh, well, standing around feeling lonesome wasn't going to get those windows repaired, and it certainly wasn't going to pay her way to Europe.

She walked over to the damaged panels and examined the casings. Although the light was poor, she was able to test the stops that held the windows in place. Prying gently with a putty knife, just one of the many tools which she always carried in her back pocket, she felt the wooden strips begin to release.

Ten minutes later, she was able to ease the first window from its frame.

There, that hadn't been so difficult. Only eight more panels to go.

"Get as much done as you can," she whispered to herself, "before the old lady comes home from the hospital."

Remembering what Nikki had said about the fleeing plumber and Granddaddy Covington's shotgun, Zoe decided it was a job that was best finished as soon as possible.

Dylan Gray had refused to leave the hospital until he was certain that all five members of the Hopkins family were going to be all right.

Although he liked to think that he loved all his parishioners, Dylan had to admit that some held a special place in his heart. The Hopkins clan were high on his list.

Thanks to a drunken driver who couldn't tell one side of the road from the other, the family had suffered a nasty trauma. But the outcome had been relatively happy. A few stitches for Dad, a cast for Mom, an ace bandage for their ten-year-old boy, and comforting hugs and kisses for the toddling twins, had set everyone right.

Dylan had remained at the hospital, offering what he could in the way of comfort and support until their uncle had arrived to drive them all home.

At the time, Dylan had been so absorbed by their predicament, that he hadn't noticed how much the experience had taken out of him until he hopped on his Harley and headed back to the church.

He was simply exhausted. Body, mind, and spirit.

Who would have thought that being a minister would be such hard work? He hadn't. Back in seminary, he had wondered if such a soft life would spoil him.

No such luck.

Needing a bit of down time to recuperate from the experience, Dylan sought the quiet of the forest. Instead of going straight to the church, he chose to detour through the pine woods behind the property. The path had been cut long ago by trail bikes, and even though it was a bit bumpy and rough on the Harley, the serenity of nature made it worth the effort.

Only a few rays from the setting sun penetrated the trees, barely lighting his way. But he had taken the path many times before and knew it well. Next to the bluff, this was his favorite place to commune with God and His creation.

By the time he had found his way to the back of the church and the rectory, the landscape was dark, the buildings black silhouettes against an inky sky. He parked the Harley in the garage behind his apartment, then walked around the building to his side door. Just as he was about to go inside, he thought he saw a movement on the porch of the Covington mansion. Instantly, his protective instincts flared.

Whether he liked the idea or not, he seemed to be responsible for the estate while its mistress was convalescing. The last thing he needed was for some neighborhood thugs to burglarize the place while he was in charge. He squinted, peering into the darkness, trying to convince himself it had been nothing but some shadows from the trees as they swayed in the evening breeze.

But no . . . there it was again . . . a distinct silhouette of a figure moving on the porch.

And it wasn't Abigail Covington, because Dylan had visited her briefly just before leaving the hospital and the Hopkins family.

Quietly, he closed the door behind him and started across the yard that separated the two properties. Approaching from the rear of the house, he crept to the side porch, keeping his steps light, ears straining for sounds of conversation.

But whoever it was appeared to be alone. He couldn't hear them speaking to anyone, and he could only distinguish one set of footsteps walking back and forth on the porch.

The thief must feel pretty comfortable, he figured, because he didn't seem even trying to be quiet. But then, no one was in sight, and the house was set well back from the road. No wonder they felt secure enough to tramp around as though they owned the place.

Indignation rose, along with his temper. Even if he didn't always approve of Abigail Covington's idiosyncrasies, he was incensed that anyone would take advantage of the woman's misfortune by raiding her house in her absence. Well, this was one would-be robber who was going to get what was coming to him—even if Dylan Gray, retired street fighter, had to give it to him personally.

Peeking around the corner of the house, Dylan saw the dark figure bend over, then he heard the squeak of rusty hinges. To his shock, the intruder seemed to disappear before his eyes.

There one moment. Gone the next. What was going on here?

A second later, he was startled to receive his answer: The trespasser suddenly appeared, only a few feet from him, crawling on hands and knees out from beneath the house.

He managed to keep out of view as he crept forward, his sneakers silent on the thick grass.

When the figure stood, Dylan braced himself, lunged

forward, and grabbed the trespasser from the back. His arms tight around the upper body, he pinned the would-be robber's arms to the side.

"Hold it right there!" he said as the individual struggled against him. "What do you think you're doing?"

Suddenly, the person twisted to the right and jabbed an elbow directly into his solar plexus. His breath left him in a whoosh, and it was all he could do not to lose his grip on the intruder. He hung on, fighting for air.

"Let go of me, you pervert!" his captive shouted. "Or, I swear, I'll do it again—only much lower next time."

In spite of his pain, several facts began to find their way through Dylan's consciousness: the voice speaking to him was undeniably feminine, the body he was holding tightly against his own was softly curved. Just below his forearms, he could feel the swell of something that—even though he had been celibate for the past four years—he recognized as a woman's breast.

"Let go of me! Now!" she demanded.

He did. So quickly that she lost her balance.

He grabbed for her and caught her arm, preventing her from falling. But she was anything but grateful.

For what seemed like an eternity of embarrassment, he stood staring at her, trying to discern her features in the darkness. He was only dimly aware of a cloud of black hair, a petite figure, and the harsh sound of her breathing and his.

"You'd better have a good excuse for mauling me like that, buddy," she said. "And you'd better not be who I think you are."

Angry, defensive words bubbled to his lips, but he choked them back. He hadn't even recovered from the last blow yet; no point in inviting another so soon.

"And just who do you think I am?" he asked.

"I'll bet dollars to donuts . . ." She stepped closer and he could see her better—the scowl, the flashing dark eyes. ". . . that you're that irresponsible nincompoop of a minister who was supposed to meet me here over three hours ago.''

Meet her? Three hours ago.

Oh, no. The recollection came flooding back. Vaguely he remembered an appointment with somebody here around four in the afternoon. But who . . . ?

"Joe Harmond?" he asked, totally confused. "The stained glass repair guy?"

"*Zoe* Harmond. The stained glass repair *woman.*" She tossed her head and turned on one heel. "But then, considering how you just groped me, I don't suppose my gender is a mystery any longer."

Without another word—or allowing him a chance to retort—she stomped away toward a van that he only now noticed standing in the driveway.

A moment later, she had slammed the door and left, spraying gravel as she peeled away.

Dylan groaned and uttered a curse under his breath—a couple of choice phrases that he hadn't used since the day he had left the streets of New York.

The words had felt perfectly natural on his tongue, he noted with dismay as he headed back to the rectory. Just as her softness had felt wonderful inside the circle of his arms.

Minister or common thug?

Sometimes he couldn't be sure.

But he was certain of one thing: It wasn't easy to leave the mean streets behind.

Chapter Three

$\mathcal{Z}$oe knocked on the door of the rectory, her heart in her throat, her pride in her pocket. A night spent tossing and turning in her bed in the back of the van had convinced her that she needed to make an appearance this morning— even if it meant she would be fired on the spot. Too much money was involved to stand on principle. Her European trip was at stake, and all the freedom and adventure it represented.

Besides, she probably owed him an apology.

Okay, she *did* owe him one. After all, she had been trespassing—sort of—and in the dark, she could understand how he might have thought she was a burglar.

Once again, her temper had gotten the better of her, and she hadn't even given him a chance to explain before she had marched away.

Sometimes, Zoe had to admit that "leaving" was something she was very good at, having had a lot of practice. "Staying" was much harder.

Mentally practicing her apology, she knocked several more times, but no one answered.

The morning sun was warm on her back, the breezes gentle and heavy with the perfume of nearby lilac bushes that climbed trellises on either side of the doorway.

Like the church itself, the rectory was built of stone, weathered and grayed over the years. It looked solid, peaceful, quaint, and inviting . . . just as a church should.

Zoe tried to remember when she had last seen the inside of a church. It had been too long, for sure. She found that she missed the quiet solace to be found inside a house of worship. Maybe she would go again . . . soon . . . but certainly not here, considering her close encounter with the preacher.

She knocked again. Less patiently this time.

Where was he?

Zoe was beginning to feel as though she had spent half of her life waiting for this man to appear.

Across an asphalt parking lot behind the chapel, she could see a half-dozen or so teenage boys running around and tossing a basketball through a hoop. Maybe they knew where the old fellow was this morning.

The old fellow. The phrase jarred her the moment it crossed her mind. In the dim light last night, she hadn't been able to see his features clearly, but there was no mistaking that thick silver hair. He must be elderly, she thought, but his arm wrapped around her chest had been anything but feeble. His voice had been strong and authoritative.

Okay, so he's an incredibly fit old fellow, she silently amended as she walked across the parking lot toward the players.

Several of them turned to look her way, and she heard a couple of adolescent hoots of approval. Although she was at least ten years their senior, she had captured their interest.

Lest the attention go to her head, Zoe reminded herself of how little it took to catch the fancy of a pubescent male. Anything slightly more vivacious and curvaceous than a fence post was likely to do the trick.

As she drew closer, Zoe realized that the one player, who appeared to be blond, was actually silver-haired. She had found her "old fellow" after all.

But he certainly wasn't moving like an elderly gentleman. Having snatched the ball from under the nose of the nearest boy, he spun toward the hoop, jumped, and slam-dunked it.

Cheers and accompanying groans sounded through the group, and Zoe heard someone say, "Hey, Rev . . . smooth movin'."

Although his back was toward her, Zoe was astonished to see just how "fit" her senior citizen really was. He wore a pair of cutoff jeans that revealed tanned, heavily muscled thighs and calves. His black T-shirt was just snug enough to accent broad shoulders, a strong back, and a trim waist.

Extremely fit, she observed. Since when did preachers have physiques like that? These boys must keep him in shape with all this basketball.

One by one, the players turned toward her, the game temporarily suspended. The minister was the last to notice her, and when he did face her, he flashed her an open, friendly smile that nearly took her breath away.

Old? she thought. No older than she. In fact, he seemed to be about the same age. Although his hair was, indeed, silver-white, several locks of it hung boyishly over his eyes, plastered to his forehead with perspiration. His eyes were shockingly blue, his features rugged, his complexion flushed from the exertion of the game.

"Hi," he called to her, bouncing the ball several times and walking toward her. "Can we help you?"

"Reverend Gray," she said, stating the obvious.

"That's right," he replied as though she had been inquiring. "And you are . . . ? Oh."

He halted in mid-step, recognition dawning on his face. "It's you, Ms. Harmond. Sorry, I didn't . . ." He simply shrugged instead of finishing his statement.

"Maybe you should take a nice, long look," she said sarcastically, "that way you'll be sure to know me the next time we meet."

"Good idea." For just a moment, his eyes swept up and down her figure, then they locked with hers, and he smiled his appreciation. "Okay. Now I'm not likely to forget again," he said, his voice smooth and low.

A couple of the boys heard his reply and snickered, prodding each other in the ribs with their elbows.

Zoe felt the blood rush to her cheeks and was thankful for her swarthy, gypsy coloring. Her blushes didn't show easily.

With a few more long strides, he closed the gap between them and extended his hand. "I'm really sorry . . . about last night, I mean," he said.

"Apology accepted," she replied, returning his handshake. This time his touch was gentle and firm, but friendly—quite a contrast to the previous evening's tussle.

"I never should have tackled you like that; it's just that I—" He paused and glanced over his shoulder. Eager, overly-interested faces were trained on him as the boys listened to every word.

"Well . . . I thought you were a burglar," he said, lowering his voice, "and I'm responsible for the safekeeping of Miss Covington's property while she's in the hospital."

"I figured that much out myself. But by then I was several miles down the road." Zoe hesitated, feeling a bit foolish herself. "And I had left in such a huff that I couldn't bring myself to come back and explain. It's just that, well, to be honest, you scared me half to death when you grabbed me around the . . ."

She shot another look at the boys. Their eyes were getting wider by the moment.

"Yes, I understand. Enough said, under the circumstances." He nodded toward the eavesdroppers, then used the tail of his T-shirt to wipe the sweat from his brow. For an all too brief moment she was treated to the sight of a washboard-rippled, taut stomach.

Then and there, Zoe decided that there ought to be some sort of rule against ministers who were as attractive as this one. It simply wasn't fair that a man of the cloth could incite lustful thoughts in an unsuspecting female. Especially one that was on her way to Europe to get away from everyone and everything she had ever known. One who didn't have time for such things.

"I'd like to get started on the windows as soon as possible," she said in her best "let's get down to business" voice. "I have my own table and tools, and I prefer to work outside, whenever possible, weather permitting. You know, toxic fumes from the solder smoke and caustic chemicals."

He nodded curtly, his manner suddenly as brusque as hers.

"I'll need some electricity for lights and my soldering iron," she added. "If you could just string an extension cord out to the porch for me, I'll get right to work."

"No problem. I'll be glad to, just as soon as I'm finished here." He nodded toward the players, who had moved a few feet closer, straining to hear.

"As soon as you . . . ?"

What did he mean? she wondered. He was going to finish his stupid basketball game before he provided her with the necessities she needed to get to work?

With impatience practically seeping from her pores, she was sure the Reverend Gray had to know how eager she was to get started. But his face was set in determined lines, and Zoe had the distinct feeling that if she pressed the issue, he would only take longer to do her bidding.

"Well . . . far be it from me to interrupt your important ministerial duties," she said, lifting one eyebrow indignantly.

The smile disappeared from his face and his eyes went cold so quickly she thought she had stepped into a deep freeze.

"There is a lot more," he said, "to being a minister than just conducting choir practices and organizing bingo games in the basement."

Other things . . . like tossing a basketball around? He had to be kidding.

"So I see," she replied sarcastically. "Well, whenever you're ready, I'll be waiting in my van." Turning her back to him, she stomped away.

As Zoe made what she hoped was a righteously indignant departure, she thought she heard him say something like: "Temperamental woman . . . always leaving in a huff."

A huff, indeed.

If he messed with her, she'd show him "huff."

"Not bad, Rev. Not bad at all!" One of the oldest, a tall, muscular, blond kid named Kerry Moore, elbowed Dylan in the ribs as they all watched Zoe walk away.

"Yeah . . ." added Eddie Truman. Eddie and Kerry were inseparable complementary puzzle parts. Kerry supplied the brawn, Eddie the brains. Whatever Eddie could conceive, Kerry would execute. And Eddie was excellent at instigation. Whatever he lacked in stature, he made up in street cunning and mischief. He wiggled one eyebrow. "She's hot for you, my man. I could see it in her eyes, no kidding."

Dylan threw the ball hard, a well-aimed shot that managed to bounce off both boys' foreheads—Kerry's then Eddie's. "Just because she's a bit testy doesn't mean she's not a lady," he said. "So watch your mouths."

He tossed the basketball to Steve Viceroy. As usual, Steve missed the ball and tripped over his own feet trying to retrieve it. Steve was always trying to be as "bad" as Kerry and Eddie, but with his lack of coordination, dull wit, and shortage of imagination, he wasn't likely to ever attain the high level of juvenile delinquency that his friends had.

A few of the other guys giggled, intrigued by the idea of the "Rev." having a female in his life. But their glee quickly changed to disappointment when Dylan announced that the game was over.

"Like Ms. Harmond said, I have other duties to perform—like having a heart-to-heart with you three." He pointed to Kerry, Eddie, and Steve. "Straight to my office, on the double."

"Uh-oh," Kerry said, rolling his eyes at Eddie, "busted."

"What for?" Steve demanded, instantly rattled and upset. "What did we do?"

"Crimes against humanity . . . or maybe nothing at all." Dylan slapped Eddie and Kerry on the shoulders just hard enough to convey the idea that he meant business. "That's what I intend to find out."

"Okay, what do you fearsome threesome know about the fire in Miss Covington's home?"

"Know? What do we know?" Kerry sat on the edge of the chair that Dylan had offered him, right next to the pastor's old-fashioned, burled oak desk.

The office was small but cozy, inviting a feeling of comfort and safety. Its mahogany wainscoting glowed in the light of the green-shaded banker's lamp on the reverend's desk. The overstuffed easy chairs embraced visitors in dark green and burgundy plaid softness.

As he had intended, Dylan Gray's office provided a pleasant place to relax and chat. Maybe even a refuge, where one could confess, unburden a heavy soul or find answers for a few of life's more perplexing problems.

But not everyone found solace within those mahogany walls.

"What do you mean, what do we know?" Eddie jumped up from his own chair and hurried over to the window. Staring out at the sweeping view of the pine forests, he pretended to be fascinated by the nothing that was happening there.

"What part of the question don't you understand?" Dylan asked.

Steve's ruddy complexion blushed a few shades redder as he studied the toes of his sneakers through thick, wire-rimmed glasses. "Why do you think we would know anything about that?" he asked.

"Yeah." Eddie nodded, an indignant scowl knotting his thick, black eyebrows together. "Why are you gonna come after *us*? It could've been anybody in town that started that fire."

Dylan leaned forward, his elbows on his desk, his fingers steepled in front of his chin. "I didn't accuse anyone of anything. I just asked what you know about it. It's a small town; I thought you might have heard something."

Eddie took a chair beside Kerry. "Are you saying that you want us to repeat *gossip*, Reverend Gray? I mean, isn't that what your sermon was about last Sunday?"

"Oh, get real, Ed. Like you actually hear anything I say from the pulpit. You just read the sign out front, huh?"

Eddie had the decency to at least look embarrassed for having been caught cheating.

"No, of course I would never ask you to repeat gossip." Dylan smiled, leaned forward, and dropped his voice to a whisper. "You just say it once; I'll listen hard the first time."

Just one more month, Zoe told herself as she sat in the van, mentally twiddling her thumbs, waiting for the elusive Reverend Gray to make his appearance. *One more month and I'll be exploring the highways and byways of Italy, France, and Spain. No waiting for anyone, no personal expectations that no relationship could meet, no unwanted ties or burdensome responsibilities.*

One more month.

Maybe sooner, if she could only do this job, collect her money, and be on her way.

Finally, she saw Rev. Gray walking toward her across the expansive lawn that separated the chapel from the mansion. He had changed from shorts and a T-shirt to dark gray slacks and a simple, white oxford shirt that accentuated his physique almost as well as the sports clothes.

Jumping from the van, she donned a moderately indignant, but definitely impatient, expression. They met at the porch.

"Thank you for waiting, Ms. Harmond," he said. "I had some business I had to take care of with the boys before I could—"

"Oh?" she said, interrupting him. "Was the score tied?"

He fixed her with a look that did more to intimidate her than she cared to admit. Those blue eyes could turn positively glacial in an instant. The thought occurred to her that she wouldn't want to be on the bad side of this man, minister or not.

Apparently, he chose to ignore the jab as he beckoned her to follow him and led her up the steps to the door of the porch. Unlocking it, he said, "I'll have your current out to you in five minutes, if you want to go ahead and set up your table. Or, you can wait, and I'll give you a hand with that, too."

He paused and looked back at her. She studied his expression to see if he was somehow insulting her, but he seemed sincere with his offer of assistance. She felt a pang of remorse. But not a very big one.

"I can handle it," she said. "I do it all the time."

He shrugged, walked across the porch, and slipped another key into the door lock. "Whatever you want," he replied. "I've always thought self-reliance was an underrated virtue."

She considered his words for a second or two. "I agree," she said. "I learned long ago that the only one I can count on is myself."

"Hm-m-mmm. I'd like to think that isn't true, Ms. Harmond," he said thoughtfully. "Independence is a fine, strong, admirable quality, but I'd like to think that there are good people in the world who will lend a helping hand to someone who is truly in need."

"I think it's up to each of us to make certain that we never are in need," she replied with a lift to her chin.

He gave her a strange smile that deeply upset her—far more than was logical. She could almost believe that there was a trace of pity in it. Maybe more than a trace.

Where did he get off feeling sorry for her? She didn't need his or anyone's sympathy. Not now. Not ever.

She was doing fine, just hunky-dory, supplying her own needs in every way.

"Life can be cruel and unpredictable," he said, "and I believe that everyone needs help once in a while. There's no shame in that."

"Experience has taught me," she said, "that to need something from someone else is to be disappointed every time."

He pushed the door open, revealing a sitting room that was decorated in traditional Victorian splendor. Zoe stood on the porch, but couldn't resist a peek inside. She caught intriguing glimpses of rose damask brocade, plush oriental rugs, and glittering crystal chandeliers—generations of accumulated treasures.

"You've been disappointed *every* time?" he asked, pausing in the doorway.

"Every time I can remember," she said. "But I'm not complaining. They were lessons well-learned."

He studied her closely with those pale blue eyes until she felt uncomfortable under such scrutiny. Then he said, "I'm very sorry that has been your experience." His voice was soft, his expression warm. "I'll say a little prayer for you."

Instantly, she bristled. "Are you saying that you think I *need* to be prayed for?"

"We all need to be prayed for, Ms. Harmond," he said quietly. "I'll pray that God will send you someone who won't disappoint you, someone who will meet one of your heart's deepest needs."

Without thinking, she blurted out what she was thinking, a habit she was trying—without much success—to break. "That's just what I need right now . . . to fall in love and clutter up my life."

"Oh? Is falling in love your heart's deepest need?" he asked teasingly.

"Hardly. It's just the first thing that came to mind."

He grinned, and she couldn't help noticing what a nice smile he had, even if he did seem to be mocking her. "If it was the first thing you thought of, it must be your deepest need. I'll say several prayers for you, as soon as possible.''

She stepped off the porch backward, nearly tripping over her own feet. Suddenly, she seemed to have lost all coordination, along with a generous measure of her self-composure. ''Gee, thanks,'' she said. ''I guess.''

''You're welcome . . . I guess.''

Zoe had chosen the widespread branches of a nearby oak as the roof for her temporary workshop. The foliage provided a shady refuge against the afternoon sun, and she loved the way the breeze rustled the leaves, playing the melodies of springtime.

In a month, it would still be spring in Europe. Maybe she would tour France first. Paris in May . . . strolling the West Bank on a balmy evening . . . ah, she could hardly wait! Already she could smell the perfume of the flower markets, the—

Her lovely dream evaporated at the chugging, wheezing sound of an old school bus as it rounded the corner. It screeched to a halt in front of the mansion, the side door flipped open, and several book- and lunchbox-laden children spilled out onto the sidewalk.

Zoe recognized one as the little girl who had shown her the way into the porch last night. Something told her she would have company within ten minutes.

It took only six for the girl to reappear, her school dress exchanged for a pair of too-large shorts and a faded T-shirt. In one hand she held a soda, in the other a piece of bread smeared with peanut butter.

''Hi! What'cha doin'?'' she said as she approached the table and peered over at the work Zoe had spread before her.

''I've started the repairs on the stained glass windows,'' she said, trying not to notice that Nikki's hands were badly in need of a scrubbing. Apparently, no one had impressed upon the child the need to wash before eating.

Zoe couldn't help remembering another little girl who had been similarly neglected, shuffled from one foster home to another, some better, some worse. Most of the parents had been good people, well-intentioned and loving, but overworked and underpaid. There had never been enough of anything—affection, time, money, guidance—to go around.

Funny, how the pain never really went away, no matter how many years passed.

"I *know* you're fixing the windows," Nikki said, "but I want to know *how*."

Zoe was surprised that the child's interest seemed genuine, so she decided to elaborate.

"Well, it's sort of like a giant puzzle. First I have to take it apart, then put it all back together again."

"How come some of the pieces are broken?"

"The fire was really hot, and it caused some of the glass to crack. I'll have to replace those pieces."

"Can you do that?"

"Sure can."

"Wow. That's neat. How about the pieces that are all black from the smoke?"

"Simple. I just scrub a lot. Like doing a whole bunch of really dirty dishes."

"Yuck. I hate doing dishes. I have to do *all* the dishes in my house. My mom works really hard, so I have to help her at home."

Zoe had a momentary flashback of her first home, her biological mother, no father on the scene. Mountains of food-encrusted dishes. Piles of mildewed laundry. Mom, sprawled on the sofa, "sick," again.

Fervently, she hoped this sweet child's situation was better.

"Your mom is very lucky to have such a good daughter as you," Zoe said. Reaching across the table, she retrieved two pairs of safety glasses. "Here," she said as she handed one to Nikki. "I'm getting ready to cut some glass now.

If you're going to be my assistant, you'll have to wear these.''

''Really? Neat!'' The girl shoved the last bite of sandwich into her mouth and set her soda can on the edge of the table. Carefully, she took the glasses from Zoe.

They both slipped on the wide, clear-framed spectacles, then looked at each other and giggled.

''You look like an alien,'' Nikki said, wrinkling her freckled nose.

''Oh, really? And how many aliens have you met personally?''

''Hundreds.''

Zoe raised one eyebrow. ''Hundreds?''

''Thousands.''

''I think you have an overactive imagination.''

Nikki grinned. ''I think you're right.''

''What's this I hear?'' Zoe looked up to see Dylan Gray standing nearby. He had walked so quietly across the lawn that she hadn't heard his approach. Smiling, he was obviously amused at what he had overheard.

''We're talking about aliens, Rev. Gray,'' Nikki said, her face brightening at the sight of the handsome, young minister.

Zoe had to admit, she knew how the girl felt. Suddenly, her hands were trembling ever so slightly. Holding the glass cutter steady seemed more of a challenge as he approached the work table and watched what she was doing.

''Do you believe in aliens, Rev. Gray?'' Nikki asked. ''I do.''

Dylan chuckled and shrugged his shoulders. ''I don't know, Nikki. It's a big universe. With God, all things are possible.''

''I saw the movie *ET* and *Close Encounters*, and I think aliens are cute. I wish I had one for a friend.''

Zoe pulled the cutting wheel across the glass and listened for exactly the right sound which told her she was scoring the surface properly. Picking up the piece, she deftly snapped it in half between her fingers.

"An alien for a friend?" she asked Nikki. "Why an alien and not just a regular kid like yourself?"

The sadness that crossed the girl's face went straight to Zoe's heart. The look, the emotion behind it, were all so familiar.

"I don't have any kid friends. My mom and me . . . I mean, *I* . . . we move a lot, and I'm always the new girl. Nobody likes new kids, 'cause they think they're geeks. Aliens are neat, because they're from another planet, and they don't know you're a geek."

Zoe stole a quick glance at Dylan and was surprised to see how stricken he looked. He, too, felt the depth of the child's pain. Zoe wondered if the reverend had once felt the ache of abandonment. He seemed well-acquainted with the feeling.

He walked around the table to stand beside Nikki. Gently, he tugged on one of her braids. "You are many things, Nicola Sarita Dickens. Charming, expressive, and far too cute for your own good, but you aren't a geek. Believe me, I've met some, and you aren't a bit like them."

"Really? I mean, you're a preacher, and you can't tell lies, right?"

"Absolutely right."

"Double-dog promise?"

"*Triple*-dog promise."

"Wow, thanks!"

Zoe watched the girl's russet eyes glimmer as she gazed up, star-struck and spellbound by the minister. What a charismatic character he was. No wonder she adored him so.

But then, little girls were easily taken in by a bit of blarney and blatant male charm. Unlike *big* girls, who were much wiser and more difficult to convince, of course, she told herself.

Having won the everlasting adoration of the younger set, Dylan turned his attentions to Zoe.

"How is the job coming?" he asked, picking up one of the smoke-blackened pieces and turning it over in his hand.

"It's a mess," she said, deciding to be honest. The project was going to take longer than she had planned. About three times as long. She wasn't sure if this job was going to assist her in getting to Europe, or prevent her leaving.

"Can you do it?" He sounded worried. The last thing she needed now was a customer who was as concerned as she was. One panic attack mixed into the potion was enough.

"Of course I can do it," she replied. "But, as you can see, the heat melted all of the soldered joints, as well as parts of the lead. Plus the broken pieces that have to be replaced, and all the smoke. I've tried three different chemical solvents already to take it off, but the only thing that works is steel wool and old-fashioned elbow grease."

She glanced over at Nikki and saw an unhappy expression mixed with the peanut butter on her face. Did she resent the fact that Rev. Gray was talking to the "older woman" now, instead of her?

"How did the fire start?" Zoe asked, trying not to think about the fact that her hand was unsteady as she fit the new piece of glass. If he would just move back a couple of feet. If he weren't standing so close, she wouldn't feel so awkward.

"We don't know for sure," he said. "Actually, that was why I was late getting over here to help you with the power line. I thought I should talk to the guys, find out if anyone had heard anything."

"I see." Zoe felt a little ashamed of how she had condescended to him about the basketball playing. Obviously, he was attempting to gain the kids' confidence, to bond with them any way he could. It seemed there *was* more to Rev. Gray's ministry than bingo games and choir practice.

"Did they?" Nikki leaned forward across the table, her eyes bright with interest. "Did they say if they knew who did it?"

"No, they didn't." Dylan studied her curiously. "We aren't even sure it was *somebody* who caused it. Maybe it was some*thing* . . . like a short in the house wiring. Old houses are known for their electrical problems."

"Oh, yeah, right." Nikki looked relieved. "That's probably what it was."

"Our Nikki, here, was quite a heroine, Ms. Harmond," he said. "Did you hear how she rescued Miss Covington from almost certain death?"

"No, I didn't. Is that true, Nikki? Did you save her?"

Nikki fidgeted with her soda can. "It wasn't that big a deal. I just helped her get out of the house so she wouldn't burn up or breathe too much smoke. But she had to go to the hospital anyway."

"The important thing is she's going to make a full recovery, thanks to you," Dylan told the girl. "I'm very proud of you."

"I've gotta go do my homework," Nikki said. A moment later, she was hurrying across the lawn toward the street.

"It appears our half-pint Good Samaritan is a tad shy," Dylan observed.

Zoe watched her thoughtfully as the child disappeared around the corner at a brisk trot.

"Yes, isn't she though," Zoe murmured, thinking of the secret passageway beneath the porch. "Very shy, indeed."

Chapter Four

$\mathcal{A}$s Zoe held up the first of the nine panels, she admired her craftsmanship and remembered why she had chosen this line of work five years ago. No matter how many windows she designed and built, no matter how many she repaired, restoring them to their original beauty, she never got over the glory of stained glass. The way it captured the sunlight and washed it in brilliant color, sparkling like ten thousand multifaceted jewels, amazed and fascinated Zoe.

Gazing at the ever-changing prisms of light, Zoe was transported to one of the happier aspects of her childhood: her kaleidoscope.

One Christmas, when she had been seven, Santa had brought her the beautiful toy—compliments of a local charity drive for underprivileged children. For hours she had watched the interplay of light and glass as she turned the wheel, creating more magic than she had thought existed in the world.

Now *she* was the one who brought this beauty from a dream into reality, through her own hands, with her own imagination and meticulous skill. And these patterns never changed, lost forever by the slightest jiggle of the kaleidoscope.

Another artist had created this window years ago, and she had rescued his work once again. Although the panel she held in her hands represented only one-ninth of the overall picture, she could see that it was a work of art that was well worth saving.

A car pulled into the driveway, a large, silver Bentley with graceful rounded curves and gleaming chrome. The car was an imposing presence . . . like its mistress.

At least Zoe had been forewarned, although it remained to be seen if that would mean forearmed. Between Nikki, Dylan, the workmen who were refurbishing the porch, and the occasional neighbor strolling by, she had been amply informed about the cantankerous nature of Miss Abigail Covington. Having dealt with more than one difficult client, Zoe wasn't particularly worried, but she wasn't looking forward to the meeting either.

Usually, she was straightforward and assertive with everyone she met, customers included. She treated all with civility, but she refused to take abuse from anyone. The first eighteen years of her life she had been helpless to resist; now that she was a woman, she insisted on being treated fairly. She didn't see why this situation should be any different.

Zoe continued with her work beneath the oak and watched from the corner of her eye as Dylan Gray exited the driver's side of the car and walked to the back.

He was actually playing the part of chauffeur for that spoiled old aristocrat. Zoe found the concept amusing. Like her, Zoe had the feeling that Dylan Gray wasn't accustomed to catering to anyone's frivolous whims.

Maybe he actually likes the old bat, she thought. No, not likely, she added as she watched Abigail exit the vehicle with all the pomp and circumstance of the Grand Duchess of Covington Falls.

While simple self-confidence and grace might have been endearing qualities, the lady carried the act to an extreme. Her nose was tilted much too high, her movements far too dramatic as she primped her French twist, waved Dylan away with the flick of a wrist, holding her ivory and ebony cane with one pinky extended, as though she were sipping tea.

"Good grief," Zoe muttered, "the lost Anastasia resurrected."

Zoe hoped she would go directly into the front door of the house, bypassing her and the workers who were laboring on the porch. But no such luck. In her peripheral vision, Zoe saw Abigail veering toward them, coming across the lawn with Dylan following a few steps behind. He held one hand out, as though ready to catch the Duchess if she were to stumble.

For a moment, Zoe wondered if she should leave her work and meet the woman midway across the yard. With her soldering iron heated to just the right temperature, she was ready to begin and didn't want to be interrupted right now. But, judging from the intense look on the woman's face, she was going to be interrupted, whether she liked it or not.

She caught her breath as Miss Covington seemed to snag her foot on a tree root, teeter, and grip her cane to keep from falling. In an instant, Dylan had grasped her forearm, and this time she didn't dismiss him.

That's what happens if you stick your nose too far into the air. You can't see where you're going or where you've been.

Zoe decided that, whether she wanted to or not, common courtesy demanded she go to her. Reluctantly, she unplugged the iron, replaced the cap on her bottle of liquid flux, so it wouldn't evaporate, and wiped her hands on a damp cloth. One quick look down at her faded jeans and sweatshirt told Zoe she was poorly dressed to greet royalty.

That's the way the gherkin squirts. Some of us have to actually work for a living.

They met near the porch at the side of the house. The other workers suddenly evaporated, finding things outside the vicinity that needed their immediate attention. Zoe thought she should say a quick hello and follow their lead. But before she could introduce herself, Miss Covington fixed her with a hateful glare and said, "What are you doing, picnicking under my oak tree? How many times do I have to tell you people in this neighborhood to keep off my property?"

Abigail turned to Dylan. "Honestly, Reverend, is this the way you look after my estate for me? Allowing the local rabble to make themselves at home while I'm gone?"

Dylan cleared his throat and shot Zoe an apologetic look. "Miss Covington, this lady isn't one of your neighbors and she isn't picnicking under your tree. She's repairing your stained glass windows. Remember? I told you they were damaged."

Abigail snorted. "Of course I remember. What do you think I am—feeble-minded?"

"No, Abigail," Dylan said with a smirk. "I don't think there's a feeble cell in your body."

Mollified, she turned back to Zoe. "But how can you fix my windows? You're a . . . a girl."

"No, I'm not." Zoe gathered her patience—all two teaspoons of it—and forced herself to speak slowly and respectfully at a normal level of volume. "I'm a *woman*," she continued. "A highly qualified glazier and stained glass artist. I'm more than capable of doing a complete restoration of your windows."

Abigail's only response was the slight twitch of one carefully penciled eyebrow. Then she turned to Dylan and said, "She's not only a girl, but she's an impudent one, too. Why on earth did you hire someone like this? Where is that Mr. Joe Harmond you told me about?"

"I'm Joe Harmond," Zoe interjected. "Well, I mean—"

"Her name is Joe?" Abigail was positively scandalized. Her face flushed nearly purple as she raised her cane and shook it at Dylan. "You've hired a female named Joe, who wears men's clothing and fixes windows for money. The next thing you'll be telling me is that she's one of those . . . those . . . Lebanese. And you know how I feel about all that."

Dylan sighed and took Miss Covington by the arm. Firmly. He gave Zoe a weary smile. "I'm sorry, Ms. Harmond. Miss Covington isn't herself today. Usually it takes her far less time to offend those she meets. She should be up to snuff tomorrow. With any luck you won't see her before then."

"Well! I never!" Abigail tried to jerk her arm away from Dylan but he held her fast.

"Come along, Abbie," he said. "There are lots of other workers here today for you to insult. You don't want to use it all up on Ms. Harmond."

"What are you looking at?" Abigail said over her shoulder to Zoe as Dylan led her away. "I'm not paying you to stand around gawking at me. Get back to work!"

Zoe whirled around and marched back to her table, fuming. She wouldn't even need a heated soldering iron for this job. After that charming encounter, she was hot enough to just use the tip of her finger.

Having just installed the first completed panel, Zoe stood back to enjoy the view. Even if the other eight were still melted, sagging, blackened messes, the repaired one gave more than a hint of how magnificent the finished project would be. And even if she had developed an instant dislike for the house's mistress, Zoe reveled in the joy of being able to recover this treasure.

The white lilies glowed against a rich green background. Tiny, rose-tinted jewels winked light at her from the border. The beveled square in the corner caught the sunlight and separated it into rainbow prisms which glimmered across the floor.

She was so absorbed that she didn't notice Dylan Gray until he was directly behind her. "Nice job . . . *Joe*," he said.

Giving him a crooked smile, she added, "Not bad, for an impudent girl."

"Not bad at all." He stepped up to the window and ran his fingertip over the now smooth lead and joints. Zoe had always prided herself on creating a perfectly even line in her soldering. As far as she was concerned, that was the defining difference between a hobbyist and a pro.

"Don't let Abigail get under your skin," he said. "That's what she wants to do."

"Why? What's the advantage of being so disagreeable?"

He shrugged. "I suppose it's to keep people at a distance."

"I'm sure it works—very well."

"Yes, it does. And if you don't let anyone get too close to your heart, it's less likely to be broken."

He turned from the window to look directly into her eyes. Zoe tried to glance away, anything to avoid the scrutiny, to guard the secrets of her own heart. But she couldn't. It wouldn't have done any good, she thought. He seemed to have already seen far more than she wanted him to. Did he know how true his words were . . . for Miss Abigail Covington . . . and for her?

Something in his expression told her he did, and she was extremely uncomfortable with the knowledge.

Zoe turned the conversation back to the old lady, where she figured it belonged. "How can you pretend to care about that woman? She's awful!"

"She can be, and I don't always like her. In fact, I'd say that there's very little that I do like about her. But I've decided to love her anyway."

"What do you mean, *decided*? Either you feel love for someone or you don't."

"What do feelings have to do with it?" He turned and walked toward the porch door. She followed, unable to stop herself. Even if she found his insights unsettling, he was fascinating. She couldn't remember ever talking to anyone, man or woman, like him before.

"Feelings are everything," she said. "That's what love is, an emotion."

"If you're talking about infatuation-type love, I suppose you're right," he replied. "But obviously I'm not infatuated with Miss Abigail. I doubt anyone has been for the past seventy years; she's made certain of that with her odious behavior. I'm talking about a different kind of love altogether, Ms. Harmond. It's the kind you can have for anyone, whether you like them or not."

"I don't know what you're talking about. But I do know I could never love someone as rude and unkind as that old bat." She nodded toward the house.

"But you need to," he said, "for yourself, if not for her."

"I don't think it's possible."

"All things are possible, Ms. Harmond."

She laughed. "That's from the Bible, huh?"

"All except the 'Ms. Harmond' part. So, you *have* spent some time in a church."

"Of course I have. I'm not a heathen, you know." She continued to follow him across the lawn in the direction of the rectory. "As a matter of fact, I've spent time in a lot of churches . . . and a lot of towns . . . and . . ."

"A bit of a roamer, are you?" His hands were thrust deep into his slacks pockets, his expression thoughtful.

But she didn't like the direction this conversation was taking. He always seemed to be able to bring it back to her.

"A bit," she said. "But I like it that way."

He stopped abruptly and placed his hand on her forearm the way he had Miss Covington's. "Do you?" he asked. "Do you like being on the run?"

"On the run? From what?"

"I don't know the answer to that question. But your heart does. Maybe you should ask it, instead."

"Well!" She propped her hands on her waist and gave him what she hoped was an indignant frown. "I think you're a nosy busybody."

Instead of being offended, he threw back his head and laughed heartily. "That's so true," he said. "It's part of my job description. And speaking of my job, I'm sorry to have to leave your stimulating company, but I have to work on my sermon.''

Only then did she realize that she had followed him all the way to the rectory's door. How embarrassing. The last thing she wanted to convey was the idea that she was pursuing him.

"Sure, no problem," she said. "I have work to do, too. A couple more hours of sunlight and all that."

Spinning around, she made a hasty retreat. But as she walked away, she heard him say, "Why don't you come to church this Sunday, Ms. Harmond? The sermon will be on the topic of 'Loving Your Neighbor.' I'd be very pleased to see you."

"Maybe," she called over her shoulder. *No way, not on your ever-livin' life!* she added silently.

"Besides, we're going to be honoring Nikki for rescuing Abigail. I'm sure she would be happy if you were there, too."

Darn him! Why had he added that? He knew she couldn't resist doing something to please that little girl.

It was a trap. Pure and simple.

She decided to amend her law against good-looking, sexy, young ministers. They shouldn't have pale blue eyes either . . . especially if they could see directly into your soul. Into dark, secret places you didn't even want to look yourself.

Chapter Five

*R*everend Dylan Gray sat in his usual place, a chair just in front of the choir loft, and watched Mrs. Whittle sing her opening solo hymn.

She was a soprano who had passed her prime, but no one, including Dylan, seemed to mind. What she lacked in accurate pitch, she made up in enthusiasm as she proclaimed loudly, "How Great Thou Art!"

The sunlight streamed through the window above the loft and shone on her dark chestnut hair, giving her a halo. Knowing her and her flair for the dramatic, Dylan was sure she had chosen this spot for exactly that reason. Mrs. Whittle had many virtues, but humility wasn't high on the list.

Dylan looked out across the congregation and wondered why he didn't feel some sort of thrill of accomplishment. This was his parish. His own church. Well, it was the Lord's church; daily he was made aware of that humbling fact. But he was its steward, a daunting task, even in a quiet, sleepy village like Covington Falls.

His eyes swept the members of his parish, seeing their complacent, almost apathetic faces, and he wondered—not for the first time—why he was here. What did these law-abiding, upper-middle-class families know about true spiritual deprivation? Nothing that he could see.

In his New York neighborhood, the needs had been obvious. A minister's task was clear: bring sinners to repentance, preach the practical value of moral standards and close family ties, help those who were suffering financially, physically, emotionally, and mentally, and—perhaps most difficult of all—set an example of honorable living without appearing to be too pious.

One always ran the risk of being too spiritually minded to be of any earthly good. Dylan had found it to be a tricky balance. But he had looked forward to the challenge of shepherding his own flock. And now he had it.

But here, he felt like a reverend in title only. How could you minister to a community that seemed to have no needs? With their comfortable, well-ordered lives, Dylan sometimes felt that all he did was provide a comfortable place for them to congregate and sing hymns once a week. He had hoped to lead a church that would be an invaluable part of the community's spiritual and physical well-being, not just a social center.

With a start, he realized that Mrs. Whittle had finished her song and taken her seat. Everyone was watching him expectantly—those who were actually awake—waiting for him to lead them in the opening prayer. As he took his place in the pulpit, he saw Zoe Harmond, sitting in the back pew, looking awkward, embarrassed . . . and stunningly beautiful.

Her dark hair had been released from its perpetual ponytail and floated in soft curls around her pretty face, which seemed to be enhanced with just a touch of makeup. Instead of her work clothes, she was wearing a simple spring dress of pastel yellow. She had pinned a daisy to her bodice. He thought of Miss Covington's disparaging remarks about her femininity and chuckled to himself.

Abigail Covington herself sat in the front pew, as always. He suspected she chose this spot for two reasons: One, because she was basically blind, but too vain to wear glasses in public. Two, because she felt it was a place of honor, and, therefore, hers alone to occupy. And alone, she was. No one in town cared to share the spot or even a moment of their time with her.

"Good morning," he said, his voice deep and melodic as it reverberated through the room.

Several members responded. The rest appeared to be, at least mentally, still snoring away at home in their beds.

After what he hoped was *not* a lengthy prayer, he noticed that he had lost a couple of them; they continued to nod, eyes closed, even after the "Amen."

"Today," he said, "we gather, not only to worship the Lord, but to honor one of our own."

Looking around the room, he finally spotted Nikki, sitting beside Zoe Harmond in the rear pew. She looked miserably shy, squirming in her seat, refusing to meet his eyes.

"As many of you know, we had a near tragedy a couple of nights ago."

He went on to explain, as though they weren't all well-acquainted with the gory details, how Miss Covington's home had caught fire and how Jim Pickard and his paramedic team had been summoned to administer first aid to the victim.

Sitting with his ten-member family in the third and fourth pews, Jim grinned with pride beneath his enormous, curl-tipped mustache. His children wore the same smiles, although thankfully without the facial hair.

"But their job of saving Miss Covington was made much easier by the actions of a brave and compassionate young lady by the name of Nicola Sarita Dickens."

He saw Zoe slip her arm around the reluctant heroine's shoulders and give her an encouraging hug.

"So many times, we focus only on the misdeeds of our young people," he said, resisting the urge to glance toward the unruly trio, Kerry, Eddie and Steve, who were sitting in the corner.

"I think we should publicly acknowledge this young person's valor in the face of what must have been terrifying circumstances." He reached into his pocket and withdrew the medal he had picked up from the engraver just the night before. He held it out on its red and blue satin neck ribbon. "Nikki," he said, "if you would please come forward. . . ."

At first, he thought she was going to refuse. She shook her head so hard that her braids slapped her face, then she crumpled in her seat and sank below view.

Several people murmured and everyone turned to stare at her.

He felt terrible for embarrassing the poor kid so badly. Most children, though stage shy, would have jumped at the idea of being honored in such a way.

Just when he was about to leave the pulpit and come down to her, he saw Zoe give her a whispered word of reassurance in her ear and a gentle push into the aisle.

Dragging her feet, Nikki slowly approached the front of the church. Jim Pickard's family began the round of applause and was quickly joined by the rest. When Nikki reached the pulpit, Dylan quickly dropped to one knee and held out his hand to her. Trembling she slipped her own into his palm. It was icy and damp. Again, Dylan regretted taking this step without first preparing her.

He decided to make the presentation short and sweet. Placing the ribbon around her neck and adjusting the medal so that it hung over her pounding heart, he said, "No greater love hath any man than this . . . that he lay down his life for a friend.' Those are the words of our Lord. And I think they apply to Nicola Sarita Dickens, because she risked her own life to save another. We can all aspire to her example."

He leaned over and whispered in the girl's ear, "Thank you, Nikki. You can go now."

She practically flew down the aisle and back to Zoe's arms.

"Which brings us to this morning's sermon," he said, opening his Bible and notebook and spreading them on the pulpit before him. "What is love? Hopefully, during the next hour we can all come to a better understanding of this great mystery."

*   *   *

"I don't agree with what you said this morning, Reverend. And I thought I should tell you so to your face."

Dylan sat on the end of Abigail Covington's miserably uncomfortable, high-backed Victorian sofa. Her parlor was as cold and formal as the chapel was cozy and homey. Unfortunately, even the cup of tea on the coffee table was cool and weak.

"Don't hold back, Abigail," he said, trying to sip the anemic brew. "Be sure to tell me what you think."

"Oh, I intend to." She frowned, leaned forward, and ran her fingertip along the edge of the piecrust table that stood beside her chintz chaise where she lounged like an Egyptian queen. "I really must fire that girl who supposedly 'cleans' for me. You just can't keep good help these days."

"Especially if you keep firing them every other Wednesday," he muttered into his tea cup.

She didn't seem to hear as she rattled on. "First of all, you say that love isn't an emotion, it's a commitment or some such silliness."

"There's nothing silly about commitment. Nothing changes faster than human emotions, Abigail. If love were nothing but a warm, fuzzy feeling, we'd be in love one minute and out the next. In any relationship, there are times when we don't even *like* the other person, let alone love them. But we can still abide by our decision, our commitment to seek the highest good for that person, as we see it."

She snorted and waved a hand that displayed four garish rings. But not a single one was a wedding band. It was common knowledge in Covington Falls that Miss Abigail had never even entertained a suitor . . . money not withstanding.

"Well," she said, "I think that's just a lot of hooey. To hear you tell it, I should stand on my front steps and throw money to all the lazy, do-nothing freeloaders in this town."

"Not at all," he said. "To give people money they

haven't earned would only postpone the day they learn the lesson of self-reliance. There's nothing loving about encouraging them to remain dependent on others.''

"Hmmm, well, I'm glad that isn't what you had in mind. I certainly don't intend to start throwing my granddaddy's hard earned money out the window."

"On the other hand . . ." Dylan chose his words carefully. ". . . it would be a wonderful gesture of love to give to those who truly are in need and deserving of help."

"Such as?"

"The old, the young, the sick, those who have had more than their share of tragedy and difficulties. People who really are trying, but under the circumstances need some assistance."

She eyed him suspiciously. "And I suppose you have some particular folks in mind?"

"I can think of quite a few. I'll write their names down for you, if you like."

"No, I don't like. I'll spend my money any way I want, thank you, Reverend. And I still don't agree with you. I don't think love is just giving money away to people who are too lazy to earn it."

Dylan sighed, suddenly feeling very tired. The woman could really sap his energy.

"You haven't listened to a word I've said, Abigail," he told her. "I didn't say anything about charities, or stinginess, or about people who hoard the riches that life has bestowed upon them."

He paused, letting his words sink in. When they did, he saw the flame of ill temper flare in her eyes. "I said it's a matter of seeking the higher good for yourself and someone else."

He thought she would come back at him with some sort of heated retort, but she didn't. Instead, she reached for a rosewood inlaid cigarette box and flipped it open. She withdrew one, placed it to her red lipstick smeared mouth, and waited.

"Well . . . where is your lighter, young man?"

He smiled, knowing that she was expecting him to fulfill their little ritual. From the beginning of their relationship, he had performed the duty of lighting her cigarettes with the silver, engraved lighter his father had given him on his twelfth birthday.

"Always keep this in your pocket, Dylan," his dad had told him, "and if a lady needs a light, you'll have one."

His willingness and readiness had endeared him to Abigail Covington from the first moment they had met, and she never missed the opportunity to take advantage of his chivalry.

But not tonight.

"I left it at home," he said smoothly.

She looked more than a little disappointed. "Along with your manners," she said with a sniff. "I've been smoking since I was fifteen years old, and this is the first time I've been forced to light my own cigarette in the presence of a so-called gentleman."

"I'm sorry, Abigail, but I left my lighter at home because I love you."

She gave him a look that would curdle fresh cream. "What is *that* supposed to mean?"

"Your doctor told you to stop smoking. When I was visiting you in the hospital, I overheard him say that you had inhaled more than enough smoke for the next twenty years. Didn't he?"

She pulled a long draw from the cigarette and released the smoke through her nose. "I'm eighty-four years old, you fool," she said. "What's the difference? I'll be dead in twenty years anyway."

"Probably. But it won't be from smoking, if I have anything to do with it."

"Well, you don't." For emphasis she blew a cloud directly into his face. "I'll smoke if I damned well want to."

"Obviously." He picked up a magazine from the coffee table and fanned it at her. "You can choose to kill yourself if you want. But I won't be a part of it."

"What a silly bunch of tomfoolery," she said. "I think you'd better go now."

"I agree. As charming as your company may be, I have some studying to do."

Before she knew what he was doing, he had lifted her left hand—the one without the cigarette—and planted a quick kiss on the back of it.

He didn't want her to think he had left all of his courtly gestures at home.

Wishing her a quick goodnight, he headed for the door, where he paused and looked back at her over his shoulder. It was worth the extra look, because what he saw was a rare sight, indeed.

Miss Abigail Covington was wearing a genuine, ear-to-ear smile on her face.

Wonders never ceased.

"Why do you live in a truck?" Nikki asked Zoe as they sat across from each other on Zoe's inflatable mattress in the back of her van and played a grueling game of Go Fish.

Judging from the amount of completed "books" on Nikki's side of the blanket, she was winning.

"Give me your fives," Zoe said, buying time while she thought up a good answer to the girl's question.

Nikki giggled. "Don't have any. Go fish."

Groaning, Zoe picked a card from the top of the deck.

"So, why *do* you live in a truck?" Nikki wasn't going to give up anytime soon. "Are you poor or something?"

"I'm not exactly poor but—"

"It's okay if you are. My mom and me were poor for a while last year, and we had to live in our car. Is that the same thing?"

They had lived in their car? Zoe cringed and decided it was high time to have a talk with Rev. Gray about Nikki's home situation. More and more, this appeared to be a case for Children's Protective Services.

At nearly nine o'clock this evening, Nikki had come

knocking at her van door, lonely, roaming the streets as usual. Apparently, she had no adult supervision at all during the hours her mother worked at the truck stop. It was only a matter of time until something bad happened to this little girl with the mussed braids and the peanut butter smile.

"A year ago, I decided to convert my van into a sort of recreational vehicle and travel from work site to site," Zoe began. "Usually I only stay for a few weeks, and it's much less expensive than renting hotel rooms or apartments."

She pointed out the meticulously organized and carefully constructed amenities. "See, here's my teeny, tiny refrigerator, my camper stove, my sink, and my little girls' room." They both giggled as she proudly displayed a portable toilet.

"My books are up here on this shelf, my clothes in that chest behind the driver's seat, and we're playing cards on my bed. It isn't so bad, if you're very neat and keep everything in its place."

"Why do you move around all the time? I *hate* moving. But I'm a kid and I can't help it. You're a grownup, so you get to be your own boss. How come you move?"

"That's a good question, Nikki," Zoe responded with unaccustomed candor. The child was honestly curious. The least she could do was give her an honest answer. "I moved all the time when I was growing up, and I guess it just became a habit."

"My mommy always wants to move because she thinks we'll be happier somewhere else. But once we get to the new place, it's just like the old place, and things aren't any better."

Zoe felt her face growing hot as the child's innocent words rang a bell of truth in her own heart. It was so easy to judge Nikki's mother harshly for dragging her daughter all over the country, constantly uprooting her. And it *was* wrong.

But wasn't she doing the same thing, constantly searching for something outside herself to fill an aching void?

"Give me your sevens," Nikki said.

"I just got this one!"

"I know. And I've got the other three! Ha, ha!"

Another book of four cards hit the blanket on Nikki's side.

"You're a wicked Fish player, Nicola Sarita Dickens."

"I know. I show no mercy. Give me your aces."

A few more moves, and the game was over.

"That makes three out of five, my favor," Nikki said, not bothering to hide her gloating. "Wanna go for seven out of ten?"

"No, I think I'll quit while I'm ahead."

"What makes you think you're ahead?"

"All the more reason to stop now." Zoe packed up the cards, then pulled an envelope from inside the clothing chest. "You told me one of your secrets," she said. "You know, about the trap door in the porch. Would you like to share one of my secrets?"

Nikki's eyes glimmered with clandestine delight. "Sure!"

Reaching inside the envelope, Zoe pulled out her collection of European travel brochures.

"This is the real reason why I'm living here in my van," she said. "I've been saving money for over a year now, so that I can go on a hiking tour of Europe and see all these wonderful places."

"Wow! Really? Castles and everything?" Nikki said, pointing to a picture of Notre Dame.

"Actually, that's a church. But I'm sure I'll see a castle or two while I'm there."

"I wish I could go."

"So, save up your money, and when you're a grownup, you can. It's good for people to keep a secret, special dream in their hearts. It gets them through the hard times."

"I have a secret, special dream." Nikki's eyes filled with faraway wonder.

Zoe leaned closer to her and lowered her voice to a whisper. "Would you tell me about it?"

"You have to promise not to tell anyone. 'Cause if any of those stupid boys at school find out, they'll tease me really bad."

"I promise."

Nikki settled back against a pillow and closed her eyes. "I want to be a flower girl."

"A flower girl?"

"Yeah, like in a wedding."

Zoe was surprised and touched by the simple goal, so easily attained by some little girls, but probably never for this one.

"Why do you want to be a flower girl, Nikki?"

The child sighed and opened her eyes. "Sometimes, on Saturdays, they have weddings in the chapel. They are so, so-o-o-o beautiful. The bride and the groom and all the pretty flowers. And Rev. Gray looks so handsome in his special black suit."

"A tuxedo?"

"Yeah. A tuxedo. And the piano and the organ play such pretty music." She paused to hum a few bars of the traditional wedding march. "And the flower girl gets to come down the aisle first, even before the bride. And she spreads petals all over everywhere. And she gets to wear a really neat dress with a skirt that comes out to here. And white patent leather shoes and a crown of flowers in her hair."

"It sounds lovely."

"Oh, it is. Being a flower girl is just like being a princess. I want to be one so bad! Every night I pray that I can. But I don't think I'll be able to."

"Why not?"

"Because I don't know anybody who wants to get married. My mommy's brother, my Uncle Dennis, he ran away to Las Vegas and did it there, so I didn't get to go to his wedding."

She sighed and nibbled on her lower lip. "Besides, when I told my mommy that I wanted to do it, she said the dress and the shoes and everything cost lots of money.

And we have to spend all of ours on food and rent.''

Zoe thought of several childhood dreams that had never come true, in spite of all the prayers, the hints, the outright begging. Her heart went out to the girl.

''Maybe it will still happen someday,'' she said. ''Don't give up hope.''

Zoe knew, better than most, that even if hopes didn't materialize, they kept you warm during cold, dark periods of your life.

It never hurt to hope.

An impish smile stole across Nikki's face, as though, perhaps, that seed of optimism had already sprouted. ''I was wondering,'' the girl said, ''priests can't get married, but *ministers* can, right?''

It didn't take a flash of insight to see where this was going. Zoe decided to head her off at the pass. ''They can if they want,'' she said, ''but they have to want to a lot. And I don't know any ministers who want to . . . not even a little.''

Nikki batted her long lashes. ''They might want to if some be-e-au-u-tiful lady wanted to, too.''

''Maybe. But I don't know any lady, beautiful or otherwise, who's even *thinking* about getting married.''

''Not even *one* itty bitty thought.''

''Nope.''

''Oh.''

The child sighed, visibly deflated, her hopes dashed again. Zoe decided it was time to change the subject. Tenderly, she reached over and moved Nikki's collar aside so she could see her neck. ''Hey, you aren't wearing your medal,'' she said.

Instantly, Nikki's demeanor changed. Her dreamy smile disappeared, and she began to fidget the way she had that morning during church.

''I took it off,'' she said, not meeting Zoe's eyes.

''Why? It's a beautiful medal, and you deserved it.''

''I just took it off, okay? It was too heavy, and the ribbon was scratchy on my neck. It made me itch.''

"I see."

"You do?" Nikki looked worried.

"Not really. If I were you, I'd be really proud of getting that medal."

"Well, it's no big deal, all right? And I think I should go home now."

She jumped up to leave, but Zoe caught her arm and held her lightly.

"Nikki, I'm sorry if I said something that bothered you. Can you tell me what's wrong?"

To her shock, the child began to cry. Tears streaked down her face, leaving muddy tracks among her freckles.

"Oh, sweetie, please tell me what's going on."

"It's just that . . . that . . ."

"Yes?"

"I did something really bad, and now I don't know what to do about it."

Several possibilities played through Zoe's mind, but one stood out in base relief. "Would it have anything to do with the fire on Miss Covington's porch?"

For what seemed like forever, the girl said nothing. Then she slowly nodded her head.

Without any parenting experience to rely on, Zoe searched her brain frantically for an appropriate answer to this serious situation. It wasn't as though the girl had stolen some extra cookies from the jar.

"I think the first step you should take is to talk to somebody about it. Someone you trust," she added, as she handed her several tissues.

Nikki seemed to consider the advice carefully, then she nodded, wiped her eyes, and blew her nose. "That's a good idea," she said, sounding more hopeful. "I think I'll do that."

"I'm so glad, Nikki." Zoe settled back on some pillows, ready to have the girl spill her heart to her.

But Nikki stood and opened the side door of the van.

"You've been a lot of help, Miss Zoe," she said as she climbed out. "Thanks."

Seconds later she was bounding across the lawn in the direction of the chapel. Zoe felt momentarily deflated. Even if she gave good advice, she apparently lacked what it took to play the honored role of "confidant." That part seemed to be reserved for Rev. Dylan Gray.

"Oh, well," she told herself, as she saw the girl disappear inside the front door of the church. "Leave it to a professional." Nicola Sarita Dickens was in good hands.

Chapter Six

$\mathcal{D}$ylan was on his hands and knees, head stuck beneath the pulpit, trying to fix a short in the public address system. So he didn't hear Nikki when she first called his name.

The wire he was trying to crimp wouldn't cooperate, and he could hardly see what he was doing in the dark.

"Get in there, you rotten, lousy . . ."

He let the words die in his throat as was appropriate in a house of worship. Sometimes he thought that giving up swearing was the toughest aspect of his conversion. Colorful, earthy street language had been an integral part of his upbringing. At times he felt as though he was having to learn a whole new language to express himself.

Especially when he gouged a screwdriver into his palm. "Ow-w-www! Why, I oughta—"

"Rev. Gray? Where are you?" said a tremulous voice that he recognized instantly.

"Nikki? Over here, under the pulpit."

"*Under* the pulpit?"

"Yeah, that's where I do my best praying."

A small face peeked around the side of the stand and down at him. "Really?"

"No, not really. I'm just trying to fix the microphone so that I don't sound like I have a frog in my throat when I speak."

He grunted as he crawled out from under the podium,

stood, and dusted off his jeans. "So, what's up, kiddo?" he asked, studying the expression on her face. She looked genuinely distressed, and he was afraid something serious might have happened to her.

"I . . . um . . . I need to . . ."

For a moment, he thought she might need to use the ladies' room and was too shy to ask. Then he realized it was something more.

"What is it, Nikki? What's wrong?"

"I need to . . . I think they call it . . . do a confession."

"A confession? Why? Did you pull off a bank heist or commit industrial espionage?"

She looked confused, then shook her head. "I don't know what that is, but I think that what I did was worse."

"And you want to confess it to me?"

"Yeah, like they do on television."

"On television?"

"You know . . . like when the bad guy says, 'Forgive me, Father, for I have sinned.' And then the priest tells him that God isn't mad at him anymore."

Dylan laughed and began to gather his tools and toss them into his toolbox.

"First of all, Nikki," he said as he buckled it closed, "I'm a minister, not a priest. So, I don't exactly hear the kind of confessions you're talking about."

"But I don't know any priests, and I do know you. Can you do it for me?" Tears began to well in her amber eyes.

Dylan opened his mouth to protest again, but thought better of it. If the child needed to unburden her soul, he had to offer her assistance in any form she requested.

"Okay," he said, thinking quickly. "What if you and I sit down here in the front pew, and you tell me all about it. Then we'll pray together and you can ask the Lord to forgive you. Would that be just as good?"

Giving him an appraising look from head to toe, she took in the Dodgers sweatshirt, the jeans, and sneakers. She didn't seem impressed.

"What's the matter?" he asked.

"You don't look much like a priest, wearing your grubbies."

"My grubbies! Hey, young lady, this is my favorite sweatshirt and these—" he pointed to his scuffed sneakers. "—are Nikes."

Her lower lip protruded and began to tremble.

"All right, all right," he said, thinking fast. "How about if I put on one of these?"

Hurrying over to the choir loft, he lifted one of the new robes—designed and donated by Abigail Covington—that had been draped across the piano bench.

Although he felt a bit foolish, he slipped it on over his clothes. "There. Is that better?"

He was rewarded with a bright smile and a nod.

"Thank heavens." Taking a seat in the front pew, he motioned for her to join him.

Again, there was quiet, but steadfast resistance.

"What is it now?" he asked.

"You can't *look* at me. We need a screen between us or a curtain or something."

He sighed. "Nikki, sweetheart, I don't have a proper confessional. This just isn't that kind of church. But I'm sure the Lord will be listening, no matter where we are. You're just going to have to trust me on this one."

She sat down, several feet from him, and placed her hands in her lap like a prim and proper southern belle. "Okay, I'm ready," she said, "but you can't look at me. Turn around."

"But I like to see the person I'm talking to."

Again she shook her head vigorously. "I won't be able to say it if you're looking at me."

"Are you sure?"

She nodded. "It's a really bad sin. The worst thing I've ever done in my who-o-o-le life. Trust me on this one."

He stifled a chuckle and did as she asked, turning his back to her. "Okay, let'er rip."

"I don't think you're taking this seriously, Rev. Gray," she said, obviously offended. "And you should. Just because I'm a kid doesn't mean I don't have bad sins to confess. You shouldn't make fun of me.''

Thoroughly chastised, Dylan became as somber and reverent as Nikki and her confession deserved.

''You're absolutely right, Nikki. I apologize. Now proceed.''

''What?''

''Go ahead.''

''Okay. Well . . . here it is. . . . I set fire to Miss Covington's house.''

Dylan sat there, stunned for several seconds as the words sank into his brain. Then he spun around to face her. ''You did *what*!''

Instantly, she covered her eyes with her hands and squealed. ''You weren't supposed to look!''

''You weren't supposed to set fire to anybody's house! Whatever were you thinking?''

''You aren't supposed to yell at me either,'' she whined. ''That's not the way they do it on TV. The priests are nice and quiet and they say, 'God forgives you, child. Go and sin no more.' They don't holler.''

''I'm not hollering.'' Dylan lowered his voice several decibels. ''I'm just very . . . surprised, that's all. Now why don't you tell me why you did such a thing?''

Dylan could think of a hundred reasons. After all, Abigail Covington didn't exactly inspire affection in the hearts of her fellow townspeople. But setting fire to her house?

''I didn't mean to. It was an accident,'' Nikki said, sniffling. She wiped her eyes on her sweater sleeve, and Dylan shuffled under the robe to get a tissue for her from his jeans pocket.

''Oh, well . . . that's different,'' he said with relief. ''Why don't you tell me how it happened.''

She twisted the end of the wet tissue between her fingers. ''Do I have to tell you that part, too?''

''No. You don't have to tell me anything at all. But I think you might feel better if you do. I promise I won't holler anymore.''

"Okay . . . see . . . I was trying to, you know . . . smoke a little, just to see what it was like."

"Smoke? You mean cigarettes?"

She nodded, her face crimson. "Yeah, see, that afternoon I saw some of the older boys—the ones you play basketball with—and they were smoking out in the woods and it looked like fun. And then Miss Covington was sitting on her front porch that night, smoking and drinking something from a glass that I think was wine, and it looked neat, like she was a movie star or something. So, after she went to bed, I snuck through the secret passageway—"

"Secret passageway?"

"Yeah, the one under the porch. I like to play Nancy Drew with it. Anyway, her cigarettes were there on the table where she'd left them, and her fancy lighter, too."

"And you decided to give it a try?"

She nodded.

He stifled a smile, remembering one afternoon in an alley behind a deli in Greenwich Village. He had been about her age, maybe younger.

"How did you like it?" he asked.

"It was okay, I guess," she replied, trying to look cool. "Until I threw up."

"Until you . . . ?"

"Yeah. That's when I dropped the lighter and the cigarette. I don't know which one it was, but something caught the chair cushion on fire."

He pursed his lips thoughtfully. "Ummm . . . I can see how that might happen . . . under the circumstances."

"I tried to put out the fire, but then her blanket—the one that she covers up her lap with—it started burning, too. And then one of the curtains and . . ."

"It just got out of hand, eh?"

"Yeah, and there was lots and lots of smoke. That's when I knew I had to warn Miss Covington and get her out of the house."

"How did you get through the door into the house? She always keeps it locked."

Nikki grinned and shuffled her feet. "One time when I was playing Nancy Drew, Crime Detective, I saw her slip a key under one of the flower pots next to the door. So, I knew that was where she keeps it."

"What happened once you got inside?"

"Well, the porch was right under Miss Covington's bedroom upstairs, and a bunch of the smoke had gone up there and through her window. She had left it open, see? And when I found her in her bed, she was choking something fierce. So, I grabbed her by the hand and made her come downstairs. Then I dragged her out the front door and she plopped down there on the lawn until the ambulance got there."

The thought of the dignified Abigail Covington "plopping" anywhere was enough to bring another snicker to the surface, but Dylan squelched it.

"That certainly explains it all," he told her.

"Do you think God will forgive me?"

Dylan had never seen such genuine remorse and desire for repentance on a face before. "I'm absolutely sure of it. All we have to do is bow our heads and ask Him."

She folded her hands, tilted her head, and squeezed her eyes shut. Dylan led her in a simple but heartfelt prayer.

When she raised her head and opened her eyes, the child wore the beaming smile of the redeemed.

"Wow! I feel *lots* better now!" she proclaimed. "It really works!"

"Of course, it does. Every time."

"Thank you, Rev. Gray!" She stood and threw her arms around his neck, giving him a hearty hug. He could feel the salt wetness of her tears on his cheek. But they were tears of joy, the kind that sprang from the well of a newly-cleansed soul.

He cleared his throat, which had suddenly felt clogged by his own emotion. "There's one more thing you have to do, Nikki," he said.

"Sure, what's that?"

"You've made it right with God. Now you have to

make restitution to your fellow man.''

"Fellow man? Who's that?'' Awareness dawned in her eyes and she shook her head. "Oh, no . . . you don't mean Miss Covington!''

"She's the person who was hurt by your actions. You'll need to ask her for her forgiveness, too.''

"But she a mean, mean, meany . . . and she won't *ever* forgive me!''

"Maybe, and maybe not. That's her decision, and you can't help that. But, either way, you have to give her the opportunity by asking.''

"She'll kill me! She'll kill me *dead* if I tell her it was me!''

"I'll go along with you, just to make sure that you're safe . . . although I don't think she's killed very many kids lately. She's getting old and feeble, you know.''

"Do I *have* to?''

He nodded. "And you need to make restitution.''

"Resti—what's that?''

Standing, he patted her on the head, then tweaked one of her braids. "It's something we'll take care of tomorrow morning . . . something that will probably keep you from *ever* doing anything like smoking or setting fires again.''

Chapter Seven

*O*nce, Zoe had been happy in her work, content, at peace with herself and the world. But, thanks to Abigail Covington, this morning she was just plain mad.

Who did that old biddy think she was, sitting there in her chaise lounge recliner like a czarina, smoking cigarettes and complaining about everything Zoe did to her granddaddy's precious antique windows?

"He brought them over himself on an ocean steamer just after the War Between the States," she said in that nasal, twangy, southern accent that drove Zoe bonkers. "Why, if anything bad was to happen to those windows, Benjamin Jeremiah Covington would roll over in his grave. Which, by the way, is right over there in that group of pines right behind the chapel."

"Too bad Granddaddy Covington's ship didn't hit an iceberg on the way here," Zoe mumbled under her breath as she tried to carefully fit the fourth repaired panel back into place.

"What did you say?"

"Nothing." Thank goodness the lady's hearing was slightly impaired. Because, although she knew it was a cheap shot unworthy of her, Zoe couldn't resist the occasional verbal jab. Even if it was mumbled.

"Those other workmen got their part of the porch repaired lickety-split," Abigail continued. "I don't know why you're holding up the works.''

"They rushed the job so they could get away from your griping," Zoe grumbled. "Unfortunately, this isn't the sort of work that can be hurried."

"I heard that!" Abigail reached out with her carved ivory and ebony cane and whacked Zoe across the back of the legs with it.

Unpleasant memories flashed through Zoe's mind: switches, belts, the occasional coat hanger. Her temper flared. She swung around and grabbed the cane out of Abigail's hand. A look of fear crossed the older woman's face as Zoe stood over her with the cane in hand. This time she had gone too far, and even *she* knew it.

"Don't you *ever, ever* strike me again, Miss Covington," Zoe said, her voice shaking with rage. "Because if you do, I swear, I'll . . .''

"You'll what?" Abigail asked, trying to sound defiant, but she was trembling all over. "You're going to hit an old woman?"

"No. I'm a better person than that. But I will throw your dear granddaddy's ivory cane so high up into that oak that you'll never get it down. Do you understand?"

She handed the cane back to the woman, slapping it against her outstretched palm.

"Good heavens, Miss Covington," she said, "don't you know how irresponsible it is to even use something like that these days with elephants being on the endangered list?"

Abigail's face didn't register even a shade of comprehension. "What?"

"Never mind. If you don't care about people, I doubt I can convince you to care about animals.''

"What makes you think I don't care about people?"

"Gee, just a wild guess. Or maybe I'm psychic."

Abigail's eyes narrowed as she reached for her omnipresent cigarette box. "You are a smart-mouthed, disrespectful girl, and I've had just about enough of your sass. I'm going to tell Rev. Gray to fire you."

A movement caught Zoe's eye: Dylan and Nikki coming across the lawn toward the porch.

"What perfect timing. There he is now. You can have him terminate me right now and put me out of your misery."

"You don't think I'll do it."

"I don't care if you do or not."

As soon as Zoe had uttered the words, she wanted to take them back. Of course, she cared. Paris in the spring. The glimmering beaches of the Riviera. The green highlands of Scotland.

Who was she kidding? This job meant everything. Why was she baiting the old lady this way? Few people ever got under her skin like this. Why Abigail Covington? What was it about her that brought out the worst in Zoe?

"Dylan Gray, I want you to fire this snitty bit of baggage," Abigail called out to him, before he and Nikki could even reach the porch. "Right now. I've had quite enough of her, I tell you."

Dylan turned to Nikki—who was looking a bit peaked this morning, Zoe noticed—and told her to wait for him at the bottom of the steps. Then he walked into the porch enclosure and over to Abigail's chair.

"Now, why would I want to do a thing like that?" he asked, surveying the window that was, panel by panel, coming back to life. "She's doing a great job."

"She insulted me . . . right to my face. I won't have that sort of insubordination in a servant."

"What makes you think I'm your *servant*?" Zoe exclaimed, her emotional barometer on the rise again. "I'm a skilled craftswoman who—"

"Ladies, please." Dylan held up one hand in typical New York traffic cop style. "While you may not be enjoying each other's company, you aren't intending to become roommates. You don't have to *like* each other, as long as you both get what you want out of this business deal."

He turned to Abigail. "Abbie, you want your family's

windows repaired. And it looks as though Ms. Harmond is doing that beautifully. And you, Zoe, want to be paid, I'm sure, for all the time and effort you've invested in this project so far. Plus, you probably want the satisfaction of seeing the job finished. Right?''

He waited until Zoe nodded her head, then Abigail.

''Now, if we can call a truce,'' he said, ''we have some other, more pressing business to attend to.''

Opening the porch door, he beckoned Nikki inside. The girl looked absolutely miserable, as though she were being led to the foot of a guillotine.

''Miss Nicola Sarita Dickens has something very important to tell you, Abigail. And I want you to listen carefully.'' He leaned over until his face was nearly nose to nose with Abigail's. ''I want you to listen with your ears *and* your heart. Do you understand?''

Miss Covington snorted. ''No, but get on with it. I haven't got all day, you know.''

Nikki looked terrified as she stepped a bit closer to Abigail. Zoe wondered what on earth could be wrong to upset the child so badly.

''I have to confess something to you, Miss Covington,'' she began in a small, quivering voice.

''What?'' The old lady cupped a hand to her ear. ''Speak up. I can't hear a blamed thing you're saying.''

''I said I have to tell you that I . . .'' She cast a quick, scared look at Dylan, who nodded his encouragement. ''I accidentally set fire to your house.'' Drawing a deep breath, she plunged ahead. ''I didn't mean to. I was trying to smoke your cigarettes, and then I barfed, and everything caught on fire, and I'm really, really, really just as sorry as I can be, and I'm asking you to forgive me. Pretty, pretty please.''

In the silence that followed, Zoe could hear every bird chirp for five miles around. Even the woodpecker in the oak near the porch seemed as loud as a jackhammer.

''You what! Why you destructive little hooligan!''

Eyes wide with fright, Nikki turned to Dylan. "I told you she'd holler at me."

"If she wants to holler, you have to let her," Dylan replied softly. "She has a right to be angry that you destroyed her property."

"You're darned right I do!" Abigail's perpetual scowl deepened. "And here I thought you saved my life. Instead, you almost killed me. And for that, you want to be forgiven? Not now, not ever, young lady." She raised her cane threateningly, but after a quick glance at Zoe, seemed to reconsider and lowered it. "You just get off my property," she said, "and don't ever come back!"

Nikki began to quietly sob. "But . . . but Rev. Gray said I need to make restitution to you, and I can't if—"

"Restitution? Ha! Like you could pay me one red cent, you little ragamuffin. You and your family don't have two nickels to rub together."

"But I could—"

"Get out of here, I say, and don't let me see your dirty little face again."

"Abigail, that's enough," Dylan said, placing a firm hand on her shoulder. "While you have the right to be angry, you don't need to be abusive."

Unable to control herself any longer, Zoe stepped forward, too. "Really, Miss Covington. Even if the child did start the fire, she still risked her life to save yours. Nothing changes that."

Abigail rose to her feet without the aid of her cane and tramped across the porch to the door of her house. "Get out of here, all of you. I don't want you around here, any of you. Leave me alone. I just want to be left alone."

She stomped inside the house and slammed the door behind her.

Nikki began to cry even harder, then turned and ran off the porch and across the lawn with Dylan close behind her.

Zoe stood alone on the porch that had suddenly grown very quiet.

But the emotions that swirled inside her were anything but quiet. She had just seen something that made her sick inside: the look on Abigail's face a second before she had slammed the door closed.

It was the look of pain, of fear, of a life lived in solitude.

"Leave me alone," Abigail Covington had said. "I just want to be left alone."

How many times had Zoe thought, and even said, those exact words. How many times had she retreated into her own dark den where there was no one to hurt her, no one she might disappoint?

Zoe looked out across the lawn at a little girl, sad, alone and neglected . . . and saw her own past.

And inside that big, lonely house, was her future.

Maybe the next time she started to run for cover, the next time she started to say the words, "Leave me alone," she had better decide if she really meant it or not.

Because, like Abigail Covington, she might get the life she had asked for.

"You did everything you could, Nikki," Dylan said as he knelt beside the girl who was huddled at the base of the pine tree, the same as she had been the night of the fire.

"She won't forgive me. Now what do I do?" she wailed, her face buried in her hands.

"You aren't responsible for what she does, Nikki," he said, "only for what you do. You did your part, and whether she does hers or not doesn't matter. I don't think she means to be, but Miss Covington can be a scary lady."

"No kidding! I was shaking all over, and I couldn't hardly breathe! I thought I was gonna barf again right there on her porch, and that would have made her *really* mad!"

"But you didn't get sick. You confessed your wrong and asked for forgiveness anyway, even though you were scared. That was very noble, and it took a lot of courage. I'm terribly proud of you."

She looked up at him, peeking through her fingers. "Really?"

"Absolutely. And I still think you're a hero."

"Heroine."

"Whatever." He reached over and tweaked her braid. "I wish you would wear your medal again. I really do think you deserve it, for rescuing Miss Covington before and for being honest and courageous today. You deserve two medals, but I don't think I have enough money in the church fund to pay for another one right now."

She dropped her hands from her face and smiled shyly at him. "Okay, I'll wear it," she said. "But under my shirt, where the boys won't see me and tease me about it."

Offering his hand, he helped her up from the ground. "You just let me catch those hoodlums teasing you, and I'll hang their hides on the rectory wall."

"Oooo, that's gross!"

"Or, I might give them a good talking to."

"Oh, no, not that! Not a 'talking to.' That's the worst!"

As Dylan led her back to the church and out to the sidewalk, where he told her goodbye, he decided that the one who really needed a "talking to" was Nikki's mother.

Across the lawn, they could see Zoe, working diligently at her table beneath the tree. Nikki called out to her, and she paused to wave.

"I think Miss Zoe is be-eau-tiful, don't you?" Nikki shot him a coy, sideways glance.

He grinned. "Yes, Miss Zoe is a very attractive young woman."

"So, you *have* noticed?"

Dylan raised one eyebrow. "Of course I've noticed. I may be a minister, but I don't have stones for eyes. What's your point?"

"Just that she's very pretty, and she's very, very nice . . . you know, like a preacher's wife should be."

Laughing, he reached over, grabbed her around the back of the neck and gently shook her, like a naughty puppy.

"You're a dangerous female, Nicola Sarita Dickens,"

he said. "Heaven help us men when you're old enough to be subtle."

"What does 'subtle' mean?"

"No, no. You'll learn that one soon enough. Women always do."

Dylan wasn't the only one who thought Nikki's mother should be "talked to." That night, after Zoe was sure the dinner rush would be over, she took a seat in a rear booth of the truck stop and waited for the red-haired waitress to take her order. She didn't have to ask if the woman was Nikki's mom; the family resemblance was too strong for any doubt. The waitress seemed exhausted as she moved from table to table, balancing a coffee pot in one hand and two pieces of pie and a donut in the other.

She was young and pretty, but hard living had taken its toll on her. A gray pallor, sunken dark areas under her eyes, and a figure that was too thin even for fashion, showed that she was losing her health at an early age. Zoe had no idea what she was going to say to this woman. No matter what she had rehearsed, it sounded self-righteous and critical. What did she know about being a single mother? She, who had avoided even the responsibility of owning a pet. How could she tell this young woman that she was a lousy mom, when she was working herself to death here in this dive, trying to put food on the table at home?

"What can I get 'cha, hon?" the waitress asked as she hurried over to Zoe's table and pulled out her tablet and pencil. The white tag on the front of her pink uniform said her name was Debra.

"Just some coffee, please, Debra."

"You've got it."

Zoe flipped her mug over, and it was instantly filled to the brim.

"Anything else?" Debra asked.

Zoe shook her head. "No, this will be fine. Unless you

have time to join me . . . like on your break or something. I'd like to buy you a cup.''

Debra eyed her suspiciously. ''Why?''

''It's about Nikki.''

A look of fear washed over the mother's face. ''Oh, no! Has something happened to her?''

''She's fine. But I'm a friend of hers, and well, I'd like to offer my help, if I may.''

''What are you talking about? How can you help us?''

Zoe thought of Dylan Gray's sermon about love and commitment to others. About seeking the higher good for another person.

She thought of Paris in spring, of the seven hills of Rome, and of the canals of Venice.

Then, she remembered Abigail Covington, alone in her empty house at the age of eighty-four. She remembered Nikki unsupervised, setting a fire that could have killed her.

''I don't know how I can help,'' she said. ''But I really want to, if I can. When you can take a break, sit down here with me. We'll talk.''

Chapter Eight

The golden heat of the North Carolina sun made Zoe feel lazy as it warmed her dark hair and soothed her aching shoulders. The grass was still damp with morning dew, and a soft breeze brought the scent of Abigail's rose garden to her across a small expanse of dandelion-dotted lawn.

Having just applied a weather-sealant putty to the window she had finished, she was giving it a final cleaning. After dumping a handful of dry plaster of Paris all over the glass, she began to rub vigorously with a stiff scrub brush. The powder absorbed the oil from the putty as well as from the flux and fingerprints.

The final step on the eighth panel. One more and she would be out of here.

Funny, the thought didn't thrill her the way it would have a few weeks ago, when she had started the job. For the hundredth time in the past hour, she glanced across to the chapel to the parking lot, where Dylan Gray was shooting hoops with his entourage of wanna-be juvenile delinquents.

Surely, he had nothing to do with her reluctance to leave this area. It wasn't because he was simply the most virile, sexy man she could ever remember meeting. It wasn't because her heart leapt into her throat every time he smiled at her, which he seemed to be doing more and more with each passing day. And it certainly wasn't the gentle, kind way he had with people, the words of practical wisdom he offered, the quiet, unconditional love which he seemed to extend to even the most difficult individuals.

No, she wasn't "smitten," or anything predictable like that. Not at this point in her life, with her dream practically in her hand.

One more panel to go.

Nearby, she saw a small figure crouching in the rose garden. Zoe smiled.

Nikki was weeding again.

Lately, the child had been sneaking into Abigail Covington's yard, determined to perform what she called her "res-stit-u-ation." Nikki was determined to do the right thing by the old lady, whether Miss Covington wanted it or not. She had worked her way from flower bed to flower bed, pulling grass and weeds from the badly neglected areas. All the time, she had kept a low profile, kneeling and crawling behind the plants, trying to stay out of sight of the grand old house.

Zoe wondered whether Abigail Covington had seen her or not. At least, there had been no more rude encounters and for that, Zoe was grateful. The child deserved better.

Like an unpleasant answer to an unspoken question, the porch door opened and Abigail Covington appeared. She was wearing a lavender and pink flowered dress that sprouted a ridiculous amount of ruffles from the collar and cuffs. A beribboned straw sun hat was shoved onto her head, and she waved her ivory-headed cane as she shuffled across the lawn in their direction.

Zoe saw Nikki cringe and cower deeper into the bushes.

"You there, girl! What are you doing in my rose garden?" Abigail demanded.

"Pulling weeds," came a small, quivering voice.

Zoe set her brush and powder aside, ready to do battle on Nikki's behalf if necessary. But that didn't seem to be needed this time.

From a pocket in her skirt, Abigail produced two pairs

of gloves and some garden shears. "Any ding-a-ling can pull weeds. If you're determined to be messing around out here, you might as well do something useful."

Slowly, Nikki rose from her hiding place. She gave Abigail and her shears a suspicious look, but her eyes were alight with interest. "Like what?" she said.

"Like deadheading these old blossoms."

"I don't know how."

"Of course you don't. Nobody's ever shown you how. Come here, girl. Be quiet and I'll teach you something."

Zoe watched, fascinated, as Abigail patiently showed Nikki how to snip away the dead roses above the five-leaf formations. The old lady was almost civil.

"I lo-o-ove roses," Nikki said, burying her nose in a velvety red blossom. "I think they're the most beautiful flower in the world!"

"Hmmmm, so they are."

"Brides and flower girls carry them in weddings, you know," she said.

"I suppose. But if you're going to bend my ear, we're never going to get this garden done. Get back to work and wear these gloves, or you'll look like you've wrestled with a couple of bobcats."

Slipping on the gloves, which were far too large for her, Nikki returned to her task.

"What did you say your name is, girl?" Abigail asked, studying a spot of rust on one of the leaves.

"Nikki."

"That's a boy's name. I'm not going to call you that. What's your real name?"

"Nicola Sarita Dickens."

"Then I'll call you Nicola. And you call me Miss Abigail."

Zoe glanced across the lawn toward the chapel and saw Dylan walking in their direction. He looked concerned as she had been a few minutes ago, ready to defend his little friend.

But the situation didn't need his intervention—or hers

either, for that matter. Zoe rushed to intercept him and tell him so.

Grinning broadly, she tried not to skip as she walked.

A small figure stole silently through the darkness toward the rectory door. With trembling hands, she slipped a piece of white, folded paper beneath the door, knocked timidly, then scurried behind the nearest shrub.

After a few moments, the door opened. Dylan Gray stood, silhouetted against the lamplight inside the house, wearing a sweatsuit and a curious look on his face.

He glanced around, then spotted the paper at his feet.

The little spy watched tensely as he unfolded the note and read it. She heard him chuckle and wondered what that might mean to her plan.

When he stepped back inside and closed the door, her hopes were dashed. All had been in vain.

But no.

Soon, he reappeared, shoes on, a leather jacket slung over his shoulder and his motorcycle helmet under the other arm.

Behind the bushes, she shivered deliciously as she heard the cycle roar to life and watched it pull onto the road. She watched until he had disappeared, then snuck out from behind the shrub. One down. One to go.

Crouching as she ran, she hurried across the lawn toward Zoe's van, running from bush to bush, sneakers making only the tiniest crunching sound when she reached the gravel driveway. In her grubby little hand, she clutched the other piece of paper.

An angel of mercy on a sacred mission.

It was all she could do not to cackle with glee.

She slipped up to the side of the truck, stepped on the fender and tucked the note beneath the windshield wiper.

Then the small angel rapped loudly with her fist on the van door . . . and ran like the devil.

*   *   *

Having just settled snugly into her sleeping bag, Zoe was startled to hear the loud knocking on the side of her truck.

"Who could that be?" she mumbled as she slipped on a plaid flannel shirt, a pair of jeans, and some loafers.

It wasn't particularly late, but she was exhausted from an especially trying day with the repairs and wasn't in the mood for visitors.

But when she opened the door, stepped out and looked around, there was no one to be seen.

"Hmmmm. Not amusing," she muttered as she started to climb back inside.

Then she saw the piece of paper shoved under her windshield wiper. Back inside the van, she unfolded it and read the words that were carefully printed on the three-ring loose-leaf notebook paper.

> *Dear Miss Zoe,*
>
> *Hi. How are you? I am fine. I have something very, very, very important to talk to you about. Would you please meet me right now at the top of Pine Bluff? We can be alone there and talk. Please come. Don't forget. Thank you.*
>
> *Sincerely,*
> *Reverend Dylan Gray*

Laughing, Zoe refolded the note and tucked it into her shirt pocket, next to her heart. Living the life of a gypsy, she had learned to travel light. But in the future, whether she lived in a van, a mansion, or out of a backpack, she knew she would always carry this note among her few treasured possessions.

Oh well, what the heck, she thought as she climbed into the driver's seat and started the engine. Nikki had carefully pointed the way to Pine Bluff that morning—nonchalantly, of course—so Zoe knew the way.

It wasn't as though she had anything else to do for the rest of the evening. And it *certainly* wasn't the fact that she would use any excuse, even a flimsy one, to be alone in a romantic place with the sexy, young minister.

In the shadows the conspirator watched, smiled, hummed the wedding march, and dreamed of white patent leather shoes.

By the time Zoe arrived at the top of Pine Bluff, she was beginning to have second thoughts. This was blatantly a make-out point. It was such a beautiful spot, half the population of Covington Falls had probably been conceived at this site.

The road switchbacked with tight one hundred and eighty degree turns all the way up. But the view of the valley below was worth it.

As she rounded the last curve and looked down, she saw the tiny town, twinkling like a miniature Victorian village beneath a Christmas tree. The ribbon of silver river twisted and turned, dividing the valley in neat halves, culminating at Covington Falls at the southern end of town. Even from this distance, the moon was bright enough for her to see the light mist churned by the waterfall.

Tonight the valley was inhabited by fairies . . . one little imp in particular.

Zoe's pulse was already pounding, but her heart rate nearly doubled when she pulled her van into the small parking area at the top of the crest and saw Dylan's motorcycle sitting at the curb.

He was here.

Had she really doubted he would be?

Yes, she had. Things like this didn't happen, not to her. Usually, she didn't allow them to.

She parked near his bike, got out, and looked around. There he was, standing at the edge of the bluff, his profile to her, looking out across the valley.

The moonlight caught the sheen of his hair as a night breeze brushed it back from his face. She allowed herself to enjoy the sight for a moment before calling out to him. He smiled instantly at the sight of her, which eased some of her anxiety. At least he didn't appear to think this was a ridiculous jaunt.

"Hello, yourself," he said as he strode toward her. "I was wondering if you would come."

For the briefest moment, she wondered if perhaps he *had* written that note, but he answered her question with one of his own.

"I suppose," he said, "that you received a similar summons from me?" He pulled the piece of notebook paper from his shirt pocket and handed it to her.

She unfolded it and read it by moonlight. It was addressed to him, from her, and the message was identical. So were the oh-so-carefully scribed letters. Pulling hers from her pocket, she handed it to him. "I think we have a wanna-be-cupid on the loose," she said.

"True," he said with a smirk, "but the interesting thing is . . . we both came up here anyway, even though we knew it was a ruse."

His candor left her nonplussed. This wasn't the way the game was supposed to be played. They should have both pretended to be a little duped, or just not mention it at all.

But then, he was a New Yorker, and they weren't exactly known for their subtlety.

"So, what's the very, very, very important news you have to tell me?" she said, deciding to play, whether he wanted to or not.

"Me? I thought *you* were the one with something on your mind."

Something on her mind? Oh, yes. She had several things on her mind, but none of them seemed to be appropriate, considering that he was a minister. Not to mention the fact that she would be leaving in one week, never to return to this part of the world again.

Never see him again.

Never see Nikki again.

Never stand here in this beautiful spot and look down

at the sleeping village and the misting falls.

"Actually," she said, "I *do* have something very important to discuss with you, and now is as good a time as any."

Chapter Nine

$\mathcal{D}$ylan remembered this feeling; it was good, old-fashioned lust. Sitting on a large flat boulder at the edge of the bluff with Zoe Harmond at his side, he was acutely aware of how female she was. Her dark gypsy's skin shone deep gold in the moonlight. Her black hair hung in loose curls around her face and he found himself aching to touch it and see if it was as silky as it looked.

Her rich, husky voice fell softly on his ears, even as her words touched his heart. The emotions they stirred deep within him had little to do with lust. If he wasn't careful, he could fall in love with this woman.

That wouldn't do.

Long ago, Dylan had learned that he fell in love far too easily. He had learned to guard his heart, rather than get it broken. The Lord and his ministry supplied those needs for him. Or so he prayed every day. Right now, with his own restlessness a problem, not knowing one day from the next, how could he invite a woman into his life?

He couldn't. That was all there was to it.

Besides, this particular woman had shown absolutely no sign at all of being interested in him. He had hoped that her coming to the bluff, knowing it was a ploy of Nikki's, might have shown a hint of curiosity, at least. But once they had sat down and began talking, he could see that she did, indeed, have business with him that had nothing to do with romance.

"Well, do you think it's a good idea?" she asked, her dark eyes shining with enthusiasm that touched him.

She really was a deeply caring woman, whether she wanted to admit it or not.

"I think an after school day care center at the church is a wonderful idea," he replied. "There's only one problem: We don't have the space. The congregation outgrew the small facilities long ago, and there's simply no place to put one."

"What if I could help with that?" she asked slyly.

"Are you going to build us a stained glass classroom? Maybe some Tiffany playground equipment?"

She gave him a flirtatious—at least, he wanted to believe it was flirtatious—smile that made him want to lean over and plant a few kisses on those full lips.

"Leave that part up to me," she said. "I have talents that you probably couldn't even imagine."

The low, intimate tone of her voice went through him like a hot, liquid current, and he found he had a pretty fertile imagination. He wondered if she meant to be as seductive as she appeared. To his dismay, he couldn't tell. Apparently, he had been chaste in deed and thought for too long. He no longer even knew how to play the game.

Just as well, he reminded himself, thinking of his lectures to the older boys about respecting themselves and the young ladies in their lives. There was no time like the present to be a good example. He had decided years ago that he wouldn't preach any path he didn't follow himself.

If she just weren't so lovely and so near and giving him a sideways glance that spoke volumes.

Or did it?

Naw, he decided. It was just his overactive, hormone-activated imagination.

"I hear you talked to Nikki's mother," he said, feeling an overwhelming warmth for this woman who had cared enough to become involved.

"Yes, we had a little chat there at the restaurant. I don't know if it did any good or not. But . . ."

"It helped. I dropped by their house the next morning after Nikki had left for school to talk to her myself. She told me you had been to see her. You got her thinking. Later that night, after you had left, she spoke to the restaurant manager and told him she would have to quit unless he could put her on a daytime shift."

"Really? What did he say?"

"He said, 'Okay.' Now she can be with Nikki in the evenings."

"That's terrific!" Her dark eyes shone with tears of thankfulness, and again he felt himself drawn to her and her tender feelings for a little girl in need. Yes, this was a person he could care deeply about.

"When will you be finished with Abigail's windows?" he asked. He dreaded the answer, but he had to know how much time he had.

"I'll be done this time next week."

Did she sound sorry, or did he imagine the reluctance in her voice?

One week.

Deep inside, he felt a loss so great it ached. One week, seven days . . . it wasn't enough time.

Zoe walked across Abigail's lawn toward the great house, holding a silver tea tray and accoutrements in her trembling hands. She felt more than a little foolish, not to mention hypocritical, in her flowered, ruffled dress.

I look like a geranium in high heels, she thought with a grimace as she proceeded up the steps to the door. She tried to convince herself she was playing a part and had to dress for the role. A trip to the local secondhand store had provided her with the costume. Dylan had supplied the tea service—her props—and had been sensitive enough not to ask too many questions.

As she had anticipated, Abigail Covington was sitting in her new wicker chaise lounge, smoking, staring out at the world through her porch windows.

"Good afternoon, Miss Abigail," Zoe said, summoning every friendly molecule in her being.

"What's good about it?" the old woman snapped.

"I thought I would ask you if you'd like to join me for a spot of tea. There's no sense drinking it all alone, I say."

Abigail raised herself from the chaise and shuffled over to the door. Opening it, she peered down on Zoe, her faded eyes full of suspicion.

"Since when do you have afternoon tea? Let alone want to drink it with me?"

"Now's a good time to start."

Abigail jabbed a thumb in the direction of Zoe's table beneath the oak. "Why aren't you working?"

"The putty has to set before I can install the panel and that will take a couple of hours."

"Hummmph." Abigail looked Zoe up and down, and Zoe could tell that the five dollars at the thrift store had been well-spent. Abigail approved. She also seemed interested in the tray as she craned her neck and squinted her eyes looking down at it. "What kind of tea have you got there?"

"Earl Grey."

"Are those cookies?"

Zoe held the tray higher, showing her the lovely arrangement of goodies she had bought at the local British import shop. "Chocolate-dipped Cadbury shortbread and orange sticks and raspberry truffles."

With a sigh of resignation, Abigail succumbed to temptation and waved her inside. "I suppose you're right," she said, trying not to sound too impressed. "Get in here, girl. There's no point in you eating all that yourself."

Abigail groaned as she eased her stiff body down to the sun-warmed dirt, but it felt good to be digging in the soil again. Funny, how things could change in such a short time. She actually felt ten years younger than she had this time last spring, when she had only sat on her porch, watching the weeds grow in this garden plot.

And now. . . .

Beside her, also on hands and knees, was Nicola, her constant shadow these days. Sometimes the girl got on her nerves. But for the most part, she wasn't too bad . . . for a kid.

"That hole is too deep," she told the child. "You aren't digging your way to Peking; you're planting tomatoes."

"Sorry." Nikki threw some of the dirt back into the hole and stuck the plant in. "Like this?"

"That's better. Pack the soil around it, nice and tight."

The girl's face beamed as she sat back on her heels and surveyed her accomplishment: a crookedly planted tomato bush. "Wow, neat! Will it really grow tomatoes?"

"It isn't going to sprout turnips, if that's what you mean."

"What are we going to do with them all?"

Abigail looked at the four dozen plants she had ordered from the nursery that morning. Forty-eight plants. That would be a lot of tomatoes. "I want a nice, big juicy one every evening for my dinner salad," she told Nikki. "After that, I don't care what you do with them. Give them to your mother, I suppose, or anyone else around here who wants them."

"Gee, thanks."

Abigail felt her cheeks grow warm, and the rosy flush had nothing to do with the sunlight. "It's no big deal," she snapped. "It's just tomatoes."

Nikki was undaunted and smiled brightly. "Thanks anyway."

"You're welcome. Get busy, Nicola. You have forty-seven more to go."

"Aren't you going to help me?"

"Of course, I'm helping. I'm supervising."

Nikki raised one eyebrow. "I think you should *show* me. Rev. Dylan says the best way to teach someone is by example."

Abigail glowered at her for a moment, then grabbed a

plant and a hand shovel. Her arthritis would kill her tomorrow, and it would be this little ragamuffin's fault.

"I heard Rev. Dylan and Miss Zoe talking," Nikki chattered on as she dug her next hole.

"Oh, really?" Abigail's ears perked at the prospect of gossip.

"Yes, and Miss Zoe said that she asked you to let the chapel use your carriage house for a day care center . . . for me and other kids like me."

Abigail grunted. "Your Miss Zoe has a big mouth."

"I think it's really neat that you're going to do that," the girl said. "There's a lot of kids like me around who need someplace to stay after school until our moms and dads get off work. It would be a lot of fun to have somewhere to go and do crafts and play games and . . ."

"Hold your horses, young lady. I didn't say I would do it. I told her I would think about it, but not to get her hopes up."

Nikki snickered and popped another plant into the ground. She mumbled something under her breath, which Abigail didn't quite hear.

"What did you say, girl?"

"No-o-o-o-thing."

"Speak up! What are you grumbling in your beard about?"

"I said, 'You'll do it.' "

Abigail sat back, hard, on the ground. "Oh, I will, huh? Well, how do you know, Miss Smarty Pants?"

"I know, because I know you. And you aren't half as mean as you let on. You just act cranky so that people won't like you, but I do anyway. So there."

For what seemed like forever, Abigail Covington couldn't speak. She couldn't even breathe.

Then she picked up a small dirt clod and bounced it off the top of the girl's head. "Shut up," she said, "and plant your danged tomatoes."

Nikki laughed, not even impressed, let alone intimidated. "Okey, dokey. No-o-o-o-o problem."

* * *

Dylan didn't want to have to tell Kerry that his 1956 Chevy Nomad was terminal. But considering what Kerry, Eddie and Steve had just described as its death throes, the old classic wasn't likely to be revived. With the three boys, Dylan leaned under the open hood of the car, which had just coasted into the church parking lot and given up the ghost.

Dylan had already delivered his amateur mechanic's diagnosis, but he could tell from the confused look on Kerry's face that the truth hadn't yet seeped into his brain.

"A thrown rod . . . is that bad?" Kerry asked. "Maybe me and the guys can fix it. I changed my spark plugs by myself once."

"Sorry, fellows, but this engine will have to be completely rebuilt, and that's a lot of time and money." Dylan felt Kerry's misery. He was a bit of a car buff himself and appreciated a handsome old classic.

He could still remember the sinking feeling he had experienced the day his first car, a bright red, 1966 Charger had bit the dust.

"My dad said that the next time it needed work, I'd have to pay for it myself," Kerry said with a semireproachful look at Dylan. "After your sermon a few weeks ago—you know, the one about love and seeking the higher good for other people? Well, he decided to show he loved me by making me pay my own way on stuff like my car."

Dylan suppressed a smile. Hey! Somebody in his congregation had been awake after all.

"And I just started working at the Hamburger Palace last Saturday, so I don't have enough money to fix *any-thing* yet. What am I gonna do?"

Glancing around at the three sorrowful faces beneath the hood, Dylan felt a tug of conscience. He shouldn't; the Lord knew he had plenty of other things to do, but . . .

"I'll tell you what—" he began.

"Yoo-hoo! Reverend!" The high, quivering voice

reached him from across the parking lot and the lawn. "Come here, I need you!"

Dylan growled under his breath and slid out from beneath the hood. Abigail was standing on the steps of her side porch, waving a white handkerchief at him.

"What now?" he muttered, then turned to the boys. "I'll be back in a minute." He grinned and added, "Don't take off now."

"Funny, funny," Kerry said. "Like we could go anywhere in this piece of ah . . . junk."

As Dylan walked across the lawn, he reveled in the momentary joy of knowing that his ministry seemed to be finally going somewhere. The boys were different somehow. The hard shells were slowly crumbling away, their relationships with their parents were better. He had even heard they were doing better in school.

Just last week, one of the young couples he had been counseling had told him that they had decided not to divorce, but to give their marriage another chance.

And Abigail Covington. Oh, she was still a demanding, difficult woman, and probably would be until she died. But even she seemed a bit softer these days, a glow in her eyes and a lightness to her step.

Although Dylan wasn't conceited enough to think he had much to do with Abigail's transformation. Most of that, he believed, was due to the unconditional love of a child, Nicola Sarita Dickens. And maybe some of Zoe Harmond had rubbed off on Abigail, too, when she wasn't looking.

The thought of Zoe made his heart ache. He could see her at her worktable beneath the tree, gathering up her tools, packing to leave.

Her job here was finished. Anytime now he would have to say goodbye, and he couldn't think of anything he could do to keep it from happening.

Chapter Ten

"Good morning, Abbie," Dylan said, as he joined her on the porch. "You summoned me?"

"Yes, thank you for coming." She waved a hand toward a wicker chair and a mug that contained steaming coffee. "Take a seat. I have to bend your ear."

Stunned, Dylan sat down, feeling as though he had just drifted into a strange, but pleasant, dreamscape. Since when did Miss Abigail Covington thank anyone for anything? And coffee . . . strong and black just the way he liked it. What a switch from the anemic tea she usually offered.

"I have a couple of things to tell you," she said, "so let's get on with it."

"By all means."

"First of all . . ." She sounded very businesslike, he thought. Actually, she sounded as though she were *trying* to sound businesslike, but he could almost swear he heard a tremor of emotion underneath. "First, I have to tell you that I've been speaking with my accountant, and it seems I have some . . . tax difficulties this year."

She paused and cleared her throat. "And he says I need some sort of deduction. So, I was thinking . . ."

"Yes?" Dylan tried not to hope; knowing Abigail, she was probably just toying with him.

"So, I've decided to allow the chapel use of my carriage

house for that day care center you want to start.''

"Why, Abigail, that's—"

"It's just a business decision on my part, and I want to make a few things completely clear before we go any further.''

"Of course. What is that?" He resisted the urge to jump off his chair, throw his arms around her, and give her a hearty kiss.

"The children will *not* be allowed under *any* condition to be on my lawn.''

He nodded. "That's perfectly reasonable. I can understand why you would—"

"Except for the part that reaches from the garden area to the woods.''

"Oh, well, thank you and—"

"And I certainly don't want them messing around in my garden.''

"No. We'll make sure they don't.''

"Unless they want to plant a few things, you know, like each child have their own small plot and raise a few vegetables for their families, the way Nicola has been doing. I suppose that would be all right.''

"What a nice idea, Abbie, you—"

"And if they do plant a few patches like that, I don't want to have to mess with any of the upkeep, the weeding, the watering, all that.''

"Well, no. I'm sure we can—"

"Although I could supervise some of the planting, just to make sure they get it right. Don't want them doing it wrong, because then nothing would grow, and they'd probably be disappointed and all that malarkey.''

"No, we certainly wouldn't want that. Abigail, I'm so touched by your generosity. I can't tell you how—"

"Then don't.'' She grabbed her cigarettes, popped one in her mouth, and lit up. "I told you, it's just so that I can get the tax deduction.''

"Yes, of course it is.''

"And besides, we don't have time. I have something else to discuss with you."

Abigail leaned forward in her chair and peered out the porch windows at Zoe, who was packing the boxes of tools into her van.

"I need all the deductions I can get this year, so I've decided that the chapel needs some new windows. Stained glass windows. I'm sick to death of looking at those plain old clear ones. It's high time we had the real thing."

Stained glass windows? The very thought shone a light of hope for Dylan. "Really?" he said, his eyes on Zoe.

"That's right. I've already talked to Miss Harmond about doing the job."

"That's wonderful!"

"It will be if she says 'yes.' She hasn't accepted yet—has some fool notion about traipsing around Europe for a few months."

"What's her final word so far?"

Abigail grinned and shook her head. "She said, 'I haven't made up my mind yet, but don't get your hopes up.'"

"My goodness, Abigail. That sounds like something *you* would say."

She sniffed and wiped at her nose with her lace-trimmed hanky. "Yes, doesn't it though. I'm afraid that young woman and I have far more in common than either of us would like to admit."

Dylan's face softened. He reached over and patted her hand. "And I'm very fond of you both."

It was too much. Too fast. She snatched her hand away.

"If you want those windows, you'd better have a talk with her. I figure it'll take her at least six months to make the blamed things. You know how picky I can be."

Dylan laughed. "Yes, Abbie, we all know how difficult you can be."

He stood and, whether she liked it or not, bent over to place a quick peck on her cheek.

"Thank you, Abigail. For everything."

"Hmmph. Don't thank me yet until we see if you can pull it off."

"It?"

"Don't get fresh with me, young man. We both know that I'm buying you six more months to woo that girl before she leaves for good. Don't blow it."

"I'll give it my best shot. I really will."

A few minutes later, Dylan had his head under the Chevy's hood again, his mental gears whirring.

"Okay, guys, I'll make a deal with you," he said.

Their faces lit up. A possibility of having wheels again!

"Sure, what is it?" Kerry said.

"I've just been informed that we're going to be converting Miss Covington's carriage house into an after school day care center."

"Okay . . . so?" Eddie didn't seem impressed.

"So, we're going to need a lot of grunt labor. Just the standard stuff, sawing boards, pounding nails, things like that."

"What's the deal?" Kerry looked hopeful. A good sign.

"I help you overhaul the Chev's engine. You help me with the center."

"Deal."

"Deal."

"Yeah, sure! Deal!"

Dylan felt like dancing an Irish jig right there in the parking lot. But instead, he decided to be "cool" and gave high fives all around.

Zoe was sitting at the top of the bluff, looking down on the silent valley, when the quiet was interrupted by the thrumming of a Harley-Davidson engine.

Somehow, she wasn't surprised, but her heart raced anyway.

He had come. Somehow she had known he would, but until she actually heard the sound of the bike, she wasn't sure.

He pulled the motorcycle next to her van and cut the engine. Looking around, he spotted her sitting there on the boulder. "Imagine running into you up here," he said as he climbed off and stowed his helmet behind the seat. "I mean, what are the odds?"

Sighing inwardly, she decided there was no point in pretending—even to herself—that she was anything but thrilled to see him.

"Pretty good, I'd say, if Nikki ratted on me and told you I was coming up here," she said, moving to the side of the rock to make room for him.

"She did give me a little hint."

"What kind of a hint?"

He took the seat she offered and brushed his fingers through his mussed hair. "Let's see . . . it went something like this, 'Miss Zoe is up at Pine Bluff, thinking about whether she should leave us or not, so you'd better go up there and tell her that we really, really, really want her to stay.' "

Zoe chuckled. "That sounds like Nikki, all right."

Dylan leaned forward, his elbows on his knees, and stared down at the twinkling town. "So . . . Miss Zoe, *are* you going to leave us?"

Zoe's throat suddenly tightened into a knot that hardly allowed her to breathe. Tears sprang to her eyes. "I . . . ah . . . I think so. You see, I've been planning this trip to Europe for a long time and . . ."

"I wish you wouldn't."

Four simple words. But they washed over her in a wave of emotion so strong she didn't think she could bear it.

"What are you saying?" she asked, her heart in her eyes.

He turned to face her and took both of her hands in his. She was surprised at how firm, how warm his touch was. How such a simple gesture reached deep inside her to parts she had thought were unreachable.

"I'm saying . . ." he told her, ". . . that I want you to stay. At least long enough to build us some wonderful windows. Long enough to see the day care center open and running. Long enough to give some more of your beautiful spirit to Nikki and Abigail and to me.''

He squeezed her hands, then lifted one to his lips and gently kissed its palm, giving her delicious shivers. ''We do love you, you know, Miss Zoe.''

''We?''

''Yes. And speaking for myself . . . very much.''

She allowed herself to stroke his cheek just once, feeling the masculine rasp of beard against her fingertips. ''What kind of love are we talking here?'' she asked. ''The heavenly, 'higher good' kind, or the infatuation type?''

He smiled. ''Ah, snared by my own words. I hate that.'' Twisting one lock of her hair around his forefinger he said, ''I'll have to admit that it's a good portion of both. I believe and hope I want what's best for you, what God wants for you. I want you to fulfill your highest potential and follow the path He has mapped out for you.''

Leaning over, he brushed his lips against her cheek. Like his hands, they were warm, firm, gentle but passionate. ''I also want very much to kiss you right now, to ask you to please stay and see if things might work out between us, to beg you to postpone that trip to Europe just a few more months, until we know.''

She closed her eyes for a moment and tried to summon the vision of Notre Dame, of the West Bank in Paris, or the beaches of the Riviera. Funny, they no longer seemed so clear, so inviting. Those places appeared rather lonely and impersonal now, after spending this time in Covington Falls.

''So, which do you want to do first?'' she said. ''Do you want to kiss me, ask me, or beg?''

He laughed, placed his hand beneath her chin and lifted her face to his. ''Oh, I think I'd like to kiss you first. Then, maybe I won't have to beg.''

Chapter Eleven

"*O*ooo, Miss Zoe, you look really, really beautiful!" Nikki's amber eyes were round with wonder as she looked up at the bride . . . her bride . . . dressed in a Victorian gown of ivory lace, trimmed with seed pearls.

"And you, Nicola Sarita Dickens, are the loveliest flower girl I have *ever* seen. I feel very honored to have you spread petals for me today."

They stood in the chapel foyer, listening to the deep, rich tones of the organ inside the sanctuary. Any moment now, Mrs. Whittle would stop singing, "Oh, Promise Me," and they would begin the wedding march.

"Here, let me help you with your dress," Debra Dickens said, as she bent to straighten the long train that flowed in satin ripples behind Zoe.

"And mine, too, mommy," Nikki said, pointing to the sash tied at her waist. "Is my bow straight?"

"Perfectly straight." Debra knelt to adjust the sash anyway, then placed a kiss on her daughter's cheek. "I'm so proud of you today, honey. You look so pretty with your new dress and white shoes."

For only the briefest moment, Zoe felt a small tug of jealousy. Once, she had felt as though Nikki were almost her own, ignored by her mother. But for the past few months, Debra had been taking parenting classes at the chapel and was working hard to use what she had learned with her child.

As Debra reached out to her daughter, Nikki drifted farther away from Zoe and toward her own mom.

As it should be, Zoe reminded herself. She knew that she truly did love Nikki because, even if it meant she might not see her as often, she wished the highest good for her . . . a loving family, not just adoring friends.

"Miss Covington helped me pick *all* the roses for *all* the petals," Nikki said, holding up her basket for Zoe's inspection. "And she helped me make the crown for my hair, too." She tilted her head to show off the laurel of rosebuds, babys' breath, daisies, and strands of pearls, twined around her auburn waves.

"I know," Zoe said. "I saw the two of you out in the garden all morning, giggling and picking flowers."

Reaching beneath her bouquet, Zoe withdrew a small, gleaming length of brass pipe with stained glass wheels at the end.

"I want to give you this, Nikki," she said, carefully handing it to her. "It's a kaleidoscope. I made it myself as a gift to you for being my flower girl."

"For me? You made it for me?" Nikki handed her basket to her mother and accepted the gift as though it were the finest treasure. Holding it up to the light, she turned the wheels and gasped at the beauty of the ever-changing patterns.

"This is the prettiest thing in the world!" she said. "You'll be my best friend *forever*."

"I wanted you to have it because of all the sparkle and light you've brought into my world this past year, Nikki. I wouldn't be standing here right now, if it weren't for you."

Nikki gave her mother a sly, sideways grin. "That's true. I tricked them into liking each other. But they really wanted to anyway."

"Oh, oh, oh!" Nikki's eyes twinkled. "There's the wedding march. It's time, Miss Zoe. It's time!"

Carefully handing the kaleidoscope to her mother for safekeeping, Nikki took her basket in hand and marched to the door of the sanctuary.

Zoe followed close behind, her heart pounding in double time with the music.

Head held high, Nikki, her basket full of rose petals, her white patent leather shoes, and her pale pink dress with "zillions" of petticoats, glided down the aisle as though she had been doing it all her life.

Indeed, she had, in her fantasies.

Zoe thought of her own dreams, some set aside, but other, even more precious ones, fulfilled beyond all expectation.

She turned to Debra and saw that she was watching her young daughter, tears streaming down her cheeks. Zoe thought of all the mothers who had become her friends over the past year as they had dropped their children off at the center. She thought of the kids, elbow deep in crafts that she provided for them, expressing themselves, enjoying themselves in a safe environment.

But as Zoe stepped to the door of the sanctuary and looked down the aisle, she lost all thoughts, except those of her groom, waiting for her. As Nikki had said, he *was* extremely handsome in his "special black suit."

She thought of the special gift she had tucked inside her bouquet for him. *Two* tickets to London and *two* itineraries for a one month hiking trip across Europe.

Abigail had assured her that neither the town nor the chapel would fall apart in their absence. Volunteers would fill the gaps until they returned. The community was truly beginning to work together.

From across the room, Zoe looked into her groom's eyes and whispered the words, "I love you." He smiled and did the same.

This time tomorrow, they would be on their way, exploring the world and their own relationship. But, as Zoe took the first step on Nikki's rose-strewn carpet, she knew it would take two lifetimes for them to learn the great mystery of love.

To Love And To Cherish

∾

Beverly Beaver

Chapter One

$\mathcal{L}$ara Grayson Warren's hand trembled as she punched the second floor elevator button. When the doors closed, enveloping her in the tomb-like quiet, she shut her eyes and said a silent prayer. *Please, dear God, let Mary Beth live. Don't take my little girl away from me.*

A mixture of intense emotions surged through Lara—love, anger, fear, hope and anguish. Mary Beth was the center of her universe, her very life. She couldn't lose her only child!

The elevator doors opened. Lara stepped out, glanced around at the room signs and followed the arrows pointing to the surgery area. Her three-inch navy heels clipped sharply against the polished tile floor.

Medicinal scents mingled with the strong aroma of cleaning materials, the combined odor slightly irritating. Lara glanced from side to side at the pale green and cream colored walls along the corridor as she searched for the waiting room. Her thundering heartbeat drummed in her ears. A queasy weakness swirled uneasily in her stomach.

When Trent had telephoned her, he'd said the doctor was rushing Mary Beth into surgery to remove her damaged spleen and stop the internal bleeding.

Tears gathered in the corners of Lara's eyes. She brushed them away with her fingertips. She could not fall apart. Not now. Not in front of Trent.

She hesitated momentarily at the closed waiting room door. Taking a deep breath, she squared her shoulders and grasped the handle. She had no choice but to open the door, go inside and face Trent and whatever news he had about their daughter's condition.

On the flight in to Greenbrier from Huntsville, she had fought her anger at Trent, had tried not to blame him for what had happened. Logically, she knew that Mary Beth's accident hadn't been his fault. But as a mother, she wasn't thinking rationally—she was thinking with her heart. And since Trent Warren had broken her heart five years ago, it was easy to blame him, to make him the bad guy in any situation.

She eased open the door. Trent stood with his back to her, facing the wide expanse of windows overlooking the parking lot. His broad shoulders were slumped, his dark head bowed, his big, muscular body tense.

She swallowed hard. Her feet refused to move. She'd never wanted to see him again. Not ever. In all the years since their divorce, she had made certain their paths hadn't crossed, and that hadn't been easy considering the fact they shared custody of their daughter.

"Lara!" Peg Warren jumped up off the tan vinyl sofa in the corner of the room. "We didn't expect you so soon, honey. How'd you get here so fast?"

"I chartered a plane." Lara stood frozen in the doorway, determined not to glance at Trent. She was aware that he had turned around at the mention of her name. She focused her gaze on her ex-husband's plump, petite aunt. "How is Mary Beth? Have they brought her out of surgery?"

Peg walked across the room, slipped her arm around Lara's waist and hugged her. "No word, yet. But our little girl is going to be all right. She has . . . to . . . be." Peg's voice cracked with emotion. "Come on in and sit down, honey. All we can do is wait and pray."

Forcing her legs to move, Lara allowed Peg to lead her across the room. Despite her effort not to glance at Trent, she could still see him in her peripheral vision. He stood ramrod straight, his arms crossed over his chest. She felt his heated glare. An irrational urge almost overcame her. The urge to confront him, to slap his face, beat his chest and demand how he could have allowed something like this to happen to their daughter. But she could not—would not—become hysterical.

"I don't want to sit, Aunt Peg . . . I—" Lara tensed when she realized she'd referred to her ex-husband's relative in the familiar form she'd used during her brief marriage.

"It's all right, you know. Everybody calls me Aunt Peg." Peg patted Lara on the back. "Why don't you try to relax, honey? I'll go get us all some coffee. Trent can tell you about what happened and—"

"I told her over the phone." Trent's deep voice growled the words. "She doesn't want to hear anything I have to say. She won't believe any of my explanations. She never did."

Clenching her teeth, Lara balled her hands into tight fists. "I'll believe the truth. If you're capable of telling it."

"Now, see here." Peg Warren planted her pudgy hands on her round hips and narrowed her hazel eyes. "This is neither the time nor the place for you two to rehash old grievances. You're going to have to put aside your own feelings and think about what's best for Mary Beth. When she comes out of this—and she will—she'll need to see her parents together and united in their love for her."

Reluctantly Lara nodded. "You're right. Nothing matters except Mary Beth."

"That's one thing we can agree on," Trent said.

"Good." Peg glanced from Trent to Lara. "Now, I want your assurance that y'all won't come to blows while I get us some coffee."

Trent grunted. "I've never hit a woman in my life. Not even when Lara slapped my face."

"I don't intend to get close enough to your nephew to touch him, let alone hit him."

Peg rolled her eyes heavenward, sighed loudly and left the waiting room. Lara laid her navy leather purse on the sofa, slipped out of her coat and placed it on top of her purse. Shaking her head, she flung her long blond hair off her shoulder.

"All you said on the phone was that Mary Beth had taken a bad spill off Dixie and was being rushed into surgery. That she was seriously injured." Lara spoke to Trent, but she would not look at him. "Exactly what happened?"

"I'm not sure. Not exactly. I wasn't there when it happened."

Lara gasped. "You weren't—"

"Dammit, Lara, don't say it. Don't start blaming me for something that isn't my fault. What happened wasn't anybody's fault. Aunt Peg was with her, and so was Joshua. Something spooked Dixie. Ordinarily Mary Beth would have been as safe riding that pony as she is riding her bicycle."

"Why would a fall off her pony injure Mary Beth so severely that she requires surgery?"

"Somehow Dixie rolled over on Mary Beth."

"Oh, dear God!" Lara's face paled.

Trent's gut instinct was to reach out, grab Lara and pull her into his arms. She was hurting and needed comforting. And heaven help him, after all these years, after all the pain and bitterness that stood between them, he still wanted to be the one to comfort her.

He hadn't seen Lara in nearly five years, except in the photographs Mary Beth often brought with her on her visits. His ex-wife was still beautiful, maybe a little more beautiful now that she had matured some. The young girl freshness was gone, replaced by a womanly aura.

He had taken a rich city girl to the country and put her in boots and blue jeans on his Mississippi ranch. That suntanned girl with a ponytail and happy smile was gone. Over the years since their divorce, Lara had turned into a replica of her lovely, sophisticated mother, in her neat designer suit and pearls.

''There's a chance Mary Beth suffered some spinal injury.'' Trent clenched his hands into fists in an effort to prevent himself from pulling Lara into his arms. ''We know for a fact that she has a concussion, some broken ribs and a ruptured spleen. The doctor said . . .'' Trent choked on the painful thought that his daughter might not live. ''They'll do everything they can.''

''She really could die, couldn't she?'' Lara looked at him then, her eyes wide, her vision blurred by tears. ''How could you—no, I mustn't blame you. I'm sorry. I realize this isn't your fault. I know how much you love Mary Beth.''

Averting her gaze from his face, Lara turned from him and hugged herself. Bowing her head, she cried quietly. Her shoulders trembled. If only things were different, she wouldn't feel so alone, so alienated from Trent. Now, when she so desperately needed his comfort and strength, she couldn't turn to him.

The sudden realization that she wanted Trent's arms around her, wanted to lose herself in the comforting power of his caress, shocked her. But it shouldn't have. He had always had that effect on her. Since the first moment they met, seven years ago, all he'd had to do was look at her with those captivating brown eyes and she'd been his for the taking. That's why she'd stayed away from him after their divorce, why she didn't dare lean on him now. If she ever let him touch her, she'd be lost.

Trent eased up behind her, then stopped abruptly. His muscles strained, his arms ached with the need to hold her. God, how he missed holding her. Caressing that soft, supple flesh. Kissing those warm, moist lips. Burying himself in the hot, tight sweetness of her loving body.

Damn! Trent cursed under his breath, turned abruptly and walked away from Lara. He had to be the biggest fool on the face of the earth, wanting a woman who had made it perfectly clear that she didn't want him.

He didn't love her anymore. She'd killed his love for her when she'd left him and taken away his child. But he had never been able to forget her, had never been able to forget the wild passion between them. And even now, with a bitter divorce, five long years and several other women between them, Trent still wanted Lara as much as he had the first time he saw her.

Shoving her purse and coat aside, Lara sat down on the vinyl sofa. She glanced over at Trent. He had changed very little since their last meeting—the day they had officially ended their marriage. He was older, of course, but the years had simply changed a young, ruggedly handsome man into an even more rough and rugged cowboy. And that's how she'd always think of Trent, as a cowboy—her cowboy.

She'd met him seven years ago when she'd gone to the rodeo in Muscle Shoals with some friends. She had found him utterly irresistible. Tall, broad-shouldered, lean-hipped. A rowdy, rough and tumble cowboy who lived on a small cattle ranch in Mississippi and toured the rodeo circuit as a champion.

Lara looked at Trent's feet. Big, size twelve feet. She'd never known him to wear anything other than boots. Her gaze traveled up the length of his long, jean-clad legs, across his tight, round butt and up his wide back and thickly muscled shoulders.

He wore his jet black hair shorter now. When they first met, it had curled about his collar. Memories of the times she had run her fingers through that thick unruly mane of hair flashed through her mind. She shuddered. Her body clenched and unclenched in a purely feminine way.

Don't look at him! Don't think about what it was like with him!

She glanced across the room at the small magazine-laden, metal table situated between two brown vinyl chairs. A black Stetson rested on top of the magazine stack. Trent's hat. Their first night together, after the rodeo performance, when they'd been introduced, he'd taken off his black Stetson and placed it on her head. She would never forget the way she'd felt when she looked up at him. He'd slipped his arm around her waist, pulled her up against him and smiled at her. That devastating, wide smile that created deep dimpled creases in his cheeks. She had fallen in love with him at that precise moment.

She'd been twenty-one, fresh out of college, perhaps a bit naive and oddly enough, still a virgin.

"Come get it while it's hot!" Balancing three cups of coffee in her hands, Peg Warren barreled through the door.

Standing quickly, Lara rushed to help Peg by taking two of the cups.

"You still take yours with cream but no sugar?" Peg asked.

"Yes, thank you."

"Give that one to Trent." Peg nodded at the second cup Lara held. "It's black. He won't drink this sweet, creamy stuff I like."

She could do this, she told herself. She could walk across the room and hand Trent a cup of coffee. She wouldn't have to touch him, wouldn't have to look directly at him, and didn't even have to speak to him. Yes, she could do it.

Trent reached out to take the coffee, then hesitated when he saw the way Lara's hand quivered. "If you're that afraid of my touch, just set the damn cup on the table."

Stiffening her spine, she willed her hand to stillness, then offered Trent the cup. Tilting her chin defiantly, she looked directly at him. He searched her eyes as if seeking a hidden truth. Careful not to touch her, he took the cup. Lara swallowed, thankful that his hand hadn't grazed hers, uncertain she would have been able to hide her feelings from him.

"Has there been any word?" Peg asked as she removed the plastic lid from her coffee cup.

"Nothing," Lara told her. "I wish I could see Mary Beth. I wish I could . . . hold her." Lara set her coffee on the sofa arm, then slumped down, the side of her hip resting on her coat.

Peg sat beside Lara, took a sip of her coffee and patted

Lara's knee. "She came in and out of consciousness on the ride to the hospital. She called for you, and Trent said for her not to worry, that you were on your way. He's really wonderful with her, you know. She's the moon and stars to him."

"I know Trent loves her. And she loves him." In her bitterness and anger when their marriage ended, Lara had been tempted to fight Trent for sole custody of Mary Beth. Her mother had encouraged her to do just that. But no matter how much they hated each other, they both loved their daughter, and Lara had done what she knew was best for their little girl. Lara kept Mary Beth nine months out of the year, but she lived with Trent every summer, every other holiday and one weekend each month. Aunt Peg had agreed to be their go-between, driving to Huntsville from Greenbrier and back with Mary Beth, her armload of stuffed animals and her little pink suitcases in tow.

The solution hadn't been perfect. Not for her. Not for Trent. And certainly not for Mary Beth. But it had been the best they could do, considering the circumstances. Lara knew that Mary Beth's heart's desire was to see her parents reunited—something that could never happen.

"I thought maybe your mother would come with you." Leaning her back against the sofa cushions, Peg drank her coffee.

"Oh, I didn't tell you, did I? Mother and Jonathan have gone to Europe for six weeks," Lara said. "They left three days ago."

"Who's Jonathan?" Turning around, Trent strode across the room and sat down in one of the brown vinyl chairs. He removed the lid from his coffee and lifted the cup to his lips.

"He's Liz's new husband, Jonathan Edwards," Peg said. "I thought I told you that Liz was getting married again."

"Yeah, I suppose you did," Trent said. "How many does this make? Five or six?"

Lara glared at Trent. During their divorce, Lara had

clung to her mother, heeding her advice, listening to her warnings about Trent. And Trent had ridiculed Lara for taking everything her mother said to heart. He'd laughed at her, telling her she was foolish to take marital advice from a woman who went through husbands as if they were Kleenex.

"This is Mother's sixth marriage," Lara admitted. "But since she married Brad twice, Jonathan is just her fifth husband."

Nodding, Trent grunted, then finished his coffee, tossed the cup several yards across the room and hit the waste-paper basket with ease.

What the hell was taking so long? he wondered. Why hadn't they come out and told them something? If he didn't hear some good news about Mary Beth soon, he'd lose his mind. And despite the way she was trying so valiantly to hold herself together, he knew Lara was on the verge of falling apart.

He checked the wall clock with his watch. Three minutes difference in the two timepieces. Less than twenty minutes since Lara had arrived.

"Isn't there someone we can ask about how things are going?" Nervously Lara lifted her hand, accidentally knocking her cup off the sofa arm. When the foam container hit the floor, the lid popped off and brown liquid spread across the carpet.

"Oh, no." Lara looked down at the spilled coffee. Tears flooded her eyes. "Look what a mess I've made."

She grabbed her purse, unsnapped it and pulled out a handful of tissues, then slid off the sofa and onto her knees. With blinding tears streaming down her face, she blotted at the dark, wet stain on the carpet. Her body shook with her sobs.

"Oh, honey. Don't bother with that." Peg jumped off the sofa, leaned over and tugged on Lara's shoulders. "Come on. Get up. Let me take care of it."

Sobbing uncontrollably, Lara continued furiously blotting the stain, ignoring Peg completely.

When his aunt looked pleadingly at him, Trent shook his head affirmatively, then nodded toward the ladies room. Peg patted him on the arm as she rushed past him. She hurried into the adjacent restroom, returning quickly with a handful of paper towels.

Bending on one knee beside Lara, Trent grabbed her hands. Droplets of coffee dripped from the tissues she clutched tightly. Prying her hands open, he scooped up the soaked tissues and tossed them onto the floor, then slipped one arm around her waist and lifted her to her feet.

"It's all right, babe. Go ahead and cry."

Struggling to pull away from him, she protested vehemently. "Don't touch me! Don't!" Moist streaks marred the perfection of Lara's light makeup. "Please, let me go. I have to clean up—"

Trent whirled her around and into his arms, holding her against him, stroking her hair, her back, whispering her name. "Hush, Lara. Hush, babe. Aunt Peg will clean up your spilled coffee. Don't do this to yourself."

"Oh, God, Trent, what's going on in there? Why is it taking so long?" Easing away from him, she reached out and grabbed his shoulders. "What if she's . . . Oh, Trent, don't let her die. Please, don't let her die!"

He clasped her chin in the cradle between his thumb and index finger, forcing her to look directly into his eyes. "I wish I had that kind of power, babe." Swallowing his own unshed tears, he closed his eyes for a split second and said a silent prayer, offering God anything if only Mary Beth would live.

"I know." Lara stepped away from Trent. "I'm all right now. I apologize for going to pieces like that. I'm usually in better control of myself."

"Don't apologize for acting human, Lara. Nobody around here expects you to be perfect."

He turned his back on her, then bent over to help his aunt. He took the soiled paper towels and foam cup from her and threw them into the wastepaper basket.

Lara sat down on the sofa, opened her purse and removed her hand mirror and a tissue. She wiped away her tears and patted her smeared makeup, trying to cover the stains. *Nobody around here expects you to be perfect.* Trent's words echoed in her ears. Had he intended his statement to be another dig at her mother? During their brief marriage, Trent had repeatedly tried to help Lara free herself from her mother's overbearing, manipulative influence. Liz Grayson Bentley Harrington Harrington Stevens Edwards expected nothing less than perfection from her only child, and Lara had tried to be perfect for her mother. But she had failed miserably in pleasing her mother when she'd eloped with a rodeo cowboy she'd known for less than three weeks. Liz had been appalled by Lara's choice in a husband, and had had no qualms about causing as much trouble for the young couple as she possibly could, as had Trent's father.

But in the end, it had not been her mother or his father who had destroyed their marriage. It had been Trent himself.

"Mr. Warren?" A green-garbed man in his late thirties stood in the waiting room doorway.

Trent whirled around to face the surgeon. "Dr. Milton!"

Lara jumped up off the sofa. Peg put her arm around Lara's waist. "How is Mary Beth?" Peg asked.

Lara's breath caught in her throat. She stared into the doctor's sad gray eyes.

"Are you Mary Beth's mother?" Dr. Milton asked.

"Yes." Lara's voice was weak and a bit squeaky.

Trent walked up beside Lara, reached down and took her hand into his. When she squeezed his hand, he tightened his hold, and together, as Mary Beth's parents, they waited to learn their daughter's fate.

Chapter Two

"Mary Beth is in recovery now. I can't make y'all any guarantees, but at this point, her chance of a full recovery looks good."

An insistent hum buzzed in Lara's ears. Suddenly her knees buckled and for a split second a swirling darkness encompassed her. Grabbing her around the waist just as she swayed forward, Trent supported her body against his.

"Why don't you sit down, Mrs. Warren." Dr. Milton nodded toward the area behind them. "I'll explain the situation to you and your husband and tell you what can be done for Mary Beth."

Lara wanted the doctor to know that Trent Warren was no longer her husband, that he hadn't been in five years. She had kept the Warren name only because of Mary Beth, and she preferred being called Ms. Warren. But Lara didn't say anything, and made no protest when Trent led her to the sofa, eased her down, then sat beside her. When he wrapped his arm around her shoulders, she scooted away from him.

It would be so easy to lean on him, to allow him to comfort and console her. But as much as she had once longed for his touch, she both feared and despised it now. Feared it because Trent still possessed the power to sexually arouse her, and despised it because she'd never been able to forget how she'd felt when she saw him in another woman's arms.

Dr. Milton sat on the edge of a chair directly across from Lara and Trent. Peg remained standing.

"We removed Mary Beth's spleen and made the necessary repairs to stop the internal bleeding. I don't think her concussion is serious and time will heal her broken ribs."

"But?" Trent asked. Dropping his clasped hands between his spread knees, he stared at Dr. Milton.

"To put this as simply as possible, Mary Beth has a lumbar injury with spinal instability."

Lara gasped, then bit down on her lower lip. Trent jerked his head around, his dark eyes focusing on his ex-wife's pale face.

"It sounds worse than it is," the doctor said. "Now, I'm not saying her condition isn't serious, but it won't be permanent. She did receive some lumbar nerve damage, a spinal contusion and spinal shock . . . and I'm afraid she has some ruptured spinal ligaments."

"What can done for her?" Peg asked. "Is she going to be crippled?"

"No!" Lara cried. "Please, she can't be . . ." Fighting to control her emotions, Lara swallowed her tears. "Surely you can do something. More surgery. Call in whatever experts you need. Money is no object. My mother is a very wealthy woman."

At the mention of her mother, Trent went deadly still. Turning her head sharply, Lara glared at him.

"Mary Beth doesn't need more surgery," Dr. Milton said. "And I'm considered an expert, Mrs. Warren, but if you'd like a second opinion—"

"I don't think there'll be a need for that," Trent said. "Do you, Lara?"

She glowered at him, her blue eyes fiercely bright, then she turned her attention to the doctor. "I'm sorry if it seemed that I was implying . . . well, I'm certain you're a—"

"I understand, Mrs. Warren. You want what's best for Mary Beth, and if calling in another doctor will set your mind at rest, then I think that's what you should do." Dr. Milton smiled faintly.

"Thank you," Lara said, her voice soft and apologetic. "Perhaps I did overreact. Please, tell us what sort of treatment Mary Beth will require."

"First, she'll be placed in a fiberglass body cast, made in two parts and held together with velcro. During the four weeks she'll be in the cast, she'll have to undergo rehab on her upper body to strengthen her arms and shoulders and chest muscles to prevent wasting."

"When can I have her transferred to a Huntsville hospital?" Lara asked.

"Dammit, you're not taking her back to Huntsville!" Trent shot straight up. Stomping his booted feet over the floor, he paced back and forth in front of the sofa. Pausing momentarily, he glared at Lara. "Why the hell can't you leave her here in Greenbrier?"

"I want to take her home," Lara said. "Mother can afford for us to hire a full-time nurse to help me with Mary Beth. I'll be able to keep in touch with my job by phone and make a quick trip into the bank every day or so."

"I can't leave the ranch for weeks on end." Trent shoved his hands into his pockets and arched his spine. "I want to be around to help my daughter, every day, not just an occasional visit."

"I'd rather not argue with you about this, but if you try to cause any problems, I'll call my lawyer." Standing quickly, Lara placed her hands on her hips and stared at Trent.

"I didn't realize you folks were divorced," Dr. Milton said. "I'm fairly new here in Greenbrier."

Lara turned to the doctor, smiling weakly, suddenly realizing what an ugly little scene she and Trent had created. "Please, excuse me. Excuse us. As long as my ex-husband and I manage to stay in different states, we don't fight."

"Well, whatever your differences are, I suggest you put

them on hold for the time being,'' Dr. Milton said. ''Y'all share a five-year-old daughter who's going to need a lot of love and support from both her parents to see her through her rehabilitation during the next three or four months.''

Trent removed his hands from his pockets, took a deep, calming breath and nodded agreement. ''I'll do whatever—'' he glanced at Lara ''—*we'll* do whatever is necessary to help Mary Beth. She's our top priority.''

''Glad to hear it.'' Dr. Milton rose, placed his hand on Lara's shoulder and said quietly, ''If you'd like to see her, you and your . . . that is both parents can go in and be with her while she's in recovery.''

Trent hated himself for the surge of jealousy that swelled up inside him, tightening his chest painfully. Lara was so beautiful, she'd always drawn male attention wherever she went, and it looked as if Dr. Milton wasn't immune to her feminine allure. But why the hell, after all this time, did it still bother him so damned much to see another man touch her? Even such an innocent touch? Because, fool that he was, on some primitive level, he still thought of her as his.

''You two go on in and give my baby a kiss for me.'' Peg slipped her arm around Lara's waist, then reached out and drew Trent into her embrace. ''There will be time enough tomorrow or the next day to work out arrangements for Mary Beth's care. Right now, you two have to present a united front. She's going to need all your strength as well as her own in order to recover.''

''You're right, Aunt Peg,'' Lara said. ''I'll take a week's vacation from work and stay on here in Greenbrier until Trent and I can agree on the best course of action.''

Trent knew he should be relieved that Lara was being so rational, behaving so sensibly, almost unemotionally. But instead, he felt angry. Deep, gut-wrenching anger. He hated the way Lara fought so hard to keep her emotions in check, to behave the way she thought was proper. Except for her ability to lose herself in their passionate love-making, Trent had seen Lara relinquish complete control of her emotions only once. Those few horrendous moments five years, four months and eight days ago, right after she'd caught him with Cassie Douglas.

"Thanks for not taking her away," Trent managed to say just before he walked out of the waiting room.

Lara hugged Peg Warren, then followed her ex-husband down the hallway, into the recovery area and straight to their little girl.

Trent gazed down at the child he loved more than life itself. Mary Beth. So beautiful. So perfect. So much like Lara. Trent had wanted a son, had thought he could never love a daughter the way he could a son. His own father had taught him all the old-fashioned macho prejudices by the way he lived his own life. Jess Warren had been sorely disappointed that his first grandchild had been female. But what should he have expected, he'd told Trent, the mother being a soft, pampered city girl who didn't know the first thing about being a real woman. If Trent had married somebody like Cassie Douglas, she'd have given Jess a grandson.

His father had never approved of Lara, any more than her mother had approved of Trent. Sometimes, in the dark of night, when he was all alone and feeling sorry for himself, he blamed ol' Jess and lovely Liz for everything that had gone wrong in his marriage. But most of the time he knew who was really to blame—he and Lara.

Trent caressed his sedated daughter's soft, warm cheek. God, how he loved this child. He couldn't have loved a son more. Maybe not even as much. Only a little girl could look up at her daddy with her mother's eyes and capture his heart with her smile.

"Daddy's here, sweetheart. Daddy's here."

Lara sat down beside Mary Beth and took her limp hand, holding it in a strong, gentle grasp. Glancing at Trent, she noticed the tears in his eyes.

No matter what he'd done to her, how he had betrayed her and broken her heart, Lara had to admit that Trent was a good father. And Mary Beth adored him. All women adored Trent Warren. Even she had. Once. Long ago. There had been a time when she would have walked over hot coals to be with him.

She couldn't take Mary Beth away from Trent, not now when her baby would need her father so much. Yet, she couldn't expose herself to his presence day in and day out, without slowly losing her mind. She had no earthly idea how they would solve this problem, but somehow they had to find a solution. She'd have to find a way to compromise with Trent. She'd have to do it for Mary Beth's sake.

Trent had been pleasantly surprised when Lara agreed to extend her vacation to a second week so that Mary Beth could remain in Greenbrier instead of transferring her to a Huntsville hospital. But he didn't kid himself about his ex-wife's motives. She wasn't doing this for him; she was doing it for their daughter. Mary Beth liked seeing her daddy every day. His child wanted and needed him in her life on a daily basis, now more than ever since she was confined to a body cast.

Lara had made it perfectly clear that she couldn't stand the sight of him, that she preferred they schedule their time with Mary Beth in order to avoid each other. They decided on twelve-hour shifts, occasionally allowing Aunt Peg to relieve them. Lara took most of the day shifts, while Trent took the nights. A few times, they'd passed each other in the hall, spoken briefly and hurried their separate ways.

Mary Beth would be going home in a couple of days. Even though he and Lara hadn't discussed the situation in much detail, Trent knew she planned to take their daughter back to Alabama. He supposed he should be grateful for the time he'd had with Mary Beth. But dammit, he wanted more. He wanted to be around to help his little girl recover, to give her his love, support and encouragement every single day.

How would Lara feel, he wondered, if the tables were turned and she was forced to stay away from Mary Beth during her recovery? If she weren't allowed to do everything possible to help in her rehabilitation?

He knew he was more than an hour early, that Lara wouldn't be expecting him. She wouldn't like it, but he didn't care. They needed to talk—really talk—about what would be best for Mary Beth. And the only way to do that was face to face.

He hesitated outside the half-closed door. How was he going to be able to persuade Lara to do what he wanted? There had been a time when he knew exactly what to say and do to bring her around to his way of thinking. But that had been long ago, when she'd loved him with the same wild, mindless passion with which he'd loved her.

The sound of Lara's laughter padded over Trent's nerve endings like soft, caressing fingertips. God, how long had it been since he'd heard her laugh like that? There had come a point in their marriage when he had killed that soft, pure laughter within her and replaced it with bitter, angry tears.

Easing the door open a fraction wider, Trent glanced inside. A tall, slender man with neatly styled brown hair had his arm draped casually around Lara's shoulders. He had his back to Trent, but Trent immediately knew who he was. The man in the tailored suit was Lara's boss, vice-president of the bank where Lara worked as a loan officer, the guy who had asked Lara to marry him a few months ago.

Mary Beth had told him all about Don Chapman. "Mommy likes him a lot. They go out on dates all the time." His daughter had first mentioned Don almost a year ago. "He's nice to me. He brings me presents, and tells me I look just like Mommy." Trent didn't care how *nice* the man was, he hated him. He'd hated him the moment Mary Beth mentioned Lara was dating him. He knew his hatred was irrational. Lara wasn't his wife anymore; he had no claim on her. But deep down, on a purely primitive gut level, Trent couldn't bare the thought of another man making love to Lara.

He grunted. Hell, he was a damned fool. He certainly didn't live a celibate life, why should Lara? But there hadn't been anyone permanent since the divorce. Only two relationships had been serious enough to call them affairs.

He figured Lara thought he had rushed back into an affair with Cassie Douglas. She'd probably even wondered why he hadn't married "the other woman." The truth was that his romance with Cassie Douglas had ended when he first met Lara, and despite what she believed, he'd never loved Cassie, and he'd never wanted her or any other woman after he'd fallen in love with Lara.

"Daddy!" Mary Beth cried out when she saw Trent standing in the partially open doorway.

Trent smiled despite his pain. His heart broke every time he saw his little girl cocooned in her fiberglass shell. She had adjusted far better than he would have under similar circumstances. But then Mary Beth had inherited Lara's calm, easygoing demeanor instead of his volatile, restless nature.

In less than two weeks, Mary Beth had learned how to move around in bed using her arms, and could transfer herself from the bed to the bedside potty and the wheelchair. His chest swelled with pride whenever he looked at the beautiful child he and Lara had created together. His daughter was the most important thing he'd ever done in his entire life. She was the one thing, no matter what, that he would never regret.

"Hey there, sweetheart. How's daddy's big girl this evening?" Removing his Stetson, Trent walked into the room. Ignoring everyone else, he headed straight toward Mary Beth's bed.

She eased herself up and held out her arms. "Daddy! Daddy! Don't let Mommy take me back to Huntsville. I told her I don't want to go. I want us to stay here with you."

Trent sat down on the side of the bed, took Mary Beth's tiny, cast-encased body into his arms and stroked her long blond hair lovingly. "Calm down, baby girl."

Mary Beth clung to him, big tears pooling in her blue eyes. "I don't want to stay at Grandmother's big, old house with a nurse. I just want you and Mommy to take care of me. We can go live at the ranch and I'll get better real quick. I promise."

Trent glanced over his daughter's head, his gaze trapping Lara. She swallowed, tightened her jaw and glared back at him.

"What's going on?" he asked, his voice deceptively low and steady.

"I'm afraid Mary Beth didn't react well when Lara explained the necessity of their returning to Huntsville day after tomorrow," Don Chapman said.

Clenching her teeth tightly, Lara closed her eyes. Trent barely contained a smile, knowing his ex-wife expected his temper to flare because of the other man's intrusion into something Trent considered a family matter.

Still embracing his daughter, soothing her with his strong presence, Trent tilted his head and stared at the elegant, middle-aged banker, who stood directly behind Lara, his hand on her shoulder.

"Who the hell are you?" Trent asked.

"Don't you dare make a scene," Lara warned.

"That's Don," Mary Beth said. "I told you about him, Daddy. He's Mommy's boyfriend. And it's all his fault that Mommy wants to take me away."

"Mary Beth Warren, that isn't so!" Lara said.

"Yes, it is, too. I heard him tell you that staying here was bad for your job and it was bad for you to be around my daddy so much." Mary Beth's bottom lip trembled. Huge tears dropped from her blue eyes and cascaded down her cheeks.

Don Chapman's face turned bright pink. He cleared his throat several times. Trent glowered at the man, issuing him a silent warning that if he knew what was good for him, he wouldn't interfere in his relationship with his daughter—or his ex-wife.

Lara took a deep, exasperated breath. "What are you

doing here this early?" She forced herself to take several steps toward Trent, stopping a few inches from the bedside, her legs almost brushing his. "You weren't due to relieve me for another hour and a half."

"I came in early so we could have a little talk. I thought it was time we discussed Mary Beth's immediate future." Trent grasped his daughter gently by the shoulders, kissed her forehead, then stood up.

Lara looked tired. A hint of dark circles under her eyes. A weary slump to her shoulders. An unnatural paleness beneath her makeup. All these things alerted him to the toll Mary Beth's accident had taken on Lara.

"Don't let her take me away from you, Daddy. I don't care what he says." Mary Beth pointed an accusatory finger at Don. "I don't want a nurse taking care of me instead of you and Mommy."

Lara pressed past Trent, unable to avoid brushing his body with hers as she bent over the bed and took her daughter's hand. "Please, don't act this way. You knew that sooner or later we'd have to return to Huntsville. It's our home. My job is there. Grandmother lives there."

Mary Beth jerked her hand out of her mother's grasp. "My daddy's not there! And I need my daddy if I'm going to get all better."

"See what you've done!" Lara turned abruptly, her gaze boring into Trent. "What have you been saying to her to make her act this way?"

"What have I—? Now, you wait just one damn—er—darn minute here. Are you accusing me of creating this problem?" Trent wondered why he was so surprised by her accusation? Lara was good at blaming him for everything that went wrong in her life. Everything bad was always his fault.

"I most certainly am!" Lara shot up off the bed, her index finger pointing at Trent.

"Just like so many other times, I'm not guilty."

She stuck her finger right in his face. "Somehow you've convinced her that by throwing this temper tantrum, I'll let her stay here with you. How could you do this to her? Don't you realize you're only hurting her?''

Grabbing Lara's wrist, Trent jerked her pointing finger out of his face. He gritted his teeth, then huffed loudly, desperately trying to control his temper. "Don't push me, babe.''

Blood soared through Lara's body, drumming in her ears as her heartbeat accelerated. How many times had she and Trent argued, the heated tension between them almost tangible? And how many times had those arguments ended with her in his arms, his mouth taking hers, their bodies tangled in primitive passion? At the touch of his fingers around her wrist, her body recalled past pleasures and pleaded for a repeat performance.

She saw the memories in his eyes and instinctively knew his body had responded the way hers had. For one brief, intense moment, they stared at each other, unable to break the visual contact that united them in remembered ecstasy.

She tugged on her wrist; Trent released her. She stepped away from him, her legs weak, her hands trembling. With her back to him, she closed her eyes.

"Let's discuss this outside," she said, her voice quivering.

"Mommy, please," Mary Beth begged. "Let's stay at Daddy's ranch. Just until I can walk again. I promise I'll do whatever I have to do to get better. Even if it hurts.''

"You're not being reasonable, Mary Beth," Don said. "Your mother has an important job in Huntsville. She can't just take three or four months off to play nursemaid to—''

"Don't say anymore." Lara glared at her boyfriend, then turned her attention to her daughter. "Your father and I are going outside to discuss this matter, and when we've reached an agreement on what we both think is best for you, we'll come back in here and tell you.''

"Mommy!"

"Sit tight, sweetheart," Trent said. "Your mother is going to do what's best for you, just like she always does.''

The three adults silently exited Mary Beth's hospital room. Trent closed the door.

"Is there a coffee bar around here somewhere?" Don asked. "We could have a cup of coffee and talk this over like rational adults."

Lara placed her hand on Don's arm; he smiled at her. "This isn't something the three of us are going to discuss. You aren't involved in this decision."

"Of course I'm involved, I'm your—"

"You're my friend, Don. Not my husband. Not even my fiancé." She patted his arm affectionately. "I'd like for you to go downstairs to the snack bar and wait for me. After Trent and I have talked and I've made my decision and we've told Mary Beth, I'll come down and join you for dinner."

"I don't see what there is to decide," Don said. "Before he showed up and your daughter threw her little temper fit, we had already decided the best course of action for you and Mary Beth."

"We discussed an option," Lara said. "And I presented that option to my daughter, who vehemently opposed the idea."

"Are you going to allow a five-year-old child to dictate your actions? To completely run your life?" The pulse in Don's neck bulged with agitation. "You can't possibly be considering giving up your job and spending the next few months on some two-bit cattle ranch with your ex-husband!"

"Go downstairs and wait for me." Lara spoke through clenched teeth.

Don pulled Lara into his arms; she neither resisted nor cooperated. Holding her close he whispered in her ear, "Don't be a fool, darling."

Don released her, gave Trent a menacing stare, then turned and walked down the hall toward the elevators.

"What the hell do you see in that stiff shirt?" Trent chuckled.

Lara groaned. "I'm not going to discuss Don with you."

"Fine."

"Let's walk down this way." Lara nodded to her left. "I don't want Mary Beth to overhear us, just in case we start yelling at each other."

"If we start yelling, they'll kick us out of the hospital." Trent cupped her elbow in his big hand.

Yanking her arm out of his hold, she marched down the hall. He followed, quickly catching up with her.

Lara spun around, her eyes narrowed, her body tense. "If you think that getting me to stay at the ranch with Mary Beth while she recuperates will change anything between us, then you're—"

"What are you so afraid of, babe? Not me, surely." Trent grinned, that wide, heart-stopping grin that created dimples in his cheeks. "I don't want to renew anything with you. We're divorced. We've both gone on with our lives. You've got ol' Don and I've got . . . well, let's just say I'm never lonely. I want what's best for my daughter. Nothing more. Nothing less. If you agree to stay with Mary Beth and allow her to recuperate at the ranch, I'll follow whatever rules you set. You know, deep down, that what our little girl needs right now, is you and me, working together to help her recover completely and walk again."

Damn him! Damn him for being right!

She could take an extended leave of absence from the bank. Don might not like it, but he would have no choice but to comply with her wishes. And her mother would throw a fit to end all fits. At times, Liz could act more childish than her own granddaughter. But she'd deal with her mother somehow.

Dear Lord, was she really considering doing the unthinkable? Was she really considering spending the next three or four months on Trent's ranch, in Trent's house, seeing him every day and night?

Yes, she was. Trent *was* right. Mary Beth needed them both. And it was possible for her to take a leave of absence from her job, where it would be impossible for Trent to be away from his ranch for several months.

"All right," Lara said. "When Mary Beth leaves the hospital, we'll move in with you until she recovers. I'll let you know the rules when I get them figured out."

"Come on, let's go tell Mary Beth. This news is going to make her happy." He started to grab Lara's arm, then hesitated, deciding he'd be better off not touching her again.

She realized what had almost happened, that he'd started to touch her. During the next few months, she'd have to keep up her guard, make sure she kept her distance from Trent. "When we tell Mary Beth, I want us to make sure she understands that you and I aren't reconciled, that the three of us living together is just a temporary thing," Lara said. "We have to continually remind her of the way things really are, otherwise, when she and I leave, it'll break her heart."

Chapter Three

*R*eturning to the ranch was like opening a door to the past and walking back into yesterday. The two-story farm house, which had been built by Trent's great-grandfather at the turn of the century, was still a pristine white clapboard with green shutters and a huge front porch. The crocus bloomed in profusion around the mailbox post, their tiny yellow and purple heads heralding the approach of springtime. Buds waiting to burst open weighed down the branches of the row of yellow bells planted across the south side of the house. Daffodils and tulips had burst forth from the cold, dark winter earth.

A chill racked Lara's body, despite the warmth inside the truck. Glancing down at her daughter, whose blond head rested in her lap, Lara tucked the blanket securely around her child's shoulders. Mary Beth had fallen asleep on the drive from the hospital to the ranch.

Lara deliberately avoided eye contact with Trent. She neither wanted to see him nor speak to him, and yet here she was trapped inside his truck with him, sentenced to a three-month term of daily contact while she and Mary Beth lived on his ranch.

Nothing had changed—nothing except that she and Trent were divorced now. Her dreams of happiness had been destroyed years ago when her love had turned to hate.

As Trent pulled the truck up in front of the house, Lara

tried not to remember the day he'd brought her to his home, three days after their elopement. He had opened the truck door, swooped her up in his arms and carried her onto the front porch. She'd been giddy with happiness and so in love she couldn't see straight.

"We're here," Trent said.

"I hate to wake her." Lara glanced down lovingly at her child. "She's been so brave and worked so hard to adjust."

"She's happy to be coming home to the ranch with you and me." Trent opened the truck door, reached in and lifted Mary Beth, blanket and all, into his arms. "Maybe she won't wake up."

Getting out of the truck, Lara hesitated momentarily as she looked at the front door. Peg Warren stood just inside, a warm, welcoming smile on her face. Seven years ago, Peg had stood on the porch, a spring breeze ruffling her curly red hair, an almost identical smile on her face. And Jess Warren had stood beside his sister, his face hard and unsmiling, his dark eyes boring into Lara with what she later learned was pure hatred.

"Come on in and get out of the cold," Peg called out as she held open the door.

Lara blinked her eyes, bringing her thoughts back to the present. She smiled weakly and waved, then rushed up the front steps and into the house, following Trent as he carried a sleeping Mary Beth up the stairs.

"I suppose you already know that Peg redid the old nursery for Mary Beth," Trent whispered as he eased open the door to his daughter's room.

"Yes, Peg told me."

Lara surveyed the room she had once decorated with such love and care when she'd been expecting Mary Beth. Now the room bore no resemblance to that adorable pink and white nursery. It had been replaced with decor suitable for a five-year-old, all yellow gingham and crocheted lace, as golden bright as the child to whom it belonged.

"I had Joshua take down Mary Beth's regular bed to

make room for this hospital bed." Trent laid his daughter down and pulled up the safety rails, then turned to Lara. "Just as soon as she's well again, we'll bring her bed back up."

"The room's very nice. Peg did a great job."

Trent glanced over his shoulder, checking on Mary Beth. "Can you believe she didn't wake up? She's a sound sleeper."

"Just like you." Lara hadn't meant to say it aloud, but the thought went straight from her mind to her lips. She averted her gaze, determined not to look at Trent and allow him to see the memories in her eyes.

"Yeah, like me. It'd take dynamite to wake me once I'm out cold. But you know that, don't you?"

Yes, she remembered what a sound sleeper Trent was. She remembered everything about her ex-husband. No matter how hard she had tried to forget, she had been unable to erase him from her memory.

"I'd like to freshen up and take a nap myself before dinner," Lara said. "Would you have Joshua bring up my bags?"

"I'll go get them." Trent nodded toward the hallway. "Peg put you in the room next to this one, just the way you wanted."

"I hope I won't be inconveniencing you by taking your room while I'm here." The room next to the old nursery had been Trent's boyhood bedroom, the one Jess Warren had greatly resented her redecorating after she and Trent married.

"I don't use that room anymore." Trent walked out into the hall, hesitating when Lara didn't follow immediately. "After our divorce, I didn't stay home much. Then after Pa died, I moved into his room."

"Oh, I see."

She hadn't kidded herself that he had pined away for her after she'd left him. At the time she'd been sure he was spending his nights in Cassie Douglas's bed. What she'd never been able to figure out was why he hadn't married Cassie.

"I'll go get your bags and be right back," Trent said. "Make yourself at home."

Lara waited until Trent went downstairs before she ventured into the room she had once shared with him. She didn't know what she'd been expecting, but it certainly wasn't what she found. Nothing—absolutely nothing—in the room had been altered in any way. Even the pale green moire curtains still hung at the long, narrow windows overlooking the backyard. And the patchwork quilt Aunt Peg had given them as a wedding present still adorned the Jenny Lind bed. The bed had belonged to Peg and Jess's mother, and had been stored in the attic for years before Lara discovered it and claimed it as her own.

Dear God, how could she stay in this room—this room filled with so many happy memories of her life with Trent. And one painful memory. Without closing her eyes she could see Trent, naked except for his unbuttoned and unzipped jeans, on his knees begging her to forgive him. She hadn't forgiven him. Not that morning. Not ever. She had taken Mary Beth and left the ranch forever. Or so she'd thought.

"Where do you want them?" Trent stood in the doorway, Lara's suitcase in one hand, her garment bag and cosmetic case in the other.

Gasping, she whirled around when she heard him speak. "Oh. I . . . just put them down anywhere."

"I didn't mean to startle you." He set the suitcase on the cedar chest at the foot of the bed, then tossed the garment bag on top of the suitcase. "Peg aired everything out and put fresh linen on the bed. Nobody ever uses this room." He set the cosmetic case down on the lace-covered vanity table.

"You left everything exactly as it was," Lara said, her words both statement and question.

"Yeah. At first, I kept hoping you'd come back to me, and I wanted your things to be waiting for you," he admitted. "Then, later, when I realized there was no use wishing for the impossible, I just locked the door and tried to forget this room existed."

"I'm not sure I can stay here." Lara ran her fingertips over the smooth surface of the pitcher and bowl atop the walnut dresser.

"You asked for this room. Remember? You said you wanted to be right next to Mary Beth, so you could hear her if she needed you."

"Yes, I know I did. But . . . well, I never dreamed that the room would be the same. I thought surely you would have thrown out all my old stuff."

She gazed at the row of nearly empty toiletries lined up on the vanity table and realized they were hers. Five years old. No doubt ruined. Unusable. And her silver brush and comb rested on the right-hand side, the hand-held mirror turned face down beneath them. Her heart caught in her throat. Why on earth would he have kept these things, her personal things? Clenching her teeth, she bit down hard in an effort to stop the tears from forming in her eyes.

The silver-framed photo of Trent and her, taken by Aunt Peg a few days after their arrival on the ranch, taunted Lara from its perch in the center of her small porcelain jewelry box.

Trent came up behind her, only inches separating their bodies. He was too close. She stepped forward, away from him.

"It's your room again," he told her. "While you're here, do whatever you want with it. If you don't like it the way it is, change it."

"I shouldn't be acting so silly about the room," she said. "But I might make a few minor changes since I'll be here a few months."

He moved closer, his broad chest brushing up against her back. "You have no idea how often I've thought about the good times we shared here on the ranch, in this room."

Lara's breath caught in her throat. *Please, dear Lord, don't let him touch me.* "Don't!" she said aloud.

"Ah, babe, we screwed up a good thing, didn't we?" He grasped her shoulders in his big hands.

Lara pulled away, turned abruptly and glared at him. "You screwed up a good thing when you screwed another woman!"

Trent looked at her, his dark eyes suddenly hard and cold, the warm glimmer doused by Lara's angry accusation. "There's no use beating that dead horse." He stormed out of the room, pausing briefly in the hall. "I probably won't see you at supper. I've gotten behind on my work around here. Tell Mary Beth I'll come up to see her before she goes to sleep."

Lara stood motionless and quiet. Trent slammed the door. She let out the breath she'd been holding, then slumped down on the side of the bed.

This had been a mistake. She'd been a fool to give in to her daughter's pleas. She could not live in the same house with Trent Warren and remain sane. Five years ago he had driven her to the brink of a nervous breakdown by his infidelity and lies. He had lied to her over and over again, swearing his innocence. But she knew better. She'd seen him and Cassie with her own two eyes.

"Mommy! Daddy! Mommy, where are you?" Mary Beth cried.

Lara shot up off the bed, ran down the hall and into her daughter's room. Mary Beth had pulled herself up and was sitting there holding out her arms.

"I woke up and you and Daddy weren't here. I—I didn't know where you were. I was afraid you'd gone away."

Sitting on the bed, Lara put her arms around Mary Beth and smoothed the child's long blond hair away from her round face. "I'm right here. I was just getting settled in the next room. And Daddy had to get back to work, but he said he'd drop in and say good night before you go to sleep."

"If you're in the room next to mine, then you're staying in your and Daddy's old room, aren't you?" Mary Beth looked up at her mother with hope in her big, blue eyes. "Is Daddy going to stay in there with you?"

"No, he isn't." Lara clasped Mary Beth's shoulders gently. "Your daddy and I aren't husband and wife anymore, sweetheart. Just because I'm staying here at the ranch with you doesn't mean anything has changed between your father and me."

"But things could change. If you wanted them to." Mary Beth grabbed Lara's hands, squeezing them pleadingly. "More than anything in the world I want you and Daddy and me to live here on the ranch and be a real family. Please, Mommy. Please. Couldn't you love my daddy again the way you used to love him? He doesn't have a girlfriend, nobody he wants to marry. And you said you weren't going to marry Don, and—"

"No, darling, things can never be the way they were."

Lara didn't know whether to laugh or cry. Looking at Mary Beth's pink cheeks, her glowing blue eyes, her toothy grin, Lara wished she could grant her child's most heartfelt wish.

"Listen to me." Lara tried to keep her voice calm and pleasant, but with just a hint of authority in it. "I love you and Daddy loves you. You're the most important person in the world to both of us. But Trent and I don't love each other anymore, and we're never going to get back together."

"Why did you leave Daddy when I was just a baby?"

"What?"

"I asked Daddy and he said that I'd have to ask you. So I'm asking."

Lara had known this day would come, but she hadn't been expecting it so soon. Mary Beth was just a little girl. How could she explain the actions of two grownups in a way her child could understand? She could tell her the truth, but it would be unfair to tarnish Mary Beth's white knight image of her father.

"Daddy and I argued a lot. We weren't happy. Grandmother didn't like Daddy and Grandpa Jess didn't like me, so the two of them were always causing trouble for your daddy and me, and we found that we just couldn't live together anymore.''

"I know Grandmother doesn't like my daddy," Mary Beth said. "Sometimes she says not-so-nice things about him.''

"Grandmother shouldn't do that. I'll have to talk to her about it.''

"I've already told her not to ever say anything bad about my daddy again.'' Mary Beth eased herself back down into the bed.

Lara drew the covers up to Mary Beth's waist. "Your father loves you, sweetheart. Don't ever doubt it.''

"I know.'' Mary Beth yawned and her eyelids drooped. "Why didn't Grandpa Jess like you?''

"Because he had someone else picked out to be your daddy's wife.'' Lara leaned over and kissed her daughter's forehead. "You take a nap while I go unpack and get settled in.''

"That was silly of Grandpa Jess,'' Mary Beth said sleepily. "Daddy told me that he never wanted anyone else to be his wife except you.''

"Rest, sweetheart. I'll leave the door open. Call me if you need me.''

"All right, Mommy.''

Lara dashed into her room—that damned memory-filled room—flung herself across the bed—that damned bed where Trent had made passionate love to her time and again—and wept into the lace-edged pillow.

Lara and Aunt Peg had both eaten their dinner on trays in Mary Beth's room, the three of them making a party out of the meal. True to his word, Trent hadn't made it home in time for dinner. Lara knew what long, hard hours he had to put in to keep his ranch running smoothly, but she suspected he had stayed away deliberately in order to avoid her.

He had promised to come home in time to say good

night to Mary Beth before she went to sleep, but despite her valiant efforts to stay awake, she'd fallen asleep less than an hour after dinner.

Lara sat in the cushioned rocker that she had used when Mary Beth was nursing and memories of those precious moments flooded her memory. She laid aside the paperback romance she'd been trying to read and stretched her tired muscles. Glancing down at her watch, she realized it was nearly eight. Where was Trent?

As if the thought of him had conjured him up, Trent appeared in the open doorway. God, he was a dirty mess. His clothes filthy. The shadow of his heavy black beard darkening his face. Dried mud on his work boots. He lifted the Stetson off his head.

"Damn, she's already asleep, isn't she?" He whispered the question.

"It's not your fault. She couldn't stay awake. She went out like a light about six-thirty." Lara eased up out of the rocker and stuffed her book into the side pocket of her sweater.

Trent stepped into the room and crept over to the bed. "Look at her. Isn't she the most beautiful thing you've ever seen?"

"Yes, she is. She always has been."

"She looks so much like you." Trent kept staring down at his daughter.

"She has your smile and your dimples," Lara said.

"Yeah." Trent cleared his throat. "I need to take a bath and get a bite to eat. Why don't you go on to bed? It's been a long, difficult day for you. I'll check back in on her before I hit the sack."

"All right." Lara walked out into the hall, hesitating when Trent followed her. "I've decided that I am going to make a few changes in our . . . my bedroom. Of course, I'll cover the expenses."

"Do whatever the hell you want to the room and send me the bills!" Like an angry, wounded animal, Trent stalked off down the hall and into the room Lara thought of as Jess Warren's private domain.

I can do this, Lara told herself. I can endure living in the same house with Trent. I will do it for Mary Beth's sake.

Lara awoke with a start. She'd been dreaming. Dreaming of Trent. Sleeping in their bed had awakened ghosts from the past. She hadn't had one of those dreams in a long time. An erotic dream where she and Trent were making love. Wild, hot, passionate love. She'd been on the brink of a climax when Cassie Douglas's laughing face had peered into the bed.

Flipping on the bedside table lamp, Lara looked at the clock. Ten thirty-five. She got up, then slipped on her silk robe and satin house slippers. Since she was wide awake, she decided to check on Mary Beth.

The night-light from her daughter's room cast a pale, shadowy glow into the hall. Pausing in the doorway, Lara gasped when she looked into the room.

With his hair still damp from his shower and wearing nothing but a red terry cloth robe, Trent sat in the padded rocker. He had fallen asleep slumped over, his head resting on his crossed arms that were propped on the edge of his daughter's bed.

Lara tiptoed inside, halting directly behind the rocker. When her eyes adjusted to the dim light, she noticed that Mary Beth was awake.

"Shh. He's awfully tired," she whispered. "Daddy works too hard. He needs somebody to take care of him." Mary Beth ran her little fingers through her father's thick hair, then patted him softly on the head.

"How long's he been in here with you?" Lara asked quietly.

"I don't know. He was here when I woke up a little while ago."

"He needs to be in bed." Lara reached out to touch his shoulder, but her hand wouldn't cooperate. It hovered over him, trembling.

"Give him a little shake," Lara said.

Mary Beth obeyed. Trent groaned, but didn't awaken. Mary Beth shrugged.

"You'd better try, Mommy," Mary Beth suggested. "Besides, you'll have to put him to bed. I can't."

Forcing her hand into submission, Lara shook Trent's shoulder a bit more forcefully than she'd intended. "Wake up, Trent, and go to bed."

He jerked straight up, looking all around with wild, sleepy eyes. "What the— Lara?"

"You fell asleep with your head on Mary Beth's bed." Lara stepped away from the rocker, putting some distance between Trent and her.

Trent smiled at Mary Beth. "Hey there, big girl, what are you doing awake?"

"I just woke up and there you were."

"I'm sorry I didn't make it home in time to kiss you good night."

"You can kiss me good night now, Daddy." Mary Beth held up her arms. "Then Mommy's going to put you to bed."

Grinning, Trent glanced up at Lara, who was trying to ignore him, then he leaned over and kissed his daughter on her plump, rosy cheek. "Sleep tight and don't let the bedbugs bite."

Mary Beth hung on to Trent's neck, hugging him. "I love you, Daddy."

"I love you, too," he said, then stood up straight, turned around and clasped Lara's elbow. "Come on, Mommy, and put me to bed."

Lara kept her mouth tightly closed until she and Trent were in the hall, then she jerked away from him and headed for her room. He caught up with her before she stepped over the threshold.

"Don't you want to put me to bed?" he asked innocently, his grin growing wider by the minute.

"Your daughter seems to think you need someone to take care of you, and she's under the mistaken impression that I'm willing to take on that job.''

''I can't think of anyone I'd rather have tuck me into bed than you, babe.''

''Tuck yourself in bed. Or better yet, call Cassie Douglas. I'm sure she'd love to come over and tuck you in.''

''Nope, I don't think so. Besides, Cassie's husband might object to her leaving him and their twins alone in the middle of the night to go tuck an old boyfriend into bed.''

''Cassie's married? She has twins?'' Lara couldn't believe it. She would have sworn that Cassie would go to her grave loving Trent, waiting for Trent, and destroying anyone who got in her way.

''She's been married for four years and has three-year-old identical twin boys.''

''I can't believe she gave up on you.''

''Cassie gave up on me a long time ago,'' Trent said. ''When she finally realized that there was only one woman I'd ever love.''

He went to his room and left Lara standing, open-mouthed and wide-eyed, in the hallway.

Chapter Four

$\mathcal{T}$he doctors had said Mary Beth's recovery rate was remarkable, even for a happy, healthy five-year-old. Lara liked to think that her and Trent's efforts to provide their daughter with two full-time parents had benefited her recovery. They shared all the responsibilities for Mary Beth, everything from baths and bedtime stories to the painful leg-stretching exercises that were necessary to prevent spasticity. During the weeks since Mary Beth's accident, Lara had become reacquainted with her ex-husband. As much as she hated to admit it, she found herself liking him a lot and enjoying his company. Seeing him with their daughter made Lara realize what a good father he really was. And being around him every day made her face the fact that she'd never truly gotten over him.

A part of her was still in love with him, despite everything that had happened. The part of her that was still capable of sexual love wanted Trent as much now as she ever had. Maybe that was the reason she couldn't give herself completely to Don, couldn't commit to a permanent relationship.

But how was it possible that she still loved Trent Warren after all this time? He had betrayed her with another woman and broken her heart. How could she ever trust him again? When he'd sworn his innocence, she'd wanted desperately to believe him, but she couldn't. She'd seen them together, there in Jess's office adjacent to the barn. She had found them, just where Jess had said they'd be— lying naked on a cot at the back of the room.

Lara wiped away her tears and damned herself for allowing that old wound to reopen. But it was a wound that had never truly healed, one that still hurt as if it were brand new.

"Chicken's ready," Aunt Peg said. "You 'bout got those eggs deviled?"

"What?" Lara came out of her mental walk down memory lane. "Oh, I'm sorry. I was just thinking." She added the sweet pickle relish and then a dab of mustard to the boiled egg yolks.

"Sad thoughts?" Using a large fork, Peg lifted the chicken pieces out of the frying pan and onto a paper towel square.

"No sad thoughts today. Right?" Lara beat the mayonnaise into the egg mixture. "This is a day for celebration, not unhappy memories. Trent and I have promised to make this day special for Mary Beth."

"Well, getting her body cast removed is a cause for celebration." Peg wrapped the warm chicken in aluminum foil. "I don't want Trent worrying none about neglecting his work to take you and Mary Beth on this picnic. Joshua and I will keep things running smoothly. The men know they have to listen to me when I give orders."

"I was afraid it would be too cool for a picnic." Lara filled the empty boiled egg white halves with the fluffy deviled concoction. "But the sun's warm and the wind's mild. It's a beautiful March day."

Trent opened the back door and walked into the kitchen. Lara glanced at him. Her stomach fluttered with awareness. Dammit, he wasn't the only good-looking guy in the world. So why was it that he was the only one that turned her inside out and upside down? She couldn't look at him without wanting to touch him, couldn't touch him without wanting to make love with him.

"Give me a minute to wash up." Trent removed his

Stetson and hung it on a wooden peg by the back door. "I'll put Mary Beth's wheelchair and the picnic basket in the back of the truck. I cleaned out a spot."

"Don't forget to take a couple of those old quilts," Peg reminded him. "And you two need to decide whether or not we're giving Mary Beth a birthday party. Turning six is a big thing, you know. I think we should do it up right and invite other kids in for cake and ice cream and lots and lots of presents."

"We'll discuss it with Mary Beth, Aunt Peg, and see if that's what she wants." Lara added the deviled eggs to the open picnic basket on the table. "She may feel uncomfortable and a little embarrassed at being in a wheelchair."

"I think we should encourage her to have a party." Trent turned on the faucets and washed his hands in the stainless steel sink. "She knows a lot of the kids around here. She plays with them every summer. She's gone to some of their parties." Trent dried his hands on the checkered towel hanging on a cabinet knob by the sink.

"I just don't want to push her into anything she's not ready to do," Lara said.

"I would never push her!" Trent stomped across the kitchen, then paused before entering the hall. "I just happen to think a birthday party would make her happy." Without even glancing back over his shoulder, he stormed down the hallway, his booted feet thundering loudly.

"He hasn't changed." Lara clutched the top round on the ladderback chair in front of her. "He still takes everything I say the wrong way. And I still want to strangle him when he doesn't understand me. We argue all the time now just like we used to when we were married."

"Y'all didn't argue all the time," Peg said. "Not until those last few months, when you were recovering from giving birth to Mary Beth and Trent was trying to cope with Jess's illness. He should have told you that his father was dying instead of trying to protect you."

"That was one of our problems. He never treated me as an equal partner."

"You two had everything working against you." Peg wrapped the baking powder biscuits and laid them in the picnic basket. "He was a country boy with a high school education who made his living ranching. You were a city girl with a college degree whose mama was worth millions."

"We actually thought love would conquer all."

"Maybe it could have, if Liz and Jess hadn't done everything in their power to cause trouble. I loved my brother, but he was wrong to try to break up your and Trent's marriage."

"He wanted Trent to marry Cassie."

"Trent didn't love Cassie. He loved you."

"Then why did he . . . ?"

"Why did he have sex with Cassie that night in Jess's office?" Peg wiped her hands on her apron, then sighed. "I know what you saw, what you believe happened, but I'm telling you now what I told you then. If Trent said he didn't have sex with Cassie, then he didn't."

"How can you still defend him? They were lying there naked! How stupid do you think I am? Trent hadn't touched me in weeks. He'd made it perfectly clear that he thought we might have made a mistake getting married."

"We say a lot of things we don't mean when we're under stress and frustrated over life's injustices." Peg placed her hand on Lara's shoulder. "But that's the past, hon, and right now you and Trent have to live in the present. You can't erase five years apart, but you can try to see things from each other's point of view now. It'd make things easier all around."

"I don't want to argue with Trent. And I don't in front of Mary Beth, but I suspect she feels the tension between her father and me."

Peg nodded her head in agreement. "I think there's something you should consider about Trent wanting Mary Beth to have a birthday party."

"What?"

"She's had five birthdays and five little parties up there

in Huntsville. Not once has Trent gotten to spend Mary Beth's birthday with her. He's never had the chance to give her a birthday party.''

''Oh, Lord,'' Lara groaned. ''No wonder he . . . Maybe I'm just as bad as he is at taking everything the wrong way.''

''Maybe,'' Peg said.

The March sun beamed down with a promise of spring in its warmth. Trent drove his pickup truck slowly, taking each bump as easily as possible as they rode out across his ranch, searching for the perfect picnic spot.

''Over there, Daddy!'' Mary Beth's face beamed with a pink flush. Her eyes glowed with excitement. ''I knew we could find it. It's your special place. Remember? It's where we had our picnic last summer.''

Trent knew the exact spot Mary Beth meant. They had picnicked there last summer and he'd told her it was his special place, his favorite place on the vast ranch. But that picnic had not been the first time he'd taken his daughter out to the grove of ancient oak trees. From the first time she'd come to visit, when she'd been less than a year old, he brought her out here every summer.

Maneuvering the truck across the rutted dirt road, Trent pulled off to the side by the edge of the fence. ''Do you want to ride in your chariot or do you want me to carry you?''

''Carry me, Daddy.'' She held out her arms, then looked over her shoulder. ''Mommy, you get our quilts. Okay?''

Lara nodded. She couldn't speak. Not yet. All she could manage was a nod and a weak smile. She watched while Trent lifted Mary Beth out of the truck. For one split second, their eyes met and she realized that he knew she remembered.

This had been their special spot, their lovers' hideaway when they wanted to escape and be all alone. They had spread a quilt here and made love under the stars more than once. And one hot July evening they had created a baby here, a little girl conceived in love and passion.

"Hey, Mommy. Aren't you coming?" Mary Beth called out when she saw that Lara hadn't budged from inside the truck.

"Coming, sweetheart."

Lara forced herself to get out, walk around the truck bed and pick up the quilts and picnic basket. When she turned, she saw Trent standing in front of the biggest oak tree, Mary Beth in his arms. The noon sun glimmered behind them, spotlighting them with its shimmery golden-white beams.

Lara's breath caught in her throat at the sight of her small, helpless child and that child's big, strong father. In that one timeless moment, Lara's heart filled with love. Love for Mary Beth. And love for Trent.

Heaven help her, she did still love him.

Quickening her steps, she hurried toward the waiting twosome, set the picnic basket on top of an aged tree stump and spread the two quilts on the ground.

Trent lowered Mary Beth onto the quilt, then rose, held out his hand and offered to assist Lara. She stared at his outstretched hand, part of her wanting to accept his offer and another part of her warning her to run. Trent might be her daughter's father. He might be the man she still loved. But he was also the lover who had betrayed her—the husband who had destroyed their lives.

With trepidation, she put her hand in Trent's and allowed him to assist her. He lifted the basket off the stump and placed it in the center of the two quilts, then sat down beside Mary Beth.

"Isn't this fun? All three of us together on a picnic." Grinning broadly, Mary Beth looked back and forth from one parent to the other. "And we're in your and Daddy's special place, so that makes it perfect, doesn't it?"

Lara glared at Trent. "How does she—"

"I told her this place had been special to you and me," Trent said. "I told her that this was where we decided we wanted a beautiful baby girl and made a wish on a star."

Don't do this to me, Lara wanted to scream. *Don't torture me with all those long-ago dreams.* Looking at Mary Beth, she forced a weak smile. "And we got our wish when you were born."

Lara wasn't sure how she lived through the next hour while they shared the picnic lunch. Her stomach had been tied in knots and every bite she put in her mouth tasted like cardboard. But she'd eaten because Mary Beth had watched her, and she did not want to disappoint her in any way and ruin her "perfect" day. Shortly after finishing off three of Aunt Peg's peanut butter cookies, Mary Beth yawned several times, then lay down and asked Lara and Trent to sing with her. By the time they finished singing Mary Beth's favorite tune, she had closed her eyes and curled up on the quilt.

"She's asleep." Trent eased up on his knees, lifted the side of the quilt and covered his little girl. He sat down beside Lara. "By summer she should be able to walk when we come out here for another picnic."

"I can hardly bear to watch her when we help her with her exercises. Some of them are so painful for her," Lara said. "I know it's the only way she'll completely recover, but when she cries, I die a thousand deaths."

"I know what you mean." Trent picked a tiny spring wildflower and slipped it behind Lara's ear, letting his hand linger near her face. When she gasped and stared at him with uncertainty in her eyes, he withdrew his hand. "When someone you love suffers, you'd give just about anything to take away their pain."

To erase the sight of Trent looking at her with such longing, Lara closed her eyes, then swallowed the emotions threatening to choke her.

"I wish I could change things," he said, his voice low and soft and so damned seductive Lara wanted to hit him. "I never meant to do anything to hurt you. I loved you more than my own life."

"Please, Trent, I don't want to discuss the past."

"Yeah, I guess that subject's pretty well been talked to death, hasn't it?"

Lara picked up the leftover food spread out on the quilt and returned it to the basket. "I've decided you're right about a birthday party for Mary Beth. She needs to be around children again."

"What made you change your mind?"

"I think Mary Beth should share at least one birthday with both of her parents, don't you?"

"Aunt Peg got to you, huh?" Trent grinned. "She's a great gal. I just wish my father could have been more like her."

"I'm very fond of Peg," Lara said. "She's kind and loving and very forgiving." Lara cleared her throat. "I'll leave the invitations to you and Aunt Peg, since y'all know the children to invite. But I'd like to make all the party plans and do the decorations."

"I have a gift in mind for her. It could be from both of us. But I'm not sure you'll like the idea."

Lara cleaned up the trash, tossed it into a brown paper bag and laid it on top of the basket. "Stand up. I want to shake the crumbs off this quilt."

Laughing, Trent stood while she shook the quilt, then he helped her place it back on the ground. "You used to do that whenever we picnicked. You said you didn't want crumbs scratching you when we made love."

"Trent, please—"

"Sorry. I don't mean to keep bringing up the past, but when I'm around you, all I can think about is the way it was between us."

Lara understood only too well what Trent was saying. It was the same with her. Just being around him aroused all those old feelings within her, too. But she didn't dare give in to those feelings, those wanton emotions that had made a level-headed twenty-one-year-old throw caution to the wind and marry a man she barely knew.

"No more talk about the past, remember?" Lara shifted her hips on the quilt, nervously inching away from Trent.

"Tell me about your idea for Mary Beth's birthday present."

"A dog." He avoided looking directly at Lara, glancing instead at everything around him—the quilt, the grass, the trees, the sky.

"A dog! A dog here on the ranch would be fine, but not in our apartment in Huntsville. And, Trent, you know that she'll want to take it home with us when we leave."

"So don't leave the ranch. Stay here."

She stared at him, unable to believe what she'd heard him say. "You know that isn't possible."

"Why isn't it possible?" He scooted across the quilt toward Lara. "If we both want it badly enough, we can make it happen."

Lara pushed herself backward until her hips bumped into the huge oak tree behind her. Laying her open palms flat down at her sides, she braced herself for attack. Rising onto his knees, Trent moved in, hovering over her.

"Haven't you ever thought about our getting back together?" He lowered his face toward hers.

"No . . . I—I—"

"Liar."

The word hung in the air, hot and heavy, threatening her control. She sucked in a deep breath. "I've thought about it, yes. But I knew it could never happen."

"We still want each other, babe. All that sizzling energy between us is as strong as ever."

When he zeroed in on her mouth, his lips only inches from hers, Lara shoved forcefully against his chest. "It isn't going to happen. I'm not foolish enough to ever trust you again."

Her words acted as a deterrent, as forceful as if she'd tossed cold water over his head. Leaning back, he grunted, then sat down beside her.

"Just how involved are you with this Don Chapman?" Trent asked.

"Don? We're friends. Good friends. He's asked me to marry him."

"Are you going to marry him?"

"I don't know. I . . ." She was tempted to lie, to use Don as a wedge between her and Trent. Lord only knew she needed something or someone to keep her ex-husband at arm's length; her own willpower seemed lacking in that particular department. "No, I'm not going to marry Don."

"Why not?"

"I don't see that that's any of your business."

Resting his back against the tree, Trent arched one leg and draped his hands casually around his knee. "If the man's a part of your life, he's a part of my daughter's life. So that makes your relationship with him or any other man my business."

"I don't love Don." Lara glared at Trent, hating that smirky grin he could not disguise. "I don't love him the way I loved you. I probably won't ever love anybody else that way."

Jumping up off the quilt, Lara ran several yards deeper into the grove of trees. Trent followed her. She slowed her pace, stopping abruptly. Catching her by the shoulders, he whirled her around to face him. Tears glistened in her sky blue eyes.

"Leave me alone, dammit. I told you what you wanted to hear." She tried to pull away from him, but he held her shoulders tightly.

"It's the same for me, Lara," he admitted. "You're the only woman I've ever loved, the only one I've ever wanted to spend my whole life with."

"Don't lie to me again!" She struggled to free herself, but his superior strength kept her bound to him. "You haven't been pining away for me all these years. You've probably had a hundred women in your bed since our divorce."

"You're jealous." He tried to kiss her, but she turned her head. He laughed. "For your information nobody has shared my bed, but you're right, I haven't been celibate the last five years."

"Neither have I!" She glowered at him triumphantly.

"Don't you dare tell me about any of the men you've let touch you!" He growled the words, anger contorting his facial features into a hard, bitter mask.

"And don't you dare tell me about any of the women you've pleasured."

Placing his lips against her ear, he whispered, "There haven't been a hundred you know. There were quite a few before I met you and several since our divorce, but—"

"And one particular one while we were married." She tried again to get away from him.

"No, Lara."

He hauled her up against him, capturing her in his arms, claiming her mouth in an urgent, hungry kiss. She tried desperately not to respond, to fight the raging need within her.

He felt her resistance, but would not concede to it. He plunged his tongue into her mouth, thrusting repeatedly in a mock expression of an even more intimate act. She flung her arms around his neck, surrendering as he had hoped she would. With her acceptance reassuring him, he eased his tenacious grip on her shoulders, guiding his hands downward, across her trembling body.

She was fire, burning into him like a red-hot branding iron. He cupped her hips and drew her up against his throbbing erection. She arched into him, her body seeking his, like metal to a magnet. Straining against each other, they devoured, they conquered, they ravaged, until breathless and quivering, they fell to the hard cool earth. Resting on their knees, they clung to each other. Trent licked her earlobe, her neck, her throat. She gripped his shoulders, moaning his name repeatedly. He undid the first button on her blouse, then the second, and slipped his hand inside to cover her breast. When his palm grazed her nipple through the sheer silk of her bra, Lara cried out, and Trent replaced his hand with his mouth.

He shoved her onto the ground, coming down over her, straddling her hips. Working at the tab on her jeans, he loosened it and slid down the zipper. Just as she undid his jeans, she heard a soft, frightened voice calling to her.

"Mommy? Daddy? Mommy! Where are y'all?" Mary Beth cried out from several yards away.

"Oh, God, we forgot all about Mary Beth," Lara said, staring up at Trent, who had gone deadly still.

He lifted himself off her, then helped her to her feet. "You go on over and let her see you. Reassure her that we were close by. I need a few minutes."

"Trent?"

"We'll discuss this later."

"It shouldn't have happened," Lara told him. "I can't—I won't let you hurt me again."

Trent wanted to pull her back into his arms, kiss away the pain he saw in her eyes and promise her that he'd never hurt her. But how could he make such a promise? He hadn't intentionally hurt her five years ago. The whole thing with Cassie had been one gigantic mistake from beginning to end. If he hadn't been drinking. If he and Lara hadn't had the argument to end all arguments. If she hadn't threatened to take Mary Beth and go home to her mother. If he hadn't just found out that his father was dying. If Liz hadn't called that night, stirring up trouble the way she always did. If his father hadn't called Cassie and told her in what bar she could find his unhappy son.

Until the day Trent died, he'd never forget that morning. The morning that had ruined his life. He'd been half asleep, horribly hung over and barely aware of where he was. He'd found out later that his father had told Lara where she could find her husband. His father had wanted Lara to see him in bed with Cassie.

If only he could live that one night over again. But he couldn't. All he had was today. The present. And despite her determination to never forgive him, Lara still wanted him. Maybe even still loved him.

Trent zipped up his jeans, ran his fingers through his mussed hair and strode confidently out of the oak grove. He waved a greeting the moment he saw Mary Beth, who was sitting in Lara's lap. Mother and daughter made a picture that Trent captured in his heart, a picture that he would carry there forever.

"Daddy! Come here." Mary Beth motioned to him. "Mommy says I'm going to have a big birthday party right here on the ranch and that y'all have already decided on my birthday present. She won't tell me what it is. Tell me, Daddy. Please."

Trent sat down beside his wife—correction—his ex-wife, and lifted Mary Beth onto his lap, draping his arms around her in a comforting hug. He glanced over his daughter's head, his gaze questioning Lara.

Although the old pain was still there in her eyes, she smiled at him, and it took every ounce of his willpower not to reach out and bring her into his embrace, to bring the three of them together in a family hug.

"It wouldn't be a surprise if we told you," Trent said. "You'll just have to wait a few more weeks."

"Okay. I guess I can wait." Mary Beth reached over and grasped Lara's hand. "It'll be the first birthday I've been with Daddy, and my surprise will be the first present you and Daddy have ever given me together."

"We'll make your sixth birthday very special for you." Lara squeezed Mary Beth's little hand. "I promise you that everything will be perfect."

And it would be a perfect birthday for Mary Beth, even if it killed Lara. Somehow she'd find a way to get through these next few weeks, then she'd take Mary Beth back to Huntsville. She'd stayed on the ranch too long as it was. If she didn't escape soon she'd be caught in a trap—the trap of her own uncontrollable desire for her ex-husband.

Chapter Five

"*Y*es, Mother, Mary Beth received her gift. It came yesterday." Lara sighed. "No, she hasn't opened it yet. She'll open it this afternoon at her party when she opens her other gifts."

Chuckling softly, Peg Warren shook her head and winked at Lara, then returned to her task of placing six candles on the pink and white Cinderella birthday cake.

"We'll be returning to Huntsville soon, Mother." Lara loved her mother dearly, but despised the way she tried to control her life. "Yes, I'm glad that Don has driven down for a visit every other weekend since I've been here. No, he isn't jealous of Trent."

She had tried to be as honest with Don as possible, without admitting to him that she was still in love with her ex-husband. But Don was persistent. He simply wouldn't take no for an answer. Maybe she was foolish not to marry him. He was everything a woman could want. Handsome, successful, wealthy and a darn nice guy.

"I wish you wouldn't say things like that, Mother. Trent is Mary Beth's father, and despite what happened between us, he's a good man." Lara listened patiently to her mother's tirade. "I'm sorry you feel that way, but I don't have time to discuss it with you. I love you. Give my best to Jonathan. Goodbye, Mother!"

Lara hung up the telephone, slumped down in the nearest chair and said a silent prayer for heavenly assistance. Since her mother's return from Europe, Liz had called Lara at least three times a week to remind her what a fool she was to be living under the same roof as Trent Warren. Today's phone call was to once again reprimand Lara for keeping Mary Beth away from her grandmother on the child's sixth birthday. But now, unlike in the past when her mother had tried to undermine her marriage, the more Liz criticized Trent the more Lara praised him. In defending her ex-husband to her mother and to Don Chapman, Lara discovered that she truly liked Trent and felt that she knew him better now than she had when they'd been married.

"I take it that Liz isn't too pleased about missing Mary Beth's birthday," Peg said.

"Mother has missed several of Mary Beth's birthdays." Lara picked up the small favor bags off the kitchen table and began filling them with candy and little surprise trinkets. "Mother's upset because I'm still living here on the ranch with Trent. She's afraid he'll seduce me into remarrying him."

"Any chance of that happening?" Using her index finger, Peg shoved her bifocals upward from where they had been perched on the tip of her nose.

"Not you too, Aunt Peg."

"Yes, me, too," Peg said. "But where your mother is hoping it won't happen, I'm hoping it will."

"Well, quit hoping. I'm not going to remarry Trent. Not now or ever." Lara tied a pink ribbon around a favor bag. "As a matter of fact, I plan to tell Trent tomorrow that Mary Beth and I are going to return to Huntsville as soon as I can make arrangements."

"But she's not fully recovered. She's just beginning to try walking with her crutches." Peg pulled out a chair and sat down across the table from Lara. "Have you thought this thing through, hon, or are you just running scared?"

Lara dropped a favor bag on the floor, its contents spilling over the shiny tiles. "Damn!" She got down on her knees and gathered up the items, then stood and dumped them into the trash. "What did Trent tell you?"

"He didn't tell me anything," Peg said. "He didn't have to. I've got eyes. I see the way the two of you look at each other, like a couple of half-starved dogs peering into a chicken house."

"Lord, Aunt Peg, what a thing to say."

"I call 'em like I see 'em. And what I see is two grown people acting like a couple of kids. You want Trent as much as he wants you. Neither of you will ever be happy with anybody else, but you're both so damned stubborn you let your pride come between you."

"It's not a matter of pride," Lara said. "It's a matter of trust."

"I don't think Trent had sex with Cassie that night, but even if he did have sex with her, don't you think he's paid for that one mistake long enough? Don't you think he deserves a second chance?"

"Trent and I are not the only people to consider, you know. If I gave Trent a second chance and things didn't work out, think what it would do to Mary Beth."

"Think what it's going to do to her when you take her away from Trent."

"She'll adjust," Lara said. "I've made it perfectly clear to her from the very beginning that this stay on the ranch was temporary."

"Hey, you two. Need some help?" Lara asked.

Trent glanced up to see Lara standing in the doorway of Mary Beth's room. She was so beautiful, even in her jeans and baggy top, with her hair pulled back in a ponytail. As a matter of fact Trent preferred her like this, all soft and natural and unpretentious.

"Come on in. We're almost finished," Trent said.

"I'm getting better every day, Mommy. Daddy says he's so proud of me."

Mary Beth showed Lara how she could move her legs with very little assistance from her father. Her progress had been remarkable. Together, Trent and Lara had worked tirelessly with their child.

Now, here their little girl was, three months after her accident and beginning to practice on her crutches. She could take only a few steps, but everyone was amazed that she had come so far so fast. The doctors had told them that Mary Beth would probably be walking unaided in two or three more months.

"I wish I didn't have to be in my wheelchair at the party," Mary Beth said. "I wish I could walk better with my crutches."

"Give yourself time, sweetheart," Trent said. "By this time next year, you'll be running all over the ranch." Trent helped Mary Beth out of bed, holding her steady as he reached for her crutches that were propped against the wall.

Rushing to help, Lara grabbed the crutches and handed them to Trent. He smiled at her, the look in his eyes genuinely loving. In the weeks since the picnic, they had kept their physical distance, but with every look, every unspoken word, Lara and Trent embraced each other.

"Look, Mommy. Watch me walk!"

Trent stepped aside to allow his daughter free rein. She took one tentative step, then another and another.

"Don't push yourself too hard, darling," Lara said.

Mary Beth took six steps, then groaned as she swayed. Before she crumpled to her knees, Trent scooped her up in his arms, letting the crutches fall to the floor.

"That was wonderful." Biting her bottom lip, Lara applauded.

Trent eased Mary Beth down on the edge of her bed, then sat beside her. "You're amazing, kiddo. You're the only gal I know who could be up walking around three months after her pony rolled all over her."

Looking up at Trent with eyes identical to Lara's, Mary Beth placed her tiny hand on her father's arm. "When do you think I'll be able to ride Dixie again? I really miss her."

Lara silenced the gasp on her lips. Trent glanced up at his ex-wife, then lifted Mary Beth onto his lap.

"Whenever the doctors say you're well enough to ride again," Trent said. "Maybe by this summer."

"I'm not sure—" Lara said.

"What happened was an accident." Trent spoke to Mary Beth, totally disregarding Lara's concern. "It could have happened to anyone. The best thing for you to do is ride again as soon as you can. And I know for a fact that Dixie has missed you as much as you've missed her. She told me so, just this morning."

"Ah, Daddy, Dixie can't talk."

"She speaks pony, and I understand pony very well," Trent teased.

"Isn't Daddy funny?" Mary Beth smiled at her mother, then wrapped her arms around Trent's neck. "This summer we can all go riding together, can't we? It'll be so much fun." Mary Beth frowned, crinkling her little button nose. "We'll have to get Mommy a horse 'cause she doesn't have one. Did she have a horse when she used to live here?"

"Yeah, Lucky Lucy was your mother's horse."

Trent had given the mare to Lara shortly after their marriage, and he'd taught her how to ride. They'd usually ridden out to the oak grove for their private rendezvous, and sometimes Lara rode out with him over the ranch when he made inspection rounds.

Trent realized that Lara was remembering those days, just as he was. Those sweet, happy, halcyon days when nothing mattered except being young and madly in love. Before her mother and his father had undermined their trust in each other. Before they argued more than they made love. Before they had made such a mess of their lives. Before Lara had taken Mary Beth and run home to Liz.

Trent cleared his throat, dissolving the emotional knot his memories had created. "Hey, you know what, Mary Beth? Your mother and I thought that since you can't ride

Dixie for a while, you might want another buddy to keep you company.''

''Trent?'' Lara widened her eyes, questioning his comment.

''What do you say, Mommy? How about we go ahead and give Mary Beth her birthday present from us?''

''What is it? Is it a dog? Please, tell me it's a dog.'' She clapped her hands together. ''I've wanted a doggie of my own forever and ever.''

''You sit tight,'' Trent said. ''I'll go get him.''

Within seconds Trent had raced out of the room and returned just as quickly. In his arms was a parti-mix cocker spaniel puppy, a big gold bow tied around his neck. Lara had gone with him to the breeders several weeks ago and they had chosen the dog together.

''Oh, Daddy, let me see. Bring him here. I want to hold him.''

Bending down on one knee, Trent laid the wriggling puppy in his daughter's lap. ''How do you like him?''

Hugging the puppy to her chest, Mary Beth giggled gleefully. ''I love him. He's just what I always wanted, but we couldn't keep a dog in our apartment.'' Looking up at Lara, she smiled her big, dimple-cheeked smile. ''Come see him. Sit right here.'' Mary Beth patted the edge of the bed beside her.

Lara sat down, reached out and stroked the puppy's head. Trent covered her hand with his, then quickly removed his hand to pet the dog.

''We have to give him a name,'' Mary Beth said. ''A special name.''

''It's up to you,'' Trent told her. ''He's your dog, so you get to name him.''

''I think I'll call him Happy Birthday since he's my birthday present.'' She looked at her father for approval. ''Is that all right?''

Lara smothered her laughter by covering her mouth with her hand. Trent looked up at her and shrugged.

''Well, that's a mighty big name for such a little fellow,

but if that's the name you want, I don't see why not,'' Trent said. "You can always call him Happy for short.''

Lifting the puppy in her arms, Mary Beth kissed the top of his head. "I love you, Happy. You're the bestest dog in the world.''

"Well, you'd better let Daddy take care of Happy,'' Lara said. "We have to get ready for your party. You and I need to take baths and wash our hair.''

"This is the best birthday of my whole life.'' Mary Beth looked from her mother to her father. "You know why? 'Cause we're all together. Me and my mommy and daddy.''

By quarter after three, the house was filled with children ranging in age from two to eight years old. Aunt Peg had introduced Lara to all the other mothers who had dropped their children at the party and the two fathers who had brought their youngsters, then escaped out onto the back porch where Trent had taken refuge.

Just as they started the first game, the front door opened and closed. A set of red-haired twin boys scurried into the room, followed by their mother, a redhead carrying a gaily wrapped gift.

"Sorry we're late, Aunt Peg, but I can never get anywhere on time when I've got these two in tow.''

Lara's spine stiffened, her throat tightened and knots formed in her stomach. Cassie Douglas. What was she doing here? How did she have the nerve to show up at Mary Beth's birthday party?

Mary Beth tugged on Lara's arm. "Mommy, what's the matter?''

Lara forced a smile on her face for her daughter's sake, then patted her hand. Mary Beth sat in her wheelchair, Happy nestled in her lap and nearly two dozen children circled around a pin the tail on the donkey game board.

"Nothing's wrong,'' Lara said. "I'm fine. I was just wondering who our late arrivals are.''

"Oh, that's Matt and Mark Krenshaw and their

mommy," Mary Beth said. "Their daddy's the doctor who takes care of all our cows and horses here on the ranch. He's a veter . . . veter . . . something or other."

"Veterinarian?"

"Yea, that's it." Mary Beth waved at the twins, motioning for them to join the crowd. "Give them a donkey tail apiece, Mommy. But watch Mark. He's liable to try to stick somebody instead of the donkey."

Lara went through the motions during the party. Smiling, laughing, singing. But all the while she wondered whether Cassie Douglas Krenshaw or her husband would pick up their sons after the party. She didn't want to see Cassie. Not today or tomorrow or ever again.

Cassie had tried to talk to Lara several times before and after she divorced Trent, but Lara had refused to see her. And when she'd telephoned, Lara had hung up on her. Even months after the divorce, Cassie had written to Lara, but she'd thrown the letters, unopened, into the trash. Cassie had said all there was to say that morning when she'd hugged her naked body against Trent's and purred, "He belongs to me now. He doesn't want you anymore."

The party seemed to last forever. Paper plates, empty punch cups and party hats lay scattered about the floor. Eventually mothers started stopping by, but several of them lingered to talk to Peg and Lara. The two fathers had settled at the kitchen table and were drinking coffee with Trent.

Lara had avoided Trent whenever he'd joined in the celebration. He had tried to put his arm around her when Mary Beth blew out her candles, but Lara had pulled away from him. She had noticed Peg looking at her strangely several times and knew her husband's aunt was aware of how upset she was at seeing Cassie again.

When all but four children, two of them Cassie's twins, were gone, Lara helped Peg clear away the debris from the disaster area. Carrying two sacks filled with ripped, discarded wrapping paper, Lara nudged open the kitchen door with her hip. She gasped and dropped both bags on the floor. There by the back door stood Trent and Cassie.

"Excuse me." Lara turned to flee.

"Lara, don't go," Trent said.

"I just came by to pick up the twins," Cassie said. "I came to the back door because I . . . well, I saw the look on your face earlier today when you saw me."

Lara stood frozen to the spot, wanting to run, yet unable to move. "Why did you invite her children to Mary Beth's birthday party?" she asked Trent. He had to have known Cassie would bring them, and that she'd see Cassie, that it would hurt her terribly to be reminded of the woman who had destroyed their marriage.

"Trent didn't invite the twins. I did." Peg Warren carried a tray of dirty punch cups and paper plates into the kitchen.

"Why would you do that?" Lara asked.

"Because Cassie and Johnny Krenshaw are family friends. Johnny's been our vet for over four years now, ever since his Uncle Jay retired. And the twins have played with Mary Beth before and . . ." Peg set the tray on the table. "Well, I thought it was past time for you and Cassie to meet again."

"Aunt Peg, this was a mistake," Trent said. "You should have asked me before you—"

"Hush up," Peg told him. "Come on out here and help me keep the youngsters occupied, while Lara and Cassie have a little talk."

"I'm not going to talk to that woman." Lara reached out to open the kitchen door.

Peg grabbed Lara's arm. "Don't run away again. No matter how much you hate Cassie, it's time you faced the truth. Cassie Douglas didn't destroy your marriage. You and Trent did that."

Lara turned slowly, her nerves screaming as she faced Cassie.

"You don't have to do this, Lara." Trent took several tentative steps toward his ex-wife. "I'm sorry that Aunt Peg took it upon herself to put you in this position."

"You and Peg go out in the living room and make sure the children are all right." Lara waited until Trent and Peg left the room, then she motioned toward the wooden chairs around the table. "Won't you sit down, Cassie?"

"You really hate me, don't you?" Cassie sighed. "Well, I don't suppose I can blame you."

Standing straight and tall, her chin lifted bravely, Lara surveyed the other woman. A halo of short auburn curls surrounded her china doll pretty face. A pair of skintight jeans and a clinging sweater accentuated her voluptuous figure.

"I understand you're married now. To Johnny Krenshaw. I don't remember him, but I do remember his uncle Jay."

"Johnny was living up in Tennessee when you lived here. He moved back and went to work with his uncle. That's how we met. He made a house call out to our farm." Cassie tried to smile, obviously making an attempt to be pleasant.

"What happened between you and Trent?" Lara's heartbeat roared in her ears; her chest tightened painfully. "I thought after our divorce, you two would get married."

Cassie laughed, the sound a mixture of mirth and sadness. "Yeah, well, I thought the same thing. But I was wrong. And so were you, Lara. We both made a mistake. I tried to tell you. I even tried to contact you after the divorce, but—"

"I threw your letters away unopened," Lara said. "I didn't want to read anything about you and Trent."

"You thought I was writing to tell you about an affair with Trent?"

"I didn't know for sure, but I couldn't take the chance. I couldn't bear any more pain."

"God, what a mess we made of things." Cassie pulled out a chair from the table and sat down. "I'm willing to take my share of the blame, but you were partly at fault yourself, you know."

Lara slid out a chair and sat across the table from Cassie.

"Are you implying that I drove Trent into your arms that night?"

"Look, I'd known you two weren't getting along. Jess kept me informed about your and Trent's marital problems. Jess wanted to see me and Trent together as much as I did. I'd been crazy about Trent for years, before he met you. We'd been real close—"

"You'd been lovers," Lara said.

"Yes, we'd been lovers, and I'd thought it was just a matter of time until we got married. But Trent never asked me to marry him. He never told me he loved me.

"Then out of the blue, he up and marries you. And Jess kept telling me that I had to save Trent from you, that you'd ruin his life."

"Jess Warren hated me from the moment we met," Lara said.

Cassie spread her palms down on the table. "The night you and Trent had your big blowout about your going home to your mama . . . well, Jess called me and told me that Trent had gone into town, to Calico's, and he said now was the time to make my move.

"So I went down to Calico's and found Trent. He'd been drinking. A lot. I talked him into letting me drive him home. We picked up a six-pack on the way and when we got to the ranch, I maneuvered him out to the barn and dragged him into Jess's office."

Lara closed her eyes and allowed the memories to flood her mind. And the pain returned, as cruelly devastating as it had been that morning, just after dawn, when she'd opened the door to Jess's office.

"I know you're remembering that you found me and Trent together, naked, on that cot." Cassie reached across the table, her hands open in a pleading gesture. "Trent had kissed me several times and I hoped he'd . . . well, he didn't. He kept talking about you. Ranting and raving really, saying how he wasn't going to let you leave him."

Lara balled her hands into tight fists. Despite Cassie's

gesture, Lara had no intention of accepting the other woman's plea for understanding.

"Trent told me the two of you didn't have sex, at least he didn't remember your having sex. But I didn't believe him. I know what I saw."

"You saw what you were supposed to see," Cassie said. "Trent passed out drunk. I stripped off his clothes and mine. I tried to rouse him, tried to . . . He didn't wake up until you came storming into the room, threatening to kill us both."

"I don't believe you." Lara sprung up, knocking the chair over in her haste. "This is some lie you and Trent have cooked up."

Cassie hung her head when Lara glared at her. Folding her hands in her lap, she glanced hesitantly upward, then shook her head. "You believe whatever you want to believe, Lara. You weren't woman enough for a man like Trent five years ago. If you had been, you never would have threatened to leave him and take away his child. And you certainly never would have let another woman take him away from you. I thought maybe you'd changed, but I see you haven't."

"But you didn't take him away from me, did you? You just said so. Trent loved me then, not you. He still loves—"

"Yeah, you're right. He still loves you. He's never loved another woman. Never will. But you let your mama and Jess and all your insecurities make you doubt Trent. You believed what everyone else told you, even my lies, because you didn't trust your husband, didn't trust what you two had together."

Lara couldn't bear to hear the truth; the truth was far too painful. She ran out of the kitchen, onto the back porch and into the yard. Tears blurred her vision as she ran and ran and ran. Somewhere behind her, she heard what she thought was Trent's voice. He was calling her name.

She didn't want to see him. Didn't want to talk to him. Not now. All she wanted to do was get away, to escape the pain tearing her apart inside.

Chapter Six

*L*ara couldn't see where she was going, didn't even care. All she wanted was to escape the painful truth—she had been as responsible as Trent for the destruction of their marriage five years ago.

Dark clouds swirled in the gray evening sky, creating an overcast that blocked the sun's last faint rays. In the distance thunder rumbled like barrels rolling over a wooden floor. The chilling April wind rustled through the trees, whistled around the corner of the barn and tousled Lara's hair into disarray. Flyaway strands flicked her face. When she wiped her hair out of her eyes, she felt the moisture of her own tears.

Trent's deep voice blended with the wind's roar, becoming a pleading wail. Without slowing her pace, Lara glanced over her shoulder and saw Trent only a couple of yards away. With her attention focused on the man chasing her, Lara didn't notice the downed tree limb. Before she could catch herself, she tripped over the broken branch. She hit the ground, her hands and knees taking the brunt of her fall. Her palms stung; her knees ached.

Trent caught up with Lara, bent down and lifted her to her feet. Turning her in his arms, he caught her chin between his thumb and index finger, forcing her to face him.

"What happened? What the hell did Cassie say to you?" Trent bellowed the questions, partially out of anger and fear, partially so he could be heard over the howling wind.

"Let me go! I can't . . . I don't want . . . Don't you see, it doesn't matter what she said." Tears streamed down Lara's face. "It's too late now. Too late . . ."

"What are you talking about? It's too late for what?" Trent grabbed her by the shoulders, shaking her gently. "Dammit, woman, will you tell me what Cassie did to upset you so much?"

"She told me the truth," Lara said. "She and Jess plotted against us that night. She took advantage of the fact you were drunk. She was sure she could seduce you, that you'd make love to her. And . . . and Jess sent me to find you, knowing that you'd be in bed with Cassie."

"Cassie admitted that she set me up?" Trent tightened his hold on Lara's tense shoulders. "Did she say we had sex that night?"

"You really don't remember, do you?" Lara lifted her hand to Trent's face and held it there hovering over his cheek. But she couldn't touch him; she didn't dare.

"God forgive me, babe. No, I really don't remember," he admitted. "It's just that I know—" he released one of her shoulders and hit his chest with his fist "—deep down inside me, that even if my body betrayed you, my heart didn't. If I'd known what I was doing, I never would have—"

Lara pressed her hand over his mouth, silencing his agonized confession. "You didn't have sex with Cassie that night. You passed out cold. She undressed you."

"Lara?" He looked at her, his brown eyes glowing from the passionate fire burning inside him.

"All these years I've blamed you for everything. I've hated you for betraying me. And hated myself because . . . because I couldn't stop loving you as much as I hated you."

Cupping her face in his hands, he breathed deeply, trying to control the aggressive, possessive beast inside him that wanted to take this woman, here, now, where they stood. "I've hated you and loved you, too," he said.

"You didn't destroy our marriage all by yourself," Lara told him. Her heart raced wildly; she gasped for breath. Longing stronger than any she'd ever known shot through her body, demanding release. "I'm as much at fault as you. We both paid too much attention to what our parents thought, instead of listening to our own hearts."

"I'm sorry, Lara, for not being the man I should have been. For letting my father's bitterness affect me. For allowing him to influence the way I treated you."

"And I'm sorry I ever listened to anything my mother said against you. If only I hadn't let her and Jess manipulate me into distrusting you."

"Damn, we were a couple of young fools!" Trent lowered his head, bringing his lips down on Lara's with total abandon.

She accepted the kiss, acknowledged the savage heat of it and responded with a fervor that ignited an explosion of desire inside both of them. He grabbed her by the back of the head, holding her in place for his loving assault. Slipping her arms around his waist, she clung to him, pressing her breasts into his hard chest. He gripped her hip, pushing her intimately against his arousal.

He moved his tongue in and out, in and around, possessing, claiming, dominating. Moaning, Lara caught his tongue with a sucking motion of her lips, then thrust into his mouth. Their tongues dueled; their mouths devoured.

When he broke the kiss, Lara threw back her head and gasped for air. He kissed her neck repeatedly. She purred. He nibbled his way down her throat, nuzzling at the neckline of her blue cotton sweater. Keeping one hand on her hip, he shoved her lower body as close to his as possible, then with his other hand, he lifted her sweater and covered her breast. The moment he touched her there, she groaned.

Her diamond-hard nipple jutted into his palm, pressing against the lace confinement of her bra. Searing heat spread from her aching breasts to the core of her femininity, moistening and tightening in preparation. She hadn't felt this desperate need in a long time, and never so intensely with anyone except Trent. She longed to open herself up to him, to bring him inside her body and claim the power of his masculinity, control it and make it her own.

Soft, fine, almost undiscernible raindrops anointed their heated bodies with cooling moisture. Trent lowered his head, captured her nipple through the lace and sucked greedily. Digging her nails into the tight muscles of his broad shoulders, Lara shuddered. The spiraling tension of desire rippled through her body.

The rain increased. A lightning bolt zigzagged across the charcoal sky. Thunder boomed. Trent swept Lara up into his arms and ran toward the nearby barn. Flinging open the door, he carried her inside, into the warm, dark earthy interior. The only illumination came through the door that banged open and shut in the fierce wind. Twilight and frequent lightning seeped into the old barn each time the door swung open, surrounding them with wall-climbing shadows and casting faint, recurring radiance over their bodies.

Sliding her seductively over the hardness of his big, powerful body as he eased Lara to her feet, Trent gazed into her hungry blue eyes and knew she wanted him with the same mindless desperation he felt.

"I'm not going to wait," he told her. "I've waited five years."

He pulled her sweater up; she lifted her arms and allowed him to remove it. When he stripped away her bra and covered both breasts with his big, callused hands, Lara trembled. Placing her hands together, she delved between his arms and tore at his shirt, popping several buttons in the process. She spread back his shirt and laid her hands on top of his hairy chest. Oh, how she loved the feel of him.

Lara's knees weakened. Trent caught her about the waist, drawing her close, rubbing her naked breasts against his chest. She cried out, the sensation almost unbearable in its painful pleasure.

"It has to be now, babe." His chest rose and fell with his labored breathing. "And I can't be gentle."

He took her mouth. Hot and wet and demanding. Lifting her skirt, he caressed her legs, clutched and released her buttocks, then petted her mound.

"I want you," she moaned into his mouth. "I want you inside me. All of you."

Grasping the waistband of her pantyhose and panties, he divested her of both. Kneeling before her, he removed her shoes, then dragged the bunched material over her feet. The moment he freed her, he lifted her skirt and shoved her backward, capturing her skirt between her buttocks and the barn wall.

Trent licked a fine line up one thigh and down the other to her knee. Then he buried his face in the damp triangle of golden hair between her legs. Lara shuddered as Trent urged her thighs apart. Using his fingertips, he parted the wet, hot folds of her body and lowered his mouth, sampling her sweet femininity.

Bracing her hips against the wall, Lara threaded her fingers through Trent's black hair and caressed his head. Occasionally tightening her fingers when the pleasure he gave her threatened to send her over the edge, Lara gripped handfuls of his hair. As his marauding tongue plunged her into a powerful, shuddering release, Trent unzipped his jeans and released his throbbing sex. While the aftershocks of Lara's climax rippled through her, Trent lifted her hips and thrust into her, groaning deep in his throat.

He withdrew, then rammed into her. Once. Twice. Her body sheathed him with tight, hot pleasure. She cried out, her second and even more powerful release imminent. He lunged deeply; she accepted all that he gave her. And together they shattered into a million shards of sexual ecstasy.

They clung to each other, their bodies still joined, sweat dripping, hearts hammering. Trent kissed her. Lara closed her eyes. He eased himself out of her, adjusted his jeans and zipped them, then reached over to take her into his arms. But she had turned from him and was gathering up her clothes. Finding her panties, she slipped them on. Trent picked up her lace bra and cotton sweater and handed them to her. She put them on hurriedly, not looking at him, still shaken from their wild, primitive coupling.

Trent held up her torn pantyhose. "You don't want these, do you?"

She shook her head. He tossed the pantyhose to the dirt floor. She gasped. He laughed. "All right," he said. "Are you afraid Joshua will find them and figure out what we were doing in the barn?" Retrieving the pantyhose, he stuffed them into his pocket, then put on his shirt, buttoning it halfway.

When Trent slid his arm around Lara's waist, she tensed, suddenly feeling very vulnerable. "I don't know what happened to us. To me."

"We made love, babe." Hugging her to his side, he kissed her cheek. "It was inevitable. We've wanted this since the first moment we saw each other again at the hospital the day of Mary Beth's accident."

Lara relaxed against him, breathing deeply. "It was always like that with us, wasn't it, Trent? So hungry for each other, we couldn't think straight."

"I have a feeling you're trying to tell me something." Grasping her shoulders, he turned her around. "If you're saying sex won't solve our problems now any more than it did five years ago, then you're right."

"This all happened so fast. Too fast." Lara caressed Trent's face with tenderness. "Seeing Cassie again, and listening to what she had to say. Admitting to myself that I was as guilty as you for destroying our marriage. Giving in to the desire for you I've never been able to control."

"You're not ready for us to start over again, are you, babe?" He searched her face, finding the answer in the cold, controlled look in her eyes. "You're probably right. Too much has happened. All the bitterness and hatred has taken its toll on both of us. Over the years, you and I have built up so many negative feelings about each other."

"If we do try again . . ." Lara hesitated. Then when Trent ran his fingers down her arms and took her hands in his, she sighed. "Our first consideration must be Mary Beth. If we tried again and failed again, we'd hurt her terribly. We could scar her emotionally for the rest of her life."

"There are no guarantees, Lara. There weren't any five years ago and there aren't now."

"I know." Lara squeezed his hands. "It's just that I believe we both need some time apart, to think things through, to make sure we aren't letting our hormones make our decisions for us."

Trent released her hands abruptly. "You're going to take Mary Beth and leave the ranch, aren't you?"

"Yes."

"When?" he asked.

"Tomorrow."

With her hands braced on her plump hips and a scolding glint in her hazel eyes, Peg Warren met them at the back door. Trent realized his aunt would know what had happened just by looking at them. For one thing, their hair was mussed and their clothes were wrinkled, and they were completely drenched after their walk from the barn to the house. And for another thing, Lara had the look of a woman who'd been thoroughly ravished and he the look of a satisfied predator.

They hesitated on the screened back porch while Peg inspected them. "I've spent the last thirty-five minutes trying to explain to your daughter what was taking you two so long to get back to the house. So, you'd better have a good explanation for her."

"Is Mary Beth all right?" Lara asked. "Was she terribly upset that I just disappeared the way I did?"

"She's fine. I helped her upstairs with all her presents. She's in her room with Happy. They're eating cookies and drinking milk."

"I'd better go on up," Lara said, but when she tried to

move past her, Peg blocked her path.

"I told Mary Beth that you and Trent had gone off alone to talk," Peg said. "I'm afraid she drew her own conclusions. She's certain y'all are going to reconcile."

"Oh, Lord." Lara groaned. "Thanks for taking good care of her, Aunt Peg."

Trent placed his hand on Lara's back. She closed her eyes, remembering the glory of his touch. Turning her head slightly, she looked at him and smiled.

"We'll talk to her and explain the best we can," he said.

"How about explaining to me?" Peg cast a condemning glance from Lara to Trent. "It's pretty obvious you two have been doing a lot more than talking."

"Lara has decided to take Mary Beth back to Huntsville tomorrow." Trent's dark eyes met his aunt's hazel glare.

"Damnation!" Peg stomped her foot, then moved out of Lara's way. "What's the matter with you two? What's it going to take to bring you to your senses and keep you from ruining the rest of your lives and the life of that precious child upstairs?"

"This is none of your business, Aunt Peg." Trent guided Lara past his aunt and through the kitchen.

"You two had better clean up a little before Mary Beth sees you," Peg called out to them as they exited the kitchen. "She might not realize her parents have been making out, but she's astute enough to see the look of love in your eyes."

Trent slammed the kitchen door behind him. Turning into Trent's arms, Lara lay her head on his chest. He caressed her soothingly, wondering if he dared tell her what he really thought, what he really felt about her decision to leave the ranch tomorrow.

Lifting her head, she looked up at him pleadingly. "You'll come to Huntsville to visit us, and . . . and we'll come back to the ranch this summer. We'll make Mary Beth understand that you and I are friends now, but I don't want her to expect—"

Trent had to kiss her; he couldn't have stopped himself if his life had depended on it. And Lara had to respond; she could not keep from giving herself over to the pure, sensual joy of sharing this moment with Trent.

He ended the kiss as abruptly as he'd begun it, then walked away from her. "I should shower and change clothes before we talk to Mary Beth."

Unable to speak, her throat closed with tears, Lara nodded agreement. She watched Trent go up the back stairs, then covered her face with her hands and cried.

"But I don't want to go back to Huntsville tomorrow," Mary Beth whined. "I thought we were going to stay here until I could walk again."

"We need to go home." Lara sat down on the side of Mary Beth's bed. Happy licked her hand. Lara patted the puppy's head. "Mommy needs to go back to work. And Grandmother misses us. Daddy is going to come up to see us very soon, aren't you, Trent?"

Dammit, he didn't want this any more than his daughter did, but he had no choice but to agree with Lara's wishes. He didn't dare do anything to screw up their one last chance. And Lara was right. They had loved each other seven years ago when they'd first married in a fever of sexual desire, but neither the love nor the hot sex had kept them together.

Somehow they had managed to help their daughter survive their divorce without too many scars. But if they reconciled and then messed up a second time, Mary Beth would be the one to pay the highest price for her parents' mistake.

"Yeah, I'll drive to Huntsville every couple of weeks." He swallowed hard, hating the thought of letting the two people he cared for most in the world walk out of his life again. "You and Mommy and I will be spending plenty of time together."

"But we won't be living together here on the ranch!" Mary Beth crossed her arms over her chest. "I won't leave. I'm going to stay here with Happy and Dixie. I'm not ever going to leave my daddy again.''

Lara took Mary Beth's hands in hers. ''I want you to come back to Huntsville with me, but if you'd rather stay here—'' Sighing, Lara tried to brave a smile, ''—with your father, then I'll let you stay with him, and . . . and . . . I'll . . . I'll drive down every weekend to see you.''

Mary Beth's big blue eyes widened and her little pink mouth formed a soft, crooked oval. ''You'd go away and leave me?''

Trent came up behind Lara and clasped her shoulders. ''Your mother can't stay here. She doesn't want to leave you, but if you won't go with her, she'll have no choice.''

''Are you making her leave?'' Mary Beth glared at her father. ''Did y'all have another fight? Did you tell her she had to go away?''

''No, of course he didn't,'' Lara said. ''Your daddy would never do such a thing.''

''Then it's your fault, isn't it?'' Huge tears formed in Mary Beth's eyes. ''You want to go back to your job at the bank with Don. He's more important to you than me and Daddy.''

''That's not true,'' Lara said.

''No one is more important to your mother than you,'' Trent told her.

Lara hugged her daughter to her breast, but Mary Beth hit out at Lara, shoving her away. ''I hate you.'' She looked up at Trent. ''I hate both of you. Aunt Peg said y'all went off to talk, and I thought . . . I thought that meant y'all were going to get married again.''

''Oh, Mary Beth.'' Lara tried once more to take her child in her arms.

''Don't touch me!'' Mary Beth screamed. ''Go away! Both of you. I want Aunt Peg.''

Lara stared at her daughter, her mind reeling with sorrow and regret. Trent helped Lara to her feet, slipped his arm around her waist and led her out of Mary Beth's bedroom and into the hall. He closed the door behind them.

"Go on and get your bath," he said. "I'll get Aunt Peg to come up and talk to Mary Beth. Maybe she can get through to her."

A loud crash blasted against the closed bedroom door. Lara cried out; Trent cursed quietly. He eased the door open. Mary Beth had maneuvered herself to the edge of the bed and was tossing her birthday presents, which were spread out at the foot of her bed, onto the floor.

"If you try to make me leave the ranch, I'll run away," she yelled. "I'll run far, far away and you won't ever see me again."

Trent closed the door quietly. "Let her throw her fit. She'll tire soon enough. She's not going to listen to anything we have to say right now."

"We can't allow this to affect our decision," Lara said, with more conviction than she felt. "If we let her have her way now, and things don't work out, we could cause her much more unhappiness in the long run."

"A part of me wants to spank her," Trent said. "A part of me wants to hug her, and another part of me wants to—"

"Give her what she wants." Lara exchanged a sad, knowing look with her ex-husband, then turned and ran down the hall and into her room.

Peg had come to Lara's room and told her that it was best if she and Trent wait until morning before confronting Mary Beth again, that the child had cried herself to sleep. Later, Lara went to her daughter's room and sat for several hours in the rocker by her bed, just watching her little girl sleep. Happy lay curled up beside her, his head resting on a pillow.

Finally, when she began to doze off, Lara decided to go to bed. There was nothing more she could do until morning, and only God knew what she and Trent could do then to make things right—not only for Mary Beth, but for themselves.

Weariness spread through Lara's body like a slow-acting

poison. She undressed slowly, letting her clothes fall to the floor in an unkempt pile. She'd pick them up in the morning. In the morning when she would have to make the most difficult decision of her life.

Five years ago, she'd packed her bags and taken her daughter home to Huntsville. In all the years since, she'd never once believed the day would come when she'd consider remarrying her ex-husband. Of course, Trent hadn't actually asked her to marry him.

But he wanted her to stay at the ranch. And, heaven help her, she wanted to stay. She wanted to walk down the hall right now, open the door to Trent's room and give herself to him. She wanted him to take her in his arms and make slow, sweet love to her all night long.

Would returning to Huntsville, putting a hundred and twenty miles between them, make her stop wanting him, stop needing him, stop dreaming of him? No, it wouldn't. It hadn't in the past, when there had been no hope for them, and it certainly wouldn't now.

Lara padded across the floor in her bare feet, opened the dresser drawer and pulled out her silk gown. She turned off the overhead light, leaving only the faint glow from the small bedside lamp.

The door to her room creaked when it opened. She glanced up and saw Trent standing there, his naked chest bronze in the dim light. She clutched the gown, lifting her hands to her chest.

Trent closed the door behind him. Lara trembled. He took several tentative steps toward her. The silk gown slipped through her fingers, puddling in a rumpled circle at her feet. Trent unzipped his jeans and slid them down his hips and over his legs, dropping them on the floor.

She sucked in a deep breath. He walked toward her; she didn't move. When he reached down and threaded his fingers through hers, she felt his hand shake and knew he was as scared as she was. Afraid of this wild, restless passion that ruled them.

Neither of them said a word as Lara led Trent to her

bed—the bed they had shared years ago. She lay down and held open her arms, beckoning him to come to her.

The slow steady beat of the rain outside matched the rhythmic pulsing of their hearts. Trent accepted her invitation, covering her body with his own.

Chapter Seven

Trent braced the heavy weight of his body with his arms, leaning down to take Lara's lips. He had never loved anyone else. She was the beginning and the end of everything. The alpha and omega of his world. When she'd divorced him, the light had gone out of his life. She'd left him in darkness, alone, desolate and hungry for what he thought could never be his again.

He nibbled on her lower lip, coaxing the response he wanted. She trembled beneath him, shivering from the joy of his touch, the ecstasy of his body on hers. He drank the sweetness from her mouth as his fingertips danced over her shoulders and down her arms, a featherlight touch that aroused him as much as her. She sighed, the sound deep and husky in the back of her throat. Trent's body hardened painfully, but he restrained himself, wanting to make this loving last a long, long time.

He eased his body over to lie beside hers, his hands caressing her, seducing her with reverent tenderness. Kneading her breasts, he slid his knee between her thighs, parting her legs so that he could stimulate her by pressing his leg against her and rubbing slowly, rhythmically.

Lowering his mouth to her breast, he took her rosy nipple between his teeth and tugged gently, then encompassed it, sucking hungrily. She arched up, pushing her body against his leg, squirming.

If he allowed this to continue, he'd be buried deep inside her within seconds, exploding into fulfillment. Trent flipped Lara on her side, sliding his arm beneath her so that he could continue tormenting her nipples. She murmured a protest, but cried out in acquiescence when he bit her lovingly on the back. Remembering how she enjoyed sharp, sweet love nicks, Trent covered her back and buttocks with passionate stings.

Unable to bear the arousing assault on her body, Lara turned and crawled on top of Trent. She covered him, from neck to waist, with hot, urgent kisses, taking her time to lick his tight, tiny nipples. When she kissed the tops of his thighs, he threaded his fingers in her long, golden hair.

She pleasured him with her mouth until he thought he'd die from the pleasure. When he was on the verge of release, he pulled her up his body, whispered raw, urgent words, telling her plainly what he wanted to do to her. She straddled his hips and took him into her body. He thrust to the hilt; she whimpered with the fullness spreading her to the limit.

She rested her palms on each side of his head, offering her round, full breasts for his attention. As she rode him hard and fast, then slow and steady, then hard and fast again, he petted her buttocks and suckled her breasts. The wildness grew inside them, their desire spreading tension to every nerve ending in their bodies.

Release shot through her, jolting her body. Skyrockets of fulfillment ignited in her feminine core, then spread quickly until she was shivering from head to toe. Gasping, she rode out the last throbbing pulsations, then whimpered and fell lifeless onto Trent as complete relaxation claimed her.

Trent felt his own climax tightening and intensifying as he thrust upward into her hot, wet sheath. Gasping, groaning, crying out in the final moment, he splintered into completion.

When she started to ease her body off his, he clutched her hip. "Stay where you are, babe."

She sighed, burrowing her nose into his damp chest hair. "I love you."

He stroked her back, her waist, her buttocks. "I love you. I always have. I always will."

Lifting her head, she gazed down into his dark eyes. "Don't let me go, Trent. Please, don't ever let me go."

"Can you ever forgive me for—"

She kissed him quickly, then with her lips lingering close to his, she whispered, "Let's forgive each other and start over again."

"Do you mean it, Lara? Are you willing to take a chance on us?"

"I'm scared," she admitted. "I don't want any of us to get hurt, especially Mary Beth. You see how she reacted tonight. But . . . Oh, Trent, I don't think we have any choice, do we? I was a fool to believe I could walk away from you again."

"We'll make it work this time," he said. "We're a little older and a lot wiser."

"And we have a daughter who'll keep us on our toes."

Trent flipped Lara over onto her back, then covered her with his big body, taking her mouth in a possessive kiss. Lara wrapped her arms around his neck and her legs around his hips, encompassing him, claiming him, inviting him to take her.

And he took her again and again that night as their bodies became reacquainted and their love flourished anew.

They awoke shortly after dawn and made love again, then lay in each other's arms. This was a new day, a new beginning.

"Will you marry me?" Trent stroked her arm.

Filled with happiness, Lara sighed. "I want a real wedding this time. In a church, with flowers and music and a—" She jerked upright in bed and looked down at Trent. "I don't suppose you'd wear a tuxedo, would you?"

"I'll wear my birthday suit if it'll make you happy, babe." Lifting his hand to her face, her caressed her cheek.

"God, woman, do you have any idea how much I love you?"

Tears glazed Lara's eyes. Tears of pure joy. "Yes, I think I have a pretty good idea, if you love me as much as I love you."

"I know one person who's going to be ecstatic this morning when we tell her we're getting married again." Trent kissed Lara's bare shoulder.

She shivered. Every time he touched her, she melted. "I feel so guilty for having put her through that scene last night. If only I—"

"Don't go beating yourself up over it," Trent said. "Mary Beth's going to be so happy that she'll forget all about being angry with us last night."

"Aunt Peg will be pleased, don't you think? She tried to talk some sense into me five years ago and I wouldn't listen to her. I wouldn't listen to anyone. If only I had talked to Cassie or opened one of her letters."

Trent gathered Lara close, enclosing her in his strong arms. "We've got to let it go, babe. All the regrets. We both made some big mistakes, but we have a second chance now and that's all that matters."

"We won't ever let anything go wrong again, will we?" Lara hugged him with a desperate fierceness. "We'll always love each other and trust each other and—"

"And cherish each other and the special love we share." Easing himself on top of her, he gazed down at her and his heart swelled with tenderness and the deepest, most profound love a man could feel.

Giving herself over to all the love within her, Lara whispered, "Yes, we never really cherished what we had, never appreciated how lucky we were."

Trent held Lara in his arms and vowed to God that he would never do anything to hurt her again.

Peg Warren flung open Lara's bedroom door. "Get up! Both of you. Now! Mary Beth's missing."

Trent shot straight up. Lara flung back the covers and

jumped out of bed, forgetting that she was naked. Trent
got up, retrieved his jeans from the floor and pulled them
on. He picked up Lara's gown and handed it to her. She
slipped into it quickly.

"What do you mean Mary Beth's missing?" Trent
asked as he zipped his jeans.

"She's not in her room," Peg said. "I came upstairs to
see why you hadn't come down for breakfast and I peeked
in to check on Mary Beth. She's not in her bed, and Happy
is gone, too."

"Where could she be?" Lara turned to Trent. He slid
his arm around her waist. "She can't walk without her
crutches and then only to take a few steps."

"All I know is that she's not in her room and I've
checked your bedroom, Trent, and I know she's not in my
room," Peg said. "And she's not in either of the bath-
rooms up here."

"There's no way she could have gotten downstairs and
out of the house, is there?" Lara asked Trent.

He shook his head. "I don't see how."

"Let's check her room again. Maybe she's hiding,"
Lara said. "She could still be upset about last night."

Peg followed Lara and Trent into Mary Beth's bedroom
and the three of them searched it thoroughly, even under
the bed and inside the closet.

Trent asked his aunt to go downstairs and take a look
around, just in case, by some miracle, Mary Beth had been
able to make it down to the first floor.

"I don't think she could get down the stairs," Lara said.
"And that means she's still up here somewhere. But
where?"

"Last night she told us that she wasn't going back to
Huntsville with you, that she wanted to stay here on the
ranch," Trent said. "Knowing how stubborn our daughter
can be, I'd say she's gone into hiding and taken Happy
with her."

Trent nodded to the only door they hadn't opened in

their search. Behind the door was the narrow staircase leading up to the attic.

Smiling, Lara nodded, tension draining from her body.

"Mary Beth? Mary Beth, sweetie, where are you?" Lara called out as she walked up and down the hall. "Please, answer me. Your daddy and I have something to tell you. Some good news."

"Mommy and I have decided to get married again," Trent said. "She's not leaving the ranch. You and she and I are going to live here together and be a real family again."

Trent and Lara waited, certain that Mary Beth would reveal herself once she knew her parents were reuniting. Several minutes passed, but nothing happened. Trent guided Lara toward the closed stairway door.

"This is the only place she can be," he said. "We've looked everywhere else."

Lara's hand trembled as she reached for the doorknob. Trent covered her hand and together they opened the door.

"Oh, my," Lara said.

"Our little sleeping beauty," Trent said.

Lara's heart overflowed with sweet motherly love when she looked down to where Mary Beth lay on the first step, her head resting on the second. She was sound asleep, Happy nestled at her side. Trent bent over and scooped his daughter up in his arms. Lara picked up Happy and lifted Mary Beth's crutches from the floor. Trent walked out into the hall.

Mary Beth's eyelashes fluttered, then she slowly opened her eyes. "Daddy?"

"Hello, kiddo," Trent said.

"How'd you find me? I was hiding so I wouldn't have to leave the ranch today."

Trent carried Mary Beth back to her room and placed her in the center of the bed. Lara handed Happy to Mary Beth, then sat beside her.

"You don't have to leave the ranch today," Lara said. "You can live here from now on."

"But what about you, Mommy?" Mary Beth asked. "I don't want to leave my daddy, but I don't want you to go away. I want us all to stay together."

Trent sat down on the other side of the bed, reached out and took Mary Beth's tiny hands into his huge ones. "I asked your mother to marry me this morning and you know what she said?"

Mary Beth's eyes grew huge; her lips curved into a trembling smile as she turned to look at her mother. "Are you going to marry my daddy?"

"Yes, darling, I'm going to marry your daddy."

Mary Beth flung herself into her mother's arms. "You said yes. Oh, Mommy, this is an even better birthday present than getting Happy."

As if on cue, the cocker spaniel puppy licked Mary Beth's face. She giggled joyously, nuzzling the dog with her nose.

Lara lifted her daughter onto her lap; Trent draped his arm around Lara's shoulders. "We haven't decided when we'll get married, but we've agreed to have a real wedding, in church."

"When did you and Daddy get married the first time?" Mary Beth asked.

"In May," Lara said, then glanced at Trent. "Next month. We could remarry on our anniversary."

Trent kissed Lara on the top of her head, then did the same to Mary Beth. "That would give us about three weeks to plan a wedding."

"Mother can work miracles when it comes to social events," Lara said. "I'll call her and put her to work immediately. She'll spare no expense."

"Your mother hates me," Trent said. "Do you honestly think she'll take charge of our wedding?"

"She'll get over her dislike for you or she'll lose her daughter and granddaughter. Besides, the best way to soothe her ruffled feathers will be to let her plan the wedding."

"Can I be in your wedding, Mommy? I want to wear a

dress just like yours. All white and shiny with lots and lots of lace.''

"I think that can be arranged." Lara hugged her daughter close with one arm and wrapped her other arm around Trent's waist.

The day was as perfect as the love Trent and Lara shared, as warm and filled with promise as the hope within their hearts. They chose the anniversary of their first wedding day, partly for nostalgic reasons and partly because they felt this was more a reaffirmation of their vows than a remarriage.

Liz had been furious at the thought of Lara returning to Trent, but once Lara had stood her ground, Liz had acquiesced. Being given almost free rein in planning the wedding had, as Lara predicted, softened her mother's attitude toward Trent.

Lara had given Liz two stipulations. One was that the wedding be held at the small country church in Greenbrier, thus keeping the guest list to a minimum. And two was that Mary Beth would be the only wedding attendant. No bridesmaids. No groomsmen. This was a threesome event. Mother. Father. Child.

Spring roses in white and glorious shades of pink filled the arrangements on each side of the white candelabra at the altar. Sweet strains of "Ave Maria" played on the organ permeated the sacred sanctuary where a crowd of friends and family had gathered to celebrate the reunion of a couple deeply in love.

Mary Beth Warren, wearing a floor-length gown of white satin adorned with Schiffli lace held tightly to her crutches, each decorated with pink and white roses. Ringlets of golden hair had been pulled atop her head with a band of delicate white flowers. Directly behind her stood her mother, a vision in a floor-length, white satin gown covered in ornate Venetian lace and heavy beading. She wore her hair in a soft French twist, a lacy, beaded headpiece resting on the back of her head and a chapel-length veil of finest tulle falling gracefully about her shoulders and down her back.

Mary Beth preceded her mother down the aisle. Everyone stood, all heads turning, all eyes moistening with tears. Lara had never known such pure, sweet happiness. Trent stood at the altar, waiting there, so magnificently handsome in his black tuxedo.

When Mary Beth reached the altar, Trent helped seat her in her wheelchair and laid her crutches aside, then held out his hand to his bride. He took her pink and white rose bouquet from her and laid it in their daughter's lap. Trent stood on one side of Mary Beth, Lara on the other, each of them holding one of her tiny hands.

As they exchanged their vows, Trent and Lara spoke every word with deep conviction. When they promised to love and cherish each other, they knew that, this time, they truly understood what they were pledging.

The moment the minister pronounced them man and wife, Trent took Lara in his arms and kissed her passionately. Mary Beth tugged on her father's coattail. Breaking the kiss, he glanced down at his daughter.

"What is it, kiddo?" he asked.

"Are we really married now, forever and always?"

"Yes, darling," Lara said. "We're really married now, forever and always."

Trent picked up Mary Beth's crutches and followed Lara as she pushed their child's wheelchair down the aisle and out into the glorious May afternoon sunshine.

An enormous tent had been set up on the church grounds. A small band played the old forties love song "Always." Liz had outdone herself on the reception and the guests were treated to a feast for the eye as well as the stomach. The party lasted for hours, well after sunset.

When Lara and Trent kissed Mary Beth goodbye and turned her over to Liz and Peg, twilight shadows fell across the rich, verdant earth of Greenbrier, Mississippi.

In the morning, they would return to the ranch house and take Mary Beth on a family vacation to Disney World, in place of a honeymoon. But tonight belonged only to the two of them, and they had made plans in advance.

The chauffeur pulled the limousine off the side of the road where Trent instructed, then watched for a few moments as the couple walked into the field and up a small rise. When they disappeared into a grove of oak trees, he got in the limo and drove away.

There in the moonlight, in their special place, Trent and Lara spent their wedding night. And in their hearts they somehow knew they had created a baby brother for their precious little flower girl.

SOMETHING OLD, SOMETHING NEW

Margaret Brownley

Chapter One

$\mathcal{L}$ynne Hancock was sorely tempted to grow careless. Careless as described by Oscar Wilde when he wrote, "Losing one parent may be regarded as a misfortune, but to lose both looks like carelessness."

That kind of careless!

With her forty-something father romping about in the South Seas, and her mother forever cooking up schemes to complicate her life, Lynne was ready to do a lot more than grow careless—she was ready to disown both her parents. Since their divorce some three years earlier, Rosemary and Doug Hancock had forced her patience to the limit. Now this.

Pressing her cellular phone close to her ear, Lynne tried blocking out the noisy crowd that swarmed around the steps of the old Santa Barbara mission. It was no place to have a serious telephone conversation. She wished she'd left the darn phone at home. "Mother, you didn't!"

Lynne's four-year-old daughter, Lily, sat on the crowded plaza a few feet away, carefully drawing a picture on the cement. With her curly brown hair, big blue eyes and dimpled smile, Lily was cute as a button, even if she was covered in purple chalk.

The crowd grew more noisy and Lynne was having a hard time hearing her mother on the other end of the line. "What, Mother? Speak louder!"

It was *I Madonari* day in Santa Barbara. The festival, held every Memorial Day weekend, was loosely based on an Italian street painting fete dating back to the Renaissance. Lynne and Lily were among the hundreds of weekend artists the event attracted. With close to two hundred paintings in progress, the cement skirting the old Spanish mission resembled a colorful patchwork quilt.

Lynne moved away from a group of noisy teens who were working on a life-sized painting of Elvis Presley. "Mother, I can't believe you went against my wishes."

Lily looked up from her drawing. "Can I talk to Grammy?"

Lynne covered the mouthpiece of the phone. "Not now."

Lily frowned in disappointment, but she went back to her picture without protest.

Meanwhile, her mother had begun her "you-know-I-didn't-mean-to-but-what's-a-grandmother-to-do?" monologue. "She praised Lily and I was putty in her hands."

"But . . ." Unable to get more than a word in edgewise, Lynne sat on the bottom step and shaded the horn of the unicorn that had taken her the better part of the morning to sketch. If her mother was true to form, she would soon try changing the subject by mentioning the real estate prices in Colorado.

"By the way," her mother said as if on cue, "there's a house not far from here that's a steal. It has a wonderful yard for Lily and . . ."

Lynne tossed the chalk into the cookie tin left over from last Christmas and brushed her hand on her jeans. "That's nice, Mother, but don't change the subject. You crossed the line."

"I didn't cross the line, I overshot it by a mile," her mother admitted. "But I thought you'd understand there were extenuating circumstances . . ."

Ah, yes, the old extenuating circumstances routine. Lynne knew this one well. Come to think of it, she'd used it herself a few times. She gazed beyond the red tiled roofs to the choppy blue Pacific. The ocean sparkled like a big jewel in a garden setting. A fishing boat bopped up and down in the white-crested swells. Further out, the ghostly shape of an oil tanker was outlined against the azure sky.

"Are you there?" her mother asked.

"Yes, I'm here."

"So now that I've explained everything, what do you say?"

A marmalade cat ran across the plaza, leaving paw prints on a scene from the Sistine Chapel that a group of artists had been working on for three days. One tow-headed youth chased the cat up a trellis of scarlet bougainvillea.

"The same thing I said before. No."

"You're angry."

"I'm not angry, Mother." *Irritated, maybe. Exasperated. But not angry.* Rosemary Hancock doted on her only grandchild and who could blame her? Lily, with her quick smile and friendly, outgoing nature, managed to endear herself to everyone she met. Well, maybe not everyone; Lynne recalled a certain little ring bearer who didn't appreciate Lily gluing down his cowlick with superglue.

"You know I'm only thinking of Lily. With you unmarried and me, her very own grandmother divorced, I don't want her to grow up thinking we don't believe in love and marriage."

"I doubt very much she'll think that, Mother. Besides, I told you after the last wedding, Lily's flower girl days are over." It had been more of a disaster than a wedding. The groom was late, the cake collapsed and the best man had canceled at the last minute because of chicken pox. It was not the time for Lily to announce for all the world to hear that the bride's diamond ring was actually cubic zirconia. The bride, a friend of Lynne's, hadn't talked to Lynne since.

"I still say any four-year-old who can tell the difference between cubic zirconia and real diamonds is brilliant," her mother said. "I swear she's going to be a geologist, just like you."

"Last week you said she was a born artist." Lynne had to admit Lily's chalk painting wasn't half bad. Lily had taken great pains to draw a bride and groom with the requisite flower girl. The flower girl had Lily's same short brown hair.

The bride wore her brunette hair long, just as Lynne did, but that, hopefully, was where the resemblance ended. Staring at the drawing, Lynne had an irresistible urge to check her hair to see if it really did stand straight out like uncooked spaghetti.

The bride's blue eyes were a bit crossed, but she had the widest smile possible and that was something. When Lily had first started drawing her family members, Lynne always looked like the Wicked Witch of the West. Heaven only knows what Lily's preschool teachers must have thought. Lily's mother, the witch.

The groom. Now he was a different story. He was rather nicely proportioned from the shoulders down. His head wasn't that bad either, if you discounted the ears that stuck out like the handles of an old-fashioned sugar bowl, and the fact that he didn't have a face.

"All I'm asking," her mother coaxed, "is that you help out a friend of mine. Just this one last time. Lily will be *thrilled* and I swear I'll never volunteer her to be a flower girl again—even if they *beg* me."

"You're asking Lily to be in the wedding of a total stranger?"

"The bride's not a stranger," her mother argued. "Clara's the daughter of a friend of mine. Surely you remember me telling you about Sarah Mcintyre? We met on a cruise after your father ran away to be a beach bum. She's the one who told me the quickest way to get over a broken heart was to get another broken heart. Ann Landers, she's not."

"I know who Sarah is, Mother, but . . ." Sarah owned the travel agency that had arranged the ill-fated tour of the

Colorado gold mines she took while still in college.

"Please, Lynne. Sarah's beside herself. Her daughter's one of those career-minded women who has no idea of the importance of a traditional wedding. She refuses to have more than a single bridesmaid. Have you ever heard anything so ridiculous in your life? She agreed to have a flower girl, but only to pacify her mother. Apparently, none of the children in the family is the right age, so Sarah called me and raved about the latest photos I sent her of Lily and naturally, I thought . . ."

"You thought wrong, Mother. The answer is no."

"It'll be good for Lily. What could be more uplifting than a wedding?"

Lynne gritted her teeth. "Mother. I mean it. I've got to go. Lily and I have a bridegroom who needs attention. I'll call you later." Hanging up, she turned off the phone and slid it back into the pocket of her painting smock. Lily sat on the step next to her, her eyes shining with anticipation.

"Am I going to be a flower girl, Mommy? Am I?" Lily had been the flower girl in more weddings than Lynne cared to remember, thanks to her grandmother. Amazingly enough, she'd loved every one of them. But weddings required a lot of time and energy, and frankly Lynne could think of a lot more interesting things to do on the weekends besides chauffeur Lily to weddings. Like decorating sidewalks with chalk paintings.

"Did you tell the bride I look good in pink? And does she know about the time the flower lady forgot to fill my basket and . . ."

"Florist," Lynne said gently, stalling for time. "The florist forgot to fill your basket."

"Did you tell her what the florist lady did?"

"Not yet." Lynne smoothed the dark bangs that fell across Lily's forehead. The ragged ends were all that remained of the disastrous haircut Lily had given herself awhile back.

Lynne tried rubbing the purple chalk off Lily's nose with her finger, but only made the smudge worse. "I'll tell you what. We'll talk about this later." *Much later. Some time around the year two thousand ten.* She dropped to her knees and reached for the box of colors. "Right now we've got to finish our pictures."

"I'm finished," Lily said.

"You forgot to put a face on the groom. Who wants to marry a man with no face?" She shifted into a proper British accent like on those old English mustard commercials. "Excuse me, sir, but you forgot your face."

Lily refused to smile and if anything, her frown deepened. "I don't wanna draw a face!"

Lynne sat back on her heels, not knowing what to make of Lily's sudden outburst.

"What's the matter, sweetie?" Lynne pressed her hand against Lily's smooth forehead. Lily had a fever the week prior due to a slight runny nose, but there was no sign of one now. "Why don't you want to draw a face on the groom? You drew a face on the sun."

"I don't want to."

Lynne wrapped Lily in her arms. "Tell Mommy what's wrong."

It took some coaxing, but finally Lily relented. "Miss Denise said we could bring our parents to open house."

Lynne nodded. Miss Denise was Lily's preschool teacher. "And I told you I'd be there with bells on." This old expression had gotten a laugh out of Lily when Lynne had first used it, but today it drew no reaction.

"I'll be the only one without a daddy."

Lynne felt as if someone had kicked her in the stomach. She knew the day would come when Lily raised questions about her father, questions that could no longer be satisfied with the vague answers Lynne had depended on in the past. But Lynne never dreamed that time would come so soon.

A group of mariachi players strolled through the crowd and some of the onlookers clapped to the music. Still, Lynne lowered her voice. "I told you, Lily. You don't have a daddy."

"Roxanne said everyone has a daddy. Unless he's dead." Lily suddenly looked older than her years. "Is my daddy dead?"

A hard knot formed in Lynne's chest. Whoever this Roxanne was, she certainly knew how to ruin a day. Lynne glanced around. She never expected to have this discussion while sitting on the plaza in front of an old mission, her hands and face covered with purple and green chalk. "No, Lily," she said. "He's not dead."

"Then where is he?"

His name was Jeff Blakely and the last Lynne had heard, he was living somewhere in the Los Angeles area. He was tall, dark and ruggedly handsome, and he had the same dimpled smile as the daughter he didn't know existed. "I don't know where he is."

She had met Jeff in Colorado during the most terrifying experience of her life. Jeff was an amateur photographer and she was in her second year of college. They were strangers and probably wouldn't have met had an earthquake not dislodged the whole side of a mountain, trapping the two of them in an old deserted gold mine.

For five days she and Jeff had been stranded in a dark, dank underground chamber, not knowing how much air they had left or even if anyone knew of their plight. Every hour had seemed like their last. Lord, if it hadn't been for Jeff, she might never have survived the ordeal.

"Can we find him, Mommy, eh? Can we?"

Lynne pressed her forehead next to Lily's. "No, we can't find him."

"Why?"

Because she could still hear Jeff's worried voice. *We can't let anyone know what happened between us.*

As crazy as it seemed after all this time, she could still feel his arms around her—still taste the lips that had kissed her good-bye. Moments after their vow of secrecy, rescuers had broken through the last barrier and she never saw him again unless he was surrounded by the media, or the woman he planned to marry, who had flown out to Colorado to be near him during the rescue efforts.

Forcing the memories away, Lynne hugged her little daughter tight. "We just can't, that's why." And because she really had no more answers at the moment, she changed the subject, hating the circumstances that forced her to be forever on her guard. "Grammy wants you to be the flower girl at the wedding of her friend's daughter."

Her ploy worked. A bright smile erased the frown from Lily's face. "I knew it."

Lily looked so pleased at the idea, Lynne couldn't help but smile. Secretly, she felt guilty for not being totally honest with Lily about her father. Would she ever have the strength to explain how two perfect strangers could conceive a child and then walk away from each other as if nothing had happened? How old does a child have to be to understand the complexities of the adult world? How old does anyone have to be to understand? "I'll call grammy later and remind her to tell the bride you look good in pink."

Berating herself for taking the easy way out, Lynne wondered if Oscar Wilde ever had an opinion on chickens. "Now about the groom's face . . ."

Chapter Two

*T*raffic had been surprisingly light that Saturday morning in early July. Lynne had driven the 101 Freeway along the coast to Ventura, then shot inland toward the San Fernando Valley, making the trip to Woodland Hills in little more than an hour and a half.

"Are we almost there?" Lily asked for perhaps the umpteenth time.

"Just about." Lynne couldn't believe she'd let herself be talked into letting Lily be the flower girl in a stranger's wedding. "What's the address, sweetie?" Lily could already read her numbers.

"Two, seven, oh, I mean zero, five, nine," Lily said proudly.

"This looks like it." Lynne pulled in front of a sprawling one-story flagstaff house with shiny bay windows, a three-car garage and a manicured velvet-smooth lawn.

The wedding was still a couple of weeks away, but Lily had been invited to the bridal shower to meet the bride.

Lynne parked behind a late-model Cadillac and popped open the trunk so Lily could fetch her gift for the bride. Lily had picked out the set of country kitchen placemats and matching linen napkins herself, and had insisted upon *Beauty and the Beast* wrapping paper.

The house was crammed with strangers, but her mother's friend, Sarah, greeted them warmly. A small trim woman with silver blue hair, she had a friendly smile that didn't waver in the slightest when she took Lily's gift and added it to the growing pile of elegantly wrapped presents.

"I just spoke to your mother yesterday. I'm so pleased she's traveling all the way from Colorado just for my Clara's wedding. My agency arranged for her airline ticket."

"She wouldn't miss it for the world," Lynne said.

Sarah's gaze lit on Lily and her smile broadened. "I do believe you're even prettier than the pictures your grandmother sent me. I'm so glad you're going to be my Clara's flower girl. Come along and I'll introduce you to the bride."

Lily beamed as she followed the older woman through the crowded living room and into the spacious kitchen, her little black patent shoes tapping across the marble floor. Following behind, Lynne marveled at her daughter's ability to act so natural among strangers. Glancing at the sea of unfamiliar faces around her, Lynne wished she was back in Santa Barbara.

"There you are, Clara. Look who's here. Your little flower girl."

A tall willowy blonde whose hair, makeup and white flowing chiffon pants and tunic were impeccable, Clara leveled her gray eyes upon Lily. "Oh, yes. Mother told me you were coming." Though Clara seemed friendly enough, she struck Lynne as the type who wouldn't think much of placemats decorated with cows and chickens and wrapped in *Beauty and the Beast* paper.

"What did you say your name was, little girl?"

Lily gave Clara an indignant frown. "My name is Lily and I'm four years old. I'm a great big girl, even though I'm small for my age."

Sarah laughed. "I suppose there's some logic there, somewhere. Would you like some lemonade or a soft drink?"

"Some lemonade, please," Lily said politely.

"Come along, then."

After Sarah led Lily toward the patio, Lynne introduced

herself to Clara. "I'm Lily's mother."

"Oh, yes. Your mother and my mother are friends. It's very nice of you to let Lily be in my wedding."

"Lily loves weddings. I'm afraid she has some strong ideas on how things should be done."

"Maybe I should have hired her as my wedding consultant."

Lynne smiled. "She would have loved that." She studied Clara for a moment. "I have the strangest feeling we've met before . . ."

"Really? I don't think so. Do you live in the area?"

"I live in Santa Barbara. Maybe it'll come to me later."

Their conversation was interrupted by the arrival of another guest. Clara's gaze wandered past Lynne, a quick smile flashing across her lovely smooth face. "I don't mean to rush off, but an old school chum of mine just arrived."

"Please don't let me keep you."

Lynne watched Clara float across the room and plant a kiss on the cheek of an attractive dark-haired woman. Clara still looked familiar, though she couldn't imagine where they might have met.

She wandered over to the counter and helped herself to a carrot stick, swirling a figure eight in the creamy dip before taking a bite.

Two women stood talking about their latest diet; a group of matronly women discussed tennis. Lynne glanced out the glass door that opened onto a terraced brick patio. Three brick steps led down to a sparkling blue swimming pool.

Lily stood on the patio engaged in an animated conversation with a white-haired man. Lynne quickly threaded her way toward the door to join her. Knowing Lily, she was probably playing matchmaker.

A middle-aged woman in a short pleated tennis skirt stopped her. "I don't think we've met. My name is Ginny and this is Lou-Ellen. Do you play tennis?"

"I'm afraid not," Lynne admitted.

Lou-Ellen wore a denim jumpsuit adorned with a silver belt and a stunning turquoise squash blossom necklace with matching earrings. Lynne recognized the turquoise as coming from the old Bixby mines in Arizona. "Not play tennis?" Lou-Ellen said in a southern lilt. "What do you do in your spare time?"

"When I'm not working, I try to spend as much time as possible with my daughter."

"Where do you work?" Ginny asked, sounding more polite then interested.

"I'm a geologist. I work for ..." Her voice was drowned out by a buzz of excitement. Applause broke out all around her and everyone started talking at once.

"The groom's arrived," Lou-Ellen explained. "Have you two met?"

"Not yet," Lynne said.

"Just wait till you meet him," Lou-Ellen gushed. "Clara doesn't know how lucky she is. The guy's a dreamboat. Gorgeous." She rolled her eyes and fanned herself with a paper cocktail napkin.

"Mr. Dreamboat" 's back was toward her, making it impossible to determine much more than his height and the dark, almost black color of his hair. Leaving Lou-Ellen and Ginny to continue their conversation, she helped herself to a glass of sparkling mineral water and walked past the bar.

The groom turned his head and Lynne stopped dead in her tracks, her glass slipping from her fingers. A moment of confusion followed as a young Hispanic woman dressed in a crisp white apron descended on her with a broom and dustpan.

"I'm so sorry," Lynne stammered.

"It's all right, Señorita," the woman said. "It was just a little accident. I'll get you another glass."

While the woman made quick work of the mess, Lynne chanced another look at the groom. *Dear God in heaven, it's true!*

Fearing her knees would buckle, she pressed her back

hard against the bar to keep from falling. No matter how much she wanted to believe she was imagining things, the tall, handsome, soon-to-be bridegroom stood across the room from her big as life.

Lou-Ellen was right; he *was* a dreamboat. A dreamboat who just happened to be Lily's father.

Chapter Three

*B*y the time Lynne had managed to calm down enough to move safely out of Jeff Blakely's scope of vision, her only thought was to run. At the very least, she wanted to drop through the floor. But before she could do anything rash, she first had to find Lily.

Feeling more like an intruder than a guest, she hid behind a potted palm tree and measured the distance to the open patio door.

She forced herself to breathe, then slowly inched herself around the counter, keeping her face turned away from Jeff. He hadn't changed much since she'd last seen him, but neither had she. Now she wished she'd done something different with her hair. Or makeup.

Outside, she gasped for air, but the reprieve was only temporary. Unless Jeff left the party early, it would only be a matter of time before he spotted her. That was the last thing on earth she intended to let happen.

Lily's voice rose from the center of a small gathering. "My mommy's really pretty and she caught the bride's *bowskay*. That means she's supposed to find a groom, but no one wants to marry her . . ."

Lynne rushed to her daughter's side. "Lily . . ." She smiled at the small circle of guests listening to Lily with rapt interest. "Eh . . . I'm Lily's mother."

A bald-headed man seated in a chaise longue, his leg in

a cast, studied Lynne with interest. "So *you're* this young lady's mother. Well, don't you worry. Good things happen to good people."

She forced a smile. Dear God, what else had Lily told them?

An elderly woman took hold of Lynne's hand and gazed up at her with faded blue eyes. "I can't imagine why no one would want to marry you, dearie. But don't you worry. There's a man out there somewhere, mark my words."

Lynne kept smiling, but inside she was dying. Any moment, Jeff could walk outside and spot her. She didn't need pity, she needed a miracle. Heck, she was so desperate, she wouldn't complain if the ground suddenly opened up beneath her feet. Where was a sinkhole when you needed one?

"Thank you," Lynne said, knowing the woman was only trying to be kind. She glanced nervously at the house. Any moment she expected disaster to walk out the door. "Lily, we have to go."

Lily made a face. "Do we have to?"

"I'm afraid we do."

"But you just got here," Sarah protested. "You haven't had anything to eat yet. And Lily promised to play the piano for us."

"Lily doesn't play the piano." Lily thought turning on the switch of a player piano made her a musician.

"You haven't seen the rabbit," Lily said. "Her name is Cinderella because she's gray and she's going to have baby rabbits and . . ."

"I'm sorry, Lily, but we do have to go."

Lily looked so disappointed, Lynne felt terrible. Still, it couldn't be helped.

"Can I have a rabbit, Mommy? Can I?"

"Pocahontas won't like it." Pocahontas was Lily's very independent, though jealous cat. She turned to Sarah and, not wishing to appear rude, explained, "I'm suddenly not feeling well."

"Oh, dear. I'm sorry. Can I get you something? An

aspirin? You can lay down in one of the guest bedrooms if you like.''

"No, thank you. I'm sure I'll be all right. Is there a way out front without going through the house?"

"I'm afraid not," Sarah said. "The motor home is blocking the side of the house."

Lynne would have gladly climbed over the motor home if she thought she could get away with it. She was even tempted to scale the six-foot block walls surrounding the property, even in her high heels and panty hose.

"I see." She tried not to panic, but it was hard not to. The last thing she wanted to do was go back into the house. "Come along, Lily." Anxious to make her escape, she took Lily by the hand.

"Do we have to go home, Mommy? Are you sick? Are you going to get chicken pox?"

Lynne gave her a reassuring smile. "No, I'm not going to get chicken pox. Mommy has a headache. It's nothing serious."

Despite Lynne's assurances, Lily looked worried. "Oops! I forgot to tell the bride I look good in pink."

At mention of the bride, Lynne really did feel sick. She'd almost forgotten. Even if she escaped without Jeff seeing her, the problem would only be postponed. The wedding still loomed ahead. "I think your grandmother already talked to her about your dress."

She led Lily into the kitchen, her heart pounding so fast it sounded like bongo drums. Jeff hadn't moved, which meant she had no choice but to walk right past him. There simply was no other way to the front door.

"I have to go to the bathroom, Mommy," Lily whispered.

Lynne groaned inwardly. What would be next? "Can you wait?"

Lily shook her head. "I have to go real bad."

"Do you think you can find the bathroom by yourself?"

"Yes," Lily said.

"All right. Meet me by the car." Surely by that time,

she would have figured out a way to sneak past Jeff.

Jeff's warm laughter rose above the voices of the guests, and she was suddenly thrown back in time. Even when things seemed the bleakest, and it looked as if they would never escape that mine alive, he'd made her laugh. The memory brought a warm flush to her face. It was hard to believe; after nearly five years, he could still make her feel like a schoolgirl.

Skirting the room, she practically tripped over a chair. Her back toward him, she circled the enormous dining room table. Large platters of sliced roast beef, ham and turkey and an assortment of imported cheeses were artfully arranged around a beautiful crystal basket filled with baby pink roses.

She chanced a quick glance over her shoulder and let her breath out. Just the mere sight of Jeff made her knees nearly buckle. Lord, he was every bit as handsome today as he had been five years earlier. No wonder she'd been swept off her feet.

Behind her, Clara's mother rang a crystal dinner bell. "All right everyone! Food's ready. We'll let our guests of honor go first."

Lynne momentarily panicked. Jeff gallantly tucked his bride-to-be's hand in the crook of his elbow and started toward the buffet table.

Lynne dropped to her knees and scurried beneath the floor-length tablecloth.

Trapped beneath the table, her mind spun. This was ridiculous. She was a grown woman. There had to be some proper etiquette for bumping into the long-lost father of one's child. Where was Miss Manners when you needed her?

Worried about Lily, Lynne lifted the hem of the tablecloth a few inches off the floor to see if she could spot her. Much to her horror, she inadvertently brushed her fingertips against Jeff's jean-clad leg.

Yanking her hand away and dropping the tablecloth as if it were on fire, she sat frozen in place, convinced that any second Jeff would look under the table and demand to know what the hell she was doing there.

Her mouth dry, she held her breath until her lungs screamed for oxygen. Much to her relief, Jeff didn't look beneath the table. Obviously, he was so wrapped up in his future bride, he hadn't felt her hand against his pants. That was something. Maybe he wouldn't notice if he walked right past him and out the front door. *I should be so lucky!*

Her gaze riveted to his feet, she watched him make his way slowly around the table. He wore blue jeans and white sneakers. How ironic that he wore much the same outfit he'd worn in that collapsed mine. Even now, all these years later, she could feel his jean-clad thighs against her legs as they'd clung to each other for warmth and comfort.

The thought was as depressing as it was titillating. She was stuck beneath a table and having a hormone attack. Lord, Lily was right; she did need a groom.

She forced herself to concentrate on the expensive high-heeled gold shoes she recognized as Clara's. What a contrast.

Their voices offered another contrast. Both hushed, Jeff teasingly made mention of missing a doubleheader. Lynne remembered Jeff joking about the ballgames he was missing back when they were stuck in that mine.

Clara's voice, smooth as silk, clucked sympathetically. "Don't worry, darling. You can go to an Angel game any time, but you only get married once."

"That's Dodgers," he said.

"What?"

"I've told you a hundred times, I'm a Dodger fan." He sounded slightly resigned, as if they'd had this conversation before. He and Clara moved away, but the table was still pretty much surrounded by the other guests, making it impossible for Lynne to escape. She had no choice but to wait until the others had filled their plates.

Suddenly, she heard Lily's plaintive cry. "Has anyone seen my Mommy?"

The room stilled to a deadly silence. Only Lily could

render a room full of adults totally speechless.

Jeff was the first to speak, his voice gentle now, with none of the irritation that had been evident moments earlier. "What does your Mommy look like?"

Lynne thought she was going to die on the spot. *Dear God, don't let him ask my name.*

"She has brown hair and blue eyes," Lily said. "She's very pretty."

"I'll vouch for that!" said a voice Lynne recognized as belonging to the man with the broken leg.

"Well, let's see if we can find this pretty mommy of yours," Jeff said.

Lynne had no choice but to stand up and announce her presence. An elderly woman gasped and almost dropped her plate as Lynne crawled out from beneath the table. "My word!"

Lynne smiled up at her. "Contact lens," she muttered.

Lily's face lit up. "There's my Mommy!" She dropped Jeff's hand and ran to Lynne's side. Lynne kept her head down, pretending to dig in her purse for something as she headed for the door.

"I couldn't find you, Mommy, and that nice man tried to help me and . . ."

"I know, sweetie."

Fifteen feet left to safety. Ten. Nine. Behind her, Jeff's voice rose above all the others. It might as well have been a bullet to her heart. "Lynne? Lynne Hancock? Is that you?"

Chapter Four

*L*ynne was tempted to pretend she didn't hear him call her name, and make a fast sprint for the door. If only her feet hadn't suddenly seemed cast in cement. Frozen in place, her hand wrapped tightly around Lily's, she held her breath. Any moment now someone was going to wake her up and tell her she was having a nightmare.

"Lynne?"

Desperate to recall everything she'd learned in her high school drama classes, she turned and took a stab at feigning surprise. "Jeff Blakely?" She didn't sound surprised; she sounded like a beached whale trying to send a signal of distress. No wonder she'd failed drama.

The blue of his eyes hit her like a blast from a heated oven, piercing her to the very soul. Any question in her mind as to why she had so willingly and completely given herself to him all those years ago was forever erased.

He broke into a devastating grin that made her mouth dry. "Well, I'll be." He held out his hand and because there really was no way to avoid it, she offered hers in return. He squeezed her hand tight, but it might as well have been her heart he squeezed. She recalled with startling clarity the last time he'd held her hand. Lord, she'd trembled then, too.

Clara looked from Jeff to Lynne, a frown at her forehead. "Do you two know each other?"

Jeff released Lynne's hand, but his eyes never left her face. "Darling, I want you to meet Lynne Hancock. You remember. The one who was stuck in that mine shaft with me."

"Oh, yes," Clara said, her voice sounding like something was stuck in her throat. "The famous cave-in."

"We . . . we talked earlier," Lynne stammered. No wonder Clara had looked familiar. Lynne hadn't actually met Clara, but she had watched from her hospital bed as Clara cooed into the TV cameras about how grateful she was her fiancé had survived the ordeal. That was when reality had hit Lynne like a cement truck; she and Jeff had shared but a few moments of uncontrolled lust fueled by fear—nothing more. He had his fiancé and she had Gary.

"This is a pleasant surprise," Jeff was saying. "I can't believe it. What in the world are you doing here?"

"My daughter . . . Lily . . . she . . ." Her mouth felt like it was lined in sandpaper.

"I'm going to be the flower girl in your wedding," Lily announced proudly.

Jeff's gaze shifted to Lily. "Is that so?" He glanced back at Clara. "Why doesn't anyone tell me these things?"

"We don't have to have a flower girl if you don't want," Clara said. "I only agreed to have one to please Mother."

Lily's face dropped as she gazed at Jeff.

He smiled at her and gave her full rosy cheek a playful tweak. "I think every wedding should have a flower girl. Especially one as pretty as this one."

"I think so, too," Lily agreed. For a moment father and daughter beamed at each other as if sharing some delicious secret.

"I'm afraid we're going to have to go," Lynne stammered. Her hand on Lily's shoulder, she pushed her toward the door.

"So soon?" Jeff looked genuinely disappointed.

Dozens of excuses ran through her mind. "I have a long

drive ahead of me,'' she said, picking the one closest to the truth.

''She drove up special from Santa Barbara,'' Clara's mother explained. ''She's not feeling well.''

Jeff's eyes grew smoky with concern. *Don't look at me like that,* Lynne wanted to shout. *I don't want to know you're concerned. I don't want to know anything about you at all.* ''Is there anything I can do?'' he asked.

''No, nothing,'' she stammered. ''It's just a headache.''

''It's probably the smog,'' Sarah offered helpfully. ''They keep telling us the air quality has improved but you'll never prove it by me.''

Jeff's eyes narrowed, sharp and assessing. ''Whereabouts in Santa Barbara do you live?''

''Off State Street,'' she said vaguely.

''You were studying to be a geologist.'' It was a statement rather than a question.

''My mommy's a geologist for the Benedict Oil Company,'' Lily said proudly.

''Is that so?'' He looked impressed and stared at Lynne with an intense, but secret expression that brought a blush to her face. As if to suddenly catch himself, he dipped his head slightly. ''Are you sure you're all right? I hate to think of you driving with a headache.''

''I'm fine. Really.''

''Maybe you'll visit Clara and me after we get settled. It's been what? Five years.''

Lynne nodded. Actually, it had been four years, ten months and one week. But who was counting?

''That would be nice,'' Clara said. ''We'd love to meet your husband.''

Her heart stopped. ''My . . . ?''

''Mommy doesn't—''

Lynne quickly opened the door and managed to push Lily outside. ''I'd love to talk longer, but I'm afraid I'm in a hurry. Perhaps some other time.''

''Yes, of course.'' He followed them outside, leaving

the others in the house. "It was nice seeing you again, Lynne."

"Nice seeing you, Jeff."

So polite they were; so formal.

Outside she reached for Lily's hand and resisted the urge to cross the lush velvet lawn to her car. She felt Jeff's gaze bore into her back like a branding iron as she followed the walkway, but she waited until she was behind the wheel before she chanced another look.

Jeff stood watching them, a quizzical expression on his handsome square face.

"I'm plugged in, Mommy," Lily announced, after snapping the buckle of her seatbelt together.

"Good girl."

Lily waved to Jeff as they pulled away from the curb. Lynne turned the corner and Lily folded her arms across her chest. "I want a Daddy just like that nice man."

Lynne almost didn't see the shiny red convertible pull out in front of her.

Rosemary Hancock's voice shot over the telephone line. "What do you mean you're pulling Lily out of the wedding?"

Lynne held the telephone away from her ear. Even so, she could still hear her mother's voice loud and clear. "You know that's going to break her heart."

Lynne didn't need her mother or anyone else to tell her what the news was going to do to Lily. "Yes, but, thanks to you, it can't be helped." Although Lily had been in bed for over an hour, Lynne kept her voice low.

"Can't you arrange for time off?"

"That's not the problem, Mother."

"Then what?"

Lynne glanced toward the hallway to make certain no little ears lurked in the shadows. "Do you remember Jeff Blakely?"

"I'm not likely to forget the man who made my daughter pregnant and didn't have the decency to . . ."

"Mother, we've been through this before." *Many times before.* She glanced up at the ceiling and couldn't resist giving her mother back a bit of her own medicine. "There were *extenuating* circumstances. Besides, you know darn well, I never told him about Lily."

"And you know darn well the man had a right to know he'd fathered a child."

Lynne rubbed her head. It had been a hard day and it looked as if it was going to be an even harder night. "I don't want to talk about this now."

"You're the one who brought it up." Her mother sighed. "I'm sorry, sweetie, but what does that *man* have to do with anything?"

Lynne bit her lip. "Jeff is the bridegroom!" she blurted out.

Her terse announcement was greeted by silence. Lynne never thought she'd see the day her mother was actually speechless.

When Rosemary finally managed to speak, her voice shook. "What do you mean Jeff is the bridegroom? Jeff Blakely? Lily's father? *That* Jeff?"

"That's exactly who I'm talking about." Lynne closed her eyes. Maybe she would wake up soon and this whole nightmarish day would end. "He's marrying Sarah's daughter. I couldn't believe it myself." Another silence stretched across the wire. "Mother? Are you there?"

"Yes, yes, I'm here. Are you *sure* it was Jeff? Did . . . you talk to him?"

"Lily and I both talked to him."

"Lily! Oh, lord. What did he say when you told him . . . ?"

"I didn't tell him."

"But . . . but . . . how did you explain Lily? Surely he must have guessed."

"Why would he?" *Just because he and Lily had the same big blue eyes and the same dimpled smile . . .* "Lily's small for her age. He probably thought she was younger than she is. Besides, he assumed I was married. Didn't

Sarah ever mention Jeff's name?''

''I don't know. She might have. I don't think she ever mentioned the name Blakely, though.''

''But didn't you ever tell her about the cave-in? Surely she must have thought it odd that both Clara's fiancé and your daughter were rescued from a Colorado gold mine.''

''I don't know that I ever mentioned it to her. If you recall, you never wanted me to talk about it. Besides, I didn't meet Sarah until a year or so after the cave-in, remember? Oh, dear. I don't like the sound of this, Lynne. What's he going to say when he finds out you kept this from him?''

''He's not going to find out.''

Rosemary gasped. ''You mean you're going to let Lily be the flower girl in her own father's wedding and not tell him?''

''Lily's not going to be in the wedding, Mother. You'll have to call Sarah and make up some excuse. Tell her we've gone to the Caribbean to visit Lily's grandfather. Tell her Lily and I have joined a religious sect that strictly forbids us going to weddings. Tell her what you want, but Lily can't be in Clara's wedding.''

Rosemary groaned. ''She'll *kill* me!''

''If you don't call her, I may kill you. You're the one who got me into this mess so you can get me out.''

''But maybe there's another way . . .''

''Call her, Mother. We have no choice. Please!''

After hanging up, Lynne felt like she was living on pins and needles. Cupping her face with her hands like the *Home Alone* character, she paced a circle in her small Spanish adobe, moving from room to room in a state of shock before ending up back in the kitchen.

She couldn't believe it. After all this time, who would ever think she'd run into Jeff again?

If only she'd recognized Clara earlier, she could have taken her leave of absence before Jeff's arrival, and no one would have been the wiser.

Jeff had talked about Clara during those days and nights

they'd sat huddled together in the mine. At first he'd wanted to do right by Clara—Lord knows he tried—just as she had wanted to do right by Gary. Gradually, he'd stopped talking about Clara—and she had stopped talking about Gary.

Trapped in that mine, she was so certain she'd never see Gary again. See her family. Besides, it had taken every bit of energy to cling to what little hope was left. The gold mine became their world, leaving no energy left to devote to anything outside the jagged walls that surrounded them.

The last of the candles had been used up by the third day. Even now, she could recall how dark and dank it was, and how the ceiling kept falling. Their chances of being rescued had seemed more remote with each passing hour.

Then one night, when things were the bleakest and they had all but given up hope of ever being rescued, they'd turned to each other. Seeking only comfort at first, they'd held on to each other out of desperation and fear. Protected by the warm strength of his arms she could almost believe she was safe. But safety offered its own brand of danger, for that's when desire flared between them. Passion and need soon followed.

To this day she could still feel the jolting warmth of his lips, the urgent play of his strong firm hands on her body, the ecstasy that followed.

Even now, nearly five years later, the memory of being in Jeff's arms had not diminished or grown dim. She shivered today as she'd shivered then. And despite all the trouble it had caused her—and the pain that followed—she never regretted that night.

One night—and her entire life had changed forever.

Everything had seemed so simple before that night. She and Gary had dated for nearly two years while she was in college and had planned to get married as soon as she graduated. Had it not been for the cave-in, she was convinced they would have been married long ago.

Following her rescue, Gary had been so happy to see her. The five-day ordeal had changed them both. Things that had seemed important before the accident hadn't seemed to matter much afterwards.

"Let's get married!" he'd said the day after her rescue. "I don't care if we can't afford a house and you still have two years left before you graduate. I want us to get married now."

Even her family thought it was a good idea. But something held her back. At the time, she thought her sudden restlessness was the result of having a near-death experience. She didn't want to believe Jeff was the reason for her sudden change of heart.

She and Gary had a good relationship, but hardly a passionate one. Not like the passion that had exploded when Jeff had touched her, held her, and kissed her.

The few friends she'd confided in told her that kind of passion was possible only in life and death situations. Not in real life. At the time she'd thought they might be right. But before she settled down to marry Gary, she'd been determined to find out one way or the other.

What she needed was time to sort things out. Gary couldn't have been more sympathetic. "Take all the time you need," he'd said, but she recalled with guilt how confused and worried he'd looked. Obviously, he'd sensed things had changed between them.

Three weeks after being rescued, she'd driven up to Carmel, alone. The next day, she woke to the sound of the surf pounding beneath her bedroom window. That wasn't all that woke her. That morning she had her first bout of morning sickness.

Telling Gary the baby wasn't his was the hardest thing she ever had to do.

"Try to understand," she'd pleaded.

"What's there to understand?" Gary had looked so remote, she'd wondered if she ever really knew him. "A mountain fell on top of you and you got pregnant."

He'd packed his bags and walked out of their apartment and that's when it hit her. Any man who could walk out of a two-year relationship without so much as raising his voice was a man without passion. Suddenly, everything that had happened in that cave began to make sense. Jeff wasn't so much the right man as Gary was the wrong guy.

The problem with this explanation was that nearly five years later, Jeff was still the only man who could quicken her pulse.

Soon after Gary had walked out on her, she'd called Jeff. She'd called even though they'd made a pledge not to contact each other. She couldn't seem to help herself. She hadn't known what to expect when she dialed his number. Surprise. Concern. Maybe even awkward silence. But never did she expect his anger. ''We decided to keep what happened between us secret,'' he'd all but shouted, his voice cold. That had been his decision, not hers, but she hadn't bothered to correct him. Instead, she made up some feeble excuse for having called, and hung up.

For months following the rescue, she dreamed that Jeff had tracked her down to tell her it had all been a terrible mistake, that he loved her and couldn't live without her.

Many were the nights she stared up at a dark ceiling, thinking she'd never make it through the pregnancy.

After Lily's birth, Lynne spent the next few years settling into her role as a single parent. She loved Lily dearly and never once regretted the strange and unexpected circumstances that had turned her life upside-down.

During these past years, she'd thought Jeff had happily returned to his old life. For all she knew, that's exactly what he'd done. Still, she couldn't help but wonder why it had taken him nearly five years to marry Clara.

She closed her eyes. Dear God, this was crazy. He had his life and she had hers. What happened between them had been nothing more than pure unadulterated lust.

So what if it was lust fueled by fear, by hopelessness, by desperation, it was still lust—and no amount of wistful thinking was going to change that.

With Lily no longer in the wedding there wouldn't be a single reason in the world to see Jeff again. Not ever. And that was exactly how she wanted it.

Chapter Five

$\mathcal{T}$wo days later, Lynne's assistant, an attractive young woman of Japanese heritage, stuck her head in the door of Lynne's office. "You have a call on line one."

"Thanks, Mira." Lynne turned away from the monitor of her computer and grabbed the phone. "Yes."

"Lynne?"

At the sound of the distinctive male voice, Lynne gripped the phone until her knuckles turned white. "It's Jeff Blakely. Did I catch you at a bad time?"

"No," she squeaked out. "Not at all. This is a surprise. I didn't expect to hear from you."

"I was pretty surprised myself the other day. I never expected to run into you at my future in-laws' house."

"It's a small world."

"That's what I keep hearing. Talking of which, I'm in Santa Barbara on business. I thought maybe we could have lunch together. You know . . . to talk over old times."

She swallowed hard. *Is that what he called it? Old times?* "Well . . . I . . ."

"Clara won't mind, if that's what you're worried about. If you like, you could ask your husband to join us. I'd like to meet him."

She bit her lip. "I don't have a husband."

"Oh. I'm sorry," he said, and she grimaced. Why was

everyone always sorry that she didn't have a husband? "So what do you say?"

She could think of a dozen or so reasons to say no—but every sentence that came to mind seemed to fall apart before reaching her lips. All she could think about with any real clarity was his warm smile and deep blue eyes. "I guess so . . ."

"Great! How about meeting me at Harry's At The Pier in, say, an hour?"

"An hour?" She glanced at her watch. "All right, I'll be there." She hung up the phone and sat staring at it. What was she thinking of? She couldn't meet him for lunch. Not a chance.

She picked up the phone with the intention of calling him back, then realized she had no idea how to get hold of him. She didn't even know the name of the company he worked for.

What was she going to do? Not show up? But then he'd probably drop by the office and that would only make matters worse. Better to meet him on some neutral turf—as far removed from her life as possible.

But how could she possibly have lunch with Jeff and not tell him the truth about Lily? Her mother was right; she should have told him that long-ago day when he'd sounded so cold and angry on the phone. She should have blurted it out and hung up. She should have done a lot of things.

She paced around her desk, trying to force herself to calm down. It was no big deal; she would meet him for lunch, and talk about . . . what? Not the cave-in, for that would only bring back memories too painful to deal with . . . Nor could she talk about Lily.

Her job. That's it. She'd talk about her job, or, better yet, get him to talk about his.

She glanced at her watch again. It was too soon to leave for lunch, but after returning to the computer and staring at the meaningless numbers on the monitor, she finally tore off her lab coat, flung it onto the back of her chair, and raced to the restroom for a quick makeup repair.

Jeff sat in his car staring down at the phone in his hand. He couldn't believe it. He'd done the very thing he told himself he wouldn't do.

Not that it meant anything, of course. Any feelings he had for Lynne Hancock had been soundly dealt with years ago. He couldn't afford to renew those old feelings.

The other day . . . when his blood seemed to boil at the sight of her—that was a fluke. He was surprised, that's all, astounded. He'd never expected to see her after all this time.

Besides, he'd damned near ruined his chances with Clara once. He wasn't about to jeopardize the relationship again.

He and Clara had broken up shortly after his rescue and for good reason. Despite the promise he and Lynne had made to each other, he hadn't been able to put her out of his mind. Had she not been engaged to be married, he would have tracked her to the ends of the earth. And when she had called him six months later, he very nearly did just that.

Damn, he was angry that day. Angry at his father. Angry at himself. Angry at Lynne for making it so hard. He hated knowing that he could so easily jilt Clara for someone else.

He'd tried all his life not to be his father's son. But upon hearing Lynne's voice on the phone that day, he realized, suddenly, that he was exactly like his father.

And that's why he'd pushed Lynne away, practically told her to take a hike, when all the time he was dying inside to go to her.

After the call, he made a superhuman effort to renew his affection for Clara. But things went from bad to worse. He wasn't very good at pretending.

Convinced he wasn't deserving of a woman's trust or love, he nonetheless called Lynne on a warm day in early March, nearly nine months to the day of their rescue. He wanted to apologize for his inexcusable behavior when she had called him. He never got the chance because a man answered. He was convinced it was the man she was going with, Gary, convinced they were already married. Crushed, he'd hung up.

After he and Clara had called off their engagement, it was two years before they saw each other again and two more years before they decided to get married. Not that he had any burning desire to marry, but Clara started reciting all that stuff about biological clocks and it just seemed like the right thing to do. *Was! Was the right thing to do!*

"So what the hell are you doing asking Lynne to lunch?"

He sighed and rubbed his forehead. Lynne had looked every bit as beautiful the other day as she had when he'd last seen her. Even now he recalled in minute detail how she had looked the day they'd been rescued, covered in dirt and sweat and an inner glow he had put there.

She'd since let her hair grow longer, and her face was a bit fuller, but otherwise she looked the same, even down to the fear he saw in her eyes—the same fear he saw there before the last of their candles had burned out in that mine, and it looked as if the whole damned ceiling was about to collapse. That kind of fear.

Something was wrong. He felt it in every cell of his body. That's why he had to see her again. Certainly, she wasn't afraid of him? Did she think he would say something about what had happened between them? How could he say anything when he didn't even know how to explain it himself.

He'd lost his head—they both had. Through the years he'd blamed it on a lethal combination of lust and passion, and had stoutly denied the possibility of anything more. Looking death in the face had its advantages; it sure got the adrenaline pumping and apparently a few other things as well.

Was she really worried about what he would say? It made no sense. She and that fellow she was going with at the time were apparently divorced. Judging by the fact she was using her maiden name, it must have been one of those nasty *War of the Roses* types of divorce.

So what was she afraid of? That he was going to the *National Informer?* One of those talk shows? Did she think he was going to write an exposé? What?

She had nothing to worry about from him. Not only was their secret safe, so was her virtue. He had cheated on Clara once, and, God almighty, being a Blakely, he might be tempted again. But not if he could help it.

How he hated to think he was like his father. His father had left a string of women behind him, including Jeff's mother. The idea of following in his father's footsteps was so repugnant to Jeff that he'd fought furiously in the past, as he did now, to forget how Lynne felt in his arms.

He'd honestly thought he'd put her out of his mind for good. Until Saturday, when he saw her at his in-laws'. What a shock to find she could still affect him.

It didn't matter. She could affect him all she wanted and it still wouldn't matter. He might be a Blakely, but he sure in hell didn't intend to follow in his father's footsteps—however much he was tempted.

Chapter Six

$\mathcal{H}$arry's At The Pier was a rustic restaurant on Stearns Wharf, popular with local diners and tourists alike. California sea gulls hopped onto weathered lobster traps stacked topsy-turvy along the wooden boardwalk. Two slack-pouched pelicans roosting on the shingled rooftop of the restaurant swooped down to follow a fishing boat.

Lynne pulled up in front of the restaurant next to the valet parking sign. Handing her car keys to the youthful male attendant, she turned. She spotted Jeff by the entry and her heart did somersaults.

Dressed in tan pants and a brown shirt, a sports jacket flung casually over his shoulder, Jeff's tall lean form filled the doorway. His dark hair was parted neatly at the side, a wavy swath dipping casually onto his tanned forehead.

He greeted her with a wary smile, revealing dimples almost identical to the ones she kissed every night while tucking Lily into bed. His eyes warmed appreciatively as his gaze slid down the length of her. "You look great."

She was dressed in a slim navy skirt that flared prettily at the hem. Her fitted knit top made her eyes appear more turquoise than blue and brought out the golden highlights of her hair.

He'd caught her on one of her better days. Her usual uniform, particularly when she worked in the field, was blue jeans, combat boots and a fatigue jacket. "So do you."

"Our table's ready. It's a bit cool out, so I thought you'd prefer to sit inside."

He led her to a cozy table for two by the window overlooking the white-crested sea. A strong breeze blew the yellow patio umbrellas outside.

"This is perfect," she said. He held the chair for her before draping his sports jacket over the back of his own and taking his place opposite her.

"Hope you're hungry." He fingered his menu. "I tried the seafood platter last time and it was great."

"I'm starved," she said, though in reality, she was too nervous to eat. She opened her menu. She didn't like knowing he was knowledgeable about a restaurant located within blocks of her home and even closer to her place of employment. "Do you come to Santa Barbara often?"

"About once a month or so," he said. "I envy you living here."

"I really like it."

He didn't wait long to bring up the one subject she would have given the world to ignore. In fact, he waited no longer than it took to order two seafood platters. "Clara's mother told me you decided not to let Lily be our flower girl. I hope it's not because of . . . you know . . . what happened between us."

He gazed at her with vibrant blue eyes ringed in dark lashes. Compelling and magnetic, his eyes were almost identical to Lily's at first glance. But a closer look revealed the smoldering emotions that made them very much his own eyes. Feeling as if a newly healed wound had been suddenly sliced open, she clasped her hands together in her lap.

Anger flared within her. She was tempted, so tempted to shout out. *How dare you come into my life after all this time and mention, however vague, making love to me? What gives you the right?* Instead, she forced herself to calmly reach for a dinner roll and break it in half on her bread plate.

"I would feel awful if I thought you pulled your little girl out of the wedding because of Clara. . . ."

Surprised, she looked up. "Clara?"

"She knows about us."

Her breath caught in her lungs. "I see."

He studied her intently and it felt as if he probed even the most secret part of her. "I thought maybe Clara had said something."

She shook her head. "I haven't talked to her since the bridal shower."

"I hope you're not angry with me for the way I acted the day you called me." He rearranged his knife and fork. "I had trouble adjusting after our rescue. I can't quite explain it. . . ."

She straightened the napkin on her lap, not sure she wanted to hear this. What was the point, after all this time? "My counselor said it's normal to go through a period of evaluation after a life or death situation."

"You went to a counselor?"

She nodded. "It was called trauma counseling." With more than its share of earthquakes, fires, riots and floods, it was hard to live in Southern California for any length of time without ending up in trauma counseling. She'd created quite a sensation in her support group for having been traumatized *outside* the state. "For a long time after the cave-in, I couldn't seem to concentrate . . . I began to question my life—everything."

His eyes locked with hers. "Did the counseling help?"

"It helped me sort things out."

"I was kind of mixed up myself afterwards. Clara and I had a lot of problems. She asked me outright if something had happened between you and me. I had to tell her the truth."

She liked knowing he hadn't lied. "How did she take it?"

"Not very well, I'm afraid. We broke up for a while.

It's taken us a long time to get back together."

But five years? Had it really taken that long? And what would happen if Clara found out the rest? That Lily was Jeff's daughter?

"What about your fiancé?" he asked. "Wasn't his name Gary?"

Surprised that he would remember her fiancé's name after all this time, she sat back. "It didn't work out."

"I noticed you're still using your maiden name."

"Gary and I were never married."

Something flickered in the depth of his eyes. "I see." He aligned his spoon next to his knife. "Did you break up before or after Lily was born?"

She looked at him unflinchingly. "Before."

"It must be tough. Being a single mother."

"It can be. At times."

The waitress brought their order and Lynne used the opportunity to change the subject. "Tell me about your job."

He smiled and she felt a squeezing pain inside. Lord, how could anyone see Jeff and Lily together and not guess the truth?

"There's not much to tell. I own a small computer company. I'm setting up a computer network for the Santa Barbara State College." While they ate, he talked about the plans he had for his growing company.

"It sounds exciting," she said. "Are you still interested in photography?"

His dimple deepened. "So you remembered." His heated gaze locked with hers and for the briefest moment the years seemed to melt away and she was back in his arms.

"I remember," she said, her voice barely more than a whisper. She remembered the smallest detail and probably could recite from memory every word he'd spoken during the days they'd spent together in that mine. Her counselor told her that in certain life and death situations, the senses worked overtime, but Lynne had her own theory for why everything about Jeff was so deeply ingrained in her memory.

"What else do you remember?" he asked.

It was a loaded question, but she answered it as smoothly as he asked it. "I remember your telling me you root for the Dodgers and Rams. You like country western music, old movies and love to drive the freeway during rush hour."

He shook his head in disbelief. "I can't believe you remember all that. Incidentally, I was kidding about the freeway."

She smiled. "Were you also kidding about Mexican food? You said you heartily disliked it."

"That part was true."

"What about the trip around the world? You said your dream was to photograph every corner."

"I'd hoped that was something Clara and I could do on our honeymoon. Unfortunately, she has her heart set on sitting on a beach in Maui."

Reality hit her full force. This was now and he had another life that didn't include her or Lily. "Do you and Clara plan to live in the Los Angeles area after the wedding?"

"For a while. Clara has a condo on Wilshire. It's close to where she works. She's the vice-president of one of the biggest advertising agencies in L.A."

"That's quite impressive," Lynne said.

"Getting back to Lily . . ." he began.

"What . . . what about Lily?"

"My mother said your little girl was really looking forward to being in the wedding." He hesitated. "I understand you had a conflict with work. Is that the real reason?"

"My schedule is crazy," she stammered. How she hated having to lie. "I never know from week to week if I can get Saturdays off."

"If transportation is the problem, I'm sure we can work something out." His elbow on the table, he stroked his chin. "I understand your mother insists upon staying at a hotel. Wouldn't she like having her little granddaughter with her?"

"Yes, but . . ."

"So what do you say?"

Her mind was suddenly a blank. "Say?"

"About Lily being in the wedding."

She stared down at her plate, not wanting to meet his steady gaze. "Clara couldn't possibly want a daughter of mine in the wedding."

"Clara's as anxious as I am to put the past to rest. Who knows? Maybe the three of us can become friends."

Lynne felt a sick feeling wash over her. Not only could they not be friends, but Lily could not be in Jeff's wedding. "I don't think this is a good idea, Jeff."

"There's no sense in your little girl being disappointed because of what happened years before she was born."

Years? How old did he think Lily was? Two? "I told you, Jeff. One has nothing to do with the other."

"Then it's settled?"

Nothing was settled and she didn't like feeling pressured, didn't understand it. Most men ignored the details of a wedding. They left things such as flower girls up to their brides. So why was Jeff pushing so hard? Did he suspect something? A cold shiver ran through her.

"I suppose you wonder why I care one way or the other about having a flower girl in the wedding."

She met his gaze. "It does seem rather odd."

He looked embarrassed. "I wish I understood it myself. I can't explain it. It just seems right, having her there." He shook his head. "It's the damnedest thing. I felt really crushed when Sarah told me Lily wasn't going to be in the wedding. Don't ask me why."

She stirred uneasily. "Is your family coming to the wedding?"

"No." A dark look crossed his face, but he didn't elaborate.

She remembered him saying he and his father never got

along, and she thought it best not to probe.

"So what do you say? Are you going to deny this rather confused bridegroom his flower girl?"

"I'll . . ." She swallowed hard, trying to find her voice. "I'll see what can be worked out."

Their waitress returned with their salads, but Lynne had no appetite left. She picked at the lettuce as she listened to Jeff talk, and tried to pretend she and Jeff were just two old friends having lunch together.

Only it wasn't working. Jeff was the father of her child. He was also the man who had stolen her heart all those years ago, and by the way her heart skipped a beat every time he turned his eyes on her, it was beginning to look like he still held a very large claim.

She couldn't believe it. Had she really been carrying a torch all these years? It wasn't possible. Yet there she was sitting across from him, heart pounding, knees shaking, thinking thoughts she had no business thinking.

While they ate, he talked about his job; she talked about hers. They became more comfortable with each other, less wary. Jeff shared her same fondness for Charlie Chan movies and mystery novels. She described the *I Madonari* festival and the sand castle contest in which she and Lily had recently won a ribbon for building a rather lopsided version of Sleeping Beauty's castle. "One look at that castle and you'd think Sleeping Beauty was a wino." Jeff laughed and told her about winning first place in a photograph contest.

Suddenly she noticed the lunch crowd had left the restaurant, and she quickly glanced at her watch. "Oh, no!" She was stunned to discover they had been sitting for two hours straight. She grabbed her handbag and rose from her chair. "I was due back at the office an hour ago."

"Oh, I'm sorry." He stared at his own watch. "I had no idea it was so late."

He followed her through the empty dining room, his hand touching the small of her back as she maneuvered around the tables. His fingers, light as a feather, sent a bolt of electricity shooting up her spine. She left him at the cashier after getting her parking ticket stamped and headed for the door.

She was still waiting for her car when he joined her moments later. Her gaze froze on his tall lean frame. He reached in his pocket for his sunglasses. "I really enjoyed our lunch."

"So did I."

"I hope you'll be able to attend the wedding. I'm sure your little girl will miss you if you're not there."

"Yes . . . well . . . I'll do my best. Jeff . . . in case we don't get a chance to talk before your big day, I want you to know I wish you all the happiness in the world."

The attendant drove up in her silver blue Celica and Jeff held the door for her as she slid behind the wheel. "Say hello to Lily for me."

She smiled up at him, and prayed she wouldn't do anything so foolish as to grow teary-eyed. She never thought to hear Lily's name on Jeff's lips. "I will." She waved and drove slowly along the pier. Stopping at the main gate, she opened the window and fumbled in her purse before handing the attendant her parking ticket. She was still shaking.

She forced herself to calm down. She might have succeeded had she not glanced through her side mirror. Jeff hadn't moved from the spot where she'd left him.

Chapter Seven

The wedding rehearsal was scheduled for the second Friday in August. The temperature displayed on the huge sign visible from the San Diego Freeway read 101 degrees.

Lynne had taken the day off. She was too nervous to work. Besides, she'd promised to pick her mother up at the Los Angeles International Airport. That meant she and Lily had to leave Santa Barbara by ten o'clock that morning to make it to LAX on time for her mother's one-thirty flight from Colorado.

Lily loved airports and insisted upon checking out all the Disney characters in the gift shop.

"Come on, sweetie. Your grammy's plane has probably landed."

Lily spotted her grandmother and flew past the other passengers and into Rosemary Hancock's open arms.

In her forties, Rosemary was an attractive woman with blond-streaked hair and a figure that still turned heads. "How's my big girl?"

"Did you bring me presents?" Lily asked.

"Lily!" Lynne scolded. "You know better."

Rosemary smiled. "Of course I brought you presents." She gave Lily a playful wink. "Did you bring me any?"

"I painted a picture just for you."

"Just what I need for my bedroom wall." Rosemary leaned toward Lynne, keeping her voice low so Lily couldn't hear. "I finally took down that painting your father dragged home for our fifteenth anniversary."

"The one of the hula dancer Dad thought looked like you? You liked that painting, Mother."

"That's when I was young and not nearly so blonde."

"You're still young."

Lily chattered the whole time it took to take the escalator to the lower level and walk to the baggage claim. She skipped over to the empty conveyer belt. Nothing pleased her more than to be the first one to spot her grammy's suitcases.

With Lily occupied, Rosemary immediately steered the conversation around to Jeff. "Well, what did he say when you told him?"

Lynne knew darn well her mother was referring to Jeff Blakely. "What did who say?"

"Don't play coy with me, Lynne Hancock."

"Shhhh. Keep your voice down. If you must know, I didn't tell him."

"What?" Her mother stared at her like she'd lost her wits. "You didn't tell him? Why not?"

"Do you think this is easy for me?"

"Who said it was going to be easy?" Rosemary sighed. "I should have stayed home."

"And I thought Sarah was such a good friend of yours."

"That's exactly why I shouldn't be here. Do you know what this is going to do to Sarah? She adores Jeff like he's her own son."

"There's no reason why she shouldn't. Jeff's a great guy."

"She was heartbroken when Jeff and Clara broke up a while back. If anything happens to break them up again . . . Lynne, I'm so sorry for getting you into this mess."

"Don't blame yourself, Mother. The chances of Sarah's daughter marrying Lily's father are astronomical. This makes the odds on winning the lottery seem like a piece of cake."

Rosemary's eyes filled with sympathy. "Sweetheart, what are you going to do?"

Lynne watched her little daughter and her heart ached. *I want a daddy just like that nice man. . . .* Good grief, how *was* she going to tell him?

"You *are* going to tell him, aren't you?"

"I have to. For Lily's sake. The only thing I haven't figured out is when."

Her mother studied her with a worried expression. "He'll probably be angry at you for not telling him sooner."

"I know." She only hoped any anger he felt for her wouldn't affect his feelings toward Lily. "I think it's best to wait a while. Until after Jeff and Clara have had time to settle into their new lives. I don't want to do anything to cause a problem between them."

"I hate to be the one to break the news, but Clara's not going to like this, no matter when she finds out."

"Grammy!" Lily called excitedly. "There's your suitcase!"

The wedding rehearsal was held at St. Matthew's Presbyterian Church in Woodland Hills. The church was one of those California architectural samplers that had gained popularity in the late '70s. On the outside it looked like a mass of angled redwood miraculously held together by glass. On the inside, it actually made sense. From its high beamed ceilings to its walls of glass, the entire sanctuary was built to make the most of the panoramic view of the San Fernando Valley.

Lynne stood by one of the open windows. A soft breeze traveled inland from the ocean, offering relief from the heat. The vast orange sun skirted the western horizon, and purple shadows spread across the valley floor. In the distance, the bumper to bumper traffic on the 101 Freeway wound its away across San Fernando Valley like a metallic snake as thousands of commuters made their way home.

Sarah rushed to greet them. "Rosemary! It's so good to

see you again. You look marvelous.''

''So do you.'' Rosemary exchanged a hug with her friend. ''You've met my daughter and granddaughter.''

''Indeed I have. We'll start the rehearsal just as soon as Jeff arrives.''

At the mention of Jeff's name, Lynne felt a nervous flutter in her stomach.

''Why don't you two make yourselves comfortable? Lily, come with me and I'll show you what to do.''

Sarah and Lily disappeared through the double doors and the organist began to warm up. ''Let's sit over there,'' her mother suggested, leading the way.

Lynne followed her to one of the polished oak pews. ''I wonder if I should stay with Lily.''

''Relax, Lynne. You look like you're about to face a firing squad.''

''How can I relax, Mother?'' She glanced around, but not counting the organist, she and her mother were the only ones in the sanctuary. ''You know how talkative Lily is. What if she says something?''

''Since she doesn't know who her father is, what could she possibly say?''

''She could tell Jeff her age or mention her birthdate.'' Lily had been known to announce her age to total strangers for no reason. ''He's not stupid. He could put two and two together and . . .''

''The only thing Jeff is thinking about at the moment is surviving this wedding. That's all any man thinks about at a time like this—trust me! So try not to worry about it, sweetie.''

She would if she could. The only problem was, when she wasn't worrying about Lily, her thoughts turned to Jeff, and that's when the real battle began.

Jeff was about to be married and she wished with all her heart this wasn't so. Without warning, her eyes began to blur.

''Lynne?''

His deep masculine voice floated across the empty

church and wrapped around her heart like a warm hug. She blinked back the tears before turning.

The mere sight of him made her heart do flip-flops and rendered her momentarily speechless. Thank God for her mother, who had already managed to engage Jeff in a conversation about modern architecture.

"I'm glad you like the church," Jeff said. He spoke to her mother, but his eyes never left Lynne's face. "I'm told that the windows are placed in such a way as to follow the sun from sunrise to sunset."

"What a lovely idea," her mother exclaimed. "Don't you agree, Lynne?"

"Yes," Lynne said and because his eyes seemed to probe her very soul, she forced a smile.

"Are you all right?" Jeff asked. He was bathed in the reddish light of the fast setting sun, but the warm glow in his eyes only increased the intensity of his gaze.

"Oh, you mean . . ." *The teary eyes, idiot. He wants to know why you're crying before the wedding has even begun.* "Allergies," she offered weakly.

He arched a dark brow. "In August?"

Her mother pulled out a handkerchief and dabbed at her own eyes. "August is a very bad month for allergies."

A heavy woman in a striped dress walked out to the center of the altar and began to practice her song. Her voice rose to the vaulted ceiling where it played among the rafters before fading away.

It was one of those modern songs that was more of a declaration of independence than a love song. *I'm my own woman, yeah, yeah!* Well, maybe not quite that bad, but bad enough.

"If you two ladies will excuse me, I best find out what I'm supposed to be doing." He turned on his heel and ducked through the doors.

"I didn't know you suffered from allergies," Lynne teased.

Her mother shook out her handkerchief and tucked it back into her purse. "Up until today, the only allergy I had was toward your father."

The rehearsal went without a hitch. Well, almost without a hitch. Lily wasn't particularly happy with some of the bride's choices and kept running to her mother and grandmother to complain.

"How come they're not playing 'Here Comes The Bride'?" she demanded to know on one occasion.

Lynne hushed her daughter. "Shhhh. You don't want to hurt anyone's feelings."

"But Mommy . . ."

"The bride can pick any music she wants," Lynne explained. *Even some ghastly funeral march.* "Now go back to your place."

If Lily was upset over the choice of music, she was truly mortified upon learning she was to carry a basket full of roses down the aisle, but was not to throw a single petal. However, it was seeing the dress she was going to wear that had her in tears.

Lynne quickly hustled her daughter outside to talk to her in private. They stood on the softly lit patio, Lily's sobs drowning out the loud chorus of crickets.

"I hate black," Lily cried.

Lynne had to admit it was an unusual color for a flower girl. "Lily, you have to wear whatever the bride wants you to wear . . ."

"But I look good in pink . . ."

"And you're going to look terrific in black."

Lynne stiffened at the sound of Jeff's voice floating out of the darkness. She glanced up at him just as he stepped into the light.

"But I hate black," Lily protested.

Jeff laid his hand on Lily's shoulder and winked. "Just between you and me, so do I. But I have to wear black too. I'm going to look like a penguin." His arms to his side, fingers pointing outward, he waddled like a penguin.

Lily giggled and even Lynne couldn't help but laugh.

"You look funny," Lily said, clearly charmed.

"I'm going to look a lot more funny tomorrow. So what

do you say, champ? You aren't going to let me look funny all by myself, are you?"

"But I can't throw rose petals."

Jeff leaned over until he and Lily were practically nose to nose. Seeing them together filled Lynne with unbearable guilt. They belonged together. Anyone could see that by the way they looked at each other. Lynne crossed her arm in front of her waist to ward off a sudden shiver, then pressed a tight fist over her mouth.

"I don't think Clara would mind if you threw one rose just for me."

Lily's eyes widened. "You want me to throw a whole rose?"

"The whole thing."

Lily smiled and Lynne felt a stabbing pain as Jeff matched her dimple for dimple.

Jeff straightened. "Better find your grandmother. I don't know about you, but I'm starved. We're due at the restaurant in about—" he glanced at his watch "—twenty minutes."

Lily ran off to find her grandmother, leaving Jeff and Lynne alone.

"I really appreciate you being so patient with her," Lynne began. "I'm afraid she gets a bit stubborn at times."

His straight white teeth gleamed against his suntanned skin as he smiled. "It seems to me stubbornness runs in the family. I seem to recall a certain blue-eyed brunette who refused to give up even when it looked like there was no hope."

"Me?" Lynne asked in surprise. "You're the one who kept trying to break through that rock."

"But only because you kept insisting you heard something. Okay, own-up time. Did you hear something or didn't you?"

Lynne blushed. "Well . . ."

"I thought as much."

"What better way was there to pass the time?" She bit

her lower lip. But there was no way to erase the leading words.

His eyes locked with hers for an instant before he turned his head to gaze at the shimmering lights of the city in the distance. He made no reply; he didn't have to. For she knew, knew with every cell in her body, what he was thinking.

She didn't know what to say, suddenly, where to look, what to do. It occurred to her that those first frenzied days of trying to break through solid rock had not been so insane, after all.

Working themselves into exhaustion had prevented them from focusing on each other. It worked. For a while. But on that last night together, passion and desire took precedence and nothing could have kept them apart.

"Jeff . . . I think it was a mistake for us not to talk about what happened in that mine." She hoped for an opening, however small, that would pave the way for the future. "Maybe after you've had time to settle into your new life . . ."

Jeff stood still as a statue, his eyes dark as a moonless night. "It would be an even worse mistake for us to talk about it at this late date." His voice was strangely distant, matching the aloofness on his face and sounding almost identical to the cold angry voice on the phone all those years ago. Both left no room for argument.

"Shall we?" he said abruptly. He held open the door of the church and stood waiting for her.

Not knowing what else to say, she walked past him. Her heart felt like a cement weight had settled in her chest. Maybe he was right; maybe it was too late to talk about the past.

That night, Jeff drove Clara back to her parents' house where she was spending the night.

"Coming in for a nightcap?" she asked.

He shook his head. A throbbing pain was centered over his right eye, and Clara looked pale with exhaustion. Premarital jitters, no doubt. "I think we both better get some sleep."

"Good idea." She threw him a kiss and climbed out of the car. "See you tomorrow and don't be late."

"I'll be there with bells on," he said.

Clara looked at him oddly, then backed away from the car.

How strange. Without realizing it, he'd used one of Lynne Hancock's expressions. *I'll be there with bells on,* she'd said, when he told her that one day he was going to travel back to the Pike's Peak area and put a sign up to commemorate their ordeal. How odd that he would recall her exact words, after all this time.

He waited until Clara was safely inside before pulling away from the curb. It was midnight by the time he arrived at his bachelor pad in Chatsworth. Popping the cap on a beer, he flipped on the TV and surfed through the channels.

Tomorrow at this time, he would be married and he and Clara would be starting their new life together. He took a long swig and flipped the TV off.

I think it was a mistake for us not to talk about what happened in that mine.

It had been hard for her, too. She hadn't married her boyfriend and he was only now getting around to marrying Clara. They sure in hell paid a big price for one night of lust.

For that's all it was: lust. Granted it was lust with a capital L, but that didn't change anything. They had what was equivalent to one of those shipboard romances that evaporated like sea mist almost as soon as the ship docked. That's what he and Lynne had, nothing more. Nothing less.

So what in God's name was there to talk about?

Chapter Eight

Lily jumped out of bed at dawn the following morning and peered through their hotel window, which overlooked the swimming pool. She loved staying at a hotel and had been delighted when Lynne had told her that rather than drive all the way back to Santa Barbara following the rehearsal, they would stay at the Hilton, which was only a mile from the church. "Can I go swimming, Mommy? Can I please?"

Lynne rolled to her side and buried her nose deeper into the pillow. She hadn't slept much these last few weeks, and last night she'd hardly slept at all. It wasn't just spending the night in a strange room that had kept her twisting and turning. It was Jeff, pure and simple.

Lily shook her. "It's time to wake up, Mommy."

Lynne groaned and forced herself to look at the clock. It was a little after six. The wedding was scheduled for eleven that morning. "Oh, all right." She sat up and stifled a yawn as she groped for her slippers. "We'll have breakfast downstairs. The pool doesn't open until eight."

Lily grinned a crooked smile and dug through the bureau drawer for her swimming suit.

Lynne stood and stared at the rumpled bed. Last night, she'd dreamed she was back in the gold mine with Jeff and they had made love in her dreams, just as they had all those years ago. The dream had seemed so real. She was still affected by the memory of his touch, could still recall with astounding detail how his lips had felt. She shivered and reached for her robe.

Hands behind her neck, she massaged her tight muscles. *Oh, Jeff. No man ever made love to me like you did.*

Clamping down on her thoughts, she shook her head, grabbed her overnight bag and shuffled toward the bathroom.

Dear God, help me get through the day.

Lynne and Lily arrived at the church an hour before the wedding. Lynne wore a blue summer dress with a fitted bodice, capped sleeves and a soft flaring skirt. A big picture hat framed her face, a blue ribbon trailing from its crown. It was the perfect hat for weddings, funerals and bad hair days.

No sooner had they arrived at the church than Lily remembered she'd forgotten the little jade rock she'd planned to give to the bride.

"Can we go back to the hotel? Huh, Mommy, can we?"

"We don't have time," Lynne explained.

"But I don't have anything old to give the bride."

"Maybe you can give the bride something new. I think I have a new penny in my purse."

"That's not special," Lily complained. She was dressed in shorts and a T-shirt and made a face when the wedding coordinator told her it was time to change.

Lynne gave her daughter a warning look as she led her into the dressing room. "Not a word from you, young lady," she said in a voice that plainly meant business. It wasn't like Lily to be so difficult. Lynne wondered if her own nervousness was having a negative effect on Lily. Children sensed anxiety in adults.

Lily stood silent, her lower lip in an uncharacteristic pout. Lynne worked the black organdy dress over her head and fluffed out the full gathered skirt. It really was a beautiful dress with its full skirt billowing over a frilly petticoat. Little star-shaped sequins decorated the puffy white sleeves and neckline.

"You look beautiful!" Lynne said, turning Lily around so she could see herself in the floor-length mirror.

It was clear by the look on Lily's face that she didn't agree and no matter how much Lynne tried to convince her otherwise, Lily stood by her conviction.

"I look ugly."

"No one looks ugly on a wedding day. It's against the law."

"The wicked stepsisters looked ugly at Cinderella's wedding."

"It wasn't against the law in those days."

A knock sounded at the door. "We're ready for pictures."

"We're coming," Lynne called. She reached for the little crown of red roses and pinned it on top of Lily's head. Stepping back, Lynne regarded her daughter with motherly pride. "Perfect." Now if she could just persuade Lily to flash her dazzling smile.

Confusion reigned outside the dressing room. Sarah raced about firing directions to the ushers, the florist and even the minister. The guests were starting to arrive. There was no sign of the bride, but Jeff walked out of one of the rooms and stopped to straighten his cuffs.

Watching him, Lynne suddenly recalled her dream and her face blazed. He glanced up and seeing Lily, he immediately began to walk like a penguin. Lily's frown disappeared with a giggle and she imitated him.

The photographer ordered Lily into the bride's dressing room, making Jeff stay behind.

"Why can't the groom come with us?" Lily asked.

"Some people think it's bad luck for the groom to see the bride before the wedding," Lynne explained. "Now smile pretty."

Clara stood in the center of the room looking beautiful and fragile. She wore a simple though elegant off-the-shoulder dress of silk organza with a long train. Lily stared up at the bride, a look of awe on her face.

The photographer went into action, arranging people like a florist arranged flowers. "Smile!" he'd call out from time to time and the lights flashed. "That's it." Finally, he motioned to Lily. "Now let's have the bride and the little flower girl alone."

After every possible shot had been taken, the bride was hustled through a back door only seconds before the groom walked in. Shots were taken of the groom and his best man, the groom and his soon-to-be in-laws, and the groom alone.

"How about me and the little flower girl?" Jeff asked, clapping his hands together. "Come stand by me, Lily."

Lily didn't have to be asked twice. She loved having her picture taken. She posed prettily next to Jeff's side. The camera clicked.

Suddenly as if the two of them had devised some secret language that only they could understand, they went into their penguin imitation.

Lynne knew there was a family resemblance between Lily and Jeff, but never was it so apparent as it was at that moment. Father and daughter gazed into the camera with the same mischievous look, the same dimpled smile.

Lynne glanced around, hoping no one else noticed the resemblance. Her hopes were dashed upon seeing Clara standing at the doorway. Moments earlier, Clara's face had been flushed with happiness, but now it was pale as her dress, her gray eyes dark with tortured disbelief.

Hoping against hope the look on Clara's face had nothing to do with Lily's resemblance to Jeff, Lynne started toward her.

Sarah spotted her daughter in the doorway and let out a scream. "Clara, what are you thinking? Jeff, don't look!"

But Jeff did look and Clara stared at him for a moment before turning and slamming the door shut between them.

"What the . . . ?" Jeff started toward the dressing room, but Rodney, his best man, held him back.

"This calls for a woman's touch," Rodney said. "Let Lynne handle it."

Jeff looked puzzled. "I don't understand. What happened? What's going on?"

"She's got a case of cold feet. That's all. It happens all the time. Nothing to worry about." Rodney draped his arm around Jeff's shoulder and led him away.

Lily stood by her mother, looking bewildered and worried. "The groom saw the bride," she said in a hushed voice.

"I know."

"Is that really bad luck?"

"Some people think it is, but I don't. Where's your basket?"

"Over there." Lily pointed to a table. "Oh, look, Mommy! A kitten." She dashed across the room. The kitten ran under a bookshelf and Lily dropped down on her hands and knees. "Here, kitty, kitty. I'm not going to hurt you."

"Get up, Lily. You're going to get yourself dirty."

The door of the bride's room opened and Sarah stepped out. She clapped her hands to get everyone's attention. "It's time to take your places."

Lynne straightened the crown of roses on Lily's head and brushed lint off the front of her dress. "Be a good girl now. And smile pretty." She planted a kiss on Lily's forehead. "Love you."

Leaving Lily in the care of the wedding coordinator, Lynne stopped momentarily in front of the bride's room, then turned and walked out to the narthex where she was met by one of the tuxedoed ushers. "Are you a friend of the bride or the groom?"

It was a simple question, yet it threw her into momentary panic. She quickly scanned the inside of the church and spotting her mother sitting on the bride's side, relaxed. "My mother's saving me a seat." She dodged by the usher and hurried down the aisle of the church.

"Oh, there you are," her mother said. "Where have you been?"

"Lily was having her picture taken."

Rosemary beamed. "I must remember to tell Sarah to order me a complete set." She leaned over and whispered. "This organ music would be perfect for a funeral."

"Shhhh." Lynne glanced around. The church was packed. She waited impatiently, crossing and recrossing her legs, and swung her foot in a circle. What was taking so long? She wanted so much for this day to end. Every minute seemed like eternity.

She couldn't feel any worse if she was on a speeding train that was about to collide. She would have felt a whole lot better had she talked to Clara. She tried to calm down. The look on Clara's face could have meant anything. Maybe she hadn't expected to see Jeff outside her door.

Still, something was holding up the wedding. They should have started twenty minutes ago. She glanced toward the back of the sanctuary. She couldn't shake the feeling that the speeding train was about to crash.

By eleven forty-five, a buzz of concern began to spread through the sanctuary as guests grew restless. Even the organist kept turning her head toward the back of the church.

Rosemary glanced at her watch. "What do you think is holding things up?"

Lynne looked around anxiously, no longer able to ignore the shuddering sense of foreboding that seemed to be closing in. What if Clara really had figured out the truth? What if she was confronting Jeff at that very moment with her suspicions?

Unable to think of any other logical reason for the delay, Lynne clutched her stomach. Oh, poor Clara! Poor Jeff! Their wedding day ruined all because of her. Why, oh why hadn't she told them before now? A cold chill shot down her spine. Lily!

What if Lily heard Jeff and Clara arguing over her?

Lynne began to shake as all sorts of possibilities occurred to her. Anxious to find Lily, she reached for her purse.

"Stay here, Mother."

She rose, but an usher blocked her way. "Excuse me, ma'am. Are you Lynne Hancock?"

She tried to speak but her voice caught in her throat. Soundlessly, she nodded.

"The bride would like a word with you."

Chapter Nine

$\mathcal{L}$ynne stiffened as the shock of the usher's request sank in. Panic threatened to overwhelm her, but she fought for control. *Dear God, let me be strong. For Lily's sake.*

Rosemary started to rise. "I'll go with you."

"No, stay here." She followed the usher down the aisle, through the lobby and into the wing of the church reserved for the bridal party.

She searched for Lily, but couldn't see her. Jeff looked pale and worried and her heart went out to him. How he must hate her. He broke away from the small gathering of worried-looking family members and hurried toward her.

"I don't know what's the matter with Clara," he said, his voice low. "She won't talk to anyone. For some reason, she asked to speak to you. I don't know what to think."

Lynne stared into the velvet depths of his eyes. *He doesn't know! Dear God, Clara hasn't told him yet!*

"Would you speak to her? Please?"

"What . . . what can I say to her?" Lynne stammered.

"I have no idea. The only thing I can think is that she's got a bee in her bonnet about you and me and . . . maybe you can reassure her."

She stared at him. Could that really be what this was about? A simple attack of jealousy? Somehow she doubted it. "Jeff, before I saw you at the bridal shower, we hadn't seen each other for almost five years. How could she possibly think . . . ?''

"I don't know, Lynne." He squeezed her hand tight. "Talk to her. Please, for me."

The last person she wanted to talk to was Clara. What she wanted to do was to take Lily and run. Instead, she nodded. "Do you know where Lily is?"

"She's outside with the minister's wife."

Lynne drew a deep breath and walked toward the bride's dressing room. It took a great deal of effort to knock on the door. "Clara?" Her voice was barely louder than a whisper. She cleared her throat and tried again. "It's me, Lynne Hancock."

A click sounded and the door opened a crack. Her hand shaking, Lynne reached for the handle. Jeff stood watching her, his face lined with worry.

Her gaze locked with his and that's when it hit her. She still loved this man, and had, perhaps, always loved him. And there was nothing—absolutely nothing—in the world she wouldn't do for him. Even if it meant having to convince another woman to marry him.

She entered the room quickly, while she had the nerve, then closed the door behind her. She took a moment to brace herself before turning to face Clara.

Clara's eyes were rimmed in red as if she'd been crying, but the actual tears were gone. Only anger and bitterness remained, and maybe even despair.

"When do you intend to tell him that Lily's his child?" Clara asked, her voice cold.

"I'm . . . not sure."

Surprise crossed Clara's face, followed by a look of anguish. Had Clara expected her to deny Lily was Jeff's child?

"Why haven't you told him before now?"

"I guess I was afraid to. I knew he was involved with you. . . ."

"You kept this from him because of me?" Clara's eyes snapped with anger. "How noble of you."

"It was a mistake. A stupid mistake. I had no right to keep this from him. From either one of you. Please, Clara. Don't let anything that happened in the past ruin this day for you. Jeff loves you."

Clara measured her with a cool appraising look. "Yes, he does. That's why I see no reason to tell him about Lily at this late date. It will only complicate our lives. All our lives. I've got some money put away . . . I'd be glad to put it in a trust fund for Lily."

Incredulous, Lynne stared at her. "This isn't about money. I've already robbed him and Lily of four years together. That was a mistake. It's a mistake I intend to correct as soon as possible."

"I'm asking you, no, I'm begging you, not to tell him."

"I know you love Jeff and I'm sure once you've had time to think about this—"

"There's nothing to think about!"

"I should have told him, Clara. Years ago. He has the right to know."

Clara sagged against the dressing table, her face a white mask.

Lynne felt sorry for her. "I wish you hadn't found out about Lily today, of all days. If it'll help, I'll wait until you've had time to settle in your marriage. That's all I can promise. I'm so sorry you had to find out this way."

"So am I," Clara said, her shoulders slumped forward. To her credit she didn't argue. She simply turned and stared at herself in the mirror.

"Jeff's waiting for you. I hope you don't let him down." Unable to think of anything more to say, Lynne walked out of the room and closed the door behind her. Jeff stood a short distance away, trying to comfort Clara's distraught mother.

Upon seeing Lynne, Sarah's hand flew to her chest. "Oh, thank goodness. . . . Is Clara all right?"

Lynne met Jeff's eyes, then quickly looked away. "I think so."

"I'll go to her." Jeff started for the door, but Sarah grabbed his arm.

"I'll go." After Sarah disappeared inside the dressing room, Jeff sat down on a wooden bench, his arms on his lap, and held his head with both hands.

Lily ran through the patio doors, her shiny black shoes tapping across the floor. "Is the bride okay?"

"I think so, sweetie." Lynne walked over to Jeff and put her hand on his shoulder.

"Clara's having second thoughts about marrying me. That's it, isn't it?"

Lynne tried to force a reassuring smile, but none would come. "It's not unusual for a bride to get cold feet."

"Is that what you think it is? Cold feet?"

Before Lynne could think of a reply, Sarah's mother hurried out of Clara's room. Moving in a whirlwind of activity, she clapped her hands and started issuing orders. "Everyone! Take your place. The wedding is about to begin!"

Jeff jumped to his feet and straightened his cuffs and bow tie. How handsome he looked, how relieved. He gazed down at her and she smiled back, though her heart ached. *I'm happy for you, Jeff. I really am happy.* "I told you it was just cold feet," she said, the cheerfulness in her voice belying the heaviness in her heart.

"You always did know what to say in a crisis." They stared at each other and his gaze caressed her lips before he quickly turned away. Puzzled and confused, she stared after him. So it wasn't her imagination. He did feel something for her. That explained the strong emotional pull she'd sensed between them. She resisted the idea with everything in her. She didn't want to know that the same irresistible attraction they'd felt for each other all those years ago still existed. Not now, not when he was about to wed someone else.

She turned and desperately fought against the tears that threatened to overwhelm her. Thank goodness for Lily, who stood holding onto the little white wicker basket with both hands, her knuckles white, as if she felt insecure. Not wanting to upset Lily any more than she already was, Lynne forced a smile.

The wedding coordinator swept by. "Lily, how many times do I have to tell you? Hold the basket by the handle."

Lynne hastily dropped a kiss on Lily's forehead, giving one soft rounded shoulder a tight squeeze. "Hold it by the handle," she whispered and without another word, she hurried into the church to take her place on the pew next to her mother.

Rosemary leaned toward her, her voice low. "What in the world is going on?"

"I'll tell you later," Lynne whispered. Her hands shaking, she took the program from her mother and tried to make sense of the words that swam across the page. *Dear God, please let it soon be over.*

Jeff and his best man walked out of the side door at the front of the church and joined the minister. Standing a couple of inches taller than the other two men, Jeff looked strangely somber.

Lynne quickly looked away. If Jeff had any doubts about marrying Clara, Lynne didn't want to know about it.

The matron of honor led the small procession down the aisle. Lily was next, a wide smile on her face. She stopped in her tracks and dug inside her basket. Some of the guests laughed and Lynne sat forward, wondering if Lily was having a problem. At long last Lily tossed a single red rose onto the pure white runner and Lynne breathed a sigh. Standing at the altar, Jeff winked at Lily.

"I never heard of black at a wedding," her mother whispered in her ear. "No wonder poor Sarah's been going out of her mind."

"Shhhh."

The "funeral" march grew louder and the guests promptly rose to their feet. Looking elegant and regal as she glided down the aisle on her proud father's arm,

Clara's smile, nonetheless, couldn't have looked more fake had she cut it out of a magazine and pasted it on her face.

Jeff stepped next to Clara's side and faced the minister. Next to them, Lily fiddled with her basket.

Rosemary craned her neck to better see her granddaughter. "What in the world is Lily doing?"

"I have no idea."

"Dearly beloved . . ."

No sooner had the minister started to read from the prayer book than a black streak flew out of the basket and landed on Clara's train. Clara screamed and dropped her flowers.

"It's just a kitten." Lily dashed after the kitten, but the frightened animal ran beneath the bride's dress.

Suddenly, all bedlam broke loose. The maid of honor dove after the tabby. In her haste, she knocked the candles across the organ, setting the sheet music on fire. With an audible gasp, the guests rose to their feet.

The best man leaped toward the organ, knocking over the elegant arrangement of white roses in his haste, and tripping over the vase. But Jeff was right behind him and, after pulling Lily out of danger, managed to grab the music and stomp out the flames before any further damage was done.

The maid of honor, holding the trembling kitten at arm's length so as not to get fur on her dress, walked quietly down the center aisle to deposit the cat outside and with an audible sigh, the guests took their seats.

Everyone stared at the altar that had moments earlier looked beautiful. It was now in shambles. Flowers were strewn from one end to the next. Even the minister, who hadn't moved an inch during the fracas, looked frazzled, the prayer book still clutched in his hand.

Suddenly, Clara grabbed Lily by the arms and shook her. "You little brat. If it hadn't been for you!" She raised her hand.

Jeff moved quickly and managed to pull Lily away in

time. Lily ran down the aisle and buried her face against her mother's shoulder.

Clara stared in horror at her own raised hand. Finally she turned and ran from the sanctuary.

Chapter Ten

$\mathcal{I}$t seemed like hours had passed since the guests had filed out of the church, talking in hushed voices like mourners at a funeral. Some had seemed reluctant to leave, as if they thought the bride or groom would have a change of heart. But when it became obvious that neither Jeff nor Clara intended to make an appearance, even the family members gave up and went home.

Lynne and Lily sat on the stone edge of the water fountain inside the enclosed courtyard.

Lily was inconsolable and, despite Lynne's efforts to comfort her, continued to sob her little heart out. "I didn't mean to make the bride angry, Mommy."

"I know, sweetie." Even though Clara had raised her hand at Lily, Lynne felt no ill will toward her. Today had been a bride's nightmare. First Clara discovered Lily was Jeff's daughter. Then her wedding was ruined. It was enough to make anyone snap.

"I forgot my jade rock, so I wanted to give the bride a kitten."

"A kitten?" Of course. *Something new* . . .

Lily continued to sob in her mother's arms. "I don't want them to get a . . . a . . . divorce like grammy and grampa."

"Oh, sweetie." Lynne rubbed Lily's back. "They can't get a divorce because they never got married."

Lily looked up, tears streaming down her face. "Are they going to get married, Mommy?"

Lynne glanced at the door leading to the bride's room. "I don't know. I just don't know."

Rosemary beckoned from the open church doors. "I'm ready to go back to the hotel."

Lynne wiped Lily's face with a handkerchief. "Grammy's going to take you back with her. I'll be there in a little while."

"Are you sure you don't want to come with us?" Rosemary asked. "It seems to me this is between Clara and Jeff. What could you possibly hope to accomplish by staying?"

"I don't know, Mother. I'm responsible for this whole mess." She handed her mother the keys to the car, along with her hotel key. "I . . . I have to stay . . . Just for a while."

"How are you going to get back to the hotel?"

"Don't worry, Mother. I'll take a taxi if I need to."

"Very well. Come along, Lily. That's a girl."

After her mother and Lily had left, Lynne continued to sit on the edge of the fountain. If only she hadn't been such a coward. If only she'd told Jeff the truth from the start, none of this would have happened.

The door opened and Jeff stepped outside the church, his face drawn. He looked surprised to see her and quickly glanced around as if to make certain no one else was still on the scene. He had removed his tuxedo jacket and bow tie and his hair was mussed.

"Where's Lily?"

"I sent her back to the hotel with her grandmother. She's really heartbroken, Jeff. She never meant . . ."

He held up his hand. "I know." He sat on the edge of the fountain next to her.

Her heart ached for him. At that moment she would have done anything to change things, to make him smile again. "I'm so sorry, Jeff. I blame myself for what happened. I should have watched her more carefully. I should have . . .''

''It's not your fault, Lynne. I mean . . .'' He shook his head. ''I know things got out of hand, but it's not like Clara to overreact.''

''She had every right to be upset, Jeff. Every woman dreams of having the perfect wedding. I'm so sorry.''

Jeff pressed his hands together. ''Clara wouldn't have hit Lily. I know she wouldn't have.''

Lynne recalled the look of horror on Clara's face as she stared at her own uplifted hand and knew Jeff spoke the truth. ''I know.''

''None of this makes sense to me. I never thought Clara was the type to get wedding day jitters.'' He stood. ''I'm going home. Do you have a ride back to your hotel?''

''No, but . . .'' The last thing she wanted was to be alone with him in the cramped confines of a car, not even for a short time. ''What about Clara?''

''Clara left with her parents.''

''Oh.''

''Come on. It's on my way.''

Since she couldn't think of an excuse to turn down his offer, she walked with him to the parking lot. Only four cars remained, including Jeff's white Ranger.

Seated in the passenger seat, she watched Jeff run around the front of the car and slide behind the wheel. ''Did you get a chance to talk to Clara?''

''She refuses to talk to me. I'll try to see her later, after she's had time to calm down.''

She rubbed her neck. Clara had asked Lynne not to tell Jeff about Lily. Would she change her mind now that the wedding was off? What a nightmare. Lynne was sorely tempted to drive back to Santa Barbara and barricade herself until this whole mess had blown over.

Jeff didn't say a word as he drove to the hotel and Lynne was grateful for the silence.

The hotel was little more than a mile away, but the trip

seemed to take forever, mainly because of the traffic by the mall.

Thinking she saw her mother in front of the hotel, Lynne pulled off her sunglasses. It *was* her mother, talking to a policeman. Lily was nowhere in sight.

Jeff pulled behind a long line of cars and stopped. Alarmed, Lynne jumped out of the car. "Mother? Where's Lily?"

Rosemary turned, her face white. "I hoped she was with you."

Lily was missing. The words echoed in her head, filling her with horror and a sense of helplessness. Lily was gone, missing, and not a single person in the entire hotel remembered seeing her.

Jeff, Lynne, and Rosemary met with Detective Wiselow in the manager's office on the mezzanine. Jeff sat next to Lynne, giving her arm a reassuring squeeze. "She's just wandered off somewhere," he whispered soothingly. "They'll find her."

She nodded at his comforting words, but a cold gnawing fear held her in its icy grip.

Rosemary sat directly in front of the detective. Since Lily had disappeared while under Rosemary's care, she was questioned first. "What time did you arrive at the hotel?"

Rosemary twisted a lacy handkerchief between her fingers. "I would say it was about two o'clock. Lily was hungry so I ordered us both milk and sandwiches. I promised her she could go swimming after I showered and changed."

Detective Wiselow scribbled something on his notepad. "So you left Lily alone while you showered."

"She wasn't exactly alone," Rosemary said. "The bathroom is right off the bedroom and I left the door open." Rosemary turned to Lynne. "She was watching TV. When I came out of the bathroom, she was gone."

"It's not your fault, Mother. I've done the same thing myself."

Lynne was questioned next. She searched through her wallet for a recent photograph of Lily.

"Cute little girl," Detective Wiselow said. He looked at Jeff. "You're the little girl's father?"

"No. I'm just a friend."

"Really? I could have sworn . . ."

Lynne stood abruptly. "Can't we just get on with the search?" Everything seemed to be taking so long. Jeff put his arm around her and she clung to him.

Detective Wiselow pocketed the photograph. "We're doing everything we can, ma'am. I'll have copies of this photo made and we'll send them to all the local TV stations ASAP. We should be able to make the six o'clock news." He walked out of the office and stood in the hallway, talking to a uniformed policeman.

"Come on," Jeff said. "I'll take you to your room so you can get some rest."

"Rest? Jeff, how can I rest with my daughter God knows where? You know how high the crime rate is in this area. Innocent people have been shot to death for making a wrong turn." Tears welled up in her eyes. "Oh, Lily . . ."

"Lily's going to be all right. We've got to believe that."

"Jeff's right," her mother said, sounding more confident than she looked.

Wiping her eyes, Lynne forced herself not to give in to the panic that was rising inside. She wanted to believe what Jeff said was true. She took a deep breath and reminded herself she had to be strong for Lily's sake.

Jeff stayed by Lynne's side as they took the elevator to the eighth floor. Rosemary insisted upon remaining downstairs should the detective have further questions.

After they reached Lynne's room, Jeff used the phone to call Sarah. Unable to sit still, Lynne wandered around the room. She stopped to pick up Lily's flower girl dress and buried her nose in the shiny black fabric. Wiping her tears away, she hung the dress in the closet and looked around for something else to do to keep herself busy.

She spotted the green stone on the bureau that Lily had planned to give the bride. Lily called it jade, but it was actually aventurine. *Something old . . .* If only she'd driven back to the hotel for the stone, none of this would have happened.

The hours crept by slowly. At last it was twilight and the first star appeared in the sky. Lights illuminated the kidney shaped pool and flaming torches cast dancing shadows upon the soft swaying palms. It would soon be dark and with this thought came the tears. Her little girl was gone and there was nothing she could do.

Jeff hung up the phone and joined her by the window, his face lined with concern and frustration. Lynne felt a pang of guilt for keeping him. He had his own problems. He belonged with Clara, not her. Even if he was Lily's father.

Suddenly she was reminded of another time, another place when she'd needed him every bit as much as she needed him at that moment. *We're going to die, Jeff. I just know it. . . .*

Shaken by a sense of déjà vu, a shudder shot through her. "You're cold." He glanced around the room as if searching for something to wrap around her shoulders.

She shook her head. "Oh, Jeff, where can she be?"

"The police are doing everything possible. They're going to find her, Lynne. You mustn't give up hope." *They'll find us, Lynne. You mustn't give up hope.*

"Come on." He took her hand and led her to the bed. A tray sat on the bedstand with an untouched glass of milk and a plate of stale sandwiches. "I'll call room service."

"I'm not hungry."

Ignoring her protests, he grabbed the phone and started pressing buttons. "Please send a pot of hot tea and some sandwiches to room 809."

She lay back against the pillow and closed her eyes. It had been so long since anyone had taken care of her.

A knock sounded. Lynne sat up and held her breath. It was only Rosemary. "Nothing." She crossed to the only chair in the room and collapsed. "Where could she be?"

"Does she know anyone in the area?" Jeff asked.

"No one." Lynne rubbed her head. It wasn't like Lily to run off.

"She wouldn't have tried to find her way back to Santa Barbara, would she?"

"I don't think so, Jeff. That's over a hundred miles away."

Room service arrived with their sandwiches, but Lynne didn't feel much like eating.

They talked to the detective at eight and again at nine. At nine-thirty, Lynne talked her mother into going to her room. "Try to get some rest, Mother, please. I may need you later."

"Lynne's right," Jeff said.

"All right, but promise you'll let me know if there's any word."

"You'll be the first to know."

At ten Jeff called Sarah again. He hung up the phone looking grim-faced. "I hate to leave you alone, Lynne, but . . ."

"You don't have to explain," she whispered. "Go to her. She needs you."

He studied her face. "Are you sure?"

She nodded.

His hand on the doorknob, he glanced over his shoulder. "I'll be back."

Lynne rolled on her side and stared at the silent telephone. *Dear God. Where is she?*

Chapter Eleven

*J*eff drove to Clara's parents' house and banged on the door. Sarah let him in, looking every bit as worried and distressed as she had sounded on the phone.

"Oh, Jeff. None of this makes sense. Now she's talking about breaking up with you altogether. I don't understand any of this."

"Let me see her."

"She doesn't want to see you."

He took Sarah's hands in his. "Please?"

"All right. But I'm not responsible if she throws you out."

He kissed one tear-stained cheek and ran up the stairs two at a time. Clara's old room was on the right. He banged on the door. "Clara. Open up."

To his surprise, the door sprang open. He entered the room prepared to duck. Clara stood facing the door, looking pale, but surprisingly calm, which was more than he could say for himself.

Dressed in a white satin robe, she wore no makeup and a towel was wrapped turban style around her head. She sat at her dressing table and picked up a nail file.

He pushed the door shut behind him, surprised at the sudden rage he felt. He'd been to hell and back these last few hours, imagining the worst. And what was Clara doing? Filing her nails! "Would you mind telling me what the hell is going on?"

"Let's just say I finally came to my senses," she said, her voice perfectly calm.

Jeff stared at her in disbelief. Was it asking too much to see a little emotion? "Great! Now maybe you will tell *me*, the man you left at the altar, exactly what that means?"

"I did something today I'm not proud of."

"For chrissakes, Clara. I know you wouldn't have harmed Lily. You were upset."

She tossed her nail file down. "Yes, I was upset, Jeff, but not for the reasons you think. I asked somebody to do something today that I had no right to do. And do you know why? I wanted to save our marriage."

"Save our . . ." His mind reeled in confusion. "What the hell are you talking about?"

"I asked someone to lie because I was afraid of what would happen if the truth came out."

"Are you purposely talking in circles to make me crazy?"

"I was afraid of losing you."

"Is that why you left me at the altar? Because you were afraid of losing me?"

Clara stood and walked across the room. She sat down on the edge of her bed. "Things haven't been the same between us since the cave-in."

"Dammit! Don't tell me you're going to dredge that up again!"

"I thought it would be okay," she continued. "I honestly thought we had a chance of making a life together. But that was before I realized our relationship is turning me into an insecure woman. It seems I would do anything to protect what little part of you belongs to me."

"Nothing you're saying makes sense."

"It makes perfect sense. I think you really do love me, Jeff. But not the way I need to be loved. Not the way you love her."

Jeff couldn't believe his ears. "Are you talking about Lynne?"

"Yes."

"You think I love her?"

"You *do* love her."

He threw up his hands. "Up until a couple of weeks ago, I hadn't seen her in years." He couldn't believe what he was hearing. Had Clara suddenly gone bonkers? "Who do you think I am? My father? Do you think I'm going to run off every time a pretty woman passes by?"

"You're very different than your father, Jeff. But I think you've been trying so hard not to be like him, you've forgotten how to be yourself."

His jaw clenched. "I have no idea what you're talking about."

"Why were you going to marry me?"

"You know why."

"You can't say it, can you? You can't say you love me."

"This is ridiculous . . ."

"Is it? Do you know what's on your desk at work? Not a photograph of me. Of us. No, you have a piece of quartz you saved from that cave-in."

Lynne had given it to him after she'd found it in the mine. She called it smoky quartz crystal. "So big deal. It makes a great paperweight."

"And every year, you circle June 10th on your calendar, the day you became trapped. Most people would want to forget, but you do everything to remember."

Jeff sat on the bed next to her, his elbows on his lap. Everything Clara said was true. But the part about being in love with Lynne . . . that was crazy.

He had to admit he was still very much attracted to Lynne and yes, in the days after they'd been rescued, he was tempted to see her again and maybe even pick up where they had left off. But he hadn't. He'd tried his damnedest to do right by Clara, to make up to her for his unfaithfulness, and that was a hell of a lot more than his father had ever done.

Startled by the thought, he stared unseeing at a magazine on the floor. So Clara was right. He'd been so busy trying to right the wrongs committed by his father, he'd ended up hurting a lot of people, Clara most of all.

Next to his side, Clara sighed. "Thanks for not denying it. It saves us both a lot of trouble."

"Maybe you're right. Maybe I didn't want to do to you what my father had done to my mother . . . but that was then and this is now."

"I saw the way you looked at her at our wedding shower."

"I was surprised. I hadn't expected to bump into her after all these years . . ."

"And last night? At the rehearsal?"

He jumped to his feet. "Dammit, Clara. I wanted things to work out for us."

"I know you did, Jeff. We both did." She rose to her feet and pulled off her diamond engagement ring. "You know something? I'm almost relieved it's over. I've been so busy trying to be the right woman for you, I've forgotten how to be me. I've become someone I don't even recognize and I don't much like that person." She handed him the ring.

The diamond cut into the palm of his hand. Part of him wanted to deny everything she said, but he couldn't. Good God! Could it really be true? Was he in love with Lynne? "Clara, I never meant to hurt you."

"I know." She forced a smile. "You better go before we both do something beneath our dignity. Tell Lily I'm sorry."

At the mention of Lily, Jeff felt a gut-wrenching pain, like a knife, slice through him. "Lily's missing."

"Missing?" Clara looked genuinely concerned. "Oh, no! I'll never forgive myself if something happened to her. Never!"

"No one's blaming you, Clara. It was a hard day for all

of us.'' And it was going to be an even harder night. ''Do you mind if I use your phone?''

''Of course not.'' Clara sat quietly at her dressing table and brushed her hair while Jeff called the hotel.

Lynne's voice sounded strained as if she'd been crying. ''No word yet,'' she said in reply to his question. ''Is . . . is Clara all right?''

He met Clara's eyes in the mirror. ''Yeah,'' he said. ''I'll see you later.'' He hung up. ''Nothing.''

''You better go, Jeff.''

''Will you be okay?''

''I'm fine.''

He leaned over and kissed her on the forehead. ''Take care of yourself, Clara.''

''You too. And Jeff? Good luck on finding Lily.''

He left her room and raced down the stairs. He only hoped that by the time he reached the hotel, Lily would have been found.

He took the 101 freeway from Clara's house and headed back to the hotel. Just before he pulled into the underground parking structure adjacent to the hotel, he passed a billboard advertising milk. He pulled into the first available space and suddenly recalled something Rosemary had told Detective Wiselow. His heart skipped a beat. Maybe, just maybe, he knew where to find Lily. He pulled out of the space with a squeal of his tires, and headed for the exit.

St. Matthew's Presbyterian Church was dark, except for a few security lights, and was probably locked. He should have known it was a dumb idea. He banged the steering wheel with his fist. *Where are you, Lily?*

God, he felt close to her. Who could explain it? He liked children well enough, but had never connected to one as quickly and readily as he had connected to Lily. From the first moment he'd laid eyes on her at the bridal shower, when she'd cried out for her mother, he felt like he knew her.

Tonight she seemed so close to him, he imagined he

could hear her voice. "Mommy. I want my Mommy."

His heart leaped. "Lily!" He jumped out of the car. "Lily, is that you?"

Lynne's nerves were so taut she was convinced she was about to snap. She jumped at the sound of a knock. Thinking it was Detective Wiselow or her mother, she ran to open the door, totally unprepared for the wondrous sight that greeted her. "Lily!"

"She's asleep," Jeff whispered. He brushed past her and headed toward the bed. He lay Lily on the bed and pulled off her shoes before tucking her beneath the blankets. Lily never once opened her eyes.

"Oh, God." Lynne dropped by her daughter's side. She smoothed the bangs away from Lily's forehead and ran her fingers along a sweet rounded cheek. "Oh, my dear sweet baby." She looked up at Jeff with tears of gratitude. "Where'd you find her?"

"At the church," Jeff said softly. He sat on the opposite side of the bed and gently stroked Lily's back.

"The church? Whatever made you think to look there?"

"It was something your mother told the detective. She said she ordered milk and sandwiches for the two of them. But when I saw the tray by the bed, there was only one glass of milk."

"I don't understand. Why would that make you check the church?"

"The kitten, Lynne. She took the milk to the kitten."

Lynne shook her head in disbelief. Lily never failed to amaze her. "The church is at least a mile away. It never occurred to me . . ."

"I know. By the time she reached the church, she was so tired, she fell asleep in the little courtyard. It was dark when she woke and she was too scared to walk back."

Lynne's heart ached for her daughter. Jeff's hand was on Lily's back and Lynne covered his hand with her own. "Thank you," she whispered through her tears. "Thank you for finding Lily."

He smiled. "Thank God she's all right."

She studied his face, saw the love and concern for Lily and it only deepened her conviction that she had made a terrible mistake. She should have told him years ago. "How's . . . Clara?" she stammered.

"I think she's okay. She was concerned for Lily."

"She must hate Lily. Hate me."

"She doesn't, Lynne."

"I wouldn't blame her if she did. Lily ruined her wedding."

"I think we both realize that Lily saved us from making a big mistake." His burning eyes held hers. "You know it's funny. I've known Clara for a good many years, but tonight I felt like we actually communicated for the first time." He raked his fingers through his hair. "She said something that got me to thinking. She said I tried so hard not to be like my father, I'd forgotten how to be myself."

"I'm sure Clara didn't mean it the way it sounded. After what happened today . . ."

"She did mean it and she's right. I was just six when my father left my mother for someone else. Every night she'd come into my room and cry on my pillow. I can't tell you what that did to me."

Lynne squeezed his hand. She was in college when her parents divorced, but it still hurt. "I can imagine."

"I didn't want to cheat on Clara like my father cheated on my mother. I guess that's why I was so determined to deny my feelings for you."

"Is that why you sounded so angry the day I called?"

He grimaced as if in pain and she recognized regret in the depth of his eyes. "I'd spent weeks, months battling my feelings for you. I thought I could put the memories behind me—and then I heard your voice and it was like having to start all over again. But later, after Clara and I broke up, I had the strongest urge to call you. I had wanted to call you long before then, but suddenly I was obsessed. I dreamed you needed me. This sounds crazy, but at one point I could have sworn you called my name."

"Why didn't you call?"

"I did. Sometime in the spring. I think it was March. But when a man answered, I hung up. I didn't want to make trouble for you."

"But Gary and I had already . . ." She stopped. It wasn't Gary who had answered the phone to Jeff that long-ago day. Not if it was March. And if it wasn't Jeff, the only other man it could have been was her father. She felt dizzy. Sick. She felt hot and cold. She needed air. She stood and turned toward the open window, gasping.

Her father had spent only one day at her house and that was the day she was in the hospital having Lily. Her thoughts scrambled. How she needed Jeff that day. She'd even called his name out loud during one god-awful contraction.

"Lynne? Are you all right?" He lay a hand on her shoulder. "You're shaking. Maybe you better get some sleep."

She turned to face him. Oh, God, this was crazy. To think he'd called her on the very day Lily was born. Crazy and yet . . . so right. "Jeff, there's something you need to know."

"Tell me in the morning. We'll all feel better then. I'll take you, Lily and your mother to breakfast. Speaking of which, you better call your mother and tell her the news or she'll never talk to either one of us again." He squeezed her shoulder and turned toward the door.

"I'll call her, Jeff, but first I have to tell you something. Tonight. I have to tell you tonight." She glanced down at Lily sleeping peacefully. How sweet she looked, how angelic. "I don't want to wake her."

He regarded her thoughtfully, a puzzled frown on his forehead. Obviously he sensed something was wrong. "We could talk in the bathroom." He moved silently across the room and flipped on the bathroom light.

The bathroom wasn't much bigger than the shaft of the gold mine where they had been trapped. She walked to the sink and waited for him to close the door. The last twelve hours had taken its toll. Jeff looked exhausted.

"Maybe you're right," she said. "Maybe this can wait until later." She grabbed the doorknob, but he closed his hand over her wrist.

"Tell me now, Lynne." When she failed to reply, he tilted his head back. "Are you okay?"

"No, I'm not okay, Jeff. I've made a terrible mistake."

"What are you talking about? What mistake?"

"I'm talking about you and . . ."

He rubbed his forehead. "What happened between Clara and me is not your fault."

"This has nothing to do with Clara. If you would just listen!"

He looked startled by her outburst and maybe even hurt. She felt terrible. Her nerves were frayed; she wasn't thinking right. "I didn't mean . . ."

"I know." He sat on the edge of the bathtub. "Now suppose you start at the beginning."

Steadying herself, she began. "I told you Gary and I . . . broke up."

His brow arched. Apparently he hadn't expected her to bring up Gary. "You said you broke up shortly after the cave-in."

"What I didn't tell you was why. I was pregnant . . ." Suddenly, all the pain and confusion of those early months came back to haunt her anew. She turned and pressed against the sink with the palms of her hand. "I was pregnant with your child . . ."

Only the low whirring sound of the bathroom fan broke the silence. She raised her eyes to the mirror and met his gaze.

Jeff sat frozen, his face drained of all color. His eyes were wide with shock. "Lily?"

She turned to face him. "Yes."

"Lily's my child?" He stared at her in disbelief. "But she can't be any older than . . ."

"She turned four in March."

"Four? Damn!" He stood. "I must be the world's biggest fool."

"Lily's small for her age," she said hastily. "It's only natural that you would think . . ."

"Think? That's my problem, I haven't been thinking. Why didn't you tell me?"

"I wanted to. I called . . ."

His lips thinned with anger, his eyes blazed. "You called me once, dammit! Once!"

"You sounded so angry."

"What if I was? Is that any excuse not to tell me?" Suddenly, he looked drained. "I wasn't angry." His voice broke. "Not at you. I felt guilty for cheating on Clara like my father had cheated on my mother."

"You weren't married to Clara."

"No, but we were engaged. We'd made a commitment."

"I should have tried harder, Jeff. I know that now. I should have kept calling until you listened to me. But you sounded so cold . . . so distant . . . I thought you were afraid of Clara finding out about us."

"Clara?" Something flickered in his eyes. "She knows, doesn't she?" His voice was hard with accusations. "You told Clara I was Lily's father!"

"I didn't tell her, Jeff. I wouldn't do that without talking to you first. She figured it out for herself."

He shook his head and backed away from her as if he couldn't bear to be in the same room with her.

"Jeff, please . . ."

Looking like a man trapped, he spun around, ripped open the bathroom door and stormed from the room.

Chapter Twelve

The months between August and October flew by in one crazy blur. His life was a mess. It was the worst possible time to hire a lawyer, but someone had to put a legal stamp on the chaos.

The lawyer, a humorless man by the name of Wade Nickles, explained Jeff's rights as Lily's father. Hell, the more his lawyer talked about his legal rights, the less rights it seemed Jeff had.

He wasn't sure if he was ready for visitation rights; he just wanted to do right by Lily. Help with expenses, buy her clothes, start a college fund. He sure in hell didn't want to be the kind of hands-off father his own had been, but what choice did he have?

How does one go from being a stranger to a father, especially when he wasn't even talking to the child's mother?

Talking? Hell, he'd settle for not being angry. He was angry—furious—with Lynne, no matter how much her blue eyes and sweet, curving smile haunted him. He was so angry with her he spent most of November and all of December sitting home trying to forget her. He was convinced she had no intention of telling him about Lily. If it hadn't been for the amazing events that forced her into a corner, she probably never would have! He could never forgive her. Neither, apparently, could he forget her.

Not that this surprised him. He hadn't had any luck forgetting her following their rescue. Why should this time be any different?

On Christmas Eve, he called her, just to see if Lily had received the shiny bright bicycle he had sent to their house.

It had arrived the day before. "You shouldn't have gone to all that expense," Lynne said.

"Does the safety helmet fit properly?"

"Perfectly."

"What about the knee pads?" he asked.

"They're fine."

"We didn't have all that safety gear when I was a kid," he said.

"We didn't either."

"It's a wonder we survived."

"Yeah."

He tried to think of something else to say. "I guess I better let you go."

"Jeff . . . I never had a chance to tell you . . ."

His stomach tightened. Lord, what else was there to tell?

"Do you remember when you said you called me and a man answered? That was my father."

"I don't give a—"

"He was at the house the day Lily was born. And you were right, Jeff. I *did* call out your name." Her voice broke. "During labor. I needed you, Jeff. I needed you so much."

For several minutes he couldn't speak. It was like someone had pulled his heart into a hundred different directions. He swallowed the lump in his throat and blinked against the moisture that suddenly blurred his vision. "Merry Christmas, Lynne."

"Merry Christmas to you, too, Jeff."

He hung up, but it was a long time before his breathing returned to normal. He stared down at the quartz crystal rock in his hand. He and Lynne had found the rock on the second day they were trapped. How ironic that something as solid and timeless as a rock was a memento of the only time in his life that he had acted on impulse.

He remembered the night he'd made love to Lynne as if it was yesterday. Her mouth was sweet and soft. He'd brushed her lips ever so lightly with his own, then pushed his tongue inside, triggering the smoldering spark that had simmered between them for days into an all-consuming blaze. . . .

Putting a clamp on the memory, he glanced at his watch. He was supposed to go to a party, but he wasn't in the mood. *I did call your name.*

And, dammit, he'd heard her.

With only the memory of kissing Lynne to keep him company that lonely Christmas Eve, he decided not to call her again. He still was too angry. From now on, he'd let his lawyer handle any communication between them.

Despite his resolve, he called her that first dreary week in January, but he had a good reason: he'd heard a report on TV about a flu epidemic. Lily answered the phone and after he awkwardly introduced himself, he heard her tell her mother that "Mr. Blakely" was on the phone.

God, she made him feel old. Old and very much like a stranger. Lynne's voice soon floated into his ear, and she sounded breathless.

"Are you all right?" he asked anxiously.

"I'm fine," she assured him. "I was . . . outside."

"Oh. I was just wondering if you'd had your . . ." Suddenly he felt foolish. "Eh . . . flu shot?"

"No. I thought that was only for senior citizens or people at high risk."

"I think it's for everyone," he said. "I was concerned . . . if you got sick, you know, who would take care of Lily?"

"You're right. I'll look into it then." They chatted about the weather and ski conditions. "I was thinking about taking Lily up to the snow."

He realized with a pang how much he was missing. While he was trying to come to terms with fatherhood, his little girl was growing up. He had no idea who Lily's friends were or what she liked to eat. And if he knew little about her present life, he knew nothing about her past. How much had she weighed at birth? When did she get her first tooth, take her first step, say her first word? Damn! How could Lynne have done this to him?

As if to guess his thoughts, Lynne changed the subject. "Jeff . . . I think we need to make a decision about Lily. She has the right to know who her father is."

He picked up the rock from his desk. It was a fine time for her to think about that! He squeezed the rock tight. "I'm not ready yet."

"You're still angry with me."

"No." He surprised himself with that answer, but he realized, suddenly, it was true. She hadn't told him, but he wasn't without blame.

"Then what?"

"Nothing. I've got to go." He hung up and sat holding the rock in his hand until the clock struck eleven and it was time to go to bed.

He called three times in February for no good reason, though he tried his best to make appropriate excuses. He called only twice in March, once to tell Lynne he was going to be out of town and another time to wish Lily a happy birthday.

He tried calling Lynne in April but she and Lily went away for the spring holiday and he went to a computer show in Phoenix. They played telephone tag for a week before they managed to connect—and then they talked for three hours straight.

In May, Jeff's father breezed into town on business and called to suggest they meet somewhere for dinner. His father had never visited Jeff's apartment, preferring the impersonal environment of a hotel or restaurant. Tonight, he suggested Jeff meet him at the Mexican restaurant on Old Topanga Road.

"Weren't you going to marry some girl?" Fred Blakely asked after they'd placed their order. Fred snapped his fingers as if to nudge his memory. "August, right? Hope I can get the time off."

Jeff bit back his anger. "The wedding was scheduled for last August and it was canceled."

"That's right. I remember now. I was . . ." He snapped his fingers again.

"In Mexico divorcing wife number three. Or was it four?"

Fred grinned. "I make it a practice to count only the successes. Sorry about your wedding. You win some, lose some."

"Are you going to be in town long?"

"Only until tomorrow. I promised Candy I'd be back in time for the birth of the baby."

Jeff blinked. "Candy's having a baby?"

"No. Her daughter is."

Jeff sat back in his chair and stared at his father. It occurred to him how very little he knew about his father's life. He'd not even met his father's latest wife. The sad part was, Fred Blakely knew even less about Jeff's life. He was too busy flying all over the world, making business deals and getting entangled in messy divorces.

Almost as soon as the waiter cleared away their plates, Fred glanced at his watch. "I better get back to the hotel. I've got an early business meeting tomorrow morning." He reached for the check.

"Wait," Jeff said, suddenly feeling reckless. "I want to tell you about myself."

Fred fingered the check and frowned. "What?"

"I'm twenty-eight years old, did you know that?"

"Of course I know that . . ."

"I root for the Rams and the Dodgers, and I won first place at the Los Angeles County Fair for photography. I also know how to make pizza from scratch."

"That's very interesting, but . . ."

"I like country-western music, and hate Mexican food."

"Why didn't you tell me?"

"I did tell you, Dad. The last three times you insisted upon meeting me here."

"I don't know what's gotten into you tonight, son."

"Nothing's gotten into me. I just thought it was time we got to know each other better. Maybe I'll fly out to Texas to meet Candy and see your grandchild."

"I don't have any grandchildren. It's Candy's . . ."

Jeff felt sorry for Candy and in some strange way, sorry for his father. He stood. "You're wrong, Dad. You do have a grandchild. Her name is Lily and she's the most beautiful little girl in the world. She has big blue eyes, curly hair and a dimple—an honest-to-God Blakely dimple."

"What are you saying? You have a daughter?"

"That's exactly what I'm saying and you know what? It's high time she and I got to know each other." He spun on his heel and walked out of the Mexican restaurant for what he swore would be the very last time.

Later that night, he sat in his apartment staring at the phone. He wanted to call Lynne and tell her why he'd kept her and Lily at arms' length.

During those five days they'd been trapped in that cave, he'd been closer to Lynne than he'd been to any other person in his life. He'd told her everything—things he had never told another human being.

After their rescue, things grew crazy. Newsmen swarmed the place like buzzards, rescue workers were everywhere. But between answering inane questions (yeah, it feels great to be rescued), and being probed by medical personnel, he remembered thinking he might have made a mistake in telling her good-bye.

He'd fought his way through the crowd searching for her. He was devastated to see her in her boyfriend's arms. Devastated to think she was forever lost to him.

He'd put on a good act, mainly for Clara's benefit. And the whole time Clara fluttered around him, he'd felt crushed inside because the one person in all the world who made him feel alive was gone.

The weeks that followed the rescue were a nightmare. He thought about calling Lynne, wanted to, even though he knew she was seeing someone. They were both seeing someone.

He'd felt guilty as hell for cheating on Clara. Cheating on her like his father had cheated on every woman in his life. Jeff hadn't wanted to believe it, but it appeared he was destined to follow in his father's footsteps. He'd fought against it with everything he had. Fought to forget Lynne, fought to love Clara. Fought to be the man his father had never been.

That's why he had reacted in anger when Lynne had called him. He had worked so hard to put his life back together and out of the blue, Lynne had called and his whole world came crashing down again. It wasn't long afterwards that he and Clara had split up.

Now they'd broken up again, this time for good. So what in hell was he waiting for?

He dialed Lynne's number and felt keenly disappointed when the answering machine picked up on the third ring. He hung up without leaving a message.

He squeezed the crystal in his palm and reminded of all the time he'd wasted, he threw it across the room.

Chapter Thirteen

 Dark angry clouds spread across the sky over Santa Barbara. Tall palms swayed back and forth, sweeping the sky like giant brooms. A few drops of rain had fallen earlier, sending some of the visitors to the *I Madonari* festival scrambling inside the old historical mission for cover.

Lynne glanced up at the sky, her forehead creased in a worried frown. Rain would be disastrous to the chalk paintings, but it didn't look like the dark clouds would blow over anytime soon.

She put the finishing touches on the unicorn carousel she'd been working on for the last two days.

"Mommy, Mommy! Look at my picture!"

Smiling at the excitement in Lily's voice, Lynne stood, her legs stiff from sitting too long in one place. She moved closer to Lily and regarded the cement square that was Lily's.

Lily had drawn a bride and groom with a little flower girl and a cat identical to Pocahontas. The bride had Lynne's shoulder-length brunette hair and a dazzling smile. For once, Lily had managed not to make her look cross-eyed. The little curly-haired flower girl by her side wore a pink dress. The groom still needed work.

"Aren't you going to give the poor groom a face this year, either?"

Lily folded her arms in front of her like a pint-sized

adult. ''I don't know how to draw the groom's face.''

''Sure you do, Lily. You draw very good faces.'' Lynne moved back to her own square, picked up a piece of chalk and shaded in one of the prancing horses.

''But I don't know what the groom looks like.''

''The groom can look any way you want him to look,'' Lynne said. *He could have brown, almost black hair and a dimpled smile. Just like Jeff.*

A squeezing pain reminded her that she'd vowed to put Jeff out of her mind once and for all. ''An artist can make a painting look any way she wants it to look.''

Jeff. They'd talked for hours on the phone, but never once did he make any attempt to see her or Lily. So he was angry with her. Well, she was angry too! Yes, she should have told him. But he hadn't made it easy on her. And wasn't he the one who said they should keep what happened between them secret? He had no right to take his anger out on Lily!

''Look, Mommy, there's Mr. Blakely.''

''What?'' Lynne lifted her head. No question about it. It *was* Jeff, standing tall and looking devilishly handsome, his hair blowing in the wind. ''Jeff?'' Feeling suddenly dazed, she grabbed a rag and wiped the chalk off her hands.

''I hope I'm not interrupting anything . . .''

''No, not at all,'' she said. ''We're almost finished with our pictures. But how did you find us?''

''I remembered you telling me how you and Lily always spend Memorial Day at the festival.'' He kneeled down by Lily who stood watching him with troubled eyes. ''I hear there's a little girl who doesn't have a daddy—is that true?''

Lily nodded, her eyes shining. She sensed a game in progress and was a willing participant. ''And there's a mommy who doesn't have a groom.'' She pointed to her chalk painting.

Father and daughter studied the picture.

Seeing him and Lily together filled Lynne's heart with

sadness and pain. She would never forgive herself for keeping them apart all these years. "There's also a bride-groom who doesn't have a face," she added, not wanting to miss out on the fun.

Jeff raised a dark brow. "This is worse than I thought." He pulled Lynne to her feet. "Do you think we can find a way for the three of us to work things out?"

Lynne didn't know what to say. For months, *months!* he'd kept her waiting and now he walks into her life and wants to work things out? Just like that? She threw the rag down. "So, I take it you're not mad anymore."

"I was never mad at you, Lynne."

"You could have sure fooled me!"

"I was mad at myself for letting the most wonderful thing that ever happened to me slip through my fingers. And all because of some crazy mixed-up notion that if I pursued you, I would follow in my father's footsteps."

She stared up at him, waiting for the punch line. When none came, she moistened her lip. "Your father?"

He took both her hands in his. "I know. None of this makes sense. I was closer to you than I've ever been to anyone in my life—and I ran scared. I did the same thing when I found out about Lily. It seems to be a Blakely trait. Don't get too close to anyone. If you do, take off as fast as you can." The hard lines in his face disappeared and the tenderness in his eyes melted her resistance.

He squeezed her hands. "I don't want to play that game anymore," he said. "I want us to be together forever."

"Oh, Jeff." This was a dream. She was certain of it! "I don't know what to say."

"Say you'll forgive me for making such a mess of things."

She flung herself into his arms and wrapped her hands around his neck. "I'm the one who made a mess of things!"

"No, it was me." He drew her close and kissed her, sending shivers of desire racing through her. All the anger and resentment melted away and for one fleeting moment, it seemed as if they were the only two people in the whole wide world.

Next to them, Lily jumped up and down. "Can I be the flower girl at the wedding, Mommy? Can I? And can I wear pink and . . ."

At last Jeff released Lynne, though his hand stayed firmly around her waist as he stooped down to pick up his little daughter. The three stood in the middle of the plaza hugging each other, oblivious to the stares from the milling crowd.

They paid even less attention to the cloudburst that sent artists and visitors scrambling for cover.

Buckets of rain fell on the chalk paintings and the bright colors ran together. Elvis Presley's hips gave a seductive wiggle before melting into Mona Lisa's lap.

"Look, Mommy!" Lily cried out, pointing over Jeff's shoulder. "The groom has a face."

Lynne and Jeff turned to gaze at the sidewalk. Lily was right; the rain had washed the colors from Lynne's carousel across Lily's painting, and, by some magical act of nature, the groom did, indeed, have a face.

Jeff's face.

SOMETHING
BORROWED,
SOMETHING BLUE

~

Ruth Jean Dale

Chapter One

*T*he beautiful bride hesitated halfway down the stone
staircase leading from the grassy outdoor reception area to
the church perched high on the cliffs overlooking the Santa
Barbara Harbor. Her handsome bridegroom leaned down
to whisper in her ear and she responded with a dazzling
smile meant for him alone.

But Rosemary Hancock noticed and was glad. She'd
never seen a more radiantly happy couple than this pair of
formerly star-crossed lovers. It gave her goosebumps just
thinking how close they'd come to losing each other.
They'd earned the happiness she was confident lay before
them.

Pretty confident, anyway. She'd felt the same way about
her own chances of happiness, once upon a long ago
time—and look how *that* had turned out. Not that she'd
ever regretted marriage to her childhood sweetheart, not
even when it went south on a tide of acrimony and disil-
lusionment. Seeing her daughter, Lynne, so delirious with
happiness on her wedding day more than made up for any
grief.

"Grammy, come *on!*"

At the insistent tug on her hand, Rosemary looked down
at her cherubic five-year-old granddaughter, Lily. Resplen-
dent in a pink bridesmaid's dress with a pearl-strewn bodice, the little girl had played her role in her parents' belated

wedding with considerable panache.

Now Lily frowned and cocked her head, continuing to pull steadily on her grandmother's hand.

Rosemary resisted. "Come where?"

The sparkling blue eyes widened even further. "Mama's gonna throw her flowers out and you gotta catch 'em," Lily announced, her tone determined. "Come *on*, Grammy!"

"Sweetie, you don't understand," Rosemary protested. "Only the unmarried girls get to catch the bouquet."

"You're um-married," Lily declared with unfailing logic.

"But I'm no girl!" In fact, Rosemary was none of those things *except* single—and that wasn't by choice. The sweet young things giggling and jockeying for position in the December sunshine were the rightful claimants to Lynne's bridal bouquet.

Rosemary sighed, realizing she'd been thinking about marriage all day, and specifically about Doug. She knew Lynne had invited her father to the wedding and had waited anxiously for him to reply—which he hadn't. His lack of sensitivity made Rosemary's blood boil, even while she tamped down some unworthy little voice murmuring in relief. It had been a long time since they'd met: three years, eleven months and nine days—but who was counting?

"Is everybody ready?"

Lynne's light, happy tone cut through her mother's cheerless thoughts. Feeling lost and out of place at the edge of a sea of fresh young faces, Rosemary continued to resist Lily's determined advance. Lynne turned away from the throng below and lifted the gorgeous bouquet of poinsettias and greenery.

"One . . . two . . ."

Lily's grip loosened and Rosemary relaxed, feeling equal parts relief and satisfaction now that the ceremony was over and the reception nearly so. For a native Coloradan, even one who'd lived many years in the Golden

State, December in California remained a wondrous mystery. Balmy air . . . sunlight sparkling off the water below . . . a clear blue sky unmarred by clouds or smog. Perfection.

"*Three!*"

Lynne sent the bouquet arcing high into the air. At the same moment, Lily's small hand tightened on her grandmother's wrist in a death grip.

"Grab it!" Lily shouted. "Grab it, Grammy!"

Bolting forward, she dragged her startled grandmother directly into the path of the gaggle of would-be brides. The headlong rush of woman and child caused an instant traffic jam; a couple of the bridesmaids bumped into the hurtling pair and the air filled with startled exclamations.

Releasing Rosemary's arm, Lily whirled to face the thundering herd, flinging out her arms as if to hold back the tide. "Grab the bowskay, Grammy!" she shrieked. "Quick, grab the—!"

Rosemary didn't reach for the bouquet, she reached for her less than sporting granddaughter. When she did, the bridal bouquet slapped into her open palms as if guided by divine providence. Astonished, she stared at it.

"Hooray, hooray!" Lily clapped her hands and jumped up and down in excitement. "My grammy's getting married!"

Embarrassed, Rosemary tried to calm the child. "I certainly am *not*." Impulsively, she offered the bouquet to her nearest rival, a pretty redhead with a puzzled expression. "Here, take it. If Lily hadn't interfered—"

"No way!" The redhead grinned and shoved her hands behind her back. "All's fair in love and war." Winking, she turned away.

Lily plucked the bouquet from Rosemary's hands, brown curls bouncing and deep dimples appearing in her smooth round cheeks. "This means you're gonna get married *real soon*," she announced with absolute certainty.

"I most certainly am not." At the child's crestfallen

expression, Rosemary relented. "You just don't understand, sweetie. . . ."

How could she? Rosemary didn't understand it herself,
but everything in her insisted that she'd already had her
shot at happiness—and blown it, although she still wasn't
quite sure how. She'd married and divorced the only man
she'd ever love. Nor had they had one of those "civilized"
partings. It got so bad there at the end that they'd been
communicating through lawyers.

Marry again? Not jolly likely!

Lily knew none of this. She thrust out her soft bottom
lip. "But Mama said—"

"I know, darling." Rosemary knelt before the disappointed little girl, still clutching the Christmas red and
green bouquet. "I appreciate your efforts but that doesn't
count for grandmas."

"It does," Lily insisted. Where had the child gotten that
stubborn streak? "Mama said. She said now Grampa's
gone, you gotta get married some more." She frowned.
"Where's Grampa gone to now, Grammy?" She looked
around as if expecting him to appear.

Rosemary sighed. "Heaven only knows, honey. The last
we heard he was island-hopping in the South Pacific. Now,
don't look so worried. I'm sure—"

"Congratulations."

At the unexpected sound of a deep voice, Rosemary's
heart lurched crazily. But it wasn't Doug, of course. It was
only Gordon Conway, Doug's former partner in the con-
struction company they'd started together and raised to be
a major player in the Southern California market before
Doug lost his mind and walked away.

She smiled past her relief. "Hi, Gordon. I'd hoped to
have a chance to say hello to you. I'm sorry Pam couldn't
make it, too."

He grinned. "I'm not. We've been divorced for almost
a year."

"I didn't know. I'm sorry to hear that."

"Why?"

Rosemary stood up, keeping a restraining hand on Lily's shoulder. "General principles, I guess. It's always sad when a marriage ends."

"Yeah, well sometimes it's for the best." He gave her a level, assessing look. "She wanted to *find herself*, what the hell ever that means. Sound familiar?"

Too familiar, but Rosemary had no intention of getting into anything personal with Gordon Conway. The last time they'd seen each other, they'd both been married to other people. Now that they weren't, she wasn't sure she felt comfortable with the way he was looking at her. She shrugged, giving him a faint smile that might have meant yes and might have meant no.

"Rosemary," he said suddenly, "you look great. Better than great. What have you been doing with yourself—or maybe I should say, *to* yourself?"

His question embarrassed her. "Hey," she said lightly, "I'm a 'happening' kind of '90s chick."

"Yeah, right, and I'm Little Lord Fauntleroy. One of the things I admired most about you—"

She must have reacted strongly to that for he laughed.

"Yes, I admired you. You didn't know? I admired your home-loving ways. You were never too good to bring Doug his pipe and slippers—"

"Doug didn't smoke," she interjected.

"Figure of speech. You also threw great dinner parties and charmed all his business contacts."

"You make me sound like some '50s ideal of the little woman," she said uneasily.

He cocked his head. "That's bad? I don't think so. Doug was an ingrate, if you ask me. Now that I see you again—" His gaze moved rather explicitly down the length of her in the soft fitted chiffon that flared gracefully around her legs. "You look fabulous. Say, how long will you be staying in California?"

She caught her breath, flustered that Gordon could look at her that way. Other men, yes. She'd grown accustomed to their increasing interest during the time it had taken her to reinvent herself. But not Gordon; he *knew* her.

He also knew Doug.

She cleared her throat. "Until the kids return on Christmas Eve from their honeymoon. I'll be taking care of Lily—" She glanced at the little flower girl, who'd dropped to her knees to examine a beetle climbing a blade of green California grass. "—at Lynne's little house in Santa Barbara. The day after Christmas, it'll be back home to Denver for me."

He looked pleased. "Where are the honeymooners headed?"

"Africa, if you can believe it." Rosemary shook her head in amazement. "They're going on a photo safari. Isn't that great?"

"For them. You strike me as more the Niagara Falls type."

She darted him a sharp glance. How did he know that's where she and Doug had honeymooned? Then she saw that Gordon was just guessing, which made her feel even worse. How predictable, i.e., boring, she must have been back then!

"Mrs. Hancock!"

A young woman in a red dress with flowers in her hair rushed up. It was Lynne's maid of honor.

"Yes, Terri?"

"Lynne's waiting for you inside. She'd like you to help her change."

"Tell her I'll be right there, dear." The messenger hurried away and Rosemary turned to Gordon to say her goodbyes. Before she could speak, Lily dropped her blade of grass and jumped up.

"Mama's gotta go on her honeybunch," the little girl said.

Gordon looked puzzled, then understanding dawned. "A honeybunch, is it." He grinned at Lily and bent to pat her shoulder. "Say, I meant to tell you I think you're the best flower girl I ever saw."

"Thank you," Lily said sweetly. "So many people say

that, it must be true." Turning to Rosemary, she added, "Let's go, Grammy."

Rosemary stifled a smile. "It's been nice seeing you again, Gordon."

"Very nice. Christmas Eve, huh? That means I've got a little time."

She raised her brows. "Time to do what?"

"Renew old acquaintances. May I give you a call?"

She found herself completely unmoved by his charming smile but could find no real reason to turn him down—especially after he'd been so nice to Lily. Gordon was a successful, attractive, *single* man. And best of all, he couldn't possibly expect her to play any of those "dating" games she found so repulsive. So she shrugged and said, "Why not?" and hurried away to help her daughter.

"Where's Lily?"

"With her father—with Jeff." Rosemary crossed the small dressing room and slid her arms around Lynne's waist in a fierce hug. "It was wonderful, sweetheart—the most beautiful wedding I ever saw." Except mine, of course.

Lynne's luminous smile lit the room. "Did you really think so?"

"I *know* so." Rosemary turned her daughter and began working on the long row of buttons down the back of the gown.

"If only Daddy—" Lynne broke off with a sigh.

Rosemary's breath caught in her throat but she spoke evenly. "I know you're disappointed, honey."

"It would have been hard for you if he'd shown up." Lynne gave a sad little laugh.

"No, no, it would have been fine. I'm over all that."

"Oh, Mother!" Lynne's fine brows rose above eyes as blue as her daughter's. "You know you're not!"

"Why, Lynne Hancock Blakely—I—you can't think—why—"

Lynne laughed, breaking the tension. "That's what I like about you, Mom," she teased, stepping out of the white froth pooling around her feet. "You never could lie with a straight face. The divorce was . . . messy. Daddy broke your heart, admit it."

Rosemary shrugged. "Okay, I admit it."

"And you haven't looked at another man since he left."

"I certainly have." Rosemary gathered up the gown and deposited it on a chair. "I . . . see other men." Rarely. Not very successfully. Suddenly she added, "Did you tell Lily I should get married again?"

Lynne groaned. "She overheard me talking to Jeff. I thought I'd explained it away."

"Well, you didn't." Rosemary gave an exasperated sigh. "I wish you wouldn't discuss my . . . my *love* life. I am your mother, after all. Show a little respect."

Lynne leaned forward to give her mother a kiss on the cheek. "*You* know that, and *I* know that, but the way you look these days nobody else believes it. Mother, you're a beautiful woman—I mean, you always were a beautiful person but now you're as beautiful outside as you are inside."

Rosemary squirmed before such unwarranted praise. "You're prejudiced."

"I certainly am not." Lynne gripped her mother's shoulders and spoke with conviction. "You're too young and too pretty to let life keep passing you by. I'll admit, for a while I hoped . . ."

Rosemary's heart stood still. "You hoped your father and I would get back together," she said gently.

"You knew?"

"Of course. You love us both, my darling. But obviously, that's never going to happen." Just saying the words made her stomach muscles clench—now that she *had* stomach muscles. She added helplessly, "I don't even know where he is."

Lynne sighed. "The last I heard, he was still wandering around the South Pacific teaching the natives to build structurally superior huts or some such thing. So okay, I've given up on Daddy—he didn't even respond to the wedding invitation, for heaven's sake.''

"I'm sorry, Lynne. That wasn't like him, honestly. He adores you.''

Lynne looked crestfallen. "I used to think so—just as you used to think he loved you. Well, Mother, he doesn't. But someone else will if you just give him half a chance.''

"Matchmaker!''

"Sleeping Beauty!''

They laughed together, and then Lynne changed the subject abruptly. "Before I forget . . .'' She tugged at a ring on her right hand, extending it to her mother. "Something borrowed, something blue. Thanks, Mom.''

Rosemary accepted the sky blue lapis lazuli ring, her heart skipping a beat. The ring had been the first gift Doug ever gave her, when she was only sixteen. It'd caused an awful row in her family, with her mother ordering her to return it. Rosemary refused, of course.

She'd worn it for many years, removing it only when it became too tight for her increasingly chubby fingers. Now she slipped it onto the third finger of her left hand easily, realized what she'd done and caught her breath. Before she could remove it, Lynne called to her.

"Will you give me a hand with my hair, Mom?'' And working together comfortably, they went about the business of preparing the bride for her departure.

Rosemary went to great lengths to present a calm and reasonable facade. Inside, she was furious with Doug for not showing up for this special day, although heaven knew *she* didn't want to see him. But heaven also knew, a man shouldn't disappoint a wonderful daughter like Lynne.

Buttoning her silk shirt, Lynne asked suddenly, "Aren't you curious, Mother? He . . . he could be a beach bum somewhere, or maybe he took up with some . . . some native beauty who runs around in a sarong. Don't you care what's happened to a man you lived with for almost twenty years?''

Rosemary adjusted her daughter's collar. "Not in the

slightest,'' she said carelessly.

It was a terrible lie.

Lynne and Jeff departed amidst a hail of birdseed and best wishes, leaving Rosemary to preside over the last-minute details of the occasion: the departure of guests, the dismantling of tents and tables, the disposition of flowers and decorations.

With everything finally accomplished, she approached a very blond, very young beach-boy-type valet. Ignoring his flirty glances, she sent him for her car.

With Lily beside her, she sat down to wait. The little girl yawned and leaned against her grandmother's arm.

Mind wandering, Rosemary heard one valet speaking to another: *The blue Honda over there—yeah, for the foxy chick with the little kid.*

She smiled at that characterization, idly listening: *Man, you got that right! I like older women. She might even be— hell, she might be thirty but she's well-preserved, a real looker!*

Kid must be blind, Rosemary thought, marveling at the foibles of the young.

A few minutes later, he whipped the car to the curb and climbed out, flourishing the keys. He stood there all gold and bronze and studly, as if he'd just hopped off his surfboard so he could hop onto a magazine cover.

Lily sat up, suddenly interested.

He held the keys toward her in a teasing manner. ''Give these to your good-lookin' mama, sweet thing,'' he invited.

Lily laughed and took the keys. ''That's not my mama! My mama's on her honeybunch. That's my *grammy*.''

The expression on the kid's face made Rosemary's day.

By the time Rosemary reached Lynne's cottage in the Santa Barbara hills, a mild depression had set in. Thinking about Doug always made her blue.

Well, she wouldn't stand for it! Parking in the garage

at the back of the small lot, she led Lily through the verdant yard, across the brick patio and in through the kitchen door.

Sending Lily to change into play clothes—"I can do it my own big-girl self, Grammy!"—Rosemary strode with determination into Lynne's bedroom, hers for the next couple of weeks. Quickly she took off her wedding finery and climbed into workout clothing: shiny black tights, pink shorts and T-shirt, cross-trainers and cushiony socks.

There was a time when such gear would have been completely foreign to her, but now it was as comfortable and familiar as . . . as anything left in her life. A good workout was just what she needed for a little attitude adjustment.

Hauling her hand weights out of the combination storage-pantry-laundry room near the back door, she tried to convince herself the stresses and strains of the wedding had jangled her nerves, not all those reminders of Doug. Doug was her past and she'd vowed not to look back, only forward.

The past was cakes baked from scratch and clothing sewn by loving hands, a carefully decorated home and a man to give it all meaning. The future was Nautilus machines and weight training and aerobics and a demanding job and cool new clothes and an apartment in LoDo, Denver's hippest new area, and . . .

Warm-up complete, she reached for the ten-pounders and curled them toward her shoulders.

Damn, she needed this! Tomorrow—no, tomorrow was Sunday—Monday, while Lily was in her morning kindergarten class, she'd go to the health club where she'd already taken out a temporary membership. She'd jump on those machines and work her way through all this.

With Lily playing quietly on the patio nearby with her gray cat, Pocahontas, Rosemary began counting reps.

Meanwhile, on the street above and behind the house, a man stepped from a rental car to scope out the scene below.

He'd had no idea Lynne was into weight lifting but that wasn't what made him frown while he watched the slender figure below hoist dumbbells around with practiced ease.

Why the hell, he wondered, wasn't his daughter on her honeymoon right now instead of exercising with demonic energy in her back yard?

Chapter Two

$\mathcal{D}$oug parked the rented Geo in front of Lynne's Spanish-style adobe and jumped out, slamming the car door behind him. Without locking, he sprinted up the wide steps toward the arched front door. Where he'd been living, nobody locked anything and he was out of the habit.

At the door, he turned right and followed the paved walkway around the side of the little house. A gate guarded the back yard and he threw it open. Stepping through, he ducked beneath a date palm and ran headlong into a round metal patio table surrounded by matching chairs. The ensuing clatter threw him off his course for a moment. When he finally caught his balance again, he looked up to find his beautiful daughter staring at him with one of those hand weights held like a missile ready to be hurled at his head.

Only it wasn't his beautiful daughter confronting him, it was his beautiful wife—check that, his beautiful *ex*-wife. The Amazon standing squarely in his path, wielding a potentially deadly weapon, was definitely Rosemary.

She was exactly as he remembered her: gorgeous. She might have lost a little weight but that registered only peripherally; to him, she'd always been perfect. Almost hungrily, he searched her face. He found her as he remembered, with the exception of the militant stance: Rosemary, his Rosie. He didn't know what he'd ex-

pected—maybe the wildly vindictive woman she'd turned
into as their divorce dragged through to its mind- and
body-numbing conclusion.

He thought he saw a light of welcome flicker in her face,
but then her expression altered subtly, hardened as if she'd
just identified the intruder.

Movement off to one side shocked him out of his near-
trance.

"Grampa?" an uncertain little voice inquired, then repeated more confidently, "Grampa!"

"Lily." He felt satisfaction even saying the name of his
only grandchild. With one last, beleaguered glance at Rosie's unyielding face, he turned toward the little girl.
Kneeling, he opened his arms, forcing himself to wait for
her to come to him.

She did, hurtling against his chest and flinging her arms
around his neck. He held her close to his thudding heart,
loving the little-girl innocence of his only grandchild.
Burying his face in the soft brown curls, he felt the tension
and anxiety of the past few frantic days begin to drain
away.

He'd been right to come here. Everything was going to
work out.

He kept on believing that right up until Lily leaned back
to smile at him and announce, "Guess what, Grampa?
Grammy's gonna get married!"

Rosemary hardly knew what to say or what to do. She'd
realized all along that she *might* see Doug at their daughter's wedding, but when he didn't respond to the invitation
. . . or show up at the church . . . or indicate in any way
that he was still alive and well and living on some god-
forsaken island in the middle of the ocean, well, she'd
thought she'd dodged that particular bullet with exemplary
grace.

So much for false security. Here he was, Douglas Hancock in the flesh. And what flesh it was. . . .

Sun-browned, face leaner than when he'd left, shoulders

somehow wider and posture straighter. His aura, she decided, watching him ruffle his granddaughter's silky curls, had definitely changed.

He was the same, only different. Her mouth thinned in displeasure. She wasn't going to let him get to her again—absolutely not! She would remain cool and aloof and . . . and polite as all get out. If it killed her, that's what she would do.

"Lily," he said on a sigh. "I can hardly believe how you've grown."

The girl nodded sagely. "Like a weed, Grammy says." She smiled over her shoulder at Rosemary before adding, "Did you know me, Grampa? Mama said you'd been gone so long you maybe wouldn't."

He winced and Rosemary saw the involuntary flinching for what it was: shame and regret. Not wanting to feel sympathy toward him, not wanting to feel anything toward him, she turned away to set her dumbbells on the edge of a redwood planter.

"I recognized you, baby," he said in a husky voice. "But how did you know me? You were just a little thing, last time we saw each other."

"Mama put your picture next to my bed." Lily stroked his cheek with one small hand. "When I go to bed, I say good night and sometimes I give you a kiss."

"That . . ." Doug's voice sounded even raspier. He sucked in a quick breath. "That was very thoughtful of your mother."

"Oh, yes," Lily agreed. "Uhhh . . . thoughtful?"

"That means nice." He looked straight at Rosemary. "Hi, Rosie." He sounded at once cautious and hopeful. "Aren't you going to say anything?"

She looked past him, into the tangle of palm trees and bougainvillea bushes camouflaging the fence. After a moment, she said, "I find I have nothing to say at the moment."

"Oh." He sounded disappointed. "In that case . . ." He stood up. "I guess congratulations are in order."

She frowned. "Congratulations?"

"On your forthcoming marriage."

"Oh, for—I'm not getting married."

"But Lily said—"

"Grammy caught the bride bowskay," Lily announced serenely. "Mama said anybody who catches bride flowers gets married next so it's Grammy, all right. Don't you guess it's Grammy, Grampa?"

"Lily!" Rosemary felt her cheeks warm with chagrin. The last thing she wanted was to look foolish in front of this man who had already made her look like a total fool on any number of occasions. Sucking in a deep breath, she gentled her tone. "Lily, sweetie, you know you practically got us both trampled to death over that bouquet. I'm sure under those circumstances, it won't count toward fulfilling the superstition."

Lily looked blank; she blinked her big blue eyes and announced, "Mama said!"

Doug grinned. "And if you can't trust your mama, who can you trust?"

"Stop it, Doug." He'd been here for five minutes and already managed to annoy her by slipping in one of their family catch phrases, Rosemary thought with irritation. "What are you doing here, anyway?"

"Grandpa came to see me," Lily said, as if it should be obvious.

"I sure did, sweetheart." He ruffled her curls again as if he couldn't help touching her, as if he couldn't believe he was really here. "I also came to see your mother get married?" He glanced at Rosemary, a question in his clear hazel eyes.

She nodded. "The wedding went off as planned. Lynne and Jeff are on an airplane heading for a photo safari in Africa."

"Well, I'll be damned." His smile turned nostalgic. "All her life, that girl's wanted to see the animals in Africa. Do you remember—?"

"Me, too!" Lily tugged at his arm. "Me, too, Grampa.

Mama and Daddy went on their honeybunch and I wanted to go, too, but they said I should stay with Grammy.'' She gave Rosemary a melting smile. "That's okay, but how'll they have any fun without *me*?''

"How, indeed?'' Doug's earnest gaze locked with that of his ex-wife. "Are they . . . good together, Rosie?''

Her mouth felt dry as all Colorado. "Very,'' she assured him. "They love each other.'' Which only sometimes was enough, she didn't add.

"Lily already calls him Daddy.''

"He *is* my daddy,'' Lily said.

"He really—?''

Rosemary saw the shock on his face and understood it, for he'd never been told the whole story. "It wasn't Jeff's fault, Doug. Honestly, it wasn't.'' She glanced significantly at the little girl. "I'll tell you about it later, all right?''

She saw the reluctance in his nod.

"Sure. In the meantime, do you think I could have something to drink? Anything—tea, soda, water.''

"Of course. I should have offered.'' She bit her lip, sorry she'd added that second comment. That was the old Rosemary, the solicitous hostess.

She was through anticipating his every need, she railed silently while preparing tall glasses of iced sun tea. When he wanted something, let him ask for it, just as he'd done. It wasn't her job to make life easy for him anymore.

She clunked the tray down on the patio table and began unloading tea, napkins, a plate of cookies. "Would you care for a cookie?'' she asked, adding defensively, "I thought we could all use a snack.''

"Thanks.'' He picked up a chocolate morsel and took a bite. "You make these?''

She lifted her chin, feeling petulant but helpless to control herself. "No, I did not.''

"Glad to hear it, 'cause they're lousy.'' He gave her a charming smile. "There for a minute, I thought you were losing your touch.''

"I would care for a cookie," Lily said politely, sitting down before the glass of milk intended for her. Taking a cookie, she held it in her hand and looked expectantly at her grandfather. "Mama says you've been having 'ventures," she said. "Will you tell me one?"

Rosemary couldn't help jumping in. "Yes, Doug, do tell us about the adventures which kept you away from the wedding of your only child."

That sounded bitchy and she regretted saying it the minute the words left her mouth, more so when he gave her a puzzled glance. She started to mumble an apology but caught herself. She was *not* going to apologize to this man for anything!

"I'm sorry I missed the wedding," he said simply.

"It was good." Lily broke her cookie in half. "I was flower girl and *I* was good. Wasn't I, Grammy?"

"You were wonderful, angel."

Lily nodded. "I like being flower girl," she said, a dreamy expression coming over her. "This is a bunch of times—" She frowned. "I forget how many, but I'm gonna do it lots more times, too." She nodded emphatically. "Like when Grammy gets married."

"Give it up, Lily." Rosemary was looking at Doug, annoyed by his efforts to suppress a smile. "Lynne wanted you at her wedding," she said abruptly.

The almost-smile disappeared as if it had never been. "I wanted to be there." He raked a hand through thick brown hair, longer and shaggier than she'd ever seen him wear it. "I only got the invitation two days ago, Rosemary. I moved heaven and earth to make it in time, but I had to take a seaplane from Aitutaki to Rarotonga, and from there I—"

"Where to where?" She gave him a blank look.

"The Cook Islands, Rosie. That's where I've been for the last couple of months."

"But Lynne thought you were in Samoa . . . or Tahiti, I forget which."

"I was. And in Tuvalu and the Solomons—I've been

lots of places, seen lots of islands.'' His expression suddenly became warm, almost intimate. ''Don't you remember? That's exactly what I told you I intended to do when
I asked you—''

''I don't want to remember,'' she interrupted stiffly.

''I can't believe you're still angry.''

''You mean you're not?''

He shrugged. ''You made your choice, I made mine.''

''Is that what you call it?'' She was shaking with a
reaction to thoughts and feelings suppressed far too long.
''Forget it,'' she said in a voice that shook. ''It's water
under the bridge.''

Lily looked from one grandparent to the other. ''Grammy, are you mad at Grampa?''

''No, of course not,'' Rosemary denied the obvious with
a guilty start.

''No,'' Doug agreed with saccharine sweetness, ''Grand-
ma would never get mad at me for something that wasn't
my fault. She understands that when you're at the ends of
the earth, it may take a little time to find your way back.''

There seemed to be a subtext which wasn't immediately
clear to her, so she said, ''Huh?'' and stared at him.

Doug shrugged, his expression giving nothing away.
''Lynne will understand.''

He was right about that. His daughter would be so
thrilled to find he'd cared enough to even *try* to come that
she would forgive him anything. Rosemary chewed at her
lower lip for a moment, trying to compose herself. ''Does
that mean you're staying until she gets back?'' she asked.

''After coming all this way, I'd be crazy not to.'' He
glanced around. ''I take it you're baby-sitting 'til the new-
lyweds return?''

''That's right.''

''So you've got dibs on the house.'' He raised his
brows. ''Wonder how much trouble I'll have finding someplace to sack out. It being the holiday season and all . . .''

She couldn't even consider letting him, as he put it,

"sack out" here, regardless of how broad his hints might become; no way! He could wrangle for an invitation until the cows came home and no way would she—

"Sack out?" Lily repeated.

He patted her cheek. "Sleep, honey. I just need a place to sleep while I wait for your mama to get back."

"But—" Lily glanced at her grandmother. "You can sleep here, Grampa."

"Oh, no, he can't!" Rosemary jumped in forcefully. "We don't have room for anybody else here, Lily."

"Mama's bed is *great big*," the little girl declared. "There's lots of room. You can sleep there, Grampa." She looked as if she considered the matter settled.

"Thanks, I'd love to." He said it straight-faced.

"Ha, ha, very funny." Rosemary glowered at her ex. "This is a tiny little house, only two bedrooms and one bath. We don't have room for you, Doug, even if we wanted to accommodate you."

"Which you don't," he interpreted. "Have you forgotten how little trouble I am to have around?" He tried to wheedle while flying in the face of fact. He'd always been plenty of trouble to have around.

She started to say so but fortunately, understanding hit her just in time. He was *enjoying* this. He liked watching her squirm—and for what?

One look at him and she was falling back into old, bad habits. She had nothing to be uncomfortable about in this situation. Rosemary Hancock was a free and liberated woman now, not the insecure clinging vine he'd left behind in his quest for *adventure*! She could say and do any damned thing she wanted to—including surprise *him*.

Which she would do if it killed her! "Sure, why not?" she gave in carelessly. "Stay if you want. Lily's heart is set on it—poor little thing gets to see her grandfather so *rarely*. Besides, Lynne says the couch is quite comfortable."

Rising, she picked up the tray and carried it into the kitchen, feigning indifference.

She didn't know whether she'd fooled him, but she sure hadn't fooled herself. Nevertheless, she was proud of herself for trying.

He insisted on taking them both out to dinner that night. Both adults were walking on eggs but Lily was as free and easy as a happy pixie.

They let her pick the restaurant and not too surprisingly she chose her favorite pizza place. When their order arrived—one veggie, one cheese—Doug looked down dubiously at the concoctions before him.

"It's been years since I had pizza," he explained, lifting a slice onto a paper plate and offering it to Lily.

Rosemary watched his deft handling of the spatula. "I'm surprised you didn't order one of those mega-meat things." She shuddered. "You never liked pizza much anyway but if you had to eat it—"

"No, but you did." He shoved her paper plate with its slice of pizza across the table.

"I don't eat pizza much anymore."

"That's a change." He looked astonished.

What did she have to do, hit him over the head and scream, *I've changed in lots of ways! What are you, blind? I did this to show you, you—!*

Lily saved the day. "I *love* pizza," she announced, licking her lips. "Cheese pizza is my favorite but Mama didn't have any at her re-re-resession—"

"Reception, sweetheart."

"Re-*ception*. Can I have more, Grampa? That big piece right there—"

So Lily had another wedge, and then another. Doug picked at his and Rosemary picked at hers, trying to convince herself that she couldn't afford the calories but knowing that was only half the reason.

She'd lost her appetite, thanks to the untimely appearance of her ex-husband and her own rash invitation for him to move in with her and Lily for the next couple of weeks. She was still too angry with him to let bygones be bygones. She'd thought she'd gotten past all that but here she was, just as upset and anxious as she'd been when their marriage hit the fan.

"One more slice of pizza?"

"No, thank you."

He looked down at half of one pizza and more than half of the other. "Shall we take it with us or leave it here?"

"Take it!" Lily cried. "Pizza's my favorite breakfast."

So they took it with them, along with simmering resentments and tense silences. Rosemary drove Lynne's car through the streets of Santa Barbara, hardly noticing the holiday decorations heralding the Christmas season.

What a day this had been! The wedding and reception, quickly followed by Doug's unexpected appearance, had left her drained and exhausted. And it wasn't even over. After Lily was tucked into bed, Rosemary knew she'd still have to deal with *him*. He didn't know about Lynne and Jeff and Lily and it was up to her to tell him.

There was a lot he didn't know but she'd be damned if she'd volunteer to draw him a picture. She was through handing out unsolicited advice, too. She'd changed. She really had changed.

Lord, let it be true! This kind of test she simply wasn't prepared to take.

He'd watched her go from shock to anger to resentment and right on through to a kind of cool detachment that worried him. This was *not* the Rosemary he knew: his wife, Rosie, the girl next door, the girl he'd loved and married.

And left.

But dammit, there'd been extenuating circumstances. He'd set a train wreck in motion, yeah, but it had been as much for her good as for his own.

At Lynne's house, he carried in the yawning Lily while Rosemary brought the pizza box. At her direction, he whisked the drowsy child straight on down the hall and into her small bedroom. Rosemary followed, and Doug left her to handle the nighttime ritual.

As she'd always handled Lynne's, calling him to kiss his daughter goodnight after teeth were brushed, hair combed, nightgown donned. A sweet ache for what was gone hit him somewhere in the vicinity of his heart. They'd been a real family cliché back then: a father who went out each day to earn their daily bread, a mother who stayed home to cook and clean and care for the little girl, who did what all little girls should—be adorable.

Lily was adorable. Lynne was doing a fine job with her, despite a rocky start. Had she really married Lily's biological father, as Rosie had indicated?

"Grandpa! Want to come kiss our Lily goodnight?"

Another sweet pain pierced him and he retraced his steps down the hall. He was bending over the ruffle-frosted bed when the telephone rang in the living room. He glanced at Rosemary with a question.

She shook her head. "Lynne has a machine. I'll check later."

Which she did, after the hugging and the kissing and the tucking. Back in the living room, he watched her walk to the desk and punch a flashing button.

And heard the message, in a familiar male voice:

"Hi, Rosemary. Hope I've got the right number. This is Gordon, Gordon Conway? It was great seeing you at the wedding today, just great. That guy you used to be married to was an idiot to miss it—but I digress. How about driving up the coast with me tomorrow, Lily, too, of course? I thought we might have brunch in Solvang, do the tourist thing. Why don't you give me a call—better yet, I'll just drop by. Hope that's okay. Sleep tight—"

The machine clicked off, whether because it had run out of time or that friggin' traitor Conway had run out of fast talk. Either way, Doug Hancock was *not* a happy camper.

Chapter Three

*R*osemary's guarded gaze flew to Doug's face and just as quickly, she recognized her mistake and caught herself. She had every right to receive telephone calls from men, or anybody else. She lifted her chin slightly and met his gaze, not too belligerently, she hoped.

"Gordon Conway, huh." He raised dark brows. "How's Pam?"

"They're divorced. Gordon doesn't know." She turned toward the kitchen. "I think I'll have a glass of wine. Would you like—?" She bit off the invitation, made out of her old misdirected sense of hospitality. Such rules did not apply to this man.

"I don't suppose you've got any beer."

"There's plenty of beer." She opened the refrigerator and peered inside.

"Since when did you start drinking beer?"

"This is Lynne's house, not mine. It's for Jeff."

"Ah, yes, Jeff. Sure, I'll take a beer."

She handed him a can and took out the bottle of chardonnay, closing the refrigerator door with a quick shove of one knee. Carrying the bottle to the counter, she rummaged in a cabinet for a glass. She found one with Disney cartoon characters on the side and filled it to the brim with the golden wine.

At last she glanced at Doug, only to find him staring at

her with narrowed eyes. Disconcerted, she tossed down a gulp of wine, refilling the glass before returning the bottle to the refrigerator. Sliding into a chair at the kitchen table, she set her glass on the gleaming wooden top.

Doug joined her. "So Gordy's divorced."

"That's what he said."

"You didn't keep in touch with him?"

"Why would I? I was in Colorado and he was in California. We never were all that close, if you recall."

"No?" He swallowed a slug of beer. "Sounded like he's ready to remedy that situation."

"Oh, Doug, don't be a jerk."

He blinked. She'd never said anything even remotely like that to him before but she was too tired and emotionally buffeted to censor her every word.

His jaw ridged. "Is that what's got you so riled? Are you pissed because he was at the wedding and I wasn't?"

"No!" She tossed down the last of the wine and glared at him. "I didn't want you at the wedding—there, are you satisfied? Lynne did. You broke her heart when you didn't even respond to her invitation. But me? I never wanted to lay eyes on you again as long as I lived."

"God," he said, "I never expected you to be so bitter."

"I have every right to be bitter, don't you think? You left me because I was prepared to drift gracefully into middle age—"

"Drift, hell! You were running to meet it."

"You—" She bit off sharp words with a sigh, changing the thrust of her comment in midstream. "—could be right."

She'd surprised him again, she saw without caring this time. "Look, Doug," she said, "I've had a lot of time to think about this. I know I disappointed you, but dammit, you disappointed me, too! I feel stupid admitting it, but I really was living my dream of domestic bliss." She gave a cynical little laugh. "Unfortunately, I gained twenty-five pounds in the process. I suppose you were ashamed of me—God knows, I was ashamed of myself."

He stared at her so hard she stopped speaking. "Is that what you thought?" he asked after a moment.

"It's what I knew." She set her empty glass down very gently. "Look, there's no need to talk any more about this. I'm not the same woman I was then. I'm making a fool of myself—again!—but I thought you weren't coming. I didn't have time to prepare."

"Prepare what? Jeez, Rosie." He thrust an agitated hand through his hair. "We lived together for nearly twenty years. What's to prepare? I'm still me, you're still you."

"You may still be you but I'm not me anymore. Haven't you been listening?" She stared at him in utter frustration.

After a tense moment, he said, "Do you want me to leave, then, go on back to my island and forget this ever happened?"

She didn't even have to think about that. "Of course not. It would hurt Lynne terribly, and Lily, too. I just don't want you thinking that I'm the same sad sack of—sad sack you walked away from." She found the spirit to meet his gaze. "I'll be all right tomorrow, after I get a little rest and—" She laughed suddenly. "And give myself a good talking-to."

He smiled. That had been a long-standing joke between them, her penchant for saving her best lectures for herself, for being harder on herself than on anyone else. "I . . . didn't expect this to be so complicated," he admitted. "I guess I expected us to pick right up where we left off."

"We did! That's the problem."

At her wry tone, he shook his head. "No, I mean before all the bullshit." He straightened with sudden decisiveness. "I need to think about this. But I'll do it somewhere else if you want me gone, Rosie."

"Will you stop calling me that? I'm not a Rosie anymore."

"You are to me."

She closed her eyes and groaned.

"Okay." He sighed. "If it'll make you happy, I'll try to remember to call you Rose-mary."

"Thank you—and do more than *try*."

His eyes narrowed fractionally. "Whatever you say. Now about Gordon—"

"What about him?"

"You don't really intend to go to Solvang with him tomorrow."

"Don't I?" The time when he could tell her what to do was long gone.

For a drawn-out moment, their gazes locked. Then he shrugged. "Whatever. Look, let's forget about Gordon Conway and talk about Lynne and this guy she married— Jeff, is it? He's Lily's real father, is that the deal?"

She saw one of his big fists curve around the beer can and was afraid he'd crush it. "Yes, but it isn't what you think."

"I *think* she should have told us who the turkey was at the time, instead of letting us assume it was that guy she was engaged to—Larry, Gary, whatever."

"We're the ones who jumped to conclusions. The truth is, she wasn't very proud of what had happened and it took her a long time to confide in me. They were together only once, Doug, during that cave-in—you remember."

"I'm not likely to forget," he said grimly. "I thought Lynne was a goner."

"You're kidding!" She stared at him, aghast. "You kept telling me everything would be all right. You were a rock."

"I lied. I was scared to death. I just didn't want you to know."

For a moment they sat there, reliving those horrible days. Then Rosemary sighed.

"Anyway, Jeff was the one trapped in there with her."

"The son of a—!"

"They thought they were going to die, Doug! Who could blame them for clinging to each other?"

"Clinging." He gave a short bark of something less than laughter.

"Anyone would have done the same," she said in defense of her daughter and son-in-law.

"You wouldn't. You've got a moral code reminiscent of chastity belts and scarlet A's."

"How dare you say such a thing to me!" But then the anger drained away and her shoulders slumped. Perhaps she had been that way, once. Taking a deep breath, she said, "We're not talking about me, we're talking about Lynne and Jeff. When they came out of that mine, they were whisked off in different directions and lost touch."

"So he let her have the baby alone."

"Not alone. She had us, Doug."

"She needed *him*."

"She's *got* him, now."

"I'll withhold judgment about that until I see with my own eyes." Doug rubbed the side of his neck wearily. "How'd they get together, after all that?"

"I did it." She had to smile when she claimed the credit.

"You?" His eyes widened.

She nodded. "I have a friend in Woodland Hills, a travel agent, actually, who twisted my arm to get Lynne to let Lily be flower girl at her daughter's wedding. The intended groom turned out to be none other than Jeff Blakely. . . ."

As she explained, she began to relax and soon they were huddled over the table, heads close together as they shared the one thing they'd always have between them, no matter what: a mutual love for the child they'd created together.

"So you see," she concluded a long and complicated story, "it really wasn't Jeff's fault at all, no more than it was Lynne's. It's just a miracle they finally got together. Some lucky people really are meant for each other, I truly believe that."

Doug didn't look convinced. "Sounds good, until I remember how much Lynne suffered."

"But that suffering brought her Lily," Rosemary argued, "and now a husband she adores."

Doug smiled suddenly. "You're such a romantic, Rosie—*Rosemary*. What makes you think this marriage is going to work when . . ." There was a pregnant pause. ". . . others don't?"

She'd thought about that and had her answer ready. "They not only love each other, they see things alike in the most important ways. Family's very important to both of them."

He nodded. "That's a start."

"You know, Lynne inherited your wanderlust—"

"You make it sound like a virus."

"Whatever it is, she's got it. That's why she became a geologist. Jeff is such a serious young man, so practical. I suspect that's why he went into computers. But he has his fantasies, too. They hope to travel the world together, documenting every corner on film. This safari honeymoon is the first step toward that goal."

"What about Lily?" Doug glanced toward the child's bedroom.

"What about her?" Rosemary smiled. "They'll take care of Lily, and if they ever need a backup, voilà!" She spread her arms in a welcoming gesture. "I'm only as far away as Colorado."

"And that's enough for you? Your daughter and son-in-law will be out cruising the world, living their dream. Your husband—"

"*Ex*-husband!"

"Same difference."

"Hardly."

"Whatever you want to call me, I'll be sunning myself on some tropical island and living *my* dream. Don't you have a dream, Rosie?"

"I did." She forced the admission past an aching throat. "I wanted to be a wife and mother—I wasn't kidding when I spoke of domestic bliss. I thought it was your dream, too, but somewhere along the line your dream changed—"

She stood up abruptly, biting down hard on a lip that trembled. "It's late and I'm exhausted. I'll see you tomorrow."

"Don't go." He reached out to cover her hand resting on the tabletop. With one fingertip, he touched the blue ring lightly. "There's so much we need to talk about—"

"I can't. Not now."

She slipped her hand from beneath his and whirled away, intent only upon escape. Inside Lynne's bedroom, she leaned against the door and closed her eyes while a bittersweet rush of memory swept over her.

They grew up together in Colorado, fell in love while still practically children and married young. Doug's father was a successful contractor, rough-hewn and blunt and honest to a fault. He built a considerable family fortune with his straightforward manner and sharp business acumen.

Doug and his older brother, Brad, both went into the family business. Only when their parents died within six months of each other, only when the fate of the business was at stake, did Rosemary realize that Doug hadn't been as happy with his lot as she'd thought.

When he told her he wanted to pull up stakes and move to California, she could hardly believe her ears. Start over again? Why? They had a nice home in a nice Denver neighborhood, a lovely daughter doing very well in school, everything secure and . . . and *appropriate.*

She didn't want to go; why should she? Her own family, never as squared away as his, still needed her. Her father, a postal employee, and her mother, a supermarket cashier, were on the outs again. Her older sister was in the process of a divorce, her younger sister had just been fired from her job as an advertising salesperson for a television station, and Rosemary herself was deeply involved in every "worthy" issue she could find, from her daughter's school to civic beautification.

So what else is new? he'd shot back. *It's time we lived our own lives. Didn't you ever just want to try something different?*

She hadn't, but for him, she'd try. With the financial

backing from the sale of his half of the family business to his brother, they'd moved to Encino, California. There Doug had gone into business with his old college roommate, none other than Gordon Conway.

Once again, Rosemary found her niche, at home and in the community. Once again, she concentrated on the needs of her husband and child and those around her. After a few years, memories of Denver faded and she began to feel comfortable in California.

Then Lynne graduated from high school and Rosemary found out how wrong she'd been to take her husband and life for granted. Over a candlelit dinner at an expensive restaurant, Doug had taken her hand in his, looked deep into her eyes and said, "Okay, that's over. We've raised our kid and paid our debt to society. Now we can *really* start living."

His idea of "really living" shocked her to the soles of her feet. He wanted—he actually intended!—to sell everything and move to some island in the South Pacific.

He wanted to dump her, she decided, glaring at herself in the mirror. She'd let herself go, gotten dumpy and middle-aged while he remained youthful and energetic. Had he found someone else? Was that what he *really* meant?

When she managed to put him off, when things slowly returned to what she thought of as "normal," she managed to persuade herself that it had been nothing more than a temporary aberration in the pleasant monotony of their days. He'd been going through some sort of midlife crisis, nothing more. Thank heaven that was over!

Only it wasn't. He grew ever more distant, as if preoccupied with something she could not share. She convinced herself it was nothing to worry about, but she redoubled her efforts to make his life as comfortable and serene as she possibly could.

Then Lynne had the close call in the cave-in and a few months later broke up with her steady fellow. Before her parents recovered from all that, she announced she was pregnant—and refused to discuss her baby's paternity.

Immediately Rosemary and Doug drew together to support their daughter. They were a family again, Rosemary thought with a twinge of guilt while she did what she'd always done best: offer unfailing support and loyalty to those she loved.

She was happy. Lynne would be all right, and so would the baby. Rosemary, with Doug's help, would see to it.

That's exactly what happened—and a few weeks after the baby came, with Lynne settled back in college and Rosemary handling child care and at the height of her happiness, Doug said the awful word: divorce.

On that day, Rosemary's world came to an end. They hadn't fought over money, they hadn't fought over possessions, but they had fought over broken dreams and thwarted dreams. Doug was already long gone before the divorce became final on Dec. 22, when Lily was less than a year old.

After Lynne graduated from college and found a job, Rosemary sold everything and crept back home to Denver to lick her wounds. With time to ponder, she'd gradually come to the conclusion that her first instinct had been the correct one.

Her husband had left her because she was dumpy and middle-aged and content to live in a Betty Crocker world.

So she'd changed. She'd become a woman of the '90s: pumping iron, sweating on treadmills, counting calories, turning her entire life around with a new mind-set and a new career—swimming with the sharks in real estate instead of bouncing babies on her knee at day care as most people who knew her fully expected.

She *had* changed, dammit! Yet here came Doug, treating her just as he always had, looking at her as he always had. Only now, undressing in the dark in Lynne's bedroom, Rosemary finally admitted to herself that everything she'd done, she'd done to strike back at *him*.

She'd wanted him to realize what a gigantic, horrible mistake he'd made when he left her. She'd wanted him to take one look at the new her and fall panting at her feet.

She'd fantasized about him crawling back, begging for one more chance.

That's where her fantasy had always stopped . . . until now.

Of *course* she'd give him another chance, if he'd only ask for one. She loved—

She groaned and pulled a pillow over her head but it didn't smother the realization that she loved him. She'd always loved him and apparently she always would, no matter how much he hurt her or how much their paths might diverge. She'd taken one look at him and all her carefully constructed defenses had collapsed like a tower of Tinkertoys.

So where did that leave her?

Rolling and tumbling around in an empty bed, for starters.

The prolonged squeak of a slowly opening door penetrated the fog in Rosemary's head. When no one said anything, she managed to open one eye.

Lily stood there, a bright smile on her face and one little hand disappearing into the big paw of—

Rosemary groaned and pulled the sheet over her head, well aware of how she must look after a restless night. "Go away," she croaked.

Lily's laughter penetrated Rosemary's feathery defenses. "Oh, Grammy, you're funny! It's time to get up, Grampa says."

"He does, does he." Rosemary pulled the sheet down just enough to let her peek out. Doug stood behind the child, smiling as if he were accustomed to rousing her in her bed—as indeed, he had been, once upon a time.

Back then, he'd usually employed a different method.

Lily bounced across the room and flung herself onto the bed. Rosemary grabbed her granddaughter in a bear hug and rolled back and forth, hugging the child who shrieked with delight. Finally settling onto her back, Rosemary looked up with the smile still on her face.

At the sight of Doug, all freshly shaved and showered and put together, her smile faded. She loved him. What would a woman of the '90s do about that?

She cleared her throat. "Uhhh . . . why don't you two go on out and let me get dressed. Then I'll fix breakfast."

"We already had breakfast," Lily piped up. "Grampa—"

"Cooked? I don't think so!" Rosemary had to laugh at the very idea.

Doug gave her a whimsical smile. "I opened a box of cereal and poured milk. Hey, Rosie, I've been out in the cold cruel world. I've learned to take care of myself."

But not as well as *I* used to do, she thought. Aloud she said, "So you *have* changed."

He looked confused. "I didn't say I'd changed. I always could take care of myself. It's just that with you around, I never had to."

The truth of that hit her in the gut but she pushed it aside. "Whatever—you two scram out of here and let me get dressed, okay?"

After they'd gone, she sat there on the side of her bed with her head buried in her hands, trying to unravel her tangled thoughts

What was she going to do about Doug?

Chapter Four

Coffee. She needed coffee. Following her nose, Rosemary walked out of her bedroom, cinching the belt on her blue velour robe. The peal of the doorbell brought her swinging around.

Gordon Conway stood on the other side of the screen door, smiling broadly. His gaze went past her and the smile slipped badly.

Rosemary knew without checking that Doug had appeared in the kitchen door behind her. "Uhhh . . ." she stammered. "Gordon—"

But what could she, should she, say to him? It was none of his business who she had in the house, but on the other hand, she didn't want him to think there was anything going on with her ex-husband.

Especially when there wasn't.

Gordon spoke past her. "Doug! Well, I'll be damned! When you didn't make the wedding, I naturally thought—"

"You do remember my given name, then." Doug's voice barely concealed an oily smoothness. "I thought I was going by 'idiot' these days."

Gordon's smile didn't falter. "Heard the message, did you." He grimaced. "Sorry about that, buddy. Just trying to impress the lady, you know?"

Rosemary blinked in surprise, a feeling quickly followed

by a kind of pleasure. She spared an oblique glance at Doug, standing before the entry to the kitchen like some guard dog.

"Come on in, Gordon," she invited. "Coffee's on—I think?"

Doug nodded. "Sure is."

"Don't mind if I do," Gordon acquiesced. "That is . . ." He looked from Rosemary to Doug and back again. ". . . if I'm not interrupting . . . anything."

Rosemary cinched the belt on her blue robe even tighter. "Not a thing," she said cheerily, and gestured. "After you, Gordon."

She followed him into the kitchen with head held high.

The adults were willing to go to great lengths to act as if "this sort of thing" happened every day, Rosemary quickly realized. But it didn't; she wasn't sure she'd ever entertained two eligible—well, they were—men in her bathrobe before. Only Lily was truly at ease, chattering away while she drank a glass of orange juice before dashing off after the hapless Pocahontas.

Gordon watched her go with a smile. "That's a cute grandkid you've got there," he said, including both grandparents in his praise. "Seeing her makes me realize how sorry I am that Pam and I . . ." He sighed, concentrating on his coffee mug. "Well, you know."

They did; Rosemary glanced at Doug and saw his almost imperceptible nod.

"Thanks," Doug said into the uncomfortable silence. "As they say, grandkids are so much fun you've gotta wonder why you didn't have them first."

That drew a grin from Gordon. "Lynne seems to have turned out all right." His gaze narrowed. "So how long you here for, Doug?"

"Until after the holidays, looks like."

Gordon did not appear pleased with this piece of information, although he said, "That's good." He glanced around. "Staying here with Rosemary and Lily?"

Doug *did* look pleased. "Looks like," he said again.

"Does that mean you two—?" Gordon waggled a finger between the two of them.

Rosemary let out a derisive snort. "It means *nothing*, except that I'm still a chump. What with the holidays and all . . . it seemed like the charitable thing to do."

"So you two aren't together again," Gordon interpreted with obvious approval.

"Not in the biblical sense," Doug said, all wide-eyed innocence.

"Not in any sense," Rosemary added, her mouth curling down at one sarcastic corner.

Gordon grinned. "Great," he said enthusiastically. "In that case, Doug, you won't mind if Rosemary and Lily and I take a little drive up the coast."

"He has nothing to say about it," Rosemary announced, irritated that Gordon would think so.

"She's right," Doug agreed. "And if I did, I wouldn't. In fact . . ." He gave them a luminous smile. "I think I'll go along. I haven't been to Solvang in—"

"You've *never* been to Solvang," Rosemary said in an accusing tone. "Every time I wanted to go, you started in on your 'tourist trap' lecture. Why would you want to go now?"

He shrugged. "To see if I was wrong?"

To make me crazy, she corrected mentally. But then it occurred to her that she had nothing to lose by letting him come along. She certainly didn't have any designs on Gordon; in fact, until this very minute she hadn't even seriously considered his invitation. But if seeing her with him displeased her ex, why not?

Why not indeed! Smiling, she left to dress for an outing which might turn out to be very interesting.

Doug rode in the back seat of Gordon's Cadillac, next to an excited Lily. In the front seat, Rosemary had a hard time keeping herself from constantly glancing over her shoulder at the twosome. Gordon kept up a running commentary as he drove northwest through the Santa Ynez Valley but she listened with only half an ear.

She could feel Doug's gaze on her as palpably as a touch. He watched her with almost quizzical interest as they followed the freeway through hills she'd called "golden" when she lived in this state. Now they simply looked winter-brown.

Gordon glanced at her with a tentative smile. "You'll either love Solvang or hate it," he predicted. "At least, that's how it is with most people. It kinda reminds me of a Danish Disneyland, and—"

"Disneyland!" Apparently that one word cut through Lily's back seat chatter. "Are we going to Disneyland? I *love* Disneyland!"

"No, sweetheart," Doug soothed her. "Mr. Conway's joking—I think."

"Oh." Lily sounded disappointed.

Gordon looked into the rear view mirror at the child's dejected expression. "Don't look so down at the mouth, Lily. You'll like Solvang even if it isn't Disneyland."

"What's a . . . what's a Solving?"

"That's *Solvang*. It's a little Danish village in the middle of California. Let's see, what would a kid like best? Maybe the windmills—ever see a windmill?"

"I never did," Lily admitted. She still sounded disappointed.

"You'll like 'em. Trust me. And there'll be holiday decorations and Santa Claus might even be there."

Rosemary smiled at his enthusiasm. "Gordon Conway, how did you get to be such an expert on Solvang?" she asked lightly.

He looked sheepish. "Pam and I spent our honeymoon there," he said. "I still go back every once in a while, when I want to get away from it all. I'm pretty sure you'll like it, too." He guided the car onto a freeway off ramp.

"Me, too," Lily called from the back seat. "Grampa, too."

"Yeah, right," Doug growled from the back seat. "Don't forget Grampa."

Solvang, Gordon explained as they drove into the little village with its quaint windmills and cottages with artificial nesting storks on rooftops, was established in 1911 by a group of Danish educators. Looking for a site to build a school, they settled in this inland valley. Soon they'd recruited enough fellow Danes to establish a thriving community.

It wasn't until the 1940s that residents recognized the tourist potential in making their little town reflect its ethnic heritage. Setting to work with a will, they soon transformed the typical Spanish-Californian architecture to conform to their new role as the self-proclaimed "Danish Capital of America."

Although Rosemary had never been to Denmark, she thought this little town looked just right with its cobblestone walks and old-fashioned gas lights. Shops and restaurants and bakeries crammed the downtown area, everything decorated with twinkling fairy lights and fragrant wreaths. After showing them the sights, Gordon drove into the parking lot of a large restaurant just off the main street.

"You'll enjoy the smorgasbord here," he promised, holding the door for Rosemary and pretty much ignoring Doug. "They always have a wonderful Christmas tree that Lily will like."

Rosemary followed him inside, resisting the impulse to wait for the others, or even to turn around to see if they were coming. Doug had horned in on this occasion so he could look out for himself.

As for Lily, Rosemary had no qualms. By the time they came out, she fully expected the girl to be speaking Danish.

"Do you know what *Solvang* means? Do you, Grammy? Do you?"

Rosemary tried to concentrate on Lily's excited questions but it wasn't easy. It seemed as if they'd just spent half a day eating. With absolutely no experience or knowledge of Danish food, she'd found herself devouring everything from *gule aerter*, a thick yellow split pea soup, to *flaeskesteg*, roast pork, right on to *aeblekage*, a delicious chilled apple dessert covered with whipped cream and jelly.

Tomorrow she'd have to starve herself and spend at least eight hours in the gym to make up for this pig-out, she realized.

"Grammy!"

"I'm sorry, dear. What does Solvang mean?" Rousing herself from the food-induced stupor, Rosemary tightened her grip on the little hand and led the child back toward the linen-draped table where the men waited.

"It means sunny fields!" The little girl looked delighted with herself. "That man in there said, when me and Grampa—"

"Grandpa and I."

"That's right, we went to look at the bee-oootiful Christmas tree, and he said."

"That's wonderful, sweetie."

"Yes, it is," Lily agreed, sliding back into her seat. "Can I have more of that apple stuff now?"

Rosemary laughed. "I think you've had quite enough. We don't want you to make yourself sick."

"Okay." Lily gave in cheerfully. "But can we go for a walk or something? That man said there's a sweetcar."

Doug grinned. "That's streetcar, sweetheart."

She nodded. "With horses. Can I see the horses?"

And so they went to see the horses pull a Danish street car, loaded with tourists, through the town. Then while Lily and the two men listened to carolers, Rosemary picked up a couple of hand-knit sweaters for Jeff and Lynne, a pair of little wooden shoes for Lily, and finally popped into a bakery to buy two golden crusty loaves— Doug loved fresh bread.

Well, so did she! She wasn't getting it just for him, she assured herself petulantly.

"What next?" Gordon greeted her return. Doug and Lily stood nearby, looking into a window filled with hand-made wooden toys. "Want to check out the Spanish side of local history? The old Mission Santa Ines is just down the road."

"I don't think so, Gordon. It's been lovely but—" She was watching Doug and Lily and saw him lean down and whisper something in the little girl's ear. She turned to him with a broad smile and rose on tiptoe to kiss his cheek.

Pulling herself together, Rosemary concentrated on Gordon. "I think Lily would like to see Santa and Mrs. Claus and then we should be getting home."

"All right," he agreed. "But while I have a chance . . . I want you to know I'm really glad you came along today, even if—" He darted a significant glance at the significant presence which had been underfoot.

Rosemary gave his arm a grateful pat. "You've been very patient."

"Yeah, well, I've got an ulterior motive."

Warning signals clanged. "You do?"

"Sure. I figured if I was decent about it, he might baby-sit one of these nights and let us go out alone." At her look of alarm, he added quickly, "You know, dinner? There are a ton of great restaurants in Santa Barbara. What do you say, Rosemary? Have I earned myself another chance?"

Why was she hesitating? Why was her attention drawn once more to her ex-husband and grandchild?

"Let me think about it," she said at last, hedging and knowing it.

Gordon, however, seemed satisfied.

They located Santa easily enough; all they had to do was follow the children thronging to him. There was a line, of course, but it moved more expeditiously than they could have expected. Soon Lily was bouncing up the steps to hop onto Santa's plush red knee.

He chucked her beneath the chin with practiced ease. "Hello, there, little lady. And what might your name be?"

Lily laughed. "You know," she said.

He rolled blue eyes. "One'a those, huh. Ooooky-doke. Have you been a good girl?"

"I've been *way* good," she said confidently.

"In that case, what can Santa do for you this Christmas?"

Lily grabbed hold of his snowy beard, pulled his face close to hers and shouted, *"Make my grammy and grampa get married so I can be the flower girl!"*

As a humiliated grandmother and a laughing grandfather hustled the child away, Rosemary thought she heard old Santa mutter, "And I thought grandparents had higher standards than this younger generation!"

Gordon lingered at the front door. So did Rosemary. So did Doug, since he couldn't very well leave the two of them alone . . . could he?

Only Lily was absent, already napping in her bedroom where her grandfather had deposited her minutes earlier.

"Thanks again, Gordon," Rosemary said, sounding uneasy. "You can put me squarely in the column of people who like Solvang."

"Glad to. I think you'd also like—"

The telephone rang, cutting him off. With an apologetic glance, Rosemary went to answer.

Gordon gave Doug a narrow glance. "Are you satisfied?" he demanded.

"Satisfied with what?" Doug raised his brows in an approximation of innocence.

"I always did like Rosemary. Now that she's free—"

"Free? Free!" For some reason that particular word gouged at Doug's self-possession. "Is that what she calls it?"

"Hell, that's what I call it! Relax, buddy. I'm just trying to say that now she's no longer married—"

"To me."

"To anybody. She's unattached, how's that? I always liked and admired her and now I'd like to get to know her better." Again that narrow-eyed gaze. "You got a problem with that?"

"Only one." Doug didn't even try to temper his tone. "We go back a long way—"

"Damn right! What's your point?"

"I *know* you, Gordy. I've known you since college when you were hitting on every pretty girl you met. If you get out of line with Rosie, I swear to God, I'll knock your block off. You got that?"

Gordon recoiled in something which looked like horror. "Jesus! What do you think I am? I said I respect the woman. Surely you don't think—"

"I *said*, you got that?"

"Yeah, I got it, but where do you get off telling me—"

"Doug! It's Lynne!"

Rosemary's voice, trembling with excitement, interrupted the intense, if low level, confrontation between the two men. Again, their gazes locked.

Doug jerked his chin toward the door. "Run along, Gordy. This is family business."

Gordon seemed to consider. Then he shrugged. "Yeah, you're right. Tell Rosemary I'll call her."

I'll tell Rosemary to run if you do. Doug watched his former business partner exit through the front door. And then he realized he didn't dare tell her any such thing.

The way she was acting, so out of character, she'd probably do the exact opposite.

He turned toward the interior of the house, Gordon forgotten in a sudden panic. Would Lynne forgive him for missing her wedding?

"Oh, Daddy, I'm so glad you came—and so sorry you missed the wedding!"

"Thanks for understanding, sweetheart."

"I do, honestly. Daddy, I want you to say hello to Jeff."

Doug wanted to groan but didn't. He hated having these stilted telephone conversations with perfect strangers, especially strangers with whom he already had a bone to pick.

"Mr. Hancock?"

"Hello, Jeff. I'm . . . sorry I missed the wedding."

The answering silence stretched out interminably and then his new son-in-law said, "I hope you had a good reason. Lynne was upset, whatever she says now."

Uh-oh; fences to mend here. "She had every right to be upset," Doug admitted, his jaws tight. "But I do have a good reason, Jeff."

"Will you be there to tell us about it when we get back?"

Unforgiving young pup. "Yeah, I'll be here." Doug couldn't help adding, "You've got a few explanations of your own, my man."

"I have good reasons, too," Jeff said softly. "But just so there's no mistake—I love your daughter and I'll never deliberately do anything to hurt her."

"Neither will I. Neither will I."

There seemed nothing further to say. At the conclusion of the telephone call, Doug repeated the exchange to Rosemary.

"He's very protective of her," she said. "You'll like him, when you get to know him. I'm supremely confident of that."

He shrugged, deliberately noncommittal.

She glanced around. "I didn't get a chance to say goodbye to Gordon."

"I said it for both of us."

Her gaze sharpened. "I don't know why you tagged along today. You were just a tad shy of gracious."

"Why ever would you suggest such a thing?"

"I wonder." She shrugged as if it didn't matter.

"Rosie—Rosemary, the guy's a dog. You know that, don't you?"

"I certainly don't." She looked incensed. "And even if he were, I'm well past the age where I need a chaperon."

He followed her into the kitchen. "You've led a sheltered life."

She stopped before the sink and turned to face him, hands braced behind her. "I used to be sheltered. Do you think my life's stood still since you left?"

"Well, no, but . . ." Actually, he did. He frowned. "You haven't said much about what you've been up to since . . . the divorce."

"Since . . . the *divorce*, neither have you."

"I've been doing exactly what I said I would—doing what I want when I want to."

"Must be nice."

The cynicism rocked him. Rosie had never been cynical, never. "I take it you can't say the same."

She started to speak, then stopped. A quick expression of confusion touched her face. "Actually, I guess I can say the same."

"You're working?"

"Yes."

"Doing what?"

"Guess."

He shrugged. "I don't know . . . something domestic? Child care? Interior decorating, teaching something to someone?"

She threw back her head and laughed and he found himself admiring the strong but slender column of her throat, the way her streaky blonde hair curved away from her temples. Damn, she looked good to him! But then, she always had.

"I sell real estate," she said with an impish grin.

"You're kidding. That means dealing with strangers— hell, dealing with math."

"It also means working long, strange hours and *selling*, both concepts that appalled me in the beginning."

"So why'd you do it?"

He watched the play of emotion across her still-expressive face and decided to help her out. "Because you wanted to make a complete break with the past," he guessed.

She nodded. "I told you I'd become a woman of the '90s, and I meant it. I bought a loft in LoDo—"

"LoDo?"

Her laughter this time was more sincere. "You have been gone. Lower Denver. Lots going on there these days—renovation of old buildings for businesses and apartments and condos, lots of tourist activity. You wouldn't recognize it."

Her enthusiasm slipped away. "But of course you're not interested in any of that. In a couple of weeks you'll head back to your desert island."

"Tropical island."

"Whatever." She looked at him with eyes suddenly vulnerable. "This may be the last time we ever see each other."

He flinched before her quiet statement. "Why would you think that?"

"We only have one daughter," she murmured. "We won't be meeting at any more family weddings . . . until it's Lily's turn, I suppose."

"Don't say that, Rosie."

Stepping forward, he caught her by the arms, his hands curving around the smooth—very firm—flesh. She went still, and her expression became wary.

He sucked in a quick breath but a basic, gut-deep honesty made him go on. "I've missed you," he said quietly. "Until I saw you, I didn't know how much."

"Really?"

He nodded. "I think you've missed me, too."

"Do you?"

"Stop that," he said, irritated. "I'm being serious and you're fooling around."

"Am I?"

Before he could respond, she rose on tiptoes and pressed her lips to his.

Chapter Five

*E*ven when they'd been married, Rosemary had never taken the initiative. Doug could not have been more shocked by her kiss if she'd slapped his face—or called him a jerk again.

But he didn't try to deceive himself that he hadn't been thinking about just this eventuality since receiving his daughter's wedding invitation. He'd hoped an opportunity to make a move would present itself.

Never in his wildest dreams had he imagined Rosemary, his Rosie, reaching out this way—hell, in broad daylight, yet! He'd be an idiot not to take advantage of the situation—but what if he scared her off? What if he misread the situation and really screwed up? She'd already made it plain that she hadn't forgiven him for past stupidity.

But hell, he was only human. He reached for her—at the same exact moment she jerked away. He saw on her face an expression that stopped him in his tracks.

"Wait a minute, wait a minute." His voice came out a croak. "What the hell was that all about?"

"Curiosity. Curiosity, plain and simple." She ducked beneath his arm and headed for the kitchen door.

He watched her go, feeling as if he'd just been flattened by a runaway locomotive. Was she playing games with him or what?

* * *

Rosemary knelt on the exercise mat, shins and feet flat on
the floor beneath her. Slowly she reached out with hands
sliding along the floor, head and neck relaxing between
her arms. With her forehead touching the floor, she sat
back on her heels and held the stretch.

It felt so good she groaned with pleasure. One thing
she'd learned since her divorce was the value of exercise,
not only for strength and flexibility but for stress relief.

Since Doug's unexpected appearance, stress had become
her middle name. So after delivering Lily to her kindergarten class, Rosemary had headed straight for the health
club.

Rising slowly to hands and knees, she arched her back
in a cat stretch. It hadn't taken her twenty-four hours to
make a fool out of herself. What on earth had possessed
her to kiss him? What must he think of her now?

Not that she was a happenin' chick, obviously. He
hadn't even kissed her back, not a bit. She didn't think
he'd even been tempted. He'd just stood there like a block
of wood and let her cut her own throat.

Sliding back down onto the mat, she started her
crunches, working abs, upper abs, obliques, finishing up
with hip lifts for the lower abs. The motions were auto-
matic, which unfortunately did nothing to rein in her de-
pressed thoughts.

How was she ever going to convince him that she had
a handle on her life now? Or perhaps a more important
question, she admitted, sitting up to mop at her damp face
with the fluffy white towel furnished by the club, why was
convincing him so important to her?

Thoroughly stretched, thoroughly warmed up, she
walked quickly into the next room where all the Nautilus
equipment was arrayed in sleek, metallic glory. Taking a
deep breath, she advanced on the leg extension machine.

Slipping the weight key into the appropriate slot, she sat
on the padded seat and slid her feet behind the roller pads.
Grasping the handles lightly, she swung both legs up
smoothly, feeling the large muscles on the front of her

thighs stretch and contract rhythmically.

Five years ago, she hadn't had any muscles, to speak of, on the front of her thighs or anywhere else. The first time she'd walked into a health club in Denver, she'd felt almost as foolish as she had after being rebuffed by her ex-husband.

But she'd persisted. She'd hired a personal trainer and forced her dumpling body into tights and oversized T-shirts and she'd persisted, sometimes sweating and swearing but always there.

To her astonishment, her new regime had worked far beyond her wildest dreams. Weight had begun coming off to reveal a brand new shape. Encouraged, she'd worked even harder until—voilà! The new, improved Rosemary Hancock had emerged like a butterfly from a cocoon.

Or so she'd thought until she ran afoul of Douglas Hancock once again. *He* certainly hadn't been bowled over by the new Rosemary. He didn't even seem to notice the changes.

She adjusted the weight pin at the leg curl machine and lay down on her stomach. Maneuvering her feet under the roller pads, she took a deep breath and grabbed the handles. Curling her legs, she tried to touch her heels to her backside.

Damn Doug Hancock anyway! She'd been horribly messed up after he'd divorced her and she wasn't going to let him mess her up again. Maybe—her legs froze into position only halfway up in their arc.

Maybe she'd needed this. Maybe she'd needed to see him again to put a closure to the most painful period of her life. Whether he recognized it or not, something good had come out of that horrible time for her.

She'd reinvented herself. She was a new, improved Rosemary whether anybody else realized it or not—or even cared, for that matter. She was more confident, healthier, and even—surely it wasn't *too* conceited to think it—better looking.

Maybe—she resumed the motion of her legs, not quite

so smoothly as before—maybe Doug had left her *not* because she'd lost her looks and become dull but because his interest had simply waned.

The guy using the pullover machine moved on just as Rosemary finished her twelfth leg curl rep. Swinging around, she stood up, marching on her next objective. Slipping the key into the weight stack, she hesitated, then added ten more pounds.

She'd give her latissimus dorsi a real workout, and in the doing, stop thinking about her ex-husband and all the grief ahead of her in the next twelve days.

Sure she would.

Rosemary headed toward the locker rooms, breathing hard and swabbing at her face with the towel as she went. She'd finished her weight routine in record time, pushing her muscles to the point of failure on every apparatus. She'd even managed to clear her mind by the time she'd finished.

The sight of Gordon Conway waiting for her at the head of the stairs brought everything lurching back. He grinned and she sucked in an apprehensive breath.

"Good grief, Gordon, is anything wrong?"

He pushed away from the wall, his movements casual. "Why should something be wrong?"

"Why, because—" She shrugged, aware of the way he was looking at her. She'd worn the usual club uniform: stretchy black lycra tights with a pale blue leotard, jock socks and cross trainers. So why was he—?

She laughed. Of course! Gordon had never seen her in such a get-up, doubtless had never even imagined she'd consider wearing such garb. The old Rosemary wouldn't have, that was for sure.

She tossed the towel over one shoulder. "Let's start again. What are you doing here, Gordon?"

"Waiting for you," he said without guile.

She frowned. "Why?"

"I thought I might take you to lunch."

"Why?" she asked again, genuinely puzzled.

"Why not?" He sighed. "Look, Rosemary . . ." Now he did look anxious. "I don't have enough time to beat around the bush. Seeing you like this—" He drew his appreciative glance down the length of her. "It just blows me away, how you've changed."

Yeah, and Doug hasn't even noticed. "Gordon," she began in a warning tone, "I don't know what you have in mind but whatever it is, give it up."

He blinked in surprise. "I don't know what you mean."

"It's simple. I don't fool around."

"I'd never ask you to, Rosemary."

"Then what—?"

"My intentions," he said with dignity, "are strictly honorable."

"Then I know we have nothing further to say to each other, because *I* have no intention of ever marrying again." She started past him, her chin held high.

He caught her arm, halting her flight. "Okay, that's out in the open. So what's the harm of having a bite of lunch together? And spending a little time together before you go back to Denver? For old times' sake . . ."

She shook her head. "I don't think that's such a good idea. You understand."

He looked forlorn. "Okay, it's up to you." He half-turned. "He said you'd turn me down."

Her antenna pricked up. "He—who said what?"

"Doug said you wouldn't go out with me." Gordon shrugged. "He's the one told me where you were working out."

"Why would he say such a thing?" she wondered out loud.

"I guess he thinks you're still hung up on him."

Yeah, that was logical. For a moment, Rosemary stood there in speechless fury. Then she tossed her head and glared at the hapless Gordon. "If you don't mind waiting while I shower and get dressed and call Doug to pick Lily up at school, I would be *delighted* to join you for lunch."

And dinner and just about anything else he could name. She'd be damned if she'd let Doug reject her and then expect her to hang around mooning over him!

The food was good, the surroundings delightful, the companionship pleasant. So why could Rosemary hardly wait to return to Lynne's little adobe on the hill?

Still, it was midafternoon before she made it. Pausing on the front step, she waved good-bye to Gordon on the street below.

Turning, she entered the house, suddenly wary of what she might find. Dropping her gym bag in the entry, she looked around, the murmur of voices drawing her toward the back. At the screen door, she stopped to peer through.

She saw Lily first. Wearing her pink bridesmaid dress, the little girl held her mother's bridal bouquet.

"And see, Grampa, what I do is walk along throwing flowers on the floor." She mimed that action with the drying bouquet, swooping and dipping and smiling.

Moving slightly, Rosemary spotted Doug on a patio chair to the right of the doorway, smiling and nodding at the antics of his granddaughter. A mound of fabric rested on the table beside him, a shirt perhaps, Rosemary couldn't be sure. When she walked through the doorway he jerked upright, the smile disappearing.

"Where'd you go for lunch, San Francisco?"

Crossing the patio, Rosemary dropped a kiss on Lily's curly hair. To Doug she said, "How droll."

He looked, she regretted to notice, particularly good in a pair of khaki shorts and a T-shirt that said "London—Paris—Vanuatu." His feet were bare and brown.

"How's Gordon?" he asked finally.

"He's fine."

"Grammy, was I a good flower girl or what?" Lily tugged at Rosemary's hand.

"You were fabulous, sweetheart."

"I'm surprised at you, Rosie."

"Because I think Lily is the best flower girl in the world?"

"I *am*, Grampa! I do good." The little girl looked on the verge of tears.

Doug quickly moved to rectify the misunderstanding. "I'm sure you do, Lily. I was talking about something else. Rosie—"

"You didn't see me," Lily said forlornly. "I wish you'd been there. I didn't mess up, honest. Well, maybe one time."

"I wish I'd been there, too. Rosie—"

"I could do it again," Lily said hopefully. "If somebody'd just get married—like you and Grammy!" She threw herself against Rosemary, her little arms encircling her grandmother's waist. "You're su'posed to get married real soon, Grammy—Mama said. Can I be your flower girl, please?"

Rosemary patted the girl's head. "Yes, you can be my flower girl *when* I get married, which will be *never* if I've got any sense."

"That's a relief."

At Doug's soft remark, Rosemary's head jerked up. "What's that supposed to mean?"

"Nothing. Just that the way Gordon's pursuing you—"

"Gordon is not pur—"

"I can wear this very same dress if you hurry," Lily said, looking down at her pink frock with a worried expression. "I'm growin' like a weed, you said, but maybe I can stop for a while if I try real hard."

"Oh, sweetie! You just keep on growing." Rosemary gave Lily a hug but she was watching Doug. "Is there anything else you wanted to say, Mr. This-Is-Really-None-Of-Your-Business?"

"That's not his name. His name is Grampa!"

Doug gave them both his most charming smile, the little crooked grin that used to make Rosemary's heart turn over, well, still did, actually. "My name is mud, at the moment," he suggested. "I know it's none of my business but don't forget, Rosie, I've known that guy since college. He's not to be trusted."

"Like you *are*?" Oh, why did she say that! "I'm sorry, but I'm no longer accustomed to answering to anyone. I believe you call that independence. That's the stuff you told me I didn't have enough of, remember?"

He did. She could tell by his shocked expression. But then he shrugged and smiled. "You're right, it is none of my business." Picking up the pile of fabric from the table, he extracted a needle and promptly jabbed it into his thumb. Risking a quick glance at her, he said, "I don't suppose you'd take pity and sew this button on for me, would you?"

Of course she would—of course she wouldn't! "I don't do buttons anymore," she informed him stiffly. "I don't really sew at all anymore."

"Why, Grammy, you made my flower girl dress," Lily reminded in a shocked tone.

"Yes, sweetie, but that was very very special."

"I guess you *have* changed," Doug allowed, but he didn't look happy about it. Not happy at all.

Like Rosemary was? She'd loved sewing, but it just didn't fit her new image.

"So what's for dinner?"

Rosemary looked up from her novel, displeased by the interruption. "Whatever you want," she said. "I won't be here, so—"

"Where'll *you* be?" He looked astonished at her news.

"I'll be having dinner with Gordon at some new Mexican restaurant he thinks I'll like."

"Well . . . well . . . what about us?"

She laughed at his outraged expression. "If you're not up to defrosting a package or opening a can, I'll be glad to do it for you before I go."

"That's not what I meant. I meant, why do you want to rush off and leave Lily and me—leave Lily all alone?

I thought that's why you were here, to spend time with your granddaughter?''

He looked so indignant that she had to smile. ''I've spent time with her today. I read two books to her before her nap, and we played with her rock collection after she got up. I'm having a wonderful time with her.''

''Then why do you keep rushing off, every chance you get?''

Rosemary raised her brows. ''To give *you* time alone with her, Grampa. I'm being thoughtful.'' She closed her book. ''That, and the fact that I find Gordon pleasant company.''

''Well, son of a—'' He tightened his mouth into a thin line. ''Fine, go for it. Just don't come crying to me when he makes his move.''

''I wouldn't dream of it,'' she said airily, rising from her chair. She glanced at her wristwatch. ''I see it's time for me to get dressed. Thanks for reminding me.''

And she sailed from the room, satisfied that she'd come out on top in that exchange.

''My goodness,'' the waitress said, leaning down, ''what a pretty little girl you are.''

Lily smiled angelically. ''Thank you very much, I'm sure.''

Doug patted his granddaughter's shoulder, feeling quite pleased with himself for letting her wear her flower girl dress. She might be a little overdressed for a family-style Mexican restaurant but what the hell? Better that than disappointing her.

The grinning waitress straightened. ''We gotta nice table over there by the window,'' she offered. ''In fact, it's probably the best in the house, with a view of the fountain and all.''

''Uhh . . . could we have that one instead?'' Doug pointed.

''That one?'' The waitress looked puzzled. ''Sure, but

it's not nearly as good. The only view that one's got is of the next table.''

Where, at the moment, Rosemary sat with Gordon Conway. Doug smiled sweetly. "That one will do just fine," he assured her. "Ready, Lily?"

Lily nodded but her attention was on the waitress. "Did you know I was a flower girl sometimes?" she asked earnestly. "I did reaaal good. If you want to get married, I could maybe . . ."

Chattering away, the little girl followed the waitress through the clutter of tables filled with happy diners.

Rosemary could not believe her eyes. Doug and Lily were plunking themselves down at the next table. Openmouthed, she stared.

Doug caught her gaze and grinned broadly. "Look who's here," he cued Lily. "What a surprise!"

"Surprise my—Aunt Ethel!" But still Rosemary held out her arms for Lily to rush into them. Over the girl's head, she glared at Doug. "How did you find us?"

"Would you believe this is pure accident?"

Gordon let out a scornful grunt. "No, and even if she did, I wouldn't."

"You're right." That charming smile showed itself again. "I heard Gordon mention the restaurant when he picked you up. Then when I asked Lily what she'd like for dinner, she naturally said Mexi—"

"I said pizza, Grampa! And you said, don't you like tacos, kid?" She actually did a credible imitation of him.

Rosemary didn't want to let him off the hook that easily but found herself unable to maintain her anger and outrage. She even lost the battle not to smile.

"You rat," she said to Doug, but the smile took out the sting.

He shrugged. "Sorry, we didn't mean to rain on your parade. Lily, come back over here to our own table and sit down."

"But Grampa!" She frowned. "I want to sit with

Grammy, too.'' She wiggled her fingers at him. ''You come over here, okay?''

''Well, I wouldn't mind. . . .''

''No way!'' Rosemary sat up straighter in her chair. ''You're not going to horn in on my—''

''Your what?'' Doug pressed quickly. ''Your date? Believe me, I understand completely.'' His gaze locked with Gordon's but his smile didn't extend to his eyes.

''It's not a date. It's—''

''It certainly is a date,'' Gordon interrupted emphatically. ''She's a free and independent woman, Doug, and can go out with anyone she pleases.'' He added softly to Rosemary, ''And she pleases me plenty.''

''Why, you—''

''Doug, butt out!''

''Grammy, can I sit down or *what*?'' Lily pulled out a chair, hesitating for dramatic effect. ''Because I'm really hungry!'' Suddenly she bestowed a dazzling smile on Gordon. ''How do you do, Mr. Con-Mr. Con-Mister? *You* want me to sit down, I bet.''

Gordon, like the rest of them, was putty in her hands.

Rosemary refused to ride home with her ex and her granddaughter; that was taking civility too far. Doug had dawdled as long as they could after the meal. When it became apparent that Lily was about to fall asleep in her Shirley Temple, he gave up and carried her away.

Rosemary had been glad to linger for a drink with Gordon, not so much because she was wild to be alone with him as to show Doug a thing or two. But by the time they pulled up in front of Lynne's cottage, she was beginning to question her determination to put Doug in his place.

Gordon walked her to the front door—where, she quickly noted, Doug had left the porch light on. Gordon caught both her hands in his and smiled.

''That was fun,'' he said.

She gave an uncomfortable little laugh. ''You're kidding, right?''

"Not at all." He lifted one of her hands and pressed it to his lips. "I like your granddaughter, I really do. I've always regretted . . ." His expression grew sad.

She nodded her understanding. "Kids are a pain sometimes, but I can't imagine life without them. Lily's a true joy to me."

"You're a lucky woman."

Was she? It'd been a long time since she'd felt that way. "Thank you for being so understanding," she said lightly. "And for dinner, too. It was delicious—but there was no reason for you to pay for the two stowaways!"

He laughed. "Just trying to impress you, I guess." His grip on her hands tightened. "Rosemary—"

"Please don't," she said quickly. "I'm not ready for that, Gordon. I warned you. . . ."

"No problem," he said. With a final squeeze, he released her hands. "You said you had more Christmas shopping to do. I'll take you to the mall—Lily, too, of course. We can have lunch. . . ."

As he talked, Rosemary tried to form a polite disclaimer. Before she could let him down gently, she caught movement out of the corner of her eye and stiffened. *Doug!* He was spying on her through the open window, the dirty dog.

That's why, when Gordon paused for breath, she said brightly, "Love to! Pick me up at noon and we can go pick Lily up together."

She didn't know who was more shocked: Gordon, herself—or Doug.

Chapter Six

*T*he rush was on.

Gordon reminded Doug of a jellyfish, spreading out until he surrounded everything and everybody. Good old Gordy took Rosemary everywhere: Christmas shopping at El Paseo, from whence she returned agog about winding walkways and adobe walls and balconies with wrought-iron railings; through El Presidio de Santa Barbara State Historic Park, where, according to Gordy, the city of Santa Barbara was born; and even to the Karpeles Manuscript Library Museum, which she particularly enjoyed.

"It's fabulous," she enthused to Doug. "There are all these historic documents on display in wooden cases on pedestals, and—"

"Copies," he predicted.

"Some are original. There are books, letters, treaties, music scores—"

"Yeah, I guess I've heard of it," he admitted gracelessly. "I'd probably enjoy it myself, but now that you've already been there *without me*—"

"No problem," she said brightly. She still wore the trim navy blue linen slacks and slinky short-sleeved sweater she'd put on for a day on the town. "I'll keep Lily and you can go anytime."

"Anytime—yeah, right. Lynne will be back in eight days."

Her lips parted in astonishment. "Time does fly."

Maybe for her. For Doug, who spent a good part of his time wondering what the hell she saw in Gordon, time crept past at a snail's pace.

Not that he wasn't enjoying his time with his granddaughter; he was. They were going places on their own: to the Nishiki Koi Ponds on Montecito Street, where Lily fed the brilliantly colored fish, then on to parks and to the beach. But everywhere they went, they seemed to miss Rosemary equally.

On an impulse, he said to Rosie, "Friday's Lily's last day of school before Christmas vacation. Let's pick her up together and take her on a picnic."

She looked alarmed. "Oh, I don't know if that's such a good idea."

He scowled. "Why not? Is *Gordy* coming by again?"

"As a matter of fact, he has to go into Los Angeles tomorrow," she said airily.

"Then give me one good reason why we shouldn't do something nice for our grandchild." He sounded argumentative but damn it, Gordon didn't seem to have much trouble getting her to go out with *him*.

She looked on the verge of argument but, instead, straightened her shoulders and gave a brisk nod. "You're absolutely right. I shouldn't let my personal reservations deprive Lily of having both her grandparents with her now, since this is probably the last time it'll ever happen."

"Jeez!" He stared at her. "That's a crummy attitude."

She shrugged. "It's true. In a week or so, I'll head back to Colorado and eventually you'll go wherever it is you go these days and that will be that."

"But now that we've made up our quarrel—"

"Made up our quarrel?" Her calm facade cracked. "Doug, we haven't made up *anything*. We're co-existing for Lynne's and Lily's sakes, that's all. How could you suggest otherwise?"

"Because," he said, the admission coming slow and painful, "I've discovered I don't like knowing you're out there somewhere hating my guts.''

For a moment she stared into his eyes, her own veiled and somehow mysterious. ''I don't hate your guts,'' she said at last. ''I tried—God knows I wish I could sometimes, even now. But too much—''

''Grammy!'' Lily dashed through the back door, Pocahontas draped over her arm like a gray fur stole. ''Come see my secret hideout behind the banana tree.''

Rosemary knelt to hug the child, her gaze lifting to Doug. ''Yes,'' she said, ''let's go on a picnic tomorrow. Lily would like that, wouldn't you, honey?''

''A picnic!'' Lily jumped up and down, giving Pocahontas a chance to escape, which she grabbed. ''Grampa, too? Oh, boy!''

So that's how they ended up together at Hilda McIntyre Ray Park.

Lily ran ahead, reaching the picnic table first. She plunked **down** the tote bag containing paper plates and plastic spoons and looked around happily.

''Hurry!'' she shouted to her dawdling grandparents. ''Let's sit here!''

Rosemary barely heard the child, so enthralled was she with the view. An undulating lawn sloped down, dotted by gnarled live oak trees which didn't conceal the panoramic view of the city of Santa Barbara and the Santa Ynez Mountains.

The air sparkled around them beneath a bright winter sun. A mild breeze had dictated light sweaters for them all, but didn't dim the beauty of this December day.

Doug grinned at her. ''Like it?'' he asked, indicating the small park.

''Love it.'' She turned toward the picnic table Lily had selected. ''How in the world did you find it, tucked away in a residential district like this?''

''I asked Mrs. Hughes.''

Rosemary set her picnic basket on the table. ''Who's Mrs. Hughes?''

''She's Lindsey's mother.''

''Who's Lindsey?''

He gave her a peculiar glance before lowering the insulated cooler to the grass. ''Lynne's neighbor, Rosie. She said she met you at the wedding.''

Embarrassed, Rosemary nodded. She'd been spending so much time with Gordon that she'd in effect distanced herself from her own family. And she didn't even *like* Gordon that much—well, maybe that wasn't quite fair. She liked him just fine but in a kind of take-it-or-leave-it way. The best thing about him was that he gave her a built-in excuse to avoid Doug.

''However you found it, it's great.''

''Grammy, Grampa! Can I play on the 'quipment? Will you push me on the swings, please? Come *on*, let's go!''

And as usual when Lily called, her adoring grandparents answered with alacrity.

Lily lay dozing on a picnic blanket on the grass. Rosemary and Doug sat nearby at the picnic table with the thermos of coffee between them. The remnants of the meal still lay before them: foam plates with scraps of marinated veggies and a few crusts from the deli sandwiches, orange peels and apple cores. As Rosemary and Doug talked quietly to avoid disturbing the little girl, they worked on cleaning up with desultory movements.

Rosemary felt more at ease with him than she had since . . . since before the divorce. No matter what lay between them, they were together in their love for their daughter and their granddaughter.

Giving in to impulse, Rosemary asked at last a question that had been hovering in her mind since Doug's arrival. ''You've said so little about where you've been and what you've been doing. Is there some . . . reason you don't want to talk about it?''

''I thought there was.'' He looked at her with hooded eyes.

''Okay, I accept that.'' She slid one plate beneath another, trying to shield her disappointment.

"That's not it. The truth is, I didn't think you'd want to hear about it."

She cocked her head. "Because . . . ?"

"Because it's been everything I dreamed it would be, with one rather major exception. I love to talk about it, if you're sure you want to hear."

She nodded. "I think I need to hear." She bit her lip. "So where have you been?"

The expression on his face altered subtly. "Everywhere. Through Melanesia, French Polynesia. I was in the Cook Islands when the wedding invitation tracked me down."

"I don't know anything at all about the Cook Islands but they don't sound terribly exotic," she observed.

"They are, though—the last paradise, like Hawaii used to be. Captain Cook dropped anchor in the 1770s, gave them his name and then had the decency to sail away. It was another fifty or so years before the missionaries caught up with the natives."

She smiled at his enthusiasm. "But where *are* the Cook Islands? I don't even know."

"South Pacific."

"I'm weak in geography," she reminded him. "What's it like, your typical tropical island?"

"Pretty much." His excitement came through loud and clear. "The main island is Rarotonga. A mountain range cuts down the middle with lots of lush green valleys. . . . Gardenias and ginger are blooming now, and there are spider lilies everywhere."

"It sounds lovely," she whispered, caught up in his attitude as much as his words. "What else?"

"A few animals and birds—not many, except for a lot of black mynahs brought from India a long time ago. Noisy damn things." He laughed suddenly. "And chickens, chickens everywhere. But no poisonous insects or snakes."

"That does sound like paradise."

"It is." He spoke of it with such warmth. "Everything's

so *lush*, almost overblown. Trees everywhere, palms and banyans and bananas and coconut palms, groves of papaya and pawpaw . . . lots of little taro farms . . .''

As he talked on in a low, hypnotic voice, she leaned upon her elbows and closed her eyes, trying to see what he saw. And at long last, she began to feel something of what he must have felt before he went away. . . .

After the picnic in the park, the three began to spend more time together. It was a prickly kind of togetherness, for both adults skirted very carefully around subjects which might cause conflicts.

When Gordon called now—and he often did, he was as likely to find Rosemary already committed as free to join him for some excursion or the other. She tried to let him down gently but apparently needn't have worried, for he didn't seem the least bit discouraged.

For her part, Lily was in her glory with both her grandparents for playmates. The only activity Rosemary held sacrosanct was her every other day weight training sessions at the health club.

She clung to that schedule for more than the usual reasons. Although her body profited, her mind was of more concern to her at the moment. As always when she worked the big machines, she found herself unable to concentrate on anything other than the strain of her muscles, the acceleration of her breathing.

In other words, she could forget Doug for a few minutes at least. But when she returned to Lynne's house, there he'd be, waiting to invade and conquer her consciousness all over again.

She found him just as charming as always. She'd never met a man who appealed to her as strongly as this one did. The fact that she'd loved and lost him once already was the only thing which kept her from . . . from what?

From throwing herself at him, she supposed glumly, watching him swing a happily squealing Lily around in a circle in the back yard. Regardless of what he might say, he *had* changed.

Whether for better or worse, she had no idea, but thinking in those terms gave her quite a start. Once they'd promised to love each other *for better or worse*. Perhaps that's why she found it impossible to relate to another man; she still felt married to this one, no matter what a court of law might say.

That day—Thursday the twentieth, three days before Lynne and Jeff were to return—they went to the beach, which was Lily's favorite thing to do. Nevertheless, that same night Rosemary went to dinner with Gordon while Doug and Lily stayed home with a video and a sack of microwave popcorn.

Seated in an elegant restaurant at a table overlooking the Pacific Ocean, Gordon ordered champagne before turning to Rosemary with a smile of approval. "You're looking wonderful, as usual."

She returned his smile absently. "Thank you." She'd done nothing special to deserve his praise.

He looked down at his hand, tracing patterns on the linen with a thumbnail. "So how are you and Doug getting along? Anything happening there?"

"Happen—?" She frowned, his meaning sinking in. "Hardly!" She put all the scorn she could muster into her tone.

He looked relieved. "Good. I was afraid—" He shrugged. "—you know, both of you living there in that little house . . . so much history between you, fanning old embers. I've got to admit, you had me a little worried."

"You mean you believe me?" She rolled her eyes.

"Why not?" The corners of his mouth tipped up. He really was a nice-looking man. "I see now you're both doing it for Lily, and I can't fault you for that." His expression softened. "You're really lucky to have her, Rosemary. If I had a little granddaughter like that—"

The arrival of the wine steward, the flourish of the presentation of the champagne, effectively sidetracked the conversation but not before Rosemary felt a rush of empathy for the man sitting across from her.

He might have all that money could buy—did, as a matter of fact—but he still felt the loss of family keenly. Doug, it suddenly occurred to her, had walked away from all that Gordon longed to possess.

Had she fallen in love with the wrong man?

"Thank you for a lovely evening," Rosemary said later when they stood on the front step of the cottage.

Gordon shrugged her thanks away. When she would have turned, he caught her wrist in a light grip. "Rosemary, can you wait just a minute?"

Of course she could.

"There's something I have to say to you," he went on. "I get the very strong feeling that I'm running out of time."

"Time for what, Gordon?" She spoke absently, already wondering what kind of evening those inside had had without her.

"Time to tell you what's been on my mind."

"Something's been on your mind?" She gave him her full attention at last. "Have I been insensitive? I didn't notice any difference in you tonight. You were your usual charming self."

"Thanks, but I'm not talking tonight. I'm talking since I ran into you at Lynne's wedding." He shuffled his feet with unusual awkwardness. "Rosemary, will you meet me for breakfast tomorrow morning at the beach?"

"Oh, I don't know about that." She probably should spend the morning with Doug and Lily—*Lily*, she corrected herself.

"Please."

She found herself reconsidering. "I suppose I could, if it's that important to you. I may have to bring Lily, depending upon Doug's plans."

"That's fine."

"All right, then. If that's all . . ." She turned to the door again.

"Rosemary, will you marry me?"

She froze with her hand on the doorknob, little shivers of apprehension skittering down her spine. "What did you say?"

He touched her shoulders lightly, turning her to face him. "I said, 'Rosemary, will you marry me?' "

"Gordon! I told you—"

"Don't answer now, answer tomorrow at breakfast. I want you to think about it."

"I don't need to—"

"You do!" His grip on her shoulders tightened and he spoke with fierce determination. "You're exactly what I want in a wife, which is exactly what Doug *didn't* want. I told you I'd always admired you, and I meant it. But now you're gorgeous to boot." He groaned. "Doug never appreciated you but I do. We can live anywhere you want—Colorado, California, the moon, for all I care. I'm ready to get out of the business—hell, I've got all the money we'll ever want or need."

"I don't know what to say." She didn't, either. He was offering her all that Doug had withheld . . . except love. She looked at him closely, trying to read his expression.

"Don't say anything until tomorrow."

Gently he pulled her against his chest, and because it seemed the appropriate thing to do, she let him. She even lifted her face for his kiss.

But this was Gordon! This was Doug's former partner and best friend. At the last minute, she turned her face away and his mouth brushed her cheek.

His soft sigh tickled her ear. "I don't know if I love you," he whispered, nuzzling the curve of her jaw. "But if I don't, I think I can. I know I respect you and admire you and want to spend the rest of my life making you happy."

"I'm . . . speechless."

"Nothing ventured, nothing gained." Humor had returned to his voice and he set her away from him. "I go after what I want, Rosemary, and I want you. Say yes tomorrow and I promise you'll never regret it."

She stood there alone, watching him walk down the long stairway and get into his car. Even after he drove away, she stood there, trying to rein in her stampeding thoughts.

Well, why not?

Why shouldn't she link her life to that of a man ready and willing to give her all that had been withdrawn with the collapse of her marriage? She shivered; even thinking such radical thoughts told her that perhaps she hadn't changed as much as she thought she had.

Quietly, hoping not to disturb anyone, she turned the key in the lock and opened the front door. Stepping inside, she eased it closed behind her.

She was completely unprepared for the low voice coming from the darkness.

"So will your answer be yes or no?"

She heard the sounds of a swift passage and then hard arms circled her waist. For the second time in five minutes, she was pulled into a man's embrace.

Chapter Seven

*T*he sensations that shot through her body were at once familiar and electrifyingly new. Years ago, she had found love and fulfillment in this man's arms, in this man's kiss. She'd never thought to find those things again, with him or anyone else.

So what was she doing, sliding her arms around his neck and kissing him back as if it were the right and proper thing to do?

Gordon's advances had been tolerated, easily turned aside. Doug's advances were something else entirely. Being in his arms felt so right, so incredibly right, that she was completely incapable of holding back.

Even when he guided her toward the couch she couldn't find it in herself to resist. He covered her mouth with his, sweet and sure; he slid his hands down her sides, then to her hips to crush her lower body against his, straining and ready.

Somehow she found herself flat on her back on the open sofa bed, his big body reclining beside hers with one leg thrown over her thighs. He kissed her throat, the swell of her breasts above the silk jersey, then slid a hand beneath the stretchy fabric.

Unfortunately, his earlier words sank in just about then and she stiffened. "Did you say, 'what's my answer?' "

"Don't talk, kiss me." He tried to capture her lips again

but she gave him a shove and scooted away.

"You were eavesdropping! That's what this is about."
She gestured at the rumpled bed between them.

"You've got me all wrong." His frustration shone
through his placating tone. He reached for her but she
shimmied to the edge of the bed and jumped up.

"You louse! You dog! You heard Gordon propose to
me and this is your way of screwing up my life all over
again."

It finally seemed to occur to him that any semblance of
a tender moment had passed. He sat up, shoving his hair
away from the sides of his face. In the moonlight, she saw
that the only thing he wore were short pajama pants. Sil-
very moonlight rippled over his abdomen, ridged with new
muscle.

"I'm not trying to screw up your life," he muttered at
last.

"No?" She tried for a scornful laugh but it sounded
weak. "When *I* kissed *you*, you couldn't work up any
enthusiasm at all. Yet now when you think another man
could possibly be interested in me—"

"You've got me all wrong," he said again, his tone now
coaxing. "When you kissed me—if you want to call that
little peck a kiss—I was so shocked I *couldn't* react, with
enthusiasm or otherwise. Admit it, Rosie, that was totally
out of character."

"You no longer know anything *about* my character.
How many times do I have to tell you I've changed?"

"A thousand?" He stood and started around the sofa
bed toward her.

She backed up. "Keep away from me, Douglas Hancock!"

He took another step. "C'mon, Rose, admit it. You've
been wanting to hop into the sack with me ever since I
got here."

"I have not!"

"Sure you have, and what's wrong with that? You know
and I know that you're not interested in old Gordy."

"You don't know any such thing."

"But . . ." He sounded suddenly confused. "You're not gonna meet him tomorrow, are you?"

"I certainly am, and I'll thank you to mind your own business. We're divorced! You have no right to an opinion on what I do or who I do it with. Now kindly get out of my way and let me go to bed—alone!"

For a moment she thought he would grab her again and she steeled herself to resist. Instead, he stepped aside with a sweeping gesture of one arm.

"I'll get out of your way, but I'm not quite ready to get out of your life. Dream of me, Rosie . . . sweet dreams."

She addressed the only part of his comment that she dared. "Don't call me Rosie!" Her voice trembled but she managed to sweep past with head held high.

Rosemary and Gordon sat at a table right on the edge of the walkway overlooking the broad sandy beach. They'd already turned in their order and were waiting for it to be delivered.

He hadn't pressed her for an answer to his proposal, or anything else. In fact, he'd shown such sensitivity that she couldn't help but compare it to Doug's lack of the same. Now, Gordon sat beside her in apparent contentment while she watched the people drifting past and tried not to think at all.

He leaned forward to point down the beach. "What's going on, do you suppose?"

She glanced in the direction he indicated and saw a knot of people at the very edge of the water. "I have no idea. Photo shoot, maybe? I think I see light standards."

"That must be it." He leaned back in his chair. "You look tired, Rosemary. Did my . . . uhh . . ."

"You can call it a proposal, Gordon," she suggested. "I believe that's what it was."

"Okay, my proposal—did it keep you awake last night?"

She looked past him, toward the water. "Something did."

His grin broadened. "Good! If you were just going to say no, you wouldn't have lost any sleep over it, am I right?"

"Not entirely." She traced a scratch in the plastic tabletop with one fingertip. "I—"

A kid waiter plunked down a tray holding coffee and scones and fresh fruit. "You guys see the commotion? All kinds of stuff going on." He gestured with his chin toward the mass of people on the beach.

"What is it?" Gordon slid a coffee cup closer to Rosemary.

The waiter slipped his empty tray under one arm. "Some magazine's shooting a cover, someone said. And then I guess right out front here, there was some kind of accident, or near accident anyway. Kid on a bike almost got creamed."

Rosemary felt a shaft of concern. "I hope he's all right."

The waiter shrugged. "Yeah, I guess. Anything else I can get you guys?"

Gordon glanced inquiringly at Rosemary; she shook her head and he dismissed the waiter. Picking up his coffee cup, he gave her a quizzical glance. "I'm trying to be patient," he said, "but I'm all tied up in knots, here."

"Forgive me, Gordon. I should have told you right up front that—"

"Rosemary, where's Lily?"

She had no idea where Doug had come from but there he stood beside the table, wild-eyed and somehow . . . tattered. A raw scrape reddened one cheek and his bright Hawaiian shirt hung half-untucked from the waistband of his shorts.

"Why, how would I—" And then his meaning sank in and she sprang to her feet. "What do you mean, 'where's Lily?' "

He glanced around in obvious agitation. "She was with

me but somehow I lost her in the crowd. We—''

"Doug, what have you done? Anything could happen to her! Can't I count on you for anything?"

And there it was, right out in the open—if they had time to confront it, which they didn't.

Gordon stood up, too. "Now, take it easy. She can't have gone far. We'll find her." Turning, he took a step toward the beach and stopped short. "In fact, we *have* found her."

Rosemary whirled, her heart pounding with fear. If anything happened to Lily, Rosemary would never forgive herself; she already doubted she'd ever be able to forgive Doug.

But here came Lily now, skipping up the beach, hand in hand with—

Rosemary stared. The child was hand in hand with a bride, a beautiful bride in glowing white satin, her veil streaming out behind and her bare feet flashing over the sand. Both bride and child were laughing. In her free hand, Lily carried an enormous bridal bouquet, its long satin streamers threatening to trip her up with every step.

Rosemary ran to meet them, kneeling in the sand to clutch Lily in a paralyzing embrace that made the little girl gasp in protest.

"You're hurting me, Grammy!"

"I'm sorry, but I was so worried!" Rosemary looked up at the beautiful young woman. "How—what—who—?"

The woman laughed and thrust out one slender, perfectly manicured hand. "Hi, I'm Ashlee Carrington. We were just finishing up a shoot when this little person walked up and offered to be my flower girl. She's so cute, I wanted to take her up on it but unfortunately, the wedding was all pretend."

"Ashlee Carrington!" Hearing the name of the famous model, Rosemary felt foolish for not instantly recognizing one of the most fabulous faces and figures in the world.

Ashlee shrugged. "She said she was coming here and I

thought someone might be worried, so here we are." She patted Lily's shoulder. "Sorry I couldn't use a flower girl, honey, but if I ever need one for real I'll keep you in mind."

"Ashlee, it's time to leave now!" A busy-looking individual in wire-rimmed glasses and chi-chi sport shirt bustled up. "Everybody's waiting for you, dear."

"Okay." With a smile and a wave, the model turned away.

"Don't forget your flowers," Rosemary said quickly. "Lily, give Miss Carrington back the bouquet."

Ashlee waved the offer aside. "I gave them to her. She said she knew someone who needed them." Winking at Lily, the model lifted her voluminous satin skirts with both hands to hurry back down the beach.

Lily watched with a blissful expression, hugging the bouquet of roses and lilies and baby's breath against her middle. Then she turned toward her grandmother and thrust out the flowers like an offering. "Here, Grammy, now you can get married *for sure*!"

Gordon touched Rosemary's shaking shoulders and leaned forward to whisper in her ear. "See? It's an omen!"

She heard his words but all she could see was Doug. And all she could think was, *I really can't count on you for anything, Doug. Have I finally faced that fact?*

Rosemary wouldn't let Lily out of her sight, not after what Doug had done. The fact that all had ended well did nothing to redeem him in her eyes.

"You understand," she said to Gordon, her attention on Doug and Lily. "We'll talk soon, I promise."

Gordon's eyes took on a steely glint. "Yes, we will, because I'll settle up here and be right behind you. We've got to straighten out a few things, Rosemary."

"Of course." She edged away. "But right now I've got to get Lily home." And get hold of herself. She felt as if a rug had been ripped from beneath her feet and she couldn't stop the resulting free fall. Damn Doug for being so irresponsible!

They spoke not a word on the short ride back to the house, depending upon Lily to fill the conversational void. Once inside, the little girl took off for the back yard, in pursuit of the hapless Pocahontas.

Rosemary and Doug faced each other, perhaps for the last time. She launched the first salvo.

"You followed me to the beach."

"That's right."

"And you let Lily get away from you in a crowd." She closed her eyes a moment in disbelief. "You know what might have happened. How could you?"

He hesitated for just the briefest moment, and then his mouth hardened. "I couldn't help it, Rosemary."

"Of course you could have helped it! You can always help it. Life is full of choices, Doug. Some of them are hard."

"Don't you think I know that?" For one blinding instant, his vulnerability showed. "Don't you think I was as concerned as you? Because I don't run around wringing my hands doesn't mean I don't care."

"I don't run around—oh, forget it. Just forget it. I might be able to forgive you for running out on *me* but—"

"That's what you call it, running out on you? Damn, Rosemary, I wanted you to go with me. I *begged* you to go with me, if you recall."

She gritted her teeth, well aware that they were skirting dangerously close to feelings she'd protected too long to give up easily now. "We're not talking about us, we're talking about our grandchild. You put her in danger and for that I'll never, ever forgive you."

For a moment they stood there in the middle of the living room, locked in a tormented battle neither could win. Doug turned away first.

"In that case," he said, "I'm out of here."

And within minutes, he was, carrying the small bag with which he'd arrived and nothing more. He met Gordon coming in and passed without a word.

The last thing Rosemary needed was another emotional encounter. But she owed it to Gordon to tell him he was wasting his time with her . . . or was he?

She was over Doug now, once and for all. Nothing he might say or do, nothing anyone else might say about him, could draw her back into his web. She should be grateful.

She certainly shouldn't feel like crying, which was all she *did* feel like doing at the moment.

Gordon walked inside with a final glance over his shoulder. "Where's he going?"

"Who knows? Who cares?" Rosemary bit down hard on her trembling lower lip.

"Good." That gleam reappeared in Gordon's eyes. He reached for her hands.

She moved aside skittishly. "We didn't even get a chance to drink our coffee. At least let me get you a glass of tea or juice or . . . or something."

"I don't want anything," he said, "except—"

"Well, *I* need a drink. Since it's too early for booze, I'll make it something soft."

Whirling, she hurried into the kitchen, emerging a few minutes later with a glass of orange juice and a new determination. Doug was gone. Gordon wasn't. She would listen to what he had to say. Taking a quick swallow of juice, she set the glass on an end table and faced him.

Gordon finally got her hands in his. "Rosemary, I want to marry you. Doug never was good enough for you. He never understood you."

"And you do?"

"You bet I do! I'm offering you exactly what Doug never could—a calm, well-ordered, not to mention luxurious, life. If you don't want to move back to California permanently, we can travel, live part of the year in Colorado or wherever you want. You can spend all the time you want with your daughter and granddaughter, have them with us whenever it can be arranged. I'll never try to get in the way of that. In fact . . ." He smiled. "I find your love of family to be one of your most appealing traits.''

''I . . . I don't know what to say.'' Nor did Rosemary know what to do, or even where to look. Gordon really was offering her everything she'd ever wanted from Doug . . . except love.

On the back patio, Doug stood as if turned to stone. Holding Lily's little hand in his, he strained his ears toward the conversation taking place just beyond the arch leading to the living room.

Why didn't Rosemary speak up? Why didn't she tell old Gordy to take a long walk off short Stearns Wharf? Why didn't she . . . ?

Because she was going to marry the self-serving son of a bitch. Where would that leave the man who'd just come to the most painful realization of his life—that he'd lost her and it was his own fault? He'd forced them both to make difficult choices and suddenly he regretted it more than anything he'd ever done. Now, she apparently didn't even feel a need to defend him from Gordon's attacks.

A light tug on his hand pulled his attention to the little sprite beside him.

''What's goin' on, Grampa? Let's go in.''

''In a minute, honey.'' He turned away from the scene playing out inside, the voices reduced to an indistinct murmur. ''Grandpa's got something to do, baby,'' he said to Lily. ''Why don't you go play with Pocahontas for a few more minutes, okay?''

She pursed her lips, considering. ''Okay,'' she decided.

If only . . .

''He's not worthy of you and never was, Rosemary. Marry me and you'll never regret it.''

She let her head droop until her chin rested on her chest, trying to dredge up strength to say what she must. She had no reason to defend Doug, especially after what had just happened at the beach. But loyalty . . . and love . . . didn't die all that easily, regardless of the provocation.

"I'm sorry, Gordon. My answer must be no."

He touched her chin with his fingers, tilting her face until he could peer into her eyes. What he saw there must have convinced him for he dropped his hand to his side and stepped back, grimacing. "He told you, huh."

"Told me what?"

"About what happened on the beach."

"About losing Lily?"

"Yeah."

She shrugged. What was there to tell?

Gordon looked disgusted. "I knew you'd fall for that hero b.s. Big deal—he knocked some kid on a bike out of the way of a car. Anyone would have done the same."

So that was it. Doug *hadn't* lost Lily through simple lack of attention. Even too late to do any good in their fractured relationship, she felt a deep sense of relief.

To Gordon she said, "I guess it was a pretty big deal to the kid." She hesitated before adding, "I'm sorry but the only answer I can ever give you is no." She followed him toward the door. "I'm honored you asked me, though."

He heaved a gusty sigh. "Yeah, well, you're probably doing the right thing." Turning, he caught her shoulders and lifted her up to plant a kiss on her forehead. "You're obviously still crazy about the guy—or maybe just plain crazy is the operative word here. I don't know why, when he gave you up along with everything else for some juvenile dream."

"Dreams are important, Gordon. I gave up everything trying to hang on to mine."

And she had. She'd given up on Doug because her dream of domestic bliss blinded her to *his* dream. Something to think about . . .

Once Gordon was gone, she sank into an easy chair by the window and buried her face in her hands. She was alone, and always would be.

Some slight noise brought her head swinging up. Doug

and Lily stood poised in the arched doorway leading to the kitchen.

"I thought you'd gone," she whispered, her pulse leaping into agonized drumming.

"Not without saying good-bye to Lily. I went around back . . ." He shrugged.

"I'm . . . glad you're still here." She took a deep breath. "Doug, I owe you an apology. Gordon told me what really happened at the beach."

"You should have had a little faith, Rosemary."

Rosemary. *Now* he called her Rosemary, not Rosie, and it hurt like hell. In her own defense, she had to add, "It's a little hard to have faith after everything that's happened."

"Not willing to take any more chances on me, are you."

They faced each other, farther apart than they'd ever been.

Lily looked from one to the other, her little face filled with puzzlement. Finally she said, "Grammy, Grampa says he's going somewhere. Can I go, too?"

Rosemary shook her head. "I'm afraid not, sweetheart."

"But . . . but . . . I don't want him to go without us!" A frown wrinkled Lily's brow. She turned hurt blue eyes on Doug. "D-don't you love us, Grampa?"

A stricken expression crossed his face and Rosemary expected that she wore the same look of pain and remembrance.

Doug sucked in his breath. "I love you," he said thickly.

Lily nodded encouragement. "Me 'n' Grammy."

Rosemary closed her eyes against the pain. She didn't expect Doug to respond but he did . . . at last.

"Yeah," he said in a voice she barely recognized, "you 'n' Grammy."

Rosemary's eyes flew open and she stared at him, unable to believe.

Lily was under no such restraint. "Then . . . then . . . don't you want to marry us?" she wailed. Before he could answer—if he would have—she turned to Rosemary and rushed on. "Grammy, don't *you* want to marry us so we can all be together ever and ever-more?"

Doug and Rosemary looked into each other's eyes. All at once, the horrible weight of indecision lifted from her shoulders and sailed away as lightly as a helium-filled balloon.

He was still the most important person in her life, always had been and always would be. Yes, she wanted to marry him and be together ever and ever-more. Yes!

And he wanted it, too, for as one, they began to smile—déjà vu all over again.

Epilogue

*H*ow had they made such an awful mistake? Who had said the "D" word first?

"You did," Rosemary said with absolute certainty.

Doug looked astonished. "The hell I did! I asked you to go island-hopping with me."

"And I said I had responsibilities—I couldn't."

"And then you said, 'I guess that means you want a divorce' and I said, 'I want what you want.' "

"And I said, 'No, I want what you want.' " Her eyes widened with shock. "God, Doug, how stupid could we be?"

Laughing, he held her close. "I never wanted a divorce, Rosie, but I didn't want to spend the rest of my life regretting the road not taken, either."

"But a divorce—"

"I couldn't handle a long distance marriage, either. Still can't." He kissed her cheek. "Hey, I want my old Rosie back."

"She's gone, Doug." Rosemary snuggled in his arms and pressed a kiss on the underside of his jaw. "I told you I'd changed and I have."

His arms tightened around her spasmodically. "Jeez, don't give me hope and then tell me that. I need you, sweetheart. And I need to be needed—I found that out the hard way." A shiver ran through him, then through her, as if they really were one flesh.

Rosemary cuddled her cheek against the smooth skin of his muscular chest. "I need you, too, Doug. I love you. I've learned a lot in the three years, 11 months and 20 days since you went away—not that I counted."

When the laughter passed, he said those magic words back to her. "I love you, too, Rosie—never stopped for a day or a minute. Everything just got out of hand. Let's go to Las Vegas and make it right again. Then I'll try it your way and you can try it mine and we can decide together what to do with the rest of our lives."

That's what he'd said the other time but she hadn't really heard him then.

This time, she did.

Las Vegas was the logical choice, given the circumstances—no waiting period, no blood test, no questions asked. Getting there was easy, fending off the possibilities more difficult.

They didn't want to get married in a drive-up ceremony, in a helicopter, in a winery or a saloon or a hot air balloon. They didn't want an Elvis impersonator singing "The Hawaiian Wedding Song" nor did they want to wear funny costumes or write their own vows. They wanted a plain, simple, traditional ceremony—with a little flower girl preceding them down the aisle.

Standing beneath a stained glass window in the vestibule of the Little Chapel of Happily Ever After on Dec. 22, waiting for the minister to appear, Rosemary found herself unable to stop smiling. She'd been that way since the moment she realized she and Doug would get a second chance, thanks to a certain little flower girl.

That little flower girl now capered around the happy couple, smoothing the bride's blue dress—the same one she'd worn only days earlier as mother of the bride—and patting imaginary lint off the bridegroom's new dark suit. She carried a basket of rose petals in one hand and waved it around enthusiastically.

Finally planting herself in front of her grandparents, she put her hands on her hips and cocked her head. "Could I have some of your minutes?" she inquired.

Rosemary tore her gaze away from that of the man she adored. "Of course, darling."

Lily pursed her lips. "Do you have something old 'n' new?"

Rosemary and Doug exchanged amused glances. "I guess you could say my love for Grandpa is old and new at the same time," she suggested.

Lily seemed to have a bit of trouble with that concept. "You sure that counts?" she asked at last.

Doug slid his arm around his once and future bride. "*Real* sure," he said.

"Okay." Lily gave in with good grace. "Then what about something borrowed-blue?" Grabbing Rosemary's naked hands, she examined them carefully. "Where's that borrowed-blue ring?" she demanded. "The one Mama wore? Quick, where is it, Grammy?"

Lily looked completely unstrung. "That couldn't count as borrowed, sweetie," Rosemary soothed. "Grandpa gave me that ring a very long time ago."

"But . . . but . . ." Lily's face clouded up. "You've got to have a borrowed-blue!"

"Let me think." Rosemary made a great show of concentration. "Well," she said at last, "I'm wearing a blue dress."

"But you got no borrowed, Grammy!"

Inspiration came in a flash. Rosemary knelt. "Yes, I do," she said with certainty. "I've got *you*! I borrowed you from your mama and look how well it's turned out. Without you, I can safely say we wouldn't even be here." She gave Lily a big hug, crushing the little flower basket between them.

"Ow! Don't mash me," Lily cried, pulling back without the least concern for the tenderness of the moment. "I still gotta throw these flowers, you know!"

*   *   *

Throw them she did, so brilliantly that the chapel-provided witnesses actually applauded. At the conclusion of the simple ceremony, the bride, bridegroom and flower girl trooped out into the foyer for hugs and kisses all around.

"Now," Rosemary said around the lump of happiness in her throat, "we've got to hurry home so we'll be there to give your mama and papa a wonderful Christmas surprise."

Lily plucked the small nosegay of roses and baby's breath from Rosemary's hand and waved it about. "First you gotta throw your bowskay, Grammy."

Rosemary looked around; there wasn't another soul in the room except the three of them. "Who'll catch it?"

"I got that all figured out." Lily grabbed each grandparent by a hand, dragging them toward the chapel waiting room.

There stood three couples in various stages of dread and anticipation. Triumphantly, Lily thrust the bouquet into the hands of her startled grandmother.

"Get ready!" Whirling, she faced the open-mouthed group to make an important announcement.

"My name is Lily Blakely," she declared in a clear, confident voice. "If you need a flower girl, I got lots of 'sperience and I'm real good. Now get ready, 'cause my grammy's gonna *throw that bride bowskay!*"

ANITA MILLS
ARNETTE LAMB
ROSANNE BITTNER

*Join three of your favorite storytellers
on a tender journey of the heart...*

Cherished Moments is an extraordinary collection of
breathtaking novellas woven around the theme of mother-
hood. Before you turn the last page you will have been swept
from the storm-tossed coast of a Scottish isle to the fury of
the American frontier, and you will have lived the lives and
loves of three indomitable women, as they experience their
most passionate moments.

THE NATIONAL BESTSELLER

CHERISHED MOMENTS
Anita Mills, Arnette Lamb, Rosanne Bittner
_____ 95473-5 $4.99 U.S./$5.99 Can.

Against the backdrop of an elegant Cornwall mansion before World War II and a vast continent-spanning canvas during the turbulent war years, Rosamunde Pilcher's most eagerly-awaited novel is the story of an extraordinary young woman's coming of age, coming to grips with love and sadness, and in every sense of the term, coming home...

Rosamunde Pilcher

The #1 *New York Times* Bestselling Author of *The Shell Seekers* and *September*

COMING HOME

"Rosamunde Pilcher's most satisfying story since *The Shell Seekers*."
— *Chicago Tribune*

"Captivating...The best sort of book to come home to...Readers will undoubtedly hope Pilcher comes home to the typewriter again soon."
— *New York Daily News*